THE INFORMANT

BOOKS BY THOMAS PERRY

The
INFORMANT

THOMAS
PERRY

MARINER BOOKS / AN OTTO PENZLER BOOK / HOUGHTON MIFFLIN HARCOURT

BOSTON · NEW YORK

First Mariner Books edition 2012

Copyright © 2011 by Thomas Perry

www.hmhco.com

Library of Congress Cataloging-in-Publication Data
Perry, Thomas, date.
The informant / Thomas Perry.
p. cm.
ISBN 978-0-547-56933-8   ISBN 978-0-547-73743-0 (pbk.)
1. Assassins—Fiction. 2. Informers—Fiction. 3. Mafia—Fiction. 4. Government
investigators—Fiction. 5. Organized crime investigation—Fiction. I. Title.
PS3566.E718154 2011
813'.54—dc22   2010043566

Book design by Brian Moore

Printed in the United States of America

DOH 10 9 8 7 6 5 4
4500582142

To my family

THE INFORMANT

1

IT WAS MONDAY afternoon when he drove the white van up the driveway and stopped it at the side door of the house. He pulled his blue baseball cap down securely, leaned to the seat beside him, and picked up the aluminum clipboard with its layers of invoices. As he slid down from the seat to the driveway, he reached into his blue coveralls and retrieved a ballpoint pen. He hadn't had the time to stop and pick up the perfect tools for this, but what he had would probably do. If not, people often had the right things around the house. He rang the doorbell, listened for footsteps, then rang again.

Heavy footsteps, coming quickly. He could tell from their nearness that the first ring would have been enough. The door swung open. The man was taller than he was, younger and thicker around the chest. The man glowered, and the space between his dark eyebrows and his dark, wavy hair looked very small, pinched and wrinkled with annoyance. "Mr. Delamina?"

"Yeah. What can I do for you?"

"I've got a delivery for you."

"I didn't order anything." He prepared to close the door.

"It looks like a gift." He held up the clipboard. The invoice was filled out in big, clear letters. Under QUANTITY it said "1 ea." Under

1

DESCRIPTION it said "Sony Bravia EX500," and under AMOUNT it said "$2,199." But below that in big block letters, it said PAID.

"Are you sure it's the right address?" He was a bit suspicious, but he had seen the invoice, and his greed had been stimulated. He was thinking it might be a mistake, but somehow he could still end up with something valuable.

"Yes. You're Michael Delamina?"

"Right." Delamina's small eyes moved to the truck then to the invoice, not finding a reason not to be interested.

"Then you got a new high-definition flat screen. I need to take a look at where it goes." He stepped up on the porch, and something about his brusque, hurried manner made Delamina step backward, letting him inside.

It was a large, modern kitchen with black granite counters and a black granite island, with an array of copper pots hanging from a rack above it. He took two steps inward and swerved to go around the island. As he passed it, his free hand plucked one of the black-handled kitchen knives from a slot in the butcher block beside the cutting board. As he had expected from the width of the slot, it was the boning knife. When he was working, the proper tools seemed to find their way to his hand.

He pivoted to the left and brought the knife around so his body added force to the thrust, and the eight-inch blade was lodged to the handle in the space just below Delamina's rib cage. He stepped forward with it and pushed upward. As he did, he said quietly, "I'm the one you sent people to find. Go join them." Delamina went limp, fell onto the kitchen floor, and lay there, his eyes open and losing focus.

He stood above Delamina for a moment, watching. He was fairly sure that his upward, probing thrust had reached the heart. This was a crude, elementary way of killing a man. It was actually one of the things that prison inmates did to one another. When they pushed a blade upward they tried to move it around a bit, like a driver manipulating a standard transmission, so they called it "running the gears" on someone. But he hadn't wished to have

Delamina's death look like expert workmanship. That might warn the next one that he had come back to take care of this problem. He stepped to the rack by the sink, took a clean dish towel, and wiped off the handle of the knife. He knelt on the floor for a moment and looked more closely at Delamina.

The heart and the lungs had to be stopped. The human body could take an incredible amount of battering, piercing, even burning, and heal rapidly and go on with undiminished strength for another forty years. For a pro, death had to happen right away with no uncertainty. Before he left, the person had to be dead—not dying, but dead and cooling off. He couldn't have somebody get up after he was gone. None of his ever had, but it was a concern.

He put his hand on Michael Delamina's carotid artery to be sure his heart had stopped, then tugged a button from Delamina's shirt, extracted a few inches of thread, and held the thin, white filament in front of his nostrils. The thread didn't move. He dropped it on Delamina's chest with the button, touched the artery one more time, stood, and walked.

He went out the side door of the house and got into the plain white van. He had parked so close to the side door that he only had to take two steps and he was in the driver's seat behind tinted windows. He had a red shop rag caught in the back door of the van so it hung down to cover the license plate.

He backed out of the driveway, shifted and accelerated to a moderate speed, and proceeded down the street. After he had gone a mile or two, he turned into the parking lot of a supermarket, drove around to the rear of the building, got out, and stuffed the rag, the coveralls, and the clipboard into a bag in the Dumpster. He pulled back onto the road and merged into the traffic again. He drove carefully and lawfully as he always did, and never risked having a cop pull him over. He wore the blue baseball cap and a pair of sunglasses, because he knew that if anyone saw him through the windshield, what they'd remember was a baseball cap and sunglasses. In twenty minutes he was twenty miles away, and in forty he was in another county at the lot where he had rented the van a couple of hours ago. He returned it and drove the rented car he had left on a nearby street toward the airport.

The distinguishing feature of the killing business was its premeditation. Most amateurs got caught because they were too inexperienced to look far enough ahead. They made plans to kill some enemy, but didn't devote much thought to what they would do with the body. Some of them didn't even think clearly about their alibis. It was as though the killing itself were a high wall ahead of them. They thought so much about having to climb it that they couldn't get their eyes to focus on what was beyond it.

Even the ones who bothered to construct alibis often made foolish mistakes. They would go to a movie and pay with a credit card, sneak out in the middle of the film to do the killing, and then get caught on a security camera driving back into the parking lot. Or they'd kill their wives and then call their girlfriends on their cell phones, and the phone company would have a record of which repeater tower picked up the signal.

When they didn't make mistakes, they still had trouble. The truth was, if you were the police department's favorite suspect, almost any set of precautions you took would be inadequate. If there was no real evidence of guilt, the police would start finding fibers in your car or house that were "not inconsistent" with the fibers in the dead man's clothes or carpets. A pro was never the cops' favorite suspect, because he had no clear connection with the victim.

He knew a lot about the business because he had been raised in it. His parents had been killed in a car crash when he was ten. His nearest relative was his mother's younger sister, who was in college in California and barely made it to the funeral. She had no room in her schedule for raising anybody's ten-year-old child. But a neighborhood man named Eddie Mastrewski had volunteered to take the boy in, teach him some values and the habit of work. Eddie was the local butcher, a man who drove a good car, lived in a good house, and had a reputation for honest weights and fresh meat.

In those days in a working-class neighborhood, no one thought

4

much about it. There was a boy who needed a home for a few years, and Eddie had one. In later years, the boy suspected that the reason nobody had worried that this lifetime bachelor might be a child molester was the neighborhood's whispered knowledge that Eddie regularly made home deliveries of special cuts of meat to a few particularly attractive housewives.

Eddie Mastrewski did exactly as he had promised—provided a safe, happy home and taught the boy his trade. The part that the neighbors didn't know was that Eddie the Butcher wasn't just a butcher. He was a professional killer.

The boy had been a good learner. As a teenager he had a photograph on his wall taken by a news photographer in Vietnam. In the foreground there was a procession of people at some sort of religious festival. They were walking along, some beating drums, some with their mouths open wide singing, some with their heads bent in prayer. But behind them was a glaring bright-orange-and-crimson explosion spreading into the air like a monstrous flower blooming.

He knew from Eddie that the photograph must have been taken during the two-tenths of a second after the bomb's initiator had ignited the explosive, but before the minds of any of the paraders could apprehend the change. The bomb had already gone off, but none of these people had yet heard, felt, or seen anything happen. That was still in their future.

The boy had spent a great deal of time over the next few years thinking about those two-tenths of a second. If he could deliver a disabling blow in those two-tenths of a second, the adversary would literally never see it coming, never know what happened to him until he was down.

Eddie made sure the boy was proficient with knives, shotguns, rifles, and pistols of the common brands and calibers. When the boy was fifteen, Eddie began to take him out on weekend jobs. When he turned sixteen, he quit school and worked with Eddie full-time. That was when he had advanced from apprentice to journeyman.

Killing was mostly a mental business. It required thinking clearly, not quickly. Picking the time and place long before he went out to do a job gave him the chance to study the way it should be done, to find the best shooting angle, and become familiar with all of the entrances and exits. Before the time came, a professional killer could arrange almost everything in his favor. He could come through like a gust of wind—there unexpectedly, then gone—and after he disappeared, leave an impression rather than a memory.

Eddie had taught him that "It's the passion that's missing, and that protects you. You kill somebody because someone else hates him. The only time you have to feel anything is if you make a mistake and he gets the chance to fight back. Then he's your enemy and your adrenaline flows until he's dead."

Amateurs were all passion. Amateurs would plan the killing up to the moment when their enemies died and then turn stupid. They thought it would end then, that they'll toss the knife or gun away, go back to their houses, take a shower, and stuff their clothes in the washing machine.

Amateurs didn't think about the fact that as soon as the body was found, they had potent new enemies, the cops. And cops looked for connections between victims and their killers. Nine out of ten murders were done by somebody the victim knew. How many people could the average person know? The average person could only hold five hundred faces in his memory. So at the moment when the victim hit the ground, the world's six billion people narrowed down to only five hundred suspects. The police would look at how the killing was done. If it required a lot of strength, the killer was a man; about two hundred and fifty of the five hundred were eliminated. Two-thirds of the remaining two hundred and fifty would have good alibis. Make that eighty suspects. A quarter of them were too young or too old. Make that sixty suspects. By now the amateur was beginning to feel a little sick. The pro would already have counted his money and be on the way to his next job. He was one of the six billion who had already been eliminated.

He turned into the car-rental return outside La Guardia, returned his car, and rode the shuttle bus to the terminal. The people who saw him noticed only another middle-aged man with brown hair graying a bit at the temples, who wore the nearly universal travel uniform of such men—a dark-colored sport coat with gray or beige pants, a blue shirt without a tie, and rubber-soled shoes. There was no reason to look at him closely, nor did he look at them. Everyone on a shuttle bus to an airport was on the way to somewhere else, and thinking well ahead into a different time and place.

2

HE CAME ONTO the property over the neighbor's back fence and then crouched for a few minutes beside a brick barbecue, getting his eyes used to the darkness and bringing the house back from his memory. It was a warm, pleasant Monday night in September, and he took his time. He had broken into this same house about ten years ago. That night he'd had a tentative plan to kill her if she woke, but he hadn't needed to cause her or her children harm. He had only needed to steal her dead husband's identification.

When he had listened intently for a few minutes and retrieved the memory of the interior of the house, he moved slowly and steadily, still part of the shadows, to the tall windows along the side of the dining room. He knew there was an alarm system.

The way home alarm systems worked was that a contact in the windowsill had to be touching a magnetic contact in the window frame or the alarm would go off. But these tall windows had two big panes, each in its own frame, one at the bottom and one at the top. The alarm contact was in the bottom frame, so if he could get the window unlatched, he could lower the top half and leave the lower half, with its electrical contact, in place.

He had a coil of thin steel wire in his pocket. He took it out and uncoiled it, then took out the lock-blade knife that he'd brought and opened it. He inserted the blade upward between the two frames and pried them apart a bit by wedging the blade in as far as possible. He bent his wire into a loop about an inch in diameter, and then slid the wire up into the space the blade had made. He twirled the wire so the loop went around the latch, then tugged it tight and pulled the latch into the open position. He pulled his knife out, closed it, and pocketed it.

Again he took some time to remain still in the dark shadow of the roof overhang, listen, and study what he could see of the house's interior. No interior lights had been on when he'd arrived. He stepped back to look up at the second-floor windows to be sure nothing had changed, then hooked the fingers of his left hand under a clapboard to steady himself, stepped onto the windowsill, pulled down the upper window, stepped over it with one leg, then the other, and then lowered himself silently from the inner sill to the floor. He carefully closed the upper window and reset the latch. He remembered where the stairs were.

He was standing in Elizabeth Waring's bedroom when she woke. He watched her stir and become aware of him and stifle the quick reflex movement of her right arm to reach for the gun, forcing herself to go limp again to make him believe she had just stirred in a dream. She was extraordinarily disciplined to calculate that she would not have time to grasp the gun and then abandon the attempt and try to make him think she was still asleep.

"I already have the gun," he said aloud. "I don't intend to harm you. I just want to talk for two minutes."

She opened her left eye a little, then sat up slowly and reached toward the lamp by her bed.

"Don't turn it on," he said. "There's no reason for you to see me, and it will be safer for you if you don't."

"I know you," she said. "I know who you are." She paused, seeming to use her fear to make herself more alert, but forcing herself to seem calm. "You've been away a long time. Were you in prison?"

He spoke quietly, without anger. "I know you're good at your job. That's why I became aware of you years ago. You try to surprise me, push me off balance by saying you know me. Then you ask a question that will give you information to help you find me. It's what you're supposed to do, but stop. I have questions. Who does Michael Delamina work for these days?"

"Michael Delamina?" she repeated. "I don't know who that is."

"Then good night. I'll leave your gun outside in the back yard where you can find it. I remember you have kids."

In a few heartbeats, Waring sensed that he had reached her bedroom doorway, but she hadn't seen or heard him move. "Wait."

He was still. "I'm waiting."

"I do know who he is. I just needed to know what rules you were setting—what would happen if I didn't know."

"You mean would I kill you? No. Now you want to know what will happen if you tell me."

"Yes."

"Tell me, and I'll tell you something."

"Frank Tosca. He's an underboss trying to move up to be the head of the Balacontano family. He's an upstart, but he's young and energetic, and the family was stagnant, aging, and fading. Now, one by one, all of the old soldiers and their relatives and hangers-on are being gathered into the fold." She paused. "So what are you going to tell me?"

"I know Frank Tosca."

"So what?"

"I'll tell you something about him. About fifteen years ago he killed a man named Leo Kleiner on Warren Street in New York. He shot him in the left side of the head with a K-frame .38 revolver, like the cops used when we were kids. That one was originally owned by a cop. I'd be surprised if Tosca didn't still have it hidden in his house on the St. Lawrence River in Canada."

"Why are you telling me this?"

"I didn't take some oath of omertà like they did. I worked for people who had the money to hire me. What I tell you next is important. There were three men on the street that night who saw it happen—Davey Walker the driver, Boots Cavalli, and Andy Varanese. Cavalli wouldn't tell you anything if you set him on fire. Davey Walker is dead. But if you put enough pressure on Varanese, and promise him protection for the rest of his life, he'll help you out. He hated Tosca."

"Will anybody believe this after fifteen years?"

"The house in Canada used to have a hidden room. If you head down into the basement, right in the middle of the stairway before you get down there is a door built into the wall. That's where he kept his collection of things he couldn't let cops find. He figured the Canadians wouldn't be interested in raiding the house because he never did anything there, and the Americans can't do a surprise search in a foreign country. So I think what I've given you is an eyewitness and the chance to find the murder weapon in the suspect's possession."

She waited for him to say more, then sensed that he wasn't standing where he had been anymore. She stayed still, wondering what he was doing. She heard the door downstairs by the kitchen being locked. She threw off the covers, sprang from the bed, ran to the window, and looked out.

She watched him from above, a dark shadow moving across the back lawn. He stopped at the brick barbecue, opened the stainless steel lid, placed her sidearm on the grill, and closed the lid over it. He turned, looked up at her, then moved to the back of the yard, pulled himself up onto the low stone wall, and rolled over it into the next yard.

Waring snatched up the telephone and speed-dialed her office at the Justice Department. "This is Elizabeth Waring. I just had a home visit from a suspect of the very highest priority. I need a team to set up a perimeter five blocks from my house. He looks about forty-five years old, Caucasian, probably brown hair, wearing a black topcoat, dark clothing." She listened for a few seconds.

"If he looks like every man for a mile, pick up every man for a mile, and I'll try to sort them out. This is not a brainstorming session, it's an order."

• • •

11

On Tuesday morning Elizabeth Waring wore a navy blue pants suit and a pair of flat, highly shined shoes. It felt like a uniform, which was what she had designed it to be. It helped her to feel invulnerable. She was forty-six years old now, well past the age when she could be intimidated by one more meeting with a deputy assistant attorney general. But she was still watchful. When she had finished telling him the story, Dale Hunsecker made a serious face, but it was just that—arranging his features into an expression he had practiced, probably for future appearances before congressional committees.

He said, "This man just walked into your house?"

"My bedroom. The doors and windows were all locked, and the alarm system armed. But figuring out how to get around those things is part of what he does. He was also able to avoid or get through the ring of agents we set up afterward. Nobody saw him."

"And he did it just to give you an eyewitness account of a fifteen-year-old killing in New York City?" Hunsecker was about fifty and acted as though he had spent much of his time with underlings who were much younger than he was, so he had gotten used to conducting conversations as though they were seminar dialogues in which he led his pupils to a series of incontestable conclusions.

"No. He knows that my section tries to keep track of all the Mafiosi we know about. He asked me who Michael Delamina's boss was. I told him it was Frank Tosca, who has been beginning to solidify support in the Balacontano family. In return, he told me information about Frank Tosca that he knew I would want."

"Why?"

"You know who Tosca is, right?"

"I've seen his name in briefing papers. It's hard to tell these people apart sometimes, but I understand he's a boss."

She tried to keep her voice from betraying anything but information. "He's the latest incarnation of a bad old school of thought in La Cosa Nostra. He's a throwback. He's young—late thirties when he started making his move upward—physically strong and intimidating at forty-one, and just a little bit crazy. When he turns violent, it's always out of proportion to what made him mad. We think that two years ago he was the one who had Paul Millati shot. Afterward somebody flew to California and killed Millati's son, his daughter-in-law, and their two kids. Somebody in New York killed his wife, daughter, and the family dog. And six months later, when the gravestones were set up in the family plot at the cemetery, a mysterious crew in a white truck came and removed them."

"I can see he would be somebody we'd want in jail."

"We never managed to get this kind of evidence against him before. All we ever had is rumors. What the new information does is give us a chance to go back in time to the period before he and his friends all got used to living with wiretaps and tax audits, and stopped doing things in person. This is something he did himself, and if the tip is reliable, it isn't very well covered up."

"I'm not sure what you're asking permission to do. You still don't have anything to charge him with."

"I'd like to ask the New York FBI people to lay the groundwork to pick up Anthony 'Andy' Varanese. He's the one witness who supposedly saw it happen and might be induced to talk."

"Pick him up for what?"

"He's got a long record. His last conviction was for running a ring in California that stole cargo containers from the port of Long Beach. He's back in New York now, and I think we can be sure he's doing something. I'll ask them to keep him under investigation until they catch him at whatever he's up to. The operation shouldn't take more than two or three weeks."

"I think I need to speak clearly about what you're proposing, Mrs. Waring," Hunsecker said. "There are several problems with this. We're on a war footing. The FBI is just about fully occupied with protecting this country from terror attacks. After that, there's the escalating drug war on our southern border, which has already begun to move north into major cities. We don't get unlimited use of whole squads of FBI agents every day. The Organized Crime and Racketeering Division is just one small part of Justice. And

13

you're talking about wiretaps. In this political climate, if you request a domestic wiretap, it had better be on somebody who is going to be convicted of a crime in fairly short order."

"There are dozens of surveillance operations on Mafia figures right now."

"All the more reason to question why we need another, particularly if it's just a roundabout way of getting to someone else."

"Let me talk to the New York agent in charge. If they're stretched too thin, maybe we can work something out using a small number of agents from other parts of the country on temporary loan." She could see he was not interested in the idea. His sour face had returned. "Something's bothering you."

"Mrs. Waring."

"Actually, it's not *Mrs.* Waring. I'm a widow, and his name was Hart. So I'm Mrs. Hart at my kids' school. Just call me Waring."

"What's troubling me most is that this informant of yours is manipulating the Justice Department into launching an operation to put away someone he doesn't like. That's what all of this is about."

"That's probably what it's about for him, but not for us. We just happen to be lucky that he dislikes someone who is a murderer and a public menace."

"But isn't he a murderer and a public menace too? You said he was a professional hit man."

Elizabeth took in a deep breath to calm herself and let it out. "I know it may seem as though they're about the same. They aren't. My informant is a very bad man. There's no question of it. Twenty years ago I was following a series of violent incidents all over the country—some solitary killings of mob leaders, fire fights in the centers of big cities. Most of law enforcement thought it was a war between two or more families. But when I began to look into it closely, I began to hear rumors. What the minor players were most afraid of was a man called the Butcher's Boy. Nice name, isn't it? What I believe now is that this man performed a hit for the Balacontano family, and Carl Bala didn't want to pay him, so he had him ambushed in Las Vegas. It didn't work because the Butcher's Boy read the situation correctly and killed the ambushers. Then he got angry. What looked like a gang war was actually this man reacting to that betrayal."

"And now you're proposing to help what amounts to a serial killer by putting his enemies in prison."

She straightened and stared at him. "We've been handed an opportunity to put away the heir apparent of one of the five New York families—a man who is young, very violent, and growing more powerful every day. I've been trying to help dismantle the Mafia for over twenty years, and I can tell you that I haven't seen any nice snitches. Good, honest people seldom know anything useful about the Mafia. The people who have the information we need are usually criminals."

"I understand. And I caught the reminder that I'm a recent political appointee, and you're a careerist. Our differences are not imaginary. But contrary to your assumption, they're not all in your favor. What you're proposing is the old way of doing business. The government has been protecting one criminal so he'll tell on another for—what? Fifty or sixty years? And what has this gotten us?"

"Half as many criminals."

"That's hardly been demonstrated by the current pervasiveness of organized crime. And it's a deal with the devil that could make this man a bigger problem later. If he's this spectacular hired killer, he could kill anyone—a visiting dignitary, a Supreme Court justice, a president."

"He hasn't been seen in about ten years. He hasn't been working."

"You mean he's been in prison."

"I don't think he has been, or someone would have recognized him and tried to collect the price on his head, or told the guards who he was in exchange for privileges. He's been away—maybe out of the country, or maybe just living a quiet life in some backwater. Something riled him up. Whatever got him upset had to do with Michael Delamina and, therefore, with Frank Tosca. It's what brought him to me."

"You actually sound starstruck."

"I'm not. I told you, he's a bad human being—maybe psychotic. While he was working, he was almost continuously hired by organized crime bosses to do the most important hits, the ones that had to be done by an outsider so that they could never be connected to the bosses. Some of his hits probably didn't even seem to be murders. There are undoubtedly some that seemed to be heart attacks or overdoses. He's potentially the most important informant the Justice Department has ever had. He's not somebody who can tell us about a thousand-dollar drug deal or a football pool that closed down ten years ago. His only business was murder."

"And why would he tell us anything about that?"

"He was always an outsider, not a made guy. He's not even Italian. At this point he has no loyalty to anybody, and now somebody has made him very angry. I didn't find him and ask him questions. He came to me and offered me information. This is an opportunity I don't expect to see again."

Hunsecker stroked his chin and cheeks, shook his head impatiently, stood up, and paced his office. "This opportunity you're bringing me is the news that you've found an unlocked door to the madhouse. Once we're taking orders from this serial killer, arresting whomever he wants us to, we're in an entirely different universe, and it's not one we want to inhabit. If, just to get information, we're going to ignore the crimes of a man who has probably killed scores of people, then what won't we ignore?"

"He—"

"Don't," he said. "It was a rhetorical question. My answer isn't going to change. The U.S. government isn't going to be in business with a man with a name like 'the Butcher's Boy.' We won't act on his information. If you've got something more on him than third-hand stories, then arrest and charge him. If not, we'd both better get back to our responsibilities."

"Yes, sir."

16

3

ELIZABETH WARING LOOKED up from be
hind the desk in her office and saw that the wall clock said it was
after seven. She was still frustrated by this morning's conversation
with the deputy assistant, but she had managed to distract herself with work until after the official hour for closing her section.
It had been her intention to kill the extra hour or so by accomplishing a few things that would make tomorrow morning more
productive. That way she wouldn't have to go to the underground
parking garage and run into Hunsecker there, and she wouldn't
have to look at whoever came down about the same time he did
and know that Hunsecker had complained about her.

She knew that whenever he did tell someone, he would present his account as an example of the lack of ethics of some of
the Justice Department's career employees. Or maybe he would
just say that people like Elizabeth Waring, who had dealt too long
with organized crime, began to be more and more like the enemy.
Twenty years ago, when she had started out in the Justice Department, there probably would also have been an oblique hint that
there was a moral uncertainty to women. A few of the old guard
felt women didn't really belong in the Justice Department, but
had been allowed in for purely political reasons. At least that was
over.

Now she had to report to a man who really had been allowed in for purely political reasons. He had, through complicated family relationships, been made a partner in an old, respected law firm. The combination of family and law firm had made him a good fund-raiser for political candidates, and so he was a perfect choice for a post two levels down from a cabinet member. Fortunately, he could be counted on to leave eventually. He was a bit too arrogant to survive many meetings with his superiors, too unintelligent to inspire his staff to do great things he could take credit for, and too ambitious to stand still for long. Most of the value he could get from serving as a deputy assistant attorney general he'd had on the day he'd been sworn in. He would be able to play a bigger role in his law firm or sell out to a rival firm, and spend the next few years making up for a dull career by getting very rich.

She steered her mind around the inevitable comparison. She had begun as a data analyst in this same building more than twenty years ago. She had repeatedly, reliably done something that none of the political appointees had ever done: she had solved crimes and put the people who had committed them in prison. She had caused three crime families to fall into decline because of lack of leadership, then stood by to convict the followers as they made foolish mistakes and then turned informant to save themselves.

She couldn't claim she had not been rewarded. She was the highest ranking civil servant in the Organized Crime and Racketeering section. She had also had a personal life. She had met FBI agent James Hart during her first year, fallen in love with him, married, and had two beautiful children. He had died a slow, agonizing death from lung cancer just before their eighth anniversary, and if it hadn't been for the children, she might have chosen to die with him. It sometimes occurred to her that she was still in mourning. She still thought about him each morning, each night before she slept, and several times during the day. But over the past couple of years she had stopped picturing him only at the end, when he'd looked like a tormented skeleton. When he would come into her mind now, he was a tall, handsome FBI agent in his dark suit. She would think of him early in the morning while it was still dark and nobody else was awake, and she would think, *At least I had that. I had love.* Her time at Justice had brought her other things too — a modest, steady income to raise and educate her two children, a sense of purpose.

She didn't hate Hunsecker. She was just disappointed in him. She knew that if by some fluke he lasted long enough to understand his job, he would wish he had another chance at this day. Yes, arresting a young, frighteningly effective crime boss at the instigation of a killer was sure to gratify the killer. That was regrettable. But what the killer was trying to get them to do happened to be their job. It was why they came into this office each day.

She stared out the office window. She had slowly, over twenty years, moved from a shared desk in a windowless basement computer room that was freezing all the time, all the way to a pleasant office on the fifth floor, where at least her window gave a view of Pennsylvania Avenue and a corner of the neighboring J. Edgar Hoover Building. Her rise had been a long, unceasing effort. It had required enduring the periods when the administration in charge was ineffectual, fanatical, and paranoid, or unable to focus on anything but the next election. Her special part of the Justice Department remained pretty much the way it had been when Attorney General Robert Kennedy had founded it in the early 1960s. Politics could sometimes have a terrible effect on the efforts of the Justice Department, but there had been no political faction in those years that didn't at least profess to be opposed to organized crime and racketeering, so the nonsense from above was barely audible in her section.

What had bothered her was the regular infusion every four years of political appointees at the top of the system. During her time, there had been at least three attorneys general who had, at best, rudimentary knowledge of the law, and two who had never practiced law at all. Only one had ever had any experience in the sort of crime fighting that included conducting investigations of actual criminals and convicting them of crimes, but it wasn't recent and he wasn't very good at it. The AG's hired underlings were no better qualified. The lawyers who were really good at criminal law were too rich and too busy to consider taking a government job.

Elizabeth finished reading and initialing the memos and reports that her people had submitted during the afternoon, wrote a query in the margin of the last one, put them all in the outgoing office mail, and closed her office door. The more challenging pieces of paperwork she put into her briefcase with her laptop. She went to the elevator, rode it to the cavernous parking garage beneath the building, got into her car, and drove to the exit. The armed guard waved her past and she was out on the street. She was pleased to see that in waiting she had missed the worst of the evening traffic, the segment of the commuter population who were willing to take risks to get home fast.

Elizabeth had moved to McLean, Virginia, a couple of months after Jim died. Even though she had always loved being in D.C. when Jim was alive, it had seemed much better to her to raise the kids in a nice suburb if she had to do it alone. And getting out of the house where her husband had died had been good for her and for the kids, Jimmy and Amanda.

She had always thought that Special Agent James Hart had been created to use all that courage and strength in some epic struggle to vanquish evil. Thanks to the cancer, he had only used it to endure and falsify his own death, smiling at his wife and children through the pain and suffering of that horrible last year. When it was over, she had cried every night. She had waited until the children were asleep and she could lock her bedroom door and put her face in her pillow. And then, after a year or so, there was a particularly busy time in the organized crime section, and when it had passed, one day she realized she hadn't cried for a month. What she worried about most now was Jim and Amanda. The effects of the early death of a parent on children were huge and life changing, but essentially unknowable. What she had learned was that children became very adept at appearing normal and unscathed, but she could not know what sense of loss or emptiness might be hurting them inside.

As she drove home, she looked in her mirrors frequently, watching for a car that lingered too long behind her, or one that came up on her too fast. It was not out of the question that some faction that her office had targeted might be watching for her. Prosecutors in Italy had been machine-gunned in their cars a few times in recent years, and some of the American families were still in the habit of taking in apprentices and reinforcements from the old country.

Organized crime wasn't just the Italian Mafia, either. It was Canadian bikers and Mexican *narcotraficantes,* and Russian smugglers and pimps, and groups from every other country of the world. They all brought with them their own money launderers and crooked accountants and assassins. She had been successful enough to have enemies in every group, so she took precautions every day. She watched for things that weren't right, used five alternate routes to get home, and kept her purse open on the seat beside her, so she could quickly grasp the gun inside it.

When Elizabeth reached the clapboard house with the brick façade on the quiet street in McLean, it was almost eight o'clock. She could see cars in other driveways, other houses with the lights on in kitchen and dining room windows. She pulled up her driveway into the garage attached to the house and pressed the button on the remote control to close the door behind her. She carried her briefcase into the house. She smelled food. "Hi! I'm sorry I'm late."

Nobody answered. She stepped into the kitchen. She could see the kids had eaten and left one place setting for her. There was a note from her son, Jim. WENT TO SCHOOL FOR A COLLEGE WORKSHOP. He had made his own dinner and driven back to school. She felt deflated and guilty. She was sure it wasn't one

21

of the meetings that parents were supposed to attend, but she went to the bulletin board and checked anyway. The notice was still hanging there. Students only, thank God.

She kept going and followed a faint clicking to Amanda's room. She was typing at an incredible rate and staring at her computer screen, her iPod's earbuds in her ears. Elizabeth moved closer, into the periphery of Amanda's vision, and waved.

Amanda gave a little jump, smiled, and said "Hi, Mom" a little too loudly. She pulled the earbud out of one ear.

"Hi. How was your day?"

"Not bad," Amanda said. "I got a ninety-eight on that history test we took Friday."

"Wow. Keep learning those dates, Killer. What are you up to now?"

"A French paper. In French."

"What's it about?"

"I guess I'd translate it as 'The Wondrous Cheeses of France.'"

"I don't think I'd try that one on an empty stomach. Have you eaten dinner yet?"

"Hours ago, around five-thirty. Jim had to go back to school."

"I saw his note." Elizabeth paused, then realized her daughter was waiting patiently for her to leave so she could get back to work. "Well, I'm home if you need me. My French is a little last century."

"*Très mauvais* too."

"True. Somewhere they're keeping my grades to prove it. I'm going to eat something."

"See you later." Amanda stuck the earbud into her ear and stared at a handwritten note stuck in her French dictionary, then started typing again.

It occurred to Elizabeth, as it had more and more frequently, that it was going to get very lonely around here in a couple of years, just when she would really need to keep her job to put them both through college. She walked back to the kitchen, opened the refrigerator, took out some leftover vegetables and some of the chicken from tonight's dinner, put them in the microwave, and then ate while she read this morning's *New York Times* and *Washington Post*.

She started the dishwasher, went into her room, and changed into blue jeans and an old oversize gray sweatshirt of Jim's that had GEORGETOWN across the chest. Then she went to the dining room and laid out the papers she had brought home. She had requested the records on Michael Delamina, Anthony Varanese, and Frank Tosca. She began at the top of the hierarchy, with Tosca.

He was forty-one years old. He had a few convictions during his twenties and thirties for the things that young men in the Balacontano family usually did—assault, aggravated assault, and an illegal weapons violation. They weren't even youthful mistakes. They were business, the routine tasks of collecting debts for the family. They had, together, put him in prisons for six years and two months. Prison was a trade school for young Mafiosi. There they got to know important older men and the minor criminals who worked for them, and spent lots of time listening to lectures about methods and systems. They lifted weights and did pull-ups. At the end of a sentence they came out stronger, meaner, and smarter, with allies and sponsors they hadn't had before. Tosca was older and higher in the hierarchy now, and hadn't been arrested for anything in eight years.

She turned to the files on Anthony Varanese. He wasn't in the same league as Tosca. He didn't appear ever to have been in the running to become one of the little tyrants who ran the families. His life was a perfect example of something she had learned over the years: the life of a Mafioso wasn't a profession, it was an audition. Everybody was in a competition to rise in the hierarchy—to run a crew, to be a big earner, to run a network of crews, and eventually, to master the complicated web of personal and business relationships that made up a crime family. If you weren't moving up, it was just a series of ill-paid, dangerous, and unpleasant jobs. And you always worked for an employer who was volatile, suspicious, and dishonest. Varanese had fallen out of the race a long time ago. His arrests looked to her like failed starts in different parts of the country, always working for new people on some new scheme every couple of years. Tosca had shot straight up, not moving his business address more than a couple of blocks since he had begun.

It seemed so simple to do what she had asked Hunsecker for permission to do. She could have set a surveillance team on Varanese, and within a week or two she would have had a clear idea of what he was doing these days. In another week, they'd have had enough evidence to convict him of some form of larceny, since that seemed to be his specialty. With some nudging, he would agree to testify against Tosca. Meanwhile, another team could concentrate on Tosca, pursue the cold case murder of Kleiner, and see if there was a way to get the Canadians to search his summer house for the weapon.

Hunsecker was a terrible obstacle. Some day he would move on, up, and out. Until that day she would have to devise a way to live with him. She couldn't simply stop working while she waited for him to get bored with organized crime, but she couldn't circumvent him either. There had to be some middle way. She was tired now. She put away the papers, went to the living room couch, and turned on the television set.

The eleven o'clock news was on, flashing its moving logos and slogans. The teaser was already over, so she didn't know what the top stories were. The two anchor people came on, an attractive, well-dressed man named Curt Wendler, and a pretty blond woman in her late thirties named Kate Lathrop.

Kate Lathrop was frowning. "A man police believe to be a midlevel New York organized crime figure was found dead in his home on Long Island's north shore yesterday. Michael Delamina, age thirty-six, was found on the floor of his home with a single stab wound to the heart."

Elizabeth found herself standing, staring at the screen image of the front of a long, low white house across a vast green lawn shaded by tall oaks and maples. There were police cars with blue

24

stripes, and an ambulance. A couple of coroner's men pushed a wheeled stretcher down the driveway with a bagged body strapped to it.

"Police have declined to speculate on a motive for the killing. They said the victim had several felony convictions, and that he had probably made many enemies over the years. But they do confirm that he had ties to the Balacontano family."

The screen was now filled with an accident on a narrow bridge over a river somewhere. A tractor-trailer was jackknifed across three lanes, and two small cars appeared to have tried to veer around it at the same time, but Elizabeth had stopped listening because she was already dialing the phone.

She heard the voice. "Justice, this is Fulton."

"Bob."

"Hi, Elizabeth," Fulton said. "You heard about Delamina?"

"Yes. Why am I watching it on the eleven o'clock news?"

"Everything we know about it has been forwarded to you in an e-mail. It isn't much."

"Do we know when it happened, approximately?"

"Only approximately. The body temperature indicates he died yesterday, probably late in the afternoon."

Elizabeth thought. It had happened before the Butcher's Boy had come to Washington. He had killed Delamina, then decided that his next move would be to kill Delamina's boss. He had been out of the crime world for too long to know who that was, but he knew that the Justice Department would know. He had flown to Washington and asked her. She couldn't quite bring back now why she had told him.

"Bob, call the FBI office in New York and say I have a very special request. I would like them to put Frank Tosca under surveillance. He's going to need some protection — set up a perimeter around him that will alert them to anybody attempting to get to him."

"Are you thinking that Tosca had a hit man do Delamina, and now the guy is coming for his pay?"

"No," she said. "It's a long story, but the man who killed Michael Delamina went to some trouble to find out who Delamina was working for. Now he knows, so he's going to kill Frank Tosca unless we can catch him when he comes to do it."

"Oh, boy," Fulton said. "You want me to tell the FBI that?"

"We don't have any choice. Warn them that this guy is very good at what he does. If he wants Tosca, it wouldn't bother him if he also had to take out an FBI agent or two on the way in. If we can possibly capture him alive, he could be the best domestic catch we've made in about twenty years. He knows a million things we'd like to know."

"When would he be likely to get there?"

"He's probably on his way."

"All right, I'm on it."

"If there's a problem, anything at all, call and wake me, or have them do it."

"I will." He hung up.

Elizabeth stood in the middle of her living room holding the dead telephone. She put it back on its cradle and looked at the television set again, but didn't really see it. It occurred to her that what she had just done was exactly what Hunsecker had ordered her not to do.

4

HE HAD BEEN calling himself Michael Schaeffer since he had moved to England twenty years ago, so he was
comfortable with the name. It was the sort of name that wasn't
made up, and wasn't simplified or changed from something people
couldn't pronounce. Schaeffer was the sort of name that a lot of
Americans had, not an attempt to pretend he wasn't American.
The British could detect imposture, and they didn't like it.

Before he had gone to England with his Michael Schaeffer
passport, he had randomly used a number of other names. Most
were just signifiers for landlords who needed to see something
filled in on that line. The only name that had meant anything was
the one other people called him when he wasn't there. They used
the name the Butcher's Boy to refer to him behind his back. In a
way, it was the only name he'd had since he was ten that was real.
Now that he was back in the country the nickname seemed on the
verge of coming back to him like a relapse of a chronic disease.

After all of the years of quiet in the old city of Bath, he was back
in New York. He'd had to make a visit some years ago because a
couple of young guys had spotted him on a trip to England. This
time it was worse. Michael Delamina and two friends of his had
tried to sneak into a summer house he'd rented in Brighton and
kill him and his wife in their sleep.

He had taken Meg to hide in the cellar, then gone out the cellar window into the narrow space between the window and the privet hedge that surrounded the house. In a minute he had found one of the men had gone through the back door into the pantry. Schaeffer had come up behind him, dragged him outside, and cut his throat there to keep the blood out of the house. He found the second man sixty feet down the road in a car with the lights off because in the three A.M. silence he could hear the motor running. He had used the first man's silenced pistol to put a hole in the side window and through the man's temple. He had then gone back to the house to look for the third man, but he heard the car drive off. He ran to the spot and found the man he had shot lying in the gravel where his comrade had pulled him out onto the ground so he could get behind the wheel. He searched the corpses, and then drove them fifty-four miles to London and pushed them over the side of a bridge onto a stretch of railroad tracks that led up behind an old, dark factory.

He had found a business card in one of the dead men's wallets with the address of a bed-and-breakfast in Brighton run by a Russian émigré named Voltunov. On the top page of the sign-in register on a little podium in the foyer were the names of the two dead men. Between them was the name Michael Delamina.

Schaeffer had packed a suitcase while Meg looked on. "I assume you know where you're going," she said. "Somewhere in the States?"

"Yes. He brought those two here to help him look for me. He's going to run back there now. He'll bring two dozen next time. I can't let him do that."

"I should think not."

They were silent for a few minutes while he threw the rest of the clothes he'd brought from the house in Bath into his suitcase. Meg said, "I wish we were going home."

"So do I."

"Do you know how long this will take?"

"If it goes well, three days to a week. Most likely, a bit longer."

"If it doesn't go well?"

"Then I'll know you're safe in London at your parents' town house for as long as it takes," he said. "Don't go to the house in Bath until I get back. That could be where they first spotted me, and if it is, then it's not safe."

He drove her to the London house and carried her suitcase into the bedroom she had always occupied when the family was in London during her unmarried years. She looked around her unhappily. "I suppose I'll be fine. I didn't sign on in this marriage to be left in this fortress of virginity, though. So when you get back, be prepared to make amends."

He laughed. "I'll be thinking of nothing else."

"That's always been your way." She put her arms around his neck and they kissed. "I know it would be foolish to say be careful. Just come back to me."

"I'll do my best."

He boarded a plane at Heathrow and slept through the long flight to JFK. He devoted the first few hours after he got there to meeting each flight that arrived from London that morning, watching the straggling groups of people come out through the customs corridor into the international terminal. At first he didn't see anyone who looked like he might be Michael Delamina. Nobody who came to England to kill him would have traveled with a wife and children, or brought so much luggage that he had to maneuver it around precariously propped on a rented cart.

Just after noon, Schaeffer saw his mark arrive, dragging a single rolling suitcase. He seemed exhausted, and his suit looked as though it had been on him for a week. He had an irritated expression. His face seemed to be made for it, with a protruding chin, thick brows that almost met in the middle, and a low, wrinkled forehead. Schaeffer scanned the terminal and saw nobody waiting —no family happy to see the man return, no limo driver, nobody from an office.

As the man rolled his suitcase along the shiny floor, Schaeffer began to follow him. When Delamina joined the line at the taxi stand, Schaeffer joined it too. He got close enough at the cab-stand to hear him telling the driver the address, then turned and walked away and joined a group far along the drive waiting for the shuttle to the car-rental depot. When he got there, he rented a car to drive to Delamina's house on the north shore of Long Island and look it over. The house was a suburban one-story brick single-family building set on a large green lawn. It had a long driveway that led to a garage set a few feet behind the house. There seemed to be nothing about it that would present an obstacle to him.

Next he drove to a truck-rental lot in the next town, parked his car, and rented a plain white van. At an industrial supply store he bought a uniform consisting of blue coveralls and a blue baseball cap, and a clipboard. Two hours later he drove the van to Dela-mina's and pretended to be a delivery man. He made his way in-side the house to take care of Michael Delamina with one of the knives he found in a wooden block in the kitchen.

Since that afternoon he had been following the most basic strat-egy he knew. It was something he had learned from Eddie Mastrew-ski when he was a teenager. "If someone attacks you, come back at him fast. Then see who else needs it. Go from the young, low-level shooters up through the one who sent them out after you, and then the boss, the highest one you know. It's just like running up a flight of stairs. If you stop halfway up, you're dead. You have to get all the way to the top. The man who is up there will keep sending new people after you until the end of time."

In the old days he could have done that quickly, before the ones on the upper levels had time to hear what was coming and prepare. He had known enough about the Mafia families then to be able to piece together who someone like Delamina must be. But this time he'd had no idea who Delamina was, or who he had worked for. Schaeffer couldn't go to somebody who was con-nected and ask him to explain it. He had needed to fly down to Washington and get Elizabeth Waring from the Justice Depart-ment to tell him it was Frank Tosca. Tonight he was back on Long Island on his way to Frank Tosca's house.

Schaeffer didn't like being in New York. Manhattan was a tiny, crowded place, and it would be easy to get spotted on the street by somebody from the old days that he didn't even notice. People drove by in cars, or sat at restaurant windows and watched pedestrians pass. And unless the nature of the universe had changed, there were always Mafia underlings moving around the island on their constant rounds of errands, picking up and delivering—taking a rake-off from one business, giving a loan to another, bringing bribes to officials, accepting tributes from even smaller criminals. They all made themselves useful to their superiors by watching for people like him. He was avoiding Manhattan this trip. He had flown into JFK and rented a car to drive to Tosca's house.

He hadn't tried to obtain a weapon. Having to go through metal detectors to fly somewhere, then get off a plane and do a job, had always been difficult. In the old days, when he had been working for hire, the client would sometimes have what he needed waiting for him—a gun that had been stolen in a burglary and could only be traced to its last owner, or one that had temporarily disappeared from a dealer's secondhand inventory and would be cleaned up and returned the next day. There had even been a couple that had been stolen from the intended victim's own arsenal ahead of time.

But he no longer had clients. Tonight he would have to find what he needed as he went along. He stopped at a home-improvement store not far from the airport and paid in cash for a few items that might be useful—a crowbar, a box of rubber gloves, a lock-blade knife, a strong magnet used for picking up lost screws and nails.

He loaded his purchases into the rental car and drove toward Glen Cove. When he reached the little city, he drove up Glen Cove Avenue toward the neighborhood where Tosca lived. He passed the turnoff, backtracked a few blocks, and found it again. He saw a restaurant on Glen Cove Avenue that looked appealing to him, but he decided it was best not to have any contact with the locals. What he was planning to do would be big news, and he didn't want anybody to remember that a stranger had been in the restaurant that evening. He drove on. Glen Cove was a prosperous little town that seemed to be largely horizontal. It was composed of buildings that weren't higher than two stories, most of them one. There were a few banks, boutiques, and restaurants, the sort of businesses that existed in places where people lived rather than worked. He watched people walking along the sidewalks, stopping to glance in the lighted display windows or getting into cars and driving off.

He tried to locate the house where Frank Tosca lived, and eventually found it by counting the streets parallel to Glen Cove Avenue, then counting houses from the corner. There were tall, leafy old hardwood trees on the street and thick hedges that obscured the view. Some lights were on, but he could see little else about the house from the street except that it was big. When he was growing up, the capos at Tosca's level still lived in small, narrow, two-story workingmen's houses in the less desirable parts of Queens or Brooklyn. It wasn't until they got to the point where there was a rational explanation for their having so much money—a real business big enough to produce wealth—that they might settle in Manhattan. None of them lived in places like this, a suburb along the water. It just wasn't done. The old guys had been too paranoid to be away from the neighborhoods where their soldiers lived. They didn't want to take the chance that somebody was talking business without them.

Then he saw something that he hadn't expected. There were three vans parked in the quiet, tree-lined streets a few blocks away. One was a dark-colored plain one across the street from Tosca's house and about three hundred feet down. There was another at the other end of the block. There was a third on the next parallel street, behind Tosca's house.

Another house caught his eye. It was about a block and a half away, behind high hedges. The driveway went straight back from the gated entrance about a hundred feet to a circular turnaround at the front door. After all the years living in England he recognized it as a copy in miniature of the gravel drives that were built to accommodate eighteenth-century carriages visiting large homes. This house had no lights on, but there were four dark-colored cars lined up facing the street.

He found himself smiling. It was clear to him that this was the result of his nighttime visit to Elizabeth Waring in Washington. He had told her that Tosca had kept the weapon from one of his earliest murders, and here was Tosca's house, one day later, under heavy surveillance by federal agents. He was glad he had driven around looking closely at everything before he tried to get into the house. He would have ruined everything. He left Glen Cove and drove twelve miles to Hempstead, checked into a hotel, had dinner, and went to sleep.

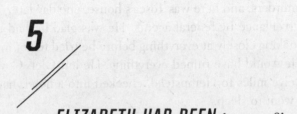

5

ELIZABETH HAD BEEN keeping files on him for more than twenty years. No, that was not exactly true. She had started a file more than twenty years ago and then, after a few years, had sent it with a number of other files to be placed in long-term storage. She had called him "unknown suspect" for the first part of the file when she was still only positing the existence of a single man who was causing so much disruption in the families. Her superiors had assured her that their long experience told them it was a real war, with the families attacking each other. He had been busy for at least a month before she got close enough to begin hearing informants talking about him and calling him the Butcher's Boy. It led up to the discovery of the body parts buried on the horse farm Carlo Balacontano, aka Carl Bala, owned at Saratoga.

The discovery was prompted by a telephone tip to the FBI. Elizabeth had said right away to anyone who would listen that it was a setup. Why would a smart strategist like Carl Bala have his men bury the head and hands of Arthur Fieldston on his own property, a hundred yards from his summer house? Why would he have them cut the body up in the first place? Weren't there a million pieces of empty land in upstate New York where nobody would find a body? Had the oceans dried up?

Her superiors had said, "He had them bury the head and hands there because it was a place he thought he could protect until he died." And she had said, "Somebody was capable of hiding the rest of the body — say, two hundred pounds of it — where nobody has ever found it. But the head and hands — the only means of identifying a murder victim — had to be right where he would walk past them every day. Carl Bala is not an idiot. He's ordered a lot of people murdered, but not this one. The person who buried the head and hands is the one who made the call to tell us where they were."

Her protests had been futile. The murder charge against Carl Bala stood. Elizabeth had been ordered to take a vacation until the trial was over. She had flown to England and walked in gardens that had been cultivated for seven hundred years and watched plays nearly every night. When she had come home, Carl Bala had been sentenced to life in prison and the Butcher's Boy was already gone, as though he had been made of smoke.

Her job in those days had been to analyze police and coroners' reports, searching for deaths that had been declared suicides or accidents that weren't, or for homicides that formed familiar patterns, or that seemed to benefit someone in organized crime. She was good at it, and she continued to scour the reports for years, but found no sign of him. He had stirred up the families with a few well-chosen murders — ones that would be almost certain to provoke retaliation against some rival group. Probably as soon as Carl Bala was arrested and denied bail as a flight risk, the Butcher's Boy disappeared.

She kept the file she had been building in a lower drawer of her desk in the back. Each time she was promoted she moved it to her new office, until she had moved from the computer rooms in the basement all the way up to the fourth floor seven years later. Only then did she send it to the archives.

Three years after that she was looking for it again. She had noticed the same kind of sudden rampage as before. This time it started with Tony Talarese dying in the kitchen of one of his restaurants. Tony Talarese had been wearing a wire for the FBI at the moment when he'd been killed. It was a macabre scene, as she pictured it while listening to the recording. His wife had been standing at the stove wearing a big pair of oven mitts when the shooter had struck. She had shrieked, rushing toward her fallen husband, flapping her arms like a bird to free her hands of the mitts. When she got to him, she hugged him, pulled up his shirt, and then screamed, "A wire! The son of a bitch is wearing a wire!" At the same time, she had spotted the out-of-proportion hysterical tears of two young hostesses and a waitress, and correctly guessed why they were so heartbroken at the death of her husband. At the moment when the FBI agents monitoring the wire burst in, she was shrieking "Whores!" and chasing them with a kitchen knife. The killing moved outward and upward from Talarese. Mafia captains died unexpected, violent deaths, and there were so many explanations for each death that there could be no explanation.

Some experts said it was the young men trying to get the old men out of the way so they could move up. But Elizabeth noticed that the first casualties had been young men. Others said outsiders must be invading the established Mafia territories, but there were no sightings of possible successors—no Latin American gangs, no black gangs, no bikers, or prison gangs. When a capo fell, nobody took over.

She was sure it had been him again. He had come back to create trouble for them once more. It had been her theory at the time, and still was, that he had gone somewhere to retire—Brazil, Thailand, Paraguay—and the Mafia, or just some part of it, really, had tried to make good on its old reputation for hunting down its enemies. They had always had great success with sticky-fingered card dealers and addicted drug runners. It would be very different trying to find and punish him. Months later she had listened to a wiretap recording in which one member of the Lorenzo family had told another, "Stay out of it. Don't look for him. If the Balacontano family still wants him, then he's theirs. If they don't get him on the first try, he'll kill some of them, and we'll see what falls out of their hands as they go down. Maybe we'll be able to pick something up—a business, a territory. But stay away from him."

He was someone they feared with an almost superstitious fear, because they knew him. When he was still in his late teens, he had been the one these men called in when they needed a truly professional murder. In his twenties he knew many of the midlevel soldiers and upper-level dignitaries, at least by sight, and had bargained with some of them, because those were the people who hired outside specialists. Her informants told her he always did what he had agreed to with an icy efficiency, took his pay, and disappeared. There was no trail to his employers, and not much chance that anyone could have followed him away from the final meeting.

Years later, when something had gone wrong and he had decided he needed to cause trouble, his reputation actually helped. When he began cutting down important men, the ones who recognized the work as his were sure that rival bosses must be employing him to destroy the competition. For a long time it had never occurred to anyone that Carl Bala had simply become so arrogant and overconfident in his growing power that rather than paying this man his fee for a hit he'd done, he had told one of his underlings to arrange an ambush in Las Vegas to kill him. It had been the most expensive act of parsimony ever.

There was a quiet buzz, and Elizabeth picked up her phone. "Yes?"

"It's the FBI New York office. Agent Holman."

"I'll take it."

When she heard the click, she said, "This is Elizabeth Waring. Is this Agent Holman?"

"Good afternoon," Holman said. "I'm calling because I was assigned to supervise the surveillance of Frank Tosca's home. I'm afraid there seems to be some kind of misunderstanding. I understood that your office had requested an intensive surveillance of Tosca."

"That's right. We appreciate your efforts very much. Has something turned up?"

"Well, yes. Special Agent Carlson, my section chief, sent a request for some paperwork—a designation of the case, some cost approvals—to Deputy Assistant Attorney General Hunsecker, and the response was 'What surveillance?' I thought the least I could do was pick up a phone and see if we could straighten this out. Mr. Hunsecker's staff seems to think he won't approve it."

"It was an emergency request," she said. "It hasn't gone through Mr. Hunsecker yet. I'm pretty sure my second, Bob Fulton, explained it to your duty agent last night. I had an inquiry from a person I know to be a professional assassin of some standing. He wanted to know who Michael Delamina's boss was. Then, late last evening we got the news that Delamina had been murdered some hours before I spoke with the assassin. What we were trying to do was prevent another murder."

"We've observed some significant security precautions around Mr. Tosca's house in Glen Cove. He seems to live at a pretty high level of alertness."

"There are a lot of people with reasons to want him dead. But at the moment, I think he's finally got one who's capable of getting in, killing him, and getting out."

"What's his reason? Is somebody paying him?"

"I don't know his reason for certain. I think he retired a long time ago. But I think that twice in the years since then, some young, ambitious soldiers have found him and tried to collect on the old contracts."

"Who put out the contracts?"

"I know Carl Bala put one out on him before he went to prison. People have said it's in the millions."

"Balacontano? Is he even alive to pay off?"

"As of this moment he is. He's safe and sound in a maximum security special wing, where nobody gets to see him but the doctors and the visitors he listed when he went in. But he'd almost certainly pay off. He's in for life, so there's no use for Bala's money that would bring him more pleasure than the death of this hit man."

Agent Holman was silent for a few seconds. "I'd hate to shut this down now. I can keep up the surveillance on Tosca's house until the end of the day. At that time, if I don't have the official approval for the operation, we'll have to stand down. Do you think you can get it?"

"All I can guarantee is that I'm going to try very hard. Thanks so much for buying me some time."

One of the other phone lines had been blinking for at least thirty seconds. She knew it must be someone from Hunsecker's office calling to find out what she was doing. She couldn't think of a way to answer that without appearing to have disregarded everything Hunsecker had said. She picked up the telephone. "Elizabeth Waring."

"Waring." It wasn't a secretary. It was Hunsecker. Waring was aware that her door was opening and that her assistant, Geoffrey, was holding a hand-scrawled note, looking worried. She nodded to him and pointed at the door. He turned and went through it.

"Hello, Mr. Hunsecker. I'm sorry if I kept you waiting. I was on another call with the FBI in New York."

"So it's true."

"Late last night we received the news that Michael Delamina had been murdered. I realized that I had to try to head off the next murder."

"You did exactly as this killer asked—you started an FBI investigation of his enemy."

"I set up a surveillance to protect Tosca, not investigate him."

"You have a team watching him twenty-four hours a day. The difference is lost on me."

"It's a big one. The target is the killer, not the probable victim."

"And if the FBI just happened to overhear the victim planning a crime, or engaging in a conspiracy, they have orders not to arrest him?"

"No. I didn't think that was necessary."

"Your humanitarian surveillance just happens to put the FBI and the target of your last request in close proximity. I've already called off your request. The FBI goes off the case at six."

"Are you sure you need to call it off? They're already in place."

"The Justice Department of the United States can't be in the position of targeting a killer's enemies, even if he's a potential informant. It's a matter of personal and professional ethics."

"We have a practical disagreement about how best to prevent a murder. That doesn't mean my ethics are any worse than yours. I think it's wrong to let anyone be murdered. For me that supersedes my previous wish to investigate this victim. If you withdraw his protection, he'll be dead in a couple of days."

"If that happens, I'll be amazed."

"As soon as it does, I'll let you know."

"If it does happen in the next couple of days, you probably won't. That will fall during your two-day suspension. You're excused until Monday."

"I can't believe this."

"You'll probably get through this, if you don't say anything else. What will it be?"

She forced herself to say nothing. She hung up, and as she stared down at her big wooden desk, she felt her stomach sink. She was almost dizzy. She had never been suspended from any job before, or even come close. Passing through her mind were the humiliation of being overruled and embarrassed in front of an FBI agent, a pure anger at Hunsecker's rigid stupidity, and fear that she was about to lose her job. She felt like crying, but she knew that Hunsecker's confidants would be looking for that, and hers would be alarmed by it. She wanted to get out of here—had to, if she wanted to keep her job.

She packed the files she'd been reading into her briefcase, turned off the lights in her office, and walked out the door. "Geoff, I've been suspended for the rest of the week. Keep track of my calls, open my mail, and sort it in my in-box in priority order. We'll have a lot of catching up to do on Monday."

6

HE WAS FEELING more relaxed now that he had found Frank Tosca's house surrounded by FBI agents. The destruction of the life Michael Schaeffer had built in England had stopped, and his trouble was contained for the moment. Delamina and the other two men who had been sent to England to find him were dead. Now Frank Tosca couldn't walk his dog without having his picture taken, and he couldn't talk to his family without having it recorded. Tosca didn't need to be dead. If the Justice Department was already preparing a murder case against him, then his brief run at being the head of the Balacontano family was over. He would be transformed from the young bull who was going to bring back the old days into a dangerous liability. Even if the FBI didn't arrest him, his closest friends would abandon him.

He checked out of his hotel Thursday morning at ten A.M. and got into his rented Toyota Avalon. Since he had moved to England he hadn't driven much. His main house was in Bath, and so he walked nearly everywhere. He kept a Jaguar in the garage because Meg liked to drive in the country sometimes and liked to have him drive her on social occasions when she had to be the Honourable Lady Margaret Susanna Moncrief Holroyd of Axeborough. He missed her this morning.

He drove in the direction of Tosca's house. Before he left for

JFK he wanted to take one look at the surveillance team in daylight. There had to be more certainty about Tosca's fate. If the feds were committed to a full-scale operation to keep Tosca in their field of vision twenty-four hours a day, then they had nearly enough evidence, and Tosca was doomed. But he had to be sure. He didn't want to be home in Bath two months from now thinking Meg was safe, and then discover more of Tosca's underlings making their way through his back garden.

He made sure he was below the speed limit, which was only twenty-five in these narrow residential streets, but he didn't spot the FBI field team. The vans with the remote listening devices and telescopic lenses were not in evidence on the streets where they had been last night. He knew the FBI preferred the use of buildings for long-term surveillance. They were less obtrusive, held more people, had a higher vantage point, provided a clearer view of the target, and supplied an inexhaustible source of electric power.

He began to look closely at the houses. He drove by the three where the vans had been parked two nights ago and studied the immediate area. There seemed to be none of the signs that would reveal the presence of FBI agents. There was no lowering of blinds or shades so there could be cameras above the rods or mountings. There were no dishes or disks that might be parabolic microphones, no cars parked in the wrong places, no crews working on the roads or on the wires, the pipes, or the landscaping of any of the houses. Most of the garage doors were open, and he could see high-end station wagons and SUVs—nothing that was either powerful or nimble. He drove to the house around the corner where two nights ago the high hedges had hidden the chase cars lined up in the driveway. He passed the entrance, and he could see the long driveway was empty. The windows had no curtains on them, and he could see into empty rooms.

He was certain now that the FBI had left. The surveillance was over. Had Tosca been so stupid or unlucky that he'd already said or done something in the few hours since Tuesday that had allowed the agents to arrest him? He drove back to the block where Tosca's house was and drove past it. There were no cops searching the house and grounds, no signs of any police vehicles anywhere. The surveillance had ended, and that meant he was going to have to take care of Tosca himself. He drove out of the residential streets to the commercial part of town. It was still before noon, so he had a lot of time to fill.

He went to a big movie theater in a shopping mall and watched a movie about bank robbers. It was so far from reality that he could watch it uncritically. The real bank robbers he had met were stupid. They all knew that bank robberies were investigated by local, state, and federal agencies. They knew that while they were committing their crime, they were being videotaped from several angles. They knew that tellers' stations had silent-alarm buttons, and that the money they got was marked and sometimes contained an ink bomb. They did it anyway and kept doing it until they were in handcuffs. But these were movie bank robbers, so they were attractive, smart, and lucky, none more so than the beautiful girl safecracker who wore the spandex catsuit and handled the explosives.

When that movie ended, he went outside again and went for a walk, then had a light lunch. After that, he went to another theater and watched another movie, this one about a high-powered woman executive who was forced to pretend she was married to her male rival. When the two finally did what everyone had been expecting for two hours and the lights went on, he walked some more, had dinner, and went to a third movie. It was about a professional killer, and he slept through most of it. When it was late enough and most of the people on the streets had already driven home, he left his car parked in the lot of the big hotel on Glen Cove that looked like a British manor and walked toward Tosca's house.

He'd been aware of the possibility that he was wrong and that the FBI agents would be back after the rest of the world was asleep so they could work unnoticed until they were established in some comfortable place and had all their gadgets working. But there were no signs of them tonight either. It had also occurred to him that if they had conclusive evidence on a man who was unlikely to be alone and sure to be heavily armed, they might pull everybody back for a day and swoop in later. But the neighborhood presented too much clear evidence against that theory. There were cars in all the driveways. Television sets projected moving glows on many white ceilings. If the FBI had planned to raid the house of a Mafia capo like Tosca, they wouldn't want civilians in the line of fire. There were no feds: he had the night to himself.

Tosca's house had a lawn that looked like a city park, with tall old trees at irregular intervals. There was a long driveway with a circle around a flower bed near the door, in nearly the same sort of grand miniaturization as the empty house around the corner.

He turned his attention to the house. The place would be filled with dozens of machines that were supposed to make the night go away, make the cold and the heat stay within a degree of each other, bring in images from everywhere in the world, and keep Frank Tosca safe. Considerable effort would be required to hide from the machines and stay invisible. He set to work on the electronic gear.

He climbed a tree at the corner of the house to reach the eaves and pulled himself up onto the roof. If there was a power failure and the phone lines were cut, the battery-operated internal modem in the security system control box in the house would begin dialing the headquarters of the security company. But the signal would be sent by a battery-operated transmitter that amounted to a cell phone mounted on the roof. He found the power cord for recharging the battery, followed it to the transmitter mounted near the peak, and disconnected both power sources.

Just beyond the edge of the roof was the tree he had climbed to get up here. He grasped a limb and lowered himself to the ground, walked around the house to the telephone circuit box, and pulled the wires from their connections. Next he went to the electrical circuit box and flipped the main circuit breaker to cut the power to the house.

He had not completely neutralized the alarm system. The security circuit box inside the house would have a rechargeable battery that would cause the alarm to sound when a breach occurred. All he had done was ensure that the signal wouldn't go to the security company and the police.

He circled the house, looking in the windows to find the easiest way in. He knew the system installed on the windows and doors. Each contact consisted of a magnet on one side and a switch on the other. If the magnet on the window frame moved away from the switch in the sill, the switch would close, the alarm circuit would be completed, and the alarm would sound. There was an alarm system box somewhere in the house, and it was possible to open it and turn off the system. But it was always hidden in a closet or cupboard, and Tosca had a big house.

After a few minutes he found the window he wanted. It was divided into four small panes on the top half and four on the bottom, and looked out onto a small garden of low, thick flowering plants. He used duct tape to cover one pane so it wouldn't shatter and make a loud noise. Then he wrapped his crowbar in his jacket and pushed it against the windowpane until it gave inward with a quiet crack. Nothing fell to the floor. He pulled the glass out and set it on the ground. Then he put his arm inside. He placed the magnet he had brought right beside the window at the center of the sill where the switch would be. Next he reached up to disengage the latch and raised the window. No alarm sounded.

He climbed inside, lowered the window again, took his magnet, and moved to stand with his back against the inner wall of the room. He stood still, looked into the dark house, and listened. When he was still a boy, Eddie Mastrewski had said, "If you want to be good at night work, watch the cat."

The cat he meant was the big yellow tomcat that Eddie allowed to live in the office of the butcher shop. Most of the time he seemed to be asleep. He slept whenever there was no strong reason not to. "You mean now?"

"He's resting. Learn from him."

The boy could tell that Eddie was serious. Eddie's lessons were also tests, and the boy knew it. He watched the cat for a long time before he was sure that the cat wasn't exactly sleeping, but not exactly not sleeping either. The cat's eyes were not quite closed, and he was still aware of the things that were going on around him. He kept watching the cat while he was working—weighing, wrapping, and labeling cuts of meat that Eddie's expert knifework placed on the cutting board—and he kept noticing other things. At the end of that day, Eddie said, "What have you learned?"

The boy said, "I'm not ready to say yet. I want to think about him and watch some more."

"Good start. That's what the cat would do."

The boy watched the cat get up at twilight and start to walk out the back door of the butcher shop. The boy reached for him to scoop him up so he could be watched, but the cat wriggled, turned its head slightly, and placed all four fangs on the boy's wrist, not quite breaking the skin, but showing him the possibility. The boy didn't let go, so the cat's claws came out to give him a quick, shallow slash that made the boy drop him.

The cat landed on his feet with a faint thump, and his body flowed around the door and into the evening.

The boy didn't know Eddie had been watching. "They're faster than we are because their nervous system is quicker. If you beat a cat to something, he's letting you win."

"Why would he do that?"

"He does it for his own reasons, and he doesn't talk. Go ahead. I'll clean up."

It was not a small favor. Every night each surface of the shop had to be cleaned and washed, and all the metal polished before they locked the door. The boy went down and out into the weedy empty lot behind the shop, sat down on a cinder block, and waited, trying to catch sight of the cat.

It took him minutes of patient staring at denser spots in the general darkness, but then a car went by and the light of its headlights reflected off the cat's amber eyes. The boy stayed where he was, watching for three hours while the cat waited in ambush for small creatures of the night, or took up a new position and then melted into nothing more than a concentration of the darkness, something that might be a rock or a clump of grass or a piece of wood—but not a cat. And then, when the cat knew that the prey was too close to escape, it moved like electricity or a thought, and grasped the animal. The cat would hold the prey with its foreclaws and kick with the rear claws to gut it. As the boy got used to watching the cat, he began to learn the things that Eddie wanted him to see, the secrets. A cat could shape himself into a hundred motionless not-cat silhouettes. And the cat could shape time. He would wait as long as the prey thought a cat might wait, and then longer. Then he could move so quickly that the only view the boy had was a memory, an impression of something that had already happened.

When he was finally ready to tell Eddie what he had observed, Eddie said, "Remember that you and the cat are in the same business, and he's the grand champion. He was born into it, kind of like you. People say cats are cruel because they'll play with a mouse, pretend to let him go, and then catch him again. It's not cruelty. He's practicing, trying to get better at being what he is. If you could move through the dark like a cat does, you'd live forever."

Eddie had practically lived forever, long enough to die of his other job. Eating all those precious cuts of meat, marbled with fat and cooked over a flame, had ultimately given him a heart attack. When he finally died, Eddie's funeral was arranged by the same local undertakers who had arranged his parents' funeral, but there was a different feeling to it.

All of the women who had received special attention from Eddie, the wives who had him deliver special cuts of meat to their back doors while their husbands were away at work, showed up.

So did a couple of divorcées and a widow Eddie would let come into the back of the shop to pick out their own delicacies. It was as though Eddie's secret girlfriends had agreed that if they all showed up, no gossip could possibly single out any one of them for disapproval. The boy considered their silent agreement the last noble gesture of his childhood, and was careful to be very polite and respectful to each of the ladies during the funeral and the endless reception held at Eddie's house afterward. When everyone had gone home, he went to the butcher shop and did some defrosting.

Eddie had told him at least five years earlier that when he died, the boy should thaw the big blocks of ice at the back of the freezer. The boy took the blocks to the back of the shop, and used hot water, sunshine, and a blowtorch. Inside the ice, carefully wrapped, the boy found several sealed plastic boxes. Each was labeled GIBLETS AND GIZZARDS FOR CAT. In them were stacks of hundred-dollar bills.

The next day the boy gave all the meat in the shop to neighborhood families, gave the shop and its equipment one last cleaning as Eddie had taught him, and put the house and the shop up for sale. He gave the cat to the lady florist two doors down from the shop who always bought cat treats for his daily visits to her store.

In the darkness, inside of a strange house all these years later, he used what he had learned about the night. He had been immobile long enough for his eyes to get used to the dark, and he'd heard no sounds of people. He began to move. He kept the surface of the wall three inches from his right shoulder and never stepped on the hardwood floor except at the edges, avoiding the center where loose boards might creak. His stronger arm and leg were near the wall, where an opponent couldn't neutralize them easily, and he could use them to push off. His knees were bent slightly so he could jump, duck, or dive quickly.

His breathing was even and deep, and his movements were patient. He simply stayed in one place long enough to feel and hear the void before him and then move forward to fill it. Many years earlier, when he was just learning to move in the night, he would stop in a hallway, listen for the sounds of the house, and count to a hundred or two hundred before he moved again. He did these things without having to calculate now. He was living in these seconds, but also sending his mind on ahead, searching for Frank Tosca.

He had to get a feel for the rooms. The living room was sure to be at the front of the house, and a house this size would probably have a foyer at the entrance. The kitchen and pantry would be at the back of the house and have their own entry. Coming forward from the kitchen there would be a formal dining room, so people could enter it from the living room and be served from the kitchen. In a one-story house the bedrooms would be toward the back, probably off a single corridor. That corridor would be the most dangerous part of the house tonight.

He moved in the direction where he predicted the corridor would be and verified that he had found it. The hallway was a single, straight one with three doors on each side. He stopped beside the first door.

He was eager to find Frank Tosca. He had met him a few times when they were both in their twenties. Tosca had been arrogant and sullen, with a habitual expression that hinted he was contemplating violence. But he had managed to endear himself to senior people in the Balacontano family. Tosca had been a particular favorite of Vincent, Carlo's younger brother, who had a reputation for throwing money around, partying, and drinking too much. Tosca was broad shouldered and thick necked, and Vincent liked to go to clubs with two men who looked like that as his bodyguards. It gave Tosca a chance to watch the old capos when they were still near their prime, and his proximity made some of their legitimacy rub off on him. In retrospect, it probably shouldn't have been surprising that he had risen so high in his early forties, but it also wouldn't have been surprising if he had been killed.

Schaeffer stuck his head in the first doorway and saw an empty bed. It was flat, still made. He studied the room in the moonlight from the window and saw that it had nothing out of place, and that there was nothing in it that seemed to belong to anyone in particular. The dresser held a white antimacassar and an empty tray for jewelry or pocket change, but there was nothing in it. The bathroom counter by the sink was bare. He moved to the room across the hall, and found it empty too. These were guest rooms, each with its own bath, a dresser, a chair, and no sign that anyone had stayed there recently. He checked a third room and then moved toward the fourth. He needed to be sure he wasn't leaving anyone behind him as he advanced.

The fourth room was a child's bedroom, a boy's room with an aquarium, an electric guitar on the wall, some posters, and a clothes hamper full of dirty clothes. He could smell musky sweat from ten feet away. This was a terrible discovery. He knew now that Frank Tosca had heard what had happened to Delamina and drawn the right conclusion. He had known that he had no adequate defense against a man like the one who was coming for him, so he had taken his family and left.

The room across the hall belonged to a girl. It seemed the girl was a bit older than the boy because she had abandoned any pretense of order, as though she used the room primarily as a closet. Some of the clothes that were thrown on the floor had the tags still on them, and they seemed to be women's sizes. There were dozens of photographs and clippings on the wall, but it was too dark to make out any images.

The last of the six rooms was a baby's, with a crib and mobiles hanging above it with little winged angels. Along one wall were a changing table with a foot-high cross mounted above it, a dresser, and a set of shelves that held diapers, little outfits, and supplies. Three children's rooms, but so far no master suite.

At the end of the hall, what he found was not a wall, but a door. He was almost certain that what he wanted was behind it. But if Tosca was smart enough to know that he was coming, then he was smart enough to make better use of the information than by just leaving. It was possible that what Tosca had done was set up a booby trap. It might be something as simple as a spring gun or as complicated as an ambush. The most likely place for either was behind that door.

He stood where he was and listened for a minute, then for another. He heard nothing, so he turned around and began to move along the corridor the way he had come. He passed the six bedrooms, reached the end of the hall where there was a turn, and stepped around it into the living room.

He passed into the dining room, looked through the window, and saw that he had misinterpreted something he'd seen. When he had seen the side of a building through the window in the boy's bedroom, he had thought he was looking at the neighbors' house. But it wasn't another building. It was part of this one, a wing he hadn't searched. It ran along the left side of the house and created an enclosed courtyard about fifteen feet wide and fifty feet long, so the family bedrooms looked out on a quiet, private space. The other wing was little more than a walkway, with no doors in it. There was only one curved portal that led through the wing to the other side so a gardener could slip into the enclosure, rake the leaves, and depart without ever entering the house. Tosca's suite windows could only be seen from within the courtyard, and there was no door or window across from his suite. It would be impossible to fire a round into the suite from the other wing.

Schaeffer went back to the boy's room, closed the door, put his magnet on the sill to keep the alarm from tripping, opened the sash, and climbed out. He remained still in the courtyard for a long time, listening and leaning his back against the outside of the house to feel any vibration from movement inside. Then he moved ahead past the girl's room and the baby's room, and reached a pair of French doors. He leaned close and peered in, then withdrew his head without moving his feet.

There were three men in the room, and all he had was a lock-blade knife and a two-foot crowbar. He played with the crowbar for a few seconds, swinging it, twirling it, and letting it slide through his hand and stop so he could feel the weight and balance. It was thick and heavy, with a crook at one end to gain leverage for prying. But the crook gave that end a bit of extra weight, so he held the other end to swing it.

He reached for the handle of the French doors, pushed, but found it locked. He withdrew his hand and peered inside. One man was asleep on the bed with his shoes off, one curled up on the small couch across the room, and one upright in a chair nodding off. Schaeffer could see a shotgun lying on the coffee table in front of him.

They were obviously prepared for the one thing that they thought might happen — that a man would come into the house, walk down the hallway, and enter the suite through the door. Only one man had to be awake to hear him walk down the hallway and try to enter the suite. The one on duty would yell and open fire, and the other two would jump to their feet and add unnecessary shots.

He would make things go a bit differently. He would appear to be in two places simultaneously. He picked up a couple of smooth Chinese river stones from the garden, climbed back through the window in the son's room, closed it, and took his magnet, then went to the baby's room. He placed the magnet, leaned out into the courtyard, and threw his first rock at the French doors, and the other right away at the opening in the courtyard, bouncing the stone so it sounded like someone running away.

The French doors swung open and the man with the shotgun ran along the courtyard to the arched portal, trying to get a shot at the intruder. Schaeffer stationed himself just inside the doorway of the baby's room and listened for sounds from the hallway. In a moment, the door of the master suite swung open and the two men who had been asleep ran up the hallway, trying to get around to the front of the house to head off the imaginary man their companion was chasing.

Schaeffer waited for the first man to pass his doorway, then stepped into the hall, already swinging his crowbar. His swing caught the second man just above his brow and knocked him backward onto the floor, unconscious. Schaeffer ducked back into the cover of the baby's room and used his crowbar to drag the man's pistol along the floor into his waiting hand.

The fallen man's companion was already near the end of the hall, but he had heard the sound of the crowbar blow and his companion's collapse to the floor. He fired twice, pointlessly, at the baby's room doorway.

Inside the baby's room, Schaeffer slipped out the window into the courtyard, aimed the gun in through the open window at the doorway, and removed his magnet from the sill. The alarm began to ring.

The man in the hallway, thinking Schaeffer had opened the window to escape, ran into the room, hoping to catch him in mid-climb. Schaeffer fired twice into the surprised man's chest and watched him fall. Schaeffer climbed back in, closed the baby's room window, and hurried down the hallway to the master suite. He waited just inside the French doors that led to the courtyard.

The man with the shotgun had seen no intruder, but had heard the four shots and the alarm, so he ran back through the courtyard toward the master suite. As he burst into the suite with his shotgun ready, Schaeffer put his first shot into the man's right temple. He died before he could take a second step, and sprawled forward onto the floor.

Schaeffer pulled the pistol from inside the coat of the man he had just killed and the loaded spare magazine with it. Then he left through the French doors, closing them behind him. The sound of the alarm was muffled immediately, almost silenced by the closed-up and well-insulated brick house. But he wanted to be gone in case he had missed something and some unnoticed backup to the system had transmitted the message that there had been a break-in. He found an open trash can two blocks away and dropped his crowbar into it, with the magnet stuck to it.

He made it to the hotel, got into his car, and drove. He was tired, but he drove from Long Island to New Jersey, and checked into a hotel near Trenton. The night had been a disappointment. Five days had passed since the attack in Britain, and Frank Tosca was still alive.

7

ON MONDAY MORNING at six A.M. Elizabeth walked into her office at the Justice Department. She wanted to spend the two hours before anyone else arrived getting caught up on the mail Geoff had left for her. The two hours before the phones started ringing would give her a chance to learn what she had missed and to find out what had been done about it so far. Deputy Assistant Hunsecker was acting as though disagreeing with him were a moral failing, and he'd given her the only administrative punishment she'd ever had. She wanted and needed to keep her job.

She had decided over the weekend that she would pretend to herself that it wasn't a great injustice that she was on the verge of being fired from her job after twenty years with the department. She'd worked in the bureaucracy long enough to know that allowing herself to nurse a grievance would eventually make staying at this job impossible. The only appropriate thing to do now was to pay attention to her work and do the best job she could.

She unloaded her briefcase on the desk and stopped. Her in-box had already been piled with files and memos when she'd left on Wednesday. Now it was empty. The other box was empty too, which was where she put papers that needed to be filed. Had Geoff filed everything? She recalled one of the files that had been

55

in the box on Wednesday. It was a file she had made ten years ago about the expenses involved in centralizing the information obtained on organized crime wiretaps. Since another set of centralizations was coming, she wanted to refresh her memory of what was involved and how much it had cost the last time. She went to the correct filing cabinet, opened the drawer, and found the red card she had placed between two other files when she had taken that one so she could replace it easily.

She remembered a couple of other files and checked for them. None of them had been returned to the cabinets. They were simply gone. As she continued her search, she tried to delay the slowly growing conviction that this was Hunsecker's work. She looked around in Geoffrey's space for signs of whatever must have come in for her since Wednesday afternoon. There were no reports, no memos, no inquiries, not even a phone message. She went back to her office to see if anything had been stored in the locked file drawer in the left side of her desk.

At seven, Geoff came in. He was carrying the briefcase that he seemed to bring primarily to hold his snacks and newspapers. "Good morning, Elizabeth. Get through the exile okay?"

"It wasn't as bad as I'd feared or as good as I'd hoped. Have a good weekend?"

"Sure." He finished putting away his things, then said, "What's wrong?"

"I can't seem to find anything. I expected quite a pile of mail and stuff. Where is it?"

He came into her office and looked at her desk. "I had all of it right here and in order on Friday afternoon." He pointed at an empty space. "Right here."

"You didn't leave anything in the pile that was classified or sensitive, did you?"

"No," he said. "Everything like that is locked up in the reading-room safe."

She shrugged. "Then it probably isn't important. But I'll let you know when I find out what became of it." She went into her office and closed the door. It had occurred to her that having some-one remove the files for her current cases was exactly what would probably happen if she were fired. Maybe Hunsecker had used her two-day suspension to get the AG's office to approve the firing. Maybe that was what the suspension had been for.

One of the buttons on her telephone lit up, then began to blink as Geoffrey put the caller on hold. She picked up the phone and hit the button. "Waring."

"This is Dale Hunsecker. I'm waiting."

She steeled herself for what she had to say. "If what you're waiting for is an apology, I know I owe you one. What happened last week was a misunderstanding that I allowed to happen. I wasn't ignoring your orders when I requested that surveillance on Frank Tosca. Conditions had changed, and I had new information that made it an emergency. I should have called you to explain before I did anything. I'm sorry."

"Well," he said. "I have to say that I'm pleasantly surprised. I expected you to say 'I told you so.'"

"About what? Don't tell me Tosca has been killed."

"No. As soon as the surveillance was lifted, Tosca took his family and slipped away. Right now we don't know where he is. He left three men in his house, apparently to guard it. They were murdered on Thursday night. Their bodies were found in various parts of the house."

"How were they killed?"

"Let's see." He seemed to be perusing something. "Two shot, one bludgeoned to death."

"Do you know where the one who was bludgeoned was found?"

"Aah, I don't see that information in this report. It does say he was unarmed."

"Of course. The killer must have gone there without a gun. He killed one and used that man's gun to kill the others."

"He would do that? He'd go to the house of a Mafia capo without bringing a gun?"

57

"I'm guessing that he did. He was here in Washington and probably flew to New York, so he couldn't have taken a weapon with him or he'd have been stopped at airport security. He must have arrived in Tosca's neighborhood after the FBI surveillance ended, and moved in. He's been doing this for a long time. I've been told by informants that he hasn't done anything but kill people since he was about fifteen."

"So he would arrive unarmed and see three armed men, and say, 'Great, they're at my mercy'? I don't see it."

"He didn't want to kill three men. He wanted Tosca. I think he arrived, determined that someone was in the house, and assumed it was Tosca. You have to realize that they wanted him to think that. They wouldn't have been there to protect the parakeet. They were there to ambush him."

"So he went through with it and killed them all. I still find it difficult to understand why he'd do that."

"People who kill for a living aren't exactly normal. They don't think the way we do, and they don't all think alike. This one is unusual. He was brought up to do it, and he knows instantly how to kill each opponent without having to stop and think. If he hadn't killed each person he's come up against, he'd be dead. This happened Friday?"

"Thursday night."

"Then we've got to find Tosca right away."

"Why Tosca?"

"Because that's who the killer was looking for on Thursday night. Unless Tosca's dead, he's still searching. If we want him, we'll have to be where Tosca is."

8

EDDIE MASTREWSKI HAD always had his own philosophy. "Killing is just one of a lot of things people ought to do for themselves, but end up paying somebody else to do for them. They pay some pimp to provide a woman who will go to bed with them, and they buy a fancy car and hire somebody to drive it for them. That's no way to live, but their mistake is a fortune for people like us. Do your own killing, drive your own car, find your own girls."

He started the boy in the trade by taking him along on jobs. On the first job, the target was a man who was difficult to approach. He spent his days in a corner office on the tenth floor of a well-guarded office building. There were surveillance cameras, sign-in sheets, calls made to verify appointments before anybody was permitted to go to the elevator. On the tenth floor, all the people in the reception areas, cubicles, and hallways stood between the elevator and the target. When he left work, he walked a hundred yards with a couple of colleagues and went down with thousands of people into a subway. When he came out at his stop, he was a hundred yards from his high-security apartment. The only times to get him were the walk to the subway or his walk from it. When the day came, the boy wore a baseball cap and carried his outfielder's glove. He and Eddie joined the crowd on the sidewalk and came up behind the man. Eddie reached into the boy's glove, pulled out a small pistol fitted with a silencer, shot the man twice behind the ear, and put the pistol back in the glove. The man fell onto the sidewalk, Eddie grabbed the boy and stepped around the body, as though shielding him from the sight of the man dying of a heart attack on the street. Other bystanders stepped between the boy and the dreadful spectacle, trying to get their bodies in his line of sight while others knelt beside the body. In less than a minute Eddie and the boy were down the steps to the platform and getting on the subway train.

The boy found that after a while there were very few jobs that seemed difficult to him. Most of the time it was like turning off a light. Eddie would walk up to the side window of a car stopped in traffic, pull out a pistol, fire a shot into the driver's head, and walk on. Or he would knock on an apartment door, wait until he saw the peephole turn dark because the man inside had his eye up to it, and then fire through the door into the man's chest.

"Learn your trade," Eddie said. "You do that and you'll always have the edge. You'll be luring people out into the night when your eyes are used to the dark and theirs aren't. Plan a job for days, but do it in seconds. The guy should be dead before he has the time to figure out if he should be scared or not. You walk into a store or a restaurant to get somebody, you're like an egg in a frying pan. If you take too much time, you heat up and burn. Do it fast and get out."

By the time he was sixteen, he had acquired the discipline and the skills. He had also picked up Eddie's philosophy. Eddie had said, "Everybody dies. It's just a question of timing, and whether the one who gets paid for it is you or a bunch of doctors. It might as well be you."

After all these years, the essentials of killing had not changed. He needed to kill Tosca, and if Tosca wasn't at his house in Glen Cove, the next place to look was his house in Canada. From New Jersey he drove to Rochester, New York, and found a hotel near the airport. He had always liked staying in hotels like this because they were full of men exactly like the one he was pretending to be. They were businessmen, most of them in sales, visiting their clients on regular rounds. But an increasing number of them were entrepreneurs trying to get some fledgling enterprise a loan from a bank or license some bit of software from another company. Sometimes when he was having a meal in a mediocre restaurant in an airport hotel, he would be seated near a table of five or six of them, all smiling and chuckling through the flop sweat as they tried to sell each other things. There would always be one or two so young that they looked unaccustomed to wearing suits. But there would also be a man a generation older who might be a district manager or an owner, depending on the size of the company.

When he had first started working long-distance hits, he had looked just like one of the young ones—a bit skinny and awkward. Now he looked like the older one, the boss who knew the way these trips worked. The older man knew that his side wasn't going to go home with everything they came for, but also knew the company could live without it. The older man was usually a little calmer, less eager.

He cultivated the appearance, watching the businessmen to be sure he got it right. Now at half of these business lunches there would be at least one laptop computer on the table. That night he decided that he should buy a laptop and carry it around with him. It was a small concession that would cement his identity as a business traveler. The next morning he drove to a computer store and bought one, signed on to the hotel's wireless system, and searched for news articles about the Balacontano family.

There were plenty of old articles about Carlo, some available in newspaper archives going back to the 1950s. There was a flurry of hits for the year when Carlo had been convicted of killing Arthur Fieldston and burying his head and hands and the silenced pistol on his horse farm outside Saratoga Springs. Schaeffer knew all about that because he had done the killing and the burying and made the anonymous call to the FBI. What he was looking for was new information about what was going on right now. MAFIA ON THE RUN. THE DECLINE OF A DYNASTY. There were six of that one, in three different decades. Newspaper writers had said the Mafia was dead so many times that he had sometimes wondered if the Mafia was paying them to say it.

There were hundreds of articles, but they told him virtually nothing. Some guy in California was denied a liquor license because he had been seen with members of the Balacontano family. A few basketball players who were apparently well known were under investigation because their favorite strip club was owned by a Balacontano soldier and their bills were comped. There were investigative reports about companies in the trash-hauling business, the linen-supply business, investment banking, sports, music. There was even one on the link between the Balacontanos and a company that ran prisons in Midwestern states. The search engines picked up anything with the right key words in it. Apparently there were Balacontanos who had nothing to do with the crime family, and the Internet picked up every time one of their kids pitched in a high school game, got married, or got promoted. He left the laptop plugged in to charge the battery while he lay on the bed, looked up at the ceiling, and considered.

He wasn't certain where Frank Tosca had gone, but his best guess was that he had taken his family to Canada, to the house he owned on the north shore of the St. Lawrence River. He might have noticed all the surveillance teams outside his house on Long Island and figured a good way to stop the clock on any federal proceedings against him would be to go to Canada for a while. He had owned the house on the river for a long time and could hardly be accused of fleeing the country to avoid prosecution.

Over the years in England, Schaeffer had kept renewing his U.S. passports in the names Michael Schaeffer and Charles F. Ackerman. He chose the Ackerman passport for this crossing because he didn't want to compromise the Schaeffer identity. He decided to take some minor precautions with the two pistols he had taken from Tosca's soldiers. First he drove to a sporting-goods store and shopped for something that was the right size and shape. He settled on a tennis net that had posts at either end that could be sunk into holes in a court. They were essentially two three-inch steel pipes with caps at the upper ends and plugs at the lower. He brought the set back to his hotel and opened the lower ends of the pipes.

The two pistols he dismantled on the bed. He slid the slides, springs, barrels, triggers, sears, handgrips, and magazines into the two pipes, then plugged the pipes again. That left the two flat steel pistol frames, which he placed on the floor of his car on the driver's side under the floor mat.

Two hours later, at seven in the evening, he was crossing the Rainbow Bridge over the wide, blue Niagara toward Niagara Falls, Ontario, with the daily caravan of Americans coming over the river to leave their money on the green felt tables of the casinos. He could see the incongruous new additions to the staid architecture he remembered from the time before he'd gone to England. The colored lights looked as though a small part of Las Vegas had been brought here and planted. When he got to the end of the bridge, the Canadian customs woman looked at him and barely focused her eyes on his passport, handed it back, then waved him into Canada.

He drove east on the Queen Elizabeth Way along Lake Ontario toward the St. Lawrence. As he approached Toronto, night was falling, and he was once again on a dark highway that could have been anywhere on the continent. He could remember clearly the only time he had been to Tosca's summer house. It had been a hot summer day, and they had come over the bridge at Alexandria Bay and entered Canada east of Gananoque. The house was on a narrow, pebbly beach, one of a stretch of houses that were not the usual small, wooden buildings that were everywhere on the Canadian side of the river and the Great Lakes. These belonged to prosperous people from Toronto, Ottawa, and Montreal, and they were as substantial as their houses in the city. Tosca's was made of brick, had two stories, a garage, a brick patio, and a boathouse with a ramp like a little railway to let the boat glide down over the pebbly beach into the water just beyond the shallows. Once the boat was in the water, four of Tosca's men would remove the ramp in sections, then put it back in when they were ready to take the boat back to its boathouse.

He stopped a few miles past Toronto to eat dinner. He liked to travel later at night, when traffic would thin out and little about him was visible. When he came out to the parking lot, it was full night. The sun had gone down an hour ago somewhere off in the direction of Cleveland. The diners all seemed to like to park in the lighted area near the door of the restaurant, so no one was near him in the back of the darkened lot. He opened the trunk of his car, took out his two metal posts, and brought them with him into the car. He emptied the posts onto the front seat, retrieved the frames from the floor near the gas pedal and the brake, and arranged the parts of his two guns for assembly.

The exercise brought him back again to his adolescence with Eddie Mastrewski. Eddie had been in the army, and he had been taught to fieldstrip and reassemble his rifle blindfolded. He had felt that blindfolded stripping and reassembling weapons was so valuable that he would always insist the boy do the same with whatever weapon he would be using on the next job. He had started him with a heavy Springfield Model 1911-A1 .45 automatic that was too big for his hand. The boy had protested that the whole idea was stupid, as everything teenagers didn't want to do was stupid. But after two hours of practice, he could accomplish the task quickly and efficiently. The next weapon was easier, and the one after that more so, and soon his hands were familiar with all of the minor differences between the common makes and models, the variations each company made in its products. He never forgot. As he assembled the guns tonight, he could practically see every part in the dark with his hands.

At midnight he reached the house. He went past it and drove a half mile farther down the road to an apartment complex that had not been there, could not have been there, in the old days. He parked in a space behind the building that was stenciled VISITOR, and walked back along the beach to Tosca's house. He stayed on the hard, wet stones along the line where the gentle waves sloshed in, not higher on the shore where there might be dirt that would hold his footprints.

He almost smiled. There was a light on downstairs. Someone was here. He stood still on the beach beyond the place where the glow could reach him and watched the windows. He reminded himself that he had a decision to make: Tosca was probably here, but if he was, his family could be here too. He didn't relish the idea of killing women and children, but leaving a witness alive would be insane. As he stared in the windows, he thought about it. He didn't see them. Maybe they were upstairs asleep, and he could do Tosca downstairs without waking them. He thought some more. Tosca had made a choice when he had sent his men to England to kill him. It had been Tosca's responsibility to remember he had a wife and children before he had done that.

He moved closer to the house. There were windows open on the river side of the house, with no protection except the screens. He understood the impulse. When a building on the shore had been closed for a while, the damp air seemed to find its way in through invisible cracks, or maybe moisture just precipitated out of the air trapped inside. The first thing people did was fling open the windows and let the fresh, sweet air from the water blow in and clear out the musty smells. All he could see from this window was an empty alcove. Beyond it was the dining room, furnished with fake-crude country-style furniture, half-lighted by the glow from a light in the living room.

He made a small incision in the window screen to the left, because the light from the next room was brighter on the right. He pushed the blade in, unhooked the screen, then pulled it outward and climbed in the window.

He was in an alcove off the living room. Since he had been here the room had been heavily remodeled to look like the house of an old ship's captain, with elaborate ship models, paintings of sailing ships getting tossed around on dark, angry waves, and glass cases full of scrimshaw and brass astrolabes and compasses.

There was a low conversation going on in the next room, and it rapidly rose to become two men yelling. He pulled out one of his pistols and walked toward the sound. The yelling stopped abruptly, and then was replaced by loud, brassy music. Someone was watching television.

Schaeffer took slow, quiet steps to the doorway and looked inside. He could see the head of an older man in a tall-backed leather chair facing away from him. He could see hair that was thin and white, with a few strands of black remaining. It wasn't Tosca. He stepped inside the room, and the man turned to look over his shoulder. "You!" said the man. "I never thought you'd come back a second time."

It was Mike Cavalli, twenty years older but clearly recognizable. "What are you doing in Tosca's house, Cavalli? You don't work for him."

Cavalli sat back in his chair, facing the flat surface of the television screen mounted on the wall in front of him. "None of your fucking business."

Schaeffer took the remote control from the table beside Cavalli's hand and turned off the television set so the big glass surface went black. Then he took the cell phone that was beside it and put it in his pocket. "Are you so old you don't remember who I am?"

"I remember you just fine. You'll kill me whether I tell you anything or not. You're a disease. Killing people is all you do."

"I'm not here for you. I'm looking for Frank Tosca."

"You can see he's not here."

"When did he leave?"

"Yesterday. He was taking his wife and kids someplace. They stayed here for a night and then went on."

"He didn't tell you where he was going?"

"No."

Schaeffer raised the pistol and fired four times at the back of the chair. The bullets burst out of the upholstery of the backrest on either side of Cavalli's face, each tear in the leather blossoming beside his cheek so he could feel the leather lash his skin.

"He told, he told," Cavalli said. "All right, he told me."

"Where is he?"

"He doesn't trust anybody to know where his family is, so he was hiding them himself. After that he was going to talk to a few of the old men."

"What about?"

Cavalli laughed, his eyes squinting and his mouth half open while his upper body shook. "What do you think? About this. About you."

"How long has he known I was coming?"

"When Delamina got killed. That's when he knew. He had sent a bunch of guys out to look for you. Delamina was in charge of one crew. Over the past year, people went to the places where somebody thought you were—Sydney, Melbourne, Hong Kong, Bangkok, London. They talked to people, even met some of the guys people thought might be you. Tosca kept sending people out. I guess you found Delamina before he found you, huh?"

"Why is Tosca suddenly interested in me? I never had much to do with him."

"I guess you haven't kept up with anything here. You been living in a cave in Afghanistan?"

"Tell me."

"He's been making a bid to run the Balacontano family. Nobody can do that without Carlo Balacontano's blessing."

"I'm amazed the old bastard is still alive."

"Well, he is. And even from prison he's always going to be the head. Anybody who runs that family is working for him. Now, what do you suppose old Carl Bala wants most, both as a gesture of respect to him and to prove the guy deserves to run the family?"

"Me."

"That's right. You're the one who dug the hole that got him sent away forever. He's always been pissed off that in twenty years, nobody has found you for him. He's going to be in prison until he dies, so the only thing that will make him happy is your head on a stake."

"They're all as stupid as ever. He's in prison for life. They could have told him anytime that they'd got me and shut him up. Maybe he would have died in peace by now."

"It's more complicated than that after all this time. The whole Balacontano family grew up hearing about you. You ended his life, but you ruined them too. The government got a lot of his money that would have found its way down to them. They lost soldiers, both to you and to the government, and those guys were their fathers, cousins, and uncles. People don't forget. Part of being in that family is wanting the chance to kill you. The kids pray at mass that they'll be the ones to get you."

"And why are you here, babysitting Tosca's house? You're from Chicago. You were in the Castiglione family."

"Did you forget you killed old Mr. Castiglione too?"

"He was older than God, living in a wheelchair in a place like a fort in Vegas. He hadn't run anything in a generation."

"This isn't about losing a boss. It's about honor, losing face. You killed a lot of people and nobody made you suffer for it, and everybody knows it. So the feeling gets worse, because of the shame."

"So that's what Tosca is talking to the old men about?"

"He's asking them to make you their problem. He's reminding them of what happened years ago. You didn't just duck the ambush and get out of the country. You lashed out in all directions. Some of the old men had relatives you killed. They have wives and aunts reminding them once a week that they haven't got you yet." Cavalli grinned. "He's going to raise the whole country against you, and they'll hunt you until you're dead."

"Is he going to them one at a time, or did he ask for a meeting?"

Cavalli shrugged. "I can see why you would want to know. But that's not the way this will play out. You're not going to win this time."

"How do you know?"

"You've taken on too much importance for that. You're a symbol, like the Thanksgiving turkey. Whether you like it or not, this is going to be a celebration, and you're the guest of honor. Frank Tosca is the first young, strong, smart leader the families have produced in years. He's like all our grandfathers—crazy-ambitious, strong, tough. He's acting just like them. If he can get the Balacontano family under his control, the rest will start to turn to him too. There are people who have been waiting for this for a long, long time. It'll be like turning the calendar back, so La Cosa Nostra is young again. Everybody wants that. But first, he needs you dead."

Schaeffer looked at him in silence.

"Carl Bala isn't the only one who lives in time. I can tell you from experience that every year you slow down—you lose a step here and there. Your reactions aren't as fast, and pretty soon it feels like you're always walking on sand or deep snow instead of sidewalk. Then one day, you notice that your hearing and vision are a little worse too. Pretty soon, it's not so hard for somebody to come up behind you, the way you did to me tonight. They wouldn't have gotten you easily when you were a kid. But you're not a kid now."

"I'm about to leave, and I'm taking your cell phone with me. If Tosca wants to talk about a way for this to end without anybody else dying, he can call your number anytime in the next eight hours. After that, I throw it away, and he'll lose his chance."

"When he doesn't call, don't blame me. You know he's not going to stop looking. He can't. In the past couple of days you've killed six of his guys. He can't ignore that, or he'll lose the others."

"Just tell him."

He backed away from the chair, still holding the gun on Cavalli. He glanced over his shoulder to be sure he was heading toward the door. Cavalli said, "Sure you want that?"

He said, "It's too late to keep this a secret. Everybody in the country seems to know I'm here. So just sit tight for a few minutes, and then you can call whoever you want on the house phone."

He could see Cavalli's reflection in the darkened flat screen of the television set. Cavalli was watching him the same way. He started to turn to open the door, but Cavalli's hand went to his coat pocket and came out with a gun. "Don't try that," he said, but Cavalli dropped onto his knees on the floor and brought his right hand around the chair back.

Schaeffer aimed low on the chair back and pulled the trigger six times, until Cavalli's lifeless hand released the pistol and it dropped to the floor. He could see in the reflection on the black television screen that he had hit Cavalli at least once in the head. He put the gun into his belt and went out the door.

This was exactly like all of those dumb bastards. There had been no reason for Cavalli to try that. He had just let the size of the contract on the Butcher's Boy eat away at him all the time they were talking, until he no longer had the strength to resist. He was over sixty, but he still couldn't pass up a sucker's odds to get rich by shooting a man who had just spared his life.

Schaeffer walked along the shore of the St. Lawrence until he recognized the building across the road where he had left his car. He took Cavalli's cell phone out of his pocket and pressed the wheel for the phone book. He found a number that said FRANK T CELL, selected it, and pressed the call button. He heard the ring signal, then a voice. "Yeah?"

"Hi, Frank," he said.

"Who is this?"

"I wanted Cavalli to give you a message, but he decided to be dead instead. I wanted to let you know that I'll disappear again if you'll forget the idea of tracking me down for Carl Bala. He'll die of old age soon, or be too old to remember I put him where he is."

Tosca sounded pleased. "Thanks for killing Cavalli. He had a lot of friends. In a day or two, everybody in the country who matters is going to be turning over rocks looking for you. When we've got you, I'm going to have some people dump your body outside the prison at Lompoc where Don Carlo Balacontano is so he can stand behind the fence in the exercise yard and watch the cops put you in a body bag."

"Wrong answer, Frank," said Schaeffer. "See you."

9

ELIZABETH LEFT WORK at seven in the evening and took the elevator to the level of her reserved parking space in the Robert F. Kennedy building's underground garage. There were always cars on this floor late into the night because they all belonged to people in supervisory jobs. Things didn't get easier as a person moved up in the hierarchy. This evening she had been trying to make her way through the past few daily reports from the data analysts who worked in the basement of the building.

Twenty years ago when she had first become aware of this killer, she had been a data analyst, and she still preferred double-checking the sources of her information, the raw, unedited statements of fact that came in with each morning's traffic. In Washington there were too many people who got by on briefings and executive summaries prepared by the newest and least experienced people, and never looked at what had prompted their conclusions. Proper interpretation wasn't always easy, not something every novice could do. Sometimes one bit of overlooked information could change everything. It took experience and intuition to sense when that one bit of information wasn't even present but should be.

Tonight she was dissatisfied. She was missing something important. She hadn't detected what the killer was doing or what he wanted. He had made an attempt on Frank Tosca at his house on Long Island and then dropped out of sight. It wasn't like him to give up, or even to let up—to slow down before he had accomplished what he wanted to do. So now he must be moving, doing something. But no reports had come in that might reveal to her what it could be.

Elizabeth had felt the frustration growing all day. She had been close to events of great importance to the world of organized crime before they'd happened—the return of the Butcher's Boy and the murder of Michael Delamina—but she had misinterpreted what she'd heard and seen, and finally, after she'd understood that he was after Tosca, she'd failed to persuade the deputy assistant in time to move in and take advantage of the opportunity.

She stepped out of the elevator carrying her briefcase in her left hand and her purse strap over her left shoulder so her right hand would be unencumbered if she needed to reach for the gun. She got into her car and kept the purse on the passenger seat where she could reach it.

It was dark out when she drove out onto the street. A light rain was falling, and the pavements were wet enough to show the reflections of headlights and traffic signals, and she had to listen to the constant thump-thump of her windshield wipers. She headed for McLean by the route that took her past her dry cleaners. She parked in one of the narrow five-minute spaces in the strip mall where the shop was and came out with the clothes she had left last Thursday—two suits, two blouses, two pairs of slacks, two of her daughter's dresses, and her son's sport coat. She thought about how good he looked in it, but also what the argument would be that got him to wear it for his college interviews later in the year.

He would say, "That's not how I dress."

She could say, "Whether you wear it every day is not the point. This is the right thing to wear for this occasion."

"They'll think I'm pretending to be somebody else."

"I'll write you a note to verify that you are who you say you are and that it's your coat."

She was holding the group of hangers with an upstretched arm so none of the clothes would drag on the wet pavement. She glanced to her left to see if any cars were coming and prepared to take the first step across the driveway when he appeared at her right side.

"I need to talk to you for five minutes. Get in your car." He took her free arm and guided her toward the car.

Elizabeth knew that this was one of the moments when life was shakily balanced on what she said or did next. As long as he was close enough to touch her, she was in mortal danger. He was also being hunted by his enemies, and that, for this moment at least, made them her enemies. If they came for him now, she would die too. She had no choice but to hurry through the light rain toward her car, but as she went, she said, "You and I don't have anything to talk about. You're putting me in danger, and I don't like it."

They were at the back door behind the driver's seat. The button clicked up. He took her cleaning out of her hand, hung the hangers on the hook in the back seat, and got into the car behind the wheel. He held his hand out.

She hesitated for a second, aware of all of the people who might be looking at her right now. She could scream. She could run. She placed the keys in the palm of his hand, then hurried to the passenger side and got in. She said, "If anybody sees me with you, my career is over."

He pulled the car out of the lot and drove up the street. "If anybody sees me with you, both our lives are over. They'll kill me for talking to the Justice Department, and you because you know whatever I told you." He looked in each of the mirrors, returned to the one on the left side for a few seconds, seemed to eliminate a possibility, and looked ahead again. "It doesn't look as though we've been spotted. As long as that cleaner isn't robbed so somebody has to watch the security tape, we're probably okay."

"What do you want?"

"I know we're not exactly best friends, but why are you pissed off?"

"You're a murderer. Are other people glad to see you?"

"Some are," he said. "You should be one of them."

"I would like you to pull my car over and get out. I'll give you a ten-minute head start before I call in federal officers to look for you."

"I know that you have no legal responsibility to tell the truth when you're talking to a suspect. That's what matters to you, right? Legal responsibility. You wouldn't give me ten minutes. Or any minutes."

She glared at him, then looked away, scowling out the window at the traffic.

"As soon as we're finished talking, I'll leave."

"You had already killed Michael Delamina before you asked me who he worked for. As soon as I told you, three of Tosca's men were killed in his house. I suppose you didn't do that."

"Of course I did."

"So that's all the information you will ever get from me."

"I'm not here to get information. I'm here to tell you something you don't know that might get you somewhere if you move fast. There is going to be a meeting. Among the people there will be at least some of the old men. Frank Tosca called it, and it will take place tomorrow."

"Where?"

"I don't know. I don't know how it's being done. For all I know, it may be a bunch of them chatting on video. But most of the old men are used to talking to people face-to-face."

"Does Tosca have the power to call a meeting like that?"

"He wants to be the most powerful man in the country, and he thinks he sees a way. Carlo Balacontano has been in jail for a long time. All those years he's had a succession of caretakers on the outside taking his orders to run the Balacontano family."

"I know. Tosca wants to be boss."

"To do it, he needs Carl Bala's blessing. The thing the old man wants most in the world is me."

"Oh. Of course he would." Her mind was leaping over obstacles now and ranging ahead like a hunting dog on a scent. "And killing you would prove to Bala that Tosca was loyal to him and that he was strong enough to run the family."

"Tosca has been trying to find me for the old man for a couple of years. Now I'm here and it's starting to occur to him that the one of us who dies might not be me. But he also sees that this moment could be his big chance. If he says all he wants is to kill me, he can get the rest of the Balacontano soldiers, the holdouts, to come in and take his orders. They want me dead. But if he can get the heads of the other twenty-five families to agree to hunt for me too, then he's the guy to take over for Carl Bala."

"It sounds like a great deal for him," she said. "Even if somebody Tosca doesn't know kills you, he'll still be the hero because he called the hunt. He can hardly lose."

Schaeffer turned and looked at her, his eyes alert but cold. "He can lose."

"If you're going to steal my car, let me off now. I need to start finding out what I can."

He pulled over suddenly, and she was disconcerted. She was almost thrown, first into him, and then into the dashboard. The car rocked. He flung the door open, stepped beneath the Metro sign, and then disappeared down the stairway to the station.

She snatched her BlackBerry out of her purse and pressed the number to dial the night supervisor of Organized Crime and Racketeering. "Fulton," the voice said.

"Fulton, it's Waring. The killer turned up again. He just ducked into the Metro station at L'Enfant Plaza. There's got to be a way to shut it down before he gets away."

"Hold on and let me find out." There was a click, and then a moment later he was back. "Elizabeth?"

"I'm still here."

"L'Enfant Plaza is the perfect station for him and the worst for us. He can get on the blue, orange, green, or yellow lines in either direction—every line but one—and in two stops he could get on the red line too. Keeping all the trains from leaving would shut down the whole system at rush hour. We'd have a panic. Even if capturing him wouldn't involve shooting, it's still too risky."

"But we'd have him."

"All we'd be doing is handing this guy five hundred hostages."

"I guess it was too much to hope he'd made that kind of mistake."

There was a pause. "Elizabeth?"

"What?"

"This brings up something that I think you need to know."

"What is it?"

"I'm taking a risk to say this."

"Then don't. At least don't say it on the phone. I . . . uh, forgot something at the office, so I've got to go back in anyway. I'll be there in ten minutes."

It was fifteen minutes before she walked back into the office. She went directly to Fulton's office and knocked.

"Come in."

She entered, closed the door, and sat down in front of Fulton's desk. "Tell me."

He looked at her, then at the desk, where his fingers were fiddling with his pencil. "You've given me some breaks and helped me out a number of times. Still, I almost called you back to ask you not to come in."

"It's that bad?"

"Bad enough. While you were suspended, he had a couple of his assistants search your office."

"Which he had a perfect right and excuse to do, of course. I'll admit I was surprised when I came back and saw everything in my in-box was missing."

"Did you get it back?"

"I'm pretty sure I got it all."

"Then they haven't found anything that will make you look bad."

"Is he really trying to do that? He's been friendly today. He came this close to admitting he was wrong about trying to keep

Tosca under surveillance. If he had simply let my arrangement with the FBI stand, we would have kept three men alive and possibly caught the Butcher's Boy, and he knows it."

"He's not your friend. There was an upper-level staff meeting Friday. 'Why does this professional killer know Waring? Why does he come to her after twenty years and ask for information? Why would she give it to him? How does he know where she lives?' And he's looked into the conviction of Carlo Balacontano twenty years ago. He says he's got a nose for things that don't smell right. Why would the head of one of the five New York families bury the head and hands of a Las Vegas businessman on his own horse farm in Saratoga? If he did that, then who knew about it and called in a tip to tell the FBI where to look? Why did the Justice Department buy into that?"

"It's ironic," she said. "That's exactly what I said twenty years ago. I said it over and over, but everybody said, 'That just shows how arrogant Carl Bala is.' And I kept insisting, until finally John Connor, the deputy assistant AG at the time, pressured me into taking a long vacation out of the country. If I hadn't agreed, it was pretty clear I was going to be out."

"I don't suppose anybody at the time wrote anything down about your objections."

"Of course not. At least not that I've ever seen. What Connor did was put a notation in my personnel file that said the long vacation in Europe was 'health-related.' For the next ten or twelve years I had to explain that to my new bosses during every annual evaluation and every promotion committee. I would say it was a great opportunity, and they took it to mean I was attached to some foreign police force."

"He knows about that too," said Fulton. "He thinks you had a mental breakdown and they saved your career by covering it up."

She shrugged. "What else could it be? And I must be having another one now."

Fulton shook his head. "I told him I thought it might have been a pregnancy that you weren't ready for. You were twenty-two. You

77

could have given up the baby. That's the kind of thing that doesn't get spelled out in attendance records and doesn't matter much all these years later."

"Very creative," she said. "Thanks for trying." She stood up. "And thanks for the warning too. I'll be very careful not to let him see that I know." She looked at her watch. "While I'm here, I think I'll do a little catching up on work I missed during my suspension."

Fulton stood up too. "What I was really trying to head off was your saying something to him like what you said to me tonight."

"What do you mean?"

"This killer, the Butcher's Boy. He's the real problem right now. Hunsecker's gut tells him that cops who have exclusive relationships with criminal informants almost always end up being corrupt. Pretty soon they're protecting the source from things that would normally get him and only passing on information he feeds them. Ultimately they end up working for the informant."

Elizabeth said, "We've both been around long enough to see that happen a few times. He didn't make that up."

"If you can see his point even a little, just think what it would sound like to the assistant AG or the AG. Make sure you're not vulnerable. If I were you, I wouldn't tell anybody that I'd seen that creep again and talked to him."

She said, "Oh, I didn't talk to him. I just happened to spot him on the street as I was leaving my cleaner's where I was picking up some clothes. I watched him from a distance to see where he went." She realized that she had crossed a line. She was lying to Fulton now.

"Well, if he does try to talk to you again, I'd think carefully before I told Hunsecker."

"Not much chance of either," she said. "Well, thanks. I owe you another one." She turned and left his office.

As Elizabeth walked along the hallway, she pressed the wheel on her phone to automatically dial home. After a moment she heard Amanda's voice. "Hello?"

"Hi, honey. I'm still at work. I'm afraid something new has

come in and I've got to deal with it tonight. Can you and Jim cook something up for dinner between you? There's plenty in the refrigerator."

"Sure. It was getting to be that time, so I already took a look in there and have my eye on a few things. We'll see what his majesty wants."

"Tell him I said he has to help. Or if you cook, he cleans up."

"We'll work it out," Amanda said. "I'll see you later."

"Yes," said Elizabeth. "But don't wait up for me. Tomorrow's a school day, and this could be a late one."

When they'd hung up, Elizabeth spent a minute or two walking along the nearly deserted hallway of the big building, feeling a kind of emptiness. Even the phrases were formulaic—something came up. Don't wait up for me. She sounded like a cheating husband, not a devoted mother. When things calmed down, she would do better.

She rode the elevator down to the computer rooms in the basement. She was going to see what the old men were up to. If the Butcher's Boy was right, tonight was the only chance to learn where they were going to meet. The day after tomorrow, they would all be back in their houses behind the high walls and at the ends of quarter-mile driveways. But tonight, if her source was correct, they would be on the move, like hermit crabs out for a walk without their shells. The trick was to pick them up before they could scuttle back in.

10

AS SCHAEFFER DROVE through the night back on the Canadian highway again, he thought about the life he had lived in England, and about the Honourable Meg. The Honourable Margaret Holroyd was the only child of Lord David Holroyd, Marquis of Axeborough, and Lady Anne Holroyd of Harrelsford, and she had been brought up in a house that looked like a castle and had secret rooms and a passageway that emerged outside the walls across a pond. Nonetheless, she claimed to have been a poor, sad, runny-nosed creature through most of her childhood. It was apparently true that she and her social set, all of whom seemed to share the coloring and facial characteristics of near relatives, had been ignored by their parents most of the time and sent early to cruel stone boarding schools where the rules involved being hit with sticks and bathing in cold water.

She had told Schaeffer about a friend's hideous Aunt Gwendolyn who caught Meg telling a ghost story at a party and stood her up as an example to the other children while she told them that liars went to hell. Meg told him, "But I wasn't sure I was on the Devil's side until I heard he'd invented sex. It seemed he had invented it just for me, to conform to my temperament and taste."

Even though the Holroyds and their complicated network of relations had large amounts of money that seemed to appear in their bank accounts magically from rents and royalties and interest, he was fairly certain that in being raised by Eddie Mastrewski, he had been the privileged child.

Eddie was a very tough man, and he never hid from the boy that the world they lived in was an unforgiving place. He raised the boy with foul language but no harsh words, and they spent most of their time together. He wasn't against schools, and knew that not going would lead to trouble, but he wasn't about to enforce anything the school said the boy had to do.

Eddie was born in a small Pennsylvania coal mining town, and he had started out working in the mines. He was not a genius, but at eighteen he knew that life in the mines was harder than anything he was likely to find elsewhere. He was drafted into the army, and when they let him out a couple of years later, he had learned a skill. He could kill people. He moved to a big city where there were men who would pay him well for killing people, and with practice, he got better at it. He also needed to have some profession that was legal, so he got a job working in a butcher's shop and learned to be an expert butcher. Later he passed both skills on to the boy.

Schaeffer didn't meet the Honourable Margaret Holroyd until he'd already had a fairly long career in killing. After a bad experience involving the Balacontano family, he had flown to England and retired to the picturesque and ancient city of Bath. He bought a comfortable old house and remodeled it in ways that would have horrified the architectural preservationists. He replaced perfectly functional old windows with arrays of glass bricks high on the walls that let in light but would frustrate snipers. He had unobtrusive, locked cabinets installed at various points in the house and stocked them with loaded firearms of several types. He had closed-circuit television cameras mounted on all sides of the exterior, and had impermeable steel doors on the entrances and on the room where he slept. When he had satisfied his sense of security, he settled in and began to live a quiet, solitary existence.

At the time Meg Holroyd was a bored, aristocratic young

woman who spent all of her time going to parties and outings with a shifting group of highborn young men and women who appeared to have known her since birth. The moment he first saw her he was captivated. She was not merely pretty. She had something far rarer. She was perfect. Her skin was like a baby's, but the shape of her face was a sculpture in polished ivory with delicate, straight features and brilliant, knowing eyes. She was well educated, witty, and clever. But as she freely admitted to him, she was a liar. She invented fanciful scandalous stories about her friends, neighbors, even national and historical figures.

On the day she met him at an educational lecture in Bath, she made him take her to tea and told him she had been thrown out of the local antiquarian society. She had gone to the last meeting, where she'd announced that she had put a powerful Peruvian aphrodisiac in the punch, and set off an orgy. She said the power of suggestion had caused a mass shedding of clothes as the members helped one another to disrobe and became a tangle of limbs. The respectable ladies and gentlemen, believing themselves compelled by the exotic South American drug, had lost all inhibition. Later, they had voted her out of the scholarly society on charges of mass sexual assault and adultery-by-proxy.

Her stories were always too outrageous for even a naive stranger from America to believe, but always amusingly recounted in the most vivid detail, with the names of the most unlikely people attached. He liked her stories for the same reason she told them—they should have happened. He became her favorite audience because he always listened patiently to the whole story before he laughed.

It had been a pleasant existence for him until the day, on an outing with her friends to the races at Brighton, he had been recognized. It had been an unlikely accident. He had never been to Brighton before, and he was seen by a person who fit in there as badly as he did, young Mario Talarese from New York City. The Talarese family had a connection with the Cappadocia brothers, a pair of Sicilians who ran some gambling enterprises in London, and the Cappadocias had taken on New York underboss Tony Talarese's nephew as an apprentice. When Mario Talarese saw the man who was once called the Butcher's Boy, he made a terrible error. Instead of placing an international call to his uncle, or even talking to the Cappadocias, he had gone after the Butcher's Boy with only one of the Cappadocias' waiters, who carried a straight razor, and a British bookie named Baldwin who secretly had no interest in getting into a fight with anyone who had once killed for a living. Baldwin had been right to worry, because in an hour he and the others were dead.

Afterward, Schaeffer had told Meg a lie of his own, that the men he'd just killed in front of her eyes had been Bulgarian secret agents who had recognized him as a CIA agent in deep cover. He said he needed to rush back to the United States for a few weeks to complete the mission the Bulgarians had been sent to thwart.

It wasn't until he returned to England a few weeks later that she had told him she'd never believed a word of his lie. But she had also informed him that while he'd been gone, she had realized she was so unbreakably attached to him that she had no choice but to ignore his unsuitability and marry him.

When he had left England, he'd assumed that his relationship with her was over, and he had never imagined she would ever consider marrying him. He was ten years older and of an incalculably lower social class. While he had enough money to remain idle and keep the old house he had remodeled, he didn't have enough to make him a plausible husband to the last direct descendant of a bloodline that people seemed to consider a part of the national patrimony. But when he found himself once again in the presence of the only woman who had ever fascinated him, and she seemed to be determined to marry him, he couldn't think of a reason to resist.

When people asked him what he did for a living, he had always replied that he'd retired from a business that was so spectacularly boring that he couldn't bear to ruin a pleasant evening by talking about it. After he returned from the United States, he resumed that policy, and it continued to work.

He and Meg had married as quietly as possible, with the Anglican priest who often figured in Meg's most ribald slanders presiding, and the pretty, plump Hartleby sisters, who were also prominent in the stories, playing their harps.

Since their wedding ten years ago, they had lived a quiet, unobtrusive life in Bath. He kept up a few precautions. He could never allow himself to be photographed, so they had always stayed as far as possible from anyone who appeared to be a celebrity. They gave money to charities through a trust, but never attended any of the receptions, balls, or dinners that were intended to prime the donors for the next year. On the rare occasions when pictures needed to be taken, Meg would be in them alone. Photographers didn't seem to mind because, although she was approaching forty, she was still perfect.

Tonight he drove the fast, crowded highway toward Toronto, feeling the traffic mounting every second. As he went from Hamilton to Mississauga, he thought about Meg. He had no more business being married to her than to the Queen. She had simply been so willful and contrary that she had fallen in love with the worst man she had ever met and stuck with him without delving any further into the truth about him than to tell him his lies weren't fooling her. He could see her without closing his eyes. In the silence of the closed car, he could hear her voice.

He could tell already that the way home to her was not going to be as easy or direct as it had been the last time. The ones who had come for him this time had not just stumbled on him. They had been searching. They had found him in Brighton, where Tony Talarese's nephew had found him the first time. That felt like a bad bit of luck; he and Meg seldom went down to Brighton because of the bad memory.

He knew exactly what he had to do to make his way home. It wasn't hoping they'd forget. He had to make them think about him every day and every night until they hated Frank Tosca for bringing him into their lives again.

11

IT WAS GETTING to be evening, and Elizabeth was in the Justice Department basement staring at a computer screen. In the old days they had used a single big computer down here with a lot of terminals. In that era each morning's suspicious-death lists—her specialty—were printed on wide sheets of lined paper that were attached with perforated edges so they could be separated or left folded like an accordion. They'd been unwieldy, but much easier on the eyes than the bright, pretty screens of these desktops.

The array of screens at this workstation constantly updated the status of each of the men the Organized Crime and Racketeering Division kept track of. If she had signed into these files from the computer in her office, there would be a record of it, but here the array was always on, and all she had to do was sit at this desk and wait. She watched, and the screen in front of her updated: Castiglione, Salvatore; Castiglione, Paul; Castiglione, Joseph, all checked in on a flight from Chicago to Phoenix, departing 8:14 P.M. All three of the brothers, the next generation leaders of the family, were leaving for Phoenix on the same plane.

Ten lines down, she noticed another sudden change: a private jet operated by Aviation Interests, Inc., and leased to Garden State Engineering and Construction, had taken off from Newark with a flight plan for St. Louis. Garden State was a Fibbiano operation. Everybody was heading west.

Three lines up, an agent reported that Angelo LoCicero was just seen arriving at the airport in Detroit. Stand by for ticketing information.

Everywhere on the display, the status entries for the heads of the families were being updated by the people assigned to watch them. It was evening, but still early even here in the Eastern time zone. She knew there was more to come because the Butcher's Boy had told her what was going to happen before it had begun. The old men were on the move, and they were on the way to a meeting, but she couldn't do anything to respond yet because she couldn't reveal to anyone how she knew. She would have to wait and let the movement go on long enough to be clear to anyone who looked at the data.

The Butcher's Boy had told her the truth. She had been given a chance to watch the upper echelon of the Mafia gathering for a meeting, something that hadn't happened even once during her career. And it was happening quickly. Alphonse Costananza was in JFK waiting at the gate for a JetBlue flight to Las Vegas. He was the head of the family that ran Cleveland.

Phil Langusto was already touching down at the airport in Flagstaff, Arizona. Salvatore Molinari was en route to Santa Fe, New Mexico. Giovanni "Chi-chi" Tasso had left New Orleans in the morning, but the surveillance team had not noticed his car leaving the city and had not yet seen him at an airport. Danny Spoleto had been seen in Albuquerque, and he was an underling for Mike Catania of Boston. It looked as though he was preparing to meet Catania on a later flight and drive him to wherever the meeting was going to be.

Evening was shading off into an early, rainy night in Washington. She began to check the communication channels, the e-mails and faxes and the data updates, for some sign that any of the people who monitored organized crime activity had already put together the fact that this wasn't just one big player doing some unusual travel. They all seemed to be converging on a single point somewhere in the Southwest.

She waited until she had fifteen big names on her summary screen, copied it, and attached it to an e-mail to be sent from her personal e-mail address. She typed in the address of Special Agent Holman at the FBI. He was the one who had been in charge of the night surveillance on Tosca, and when it was ordered stopped he had given her a chance to get it authorized by midnight. To Elizabeth that meant he was on duty at night. And he not only had behaved sensibly on that operation, but he would now be aware that the person at the Justice Department who had been right that time was Elizabeth Waring, and not her boss, the deputy assistant, who had made an unforgivable mistake in overruling her—a career-ending mistake for most people.

She hesitated for a second and reviewed her decision. She had been privileged to have secret information of a sort that she would probably never have again. If the configuration of power had only been slightly different, acting on this information would have made her career. Law enforcement people had been waiting for fifty years for this kind of meeting to happen again, and now it was happening, but only she knew it. Somebody had to do something now, and it wasn't going to be the Justice Department.

She typed, "Agent Holman: Please see the attached surveillance status updates snapshot 7:57 P.M. Has your office noted this sudden movement toward the Southwest? E. Waring, Justice Department Organized Crime and Racketeering." Then she slid the cursor back to the subject line at the top and typed, "URGENT. PLEASE ACKNOWLEDGE." She clicked on SEND.

She stared at the computer screen, watching as the updates continued. At least a few of these men were at the centers of ongoing criminal investigations and must have their phones tapped. There were others who hadn't left their little kingdoms in years. But at this time of night she couldn't be sure there was anyone on duty except her who had the information collected in a single place and had the experience to form a single coherent picture of the way the movements of so many men in different cities had suddenly begun to coincide.

She had given Holman the key, the way to see it. A field agent who saw one capo heading from New York to the Southwest might not perceive what was up. But if Holman saw that fifteen important men were headed there on the same night, he would have the sense to know this wasn't typical.

She had no proof that Holman was on duty right now. But after being married to an FBI agent for nearly eight years, she was pretty sure there would be someone next door in the J. Edgar Hoover Building alert enough to read a communication that was marked URGENT by a ranking official at the Justice Department.

The screens kept updating, the current entries blinking out and new, longer ones appearing. There must be at least twenty small surveillance teams working tonight, each of them convinced they were seeing their subjects behave in ways that they seldom did. It was also clear that none of them, so far, knew that all the others were having the same experience.

The FBI was taking a very long time answering. Her boss in the Justice Department was deaf to her requests. But somebody had to start mounting an operation to find out what this meeting was about and who was going to attend who wasn't already being watched, or it would be too late. The meeting was clearly going to take place in the Southwest. It would probably be somewhere outside the major cities. Maybe the Arizona State Police were the next best group to call. But the meeting still could be somewhere else. She couldn't be sure that, just because the old men had flown to Phoenix or Tucson, they would stay there.

Until she was sure where the meeting was, calling state and local authorities was a waste of time. Until then, going through the federal agencies would make the most sense. DEA? No. It would be hard for them to justify a raid unless there was some evidence of drugs. ATF? No again. Treasury would have been very interested in the tax implications of certain supposedly middle-income men being identified on tape as the heads of crime families, but that would be the IRS's problem, and the IRS wasn't capable of mounting this kind of operation.

Her BlackBerry rang. "Waring."

"Miss Waring, this is Special Agent Holman."

She realized she was smiling. "You got my e-mail."

"Yes. Are these real-time reports from agents in the field?"

"That's exactly what they are. My section monitors them, but at this time of the evening there isn't anyone I know of who is seeing all of them at once."

"Except you."

"Right. Usually our people run through them every morning at seven. But I was here catching up on some things, so I checked. As you know, there's been some unusual activity lately surrounding Frank Tosca, and I wanted to see if he's been spotted. But sometimes you don't see anything unless you can see everything."

"Do you think this sudden movement of the capos is what it looks like?"

"I think it is. I think they're gathering for a general conference. If we could only move quickly enough, we'd get a modern version of Apalachin, with the Citizens of the Year from thirty different cities on some ranch together making agreements about what happens for the next fifty years. Or what I'm saying could be wishful thinking."

"The reason I called you on the Tosca thing is that I knew who you are. You're known to be competent and cooperative and, more to the point, you're right a lot. I also met your husband a couple of times years ago, and I can tell you he was highly respected here. What do you want the Bureau to do?"

There it was again. The Bureau's insularity never went away. They all thought of the FBI as a separate entity, not a part of anything else. The fact that it was part of the Justice Department seemed to them to be just a convenience, a place to park. By virtue of her marriage she was a friend, and her competence made her a provisional ally, but only until she disappointed them.

"What would I like the Bureau to do?" she said. "I'd like you to

89

take the information I've given you—that the heads of the families are going to the Southwest on the same day—and treat it as though you got it through your own sources. Then give it the level of priority and importance the Bureau considers appropriate."

"That's all?"

"I have confidence that will be adequate."

"This is the sort of discovery that brings promotions, and you're handing it over to me. Do you mind my asking why?"

"You recall that the surveillance I requested on Frank Tosca was overruled by the deputy assistant AG. For the moment, at least, a request for a full-court press coming from me would not be approved. I think this is an opportunity that our side must not miss."

"Don't you think the evidence you sent me speaks for itself?"

"Evidence speaks to people who pay attention to it. The Bureau will do the best job with this, so it's yours. Good luck."

"One last question, and then I'll let you go. How would you proceed?"

"The first thing is to find out exactly where they're going. I would pick two of the small players—say, Dominic Locarno and Sonny Rosanti—and figure they'll be getting rental cars somewhere, probably Phoenix. Make sure the rental company gives them cars with global positioning systems and trace them. If it's a big meeting, the little guys will arrive first. That shows respect, and the big guys send them ahead to sniff around. Then the big guys get to make an entrance." She paused. "At that point it's still a cheap, low-profile operation. If I'm wrong about all of it, then some data analyst at Justice just got jumpy and started imagining the remote farmhouse again. It happens over here about once a year."

"Here too."

"Let me know when you can."

"You'll be the first."

12

ELIZABETH HAD JUST ended her call with Agent Holman when her cell phone rang. She realized it must be one of the kids. It was nearly twelve, much later than she had expected. She looked at the phone's display for the number of the caller, but it said nothing. "Waring."

"Did you find out where it is?" Of course it would be him. Who else would it be at this hour? The kids had gone to bed.

"Where what is?"

"The meeting."

She hesitated. "I think there will be one, but that's all I can say."

"How do you know?"

"Because you're calling me. It means you weren't lying the first time. I also saw reports of big people on the move." She was staring at the screens right now, even though it was nearly midnight.

"On the move to where?"

"Airports. Beyond that I don't know yet."

"If people are flying, then the Justice Department can find out where the planes are going."

"All right," she said. "I'll be candid. I can see they all seem to be headed for one part of the country. As of now they've gotten within a thousand miles of each other, but they should be closer soon. I don't know the place yet. The span between them is still too big."

"What part of the country?"

"I know that you still want to kill Frank Tosca. I can't give you any information that will help you do that."

"That was our deal."

"I wasn't aware that we had a deal."

"From before. I tell you something, you tell me something. I told you what's going to happen, and now you tell me where."

"I can't."

Elizabeth heard the click. It wasn't a man slamming down a pay phone in a rage. It was just there, not there. He was gone.

There was no way to tell what the Justice Department was doing, and he had probably been foolish to think she would tell him. He should have held something back to trade her and made her give him the location first. Dealing with law enforcement was like dealing with the Mafia. They had no innate sense of fair dealing or honor. They felt themselves subject only to judgment by the members of their own little organizations, according to their own rules. To them, betraying an outsider was an accomplishment.

Schaeffer walked away from the pay phone, got into his rental car, and drove it across the Peace Bridge from Buffalo to Fort Erie, Ontario. He hated to waste time backtracking, but he had to find out where the meeting was. The simplest way to do that was to find someone who planned to be there. Cavalli, the man he had killed in Tosca's beach house along the St. Lawrence River, had certainly expected to be there. He was an important ally of Frank Tosca's. Cavalli seemed to see himself as the ambassador of the Castiglione family to the future boss of the Balacontano family. His travel arrangements would already have been made.

After he had killed Cavalli, he should have taken the time to search the house. There might be tickets, reservations, phone numbers, or something. It was even possible that the meeting would happen somewhere in the area—maybe one of the Thousand Islands in the St. Lawrence. Most of them were privately owned and many of them had houses on them.

As he drove east along the north shore of Lake Ontario toward the St. Lawrence, he considered the possibilities. It was not out of the question that Tosca might have returned to his beach house by now. It was probably more likely that he would send a couple of men to clean the house and move the body so it would be found in a place that didn't connect his death with Tosca. The Castigliones wouldn't like it if Cavalli's body wasn't found very quickly, but Tosca's men could arrange that too. As soon as the Canadian authorities had established that the body had nine-millimeter holes in it, so there was nothing mysterious about the cause or manner of death, they would release it for burial.

Schaeffer drove the same route he had covered before, along the Queen Elizabeth Way. He was aware that time was passing while he went over old ground to do something he should have done the first time he was here. He had bet too heavily on Elizabeth Waring. He'd been sure she would find the approximate location of the meeting—a particular city—and that she would ask him to narrow down the possible meeting spots in that city that might host a large group of Mafiosi.

He was sure she didn't want Tosca to kill him and become the most powerful man in the country. A relatively young, violent leader like him in charge of one of the biggest families might reform and revitalize the whole Mafia. The old years of gang-run companies and unions, and gang-controlled city governments, would be back to stay.

He had been overconfident about her. The Justice Department must know where the meeting was by now, and they should be trying to get their people and their microphones and cameras in place before it started. She should have been excited, busy, careless about everything but the success of their raid. She should have been trying to find out anything he knew that might keep her agents safe. Instead she had been on her guard, thinking about what he would or wouldn't do if he knew where the meeting was.

He made it back to Tosca's house along the St. Lawrence River early in the morning. He drove past to see whether there were any cars parked there, or any other signs of people, but there were none. He parked a half mile up the road at the apartment building again and then walked back on the narrow, stony beach. It was still dark, just as it had been when he had come before. He watched the road for cars and studied the fronts of the houses for signs that they were occupied. There were a few with windows open to the cool night air, but only a few. The closer he got to the string of bigger brick houses where Tosca's was, the fewer signs of life. These were summer places owned by rich families, and rich families could go anywhere in the world so they probably spent less time here.

He approached Tosca's house, then stood at the edge of the water on the pebbly shore and studied it. The windows were open, just as they had been before, but there were no lights on. Could Tosca have failed to understand that he'd been here and killed Cavalli in his house? No. Maybe he had devised some way of keeping himself in the clear by having a caretaker find the body while he was somewhere far away.

Schaeffer moved forward. He found the screen he'd cut the night before last, still pulled out from the window. He went to the back door, found it still unlocked, and stepped inside. He could smell the body. The house looked just as it had when he'd left. He listened to the silence for a few seconds, then turned on the light. The body was still lying in front of the chair. The big pool of blood had dried completely around the edges, and even in the middle it was dark and congealed.

As he moved closer, the smell of the body was stronger. He was careful to stay away from the blood. That was the kind of evidence that cops all over the world dreamed about—the killer's handprint or footprint in the victim's blood. He stepped close on the side that was bloodless, reached into Cavalli's pocket, and extracted his wallet and keys. The tag said the keys were for a rental car from a lot in Toronto. He supposed it must be in the garage.

There was a lot of cash in the wallet, but nothing that would help him find some particular place—no travel agent's card, no written notation of a confirmation number, a flight number, or even a phone number with an area code.

He looked around him. It had been late night when he'd come in before, and Cavalli was alone watching TV, not visiting with anyone. He turned off the light, moved to the staircase, and climbed to the second floor. He found the room he wanted right away. There was a two-suiter suitcase open on a chest and an unmade bed. He closed the shutters and turned on a bedside lamp. He ran his hands in the outer pockets of the suitcase and felt paper.

He pulled out a thin sheaf of letter-size inkjet-printer paper. His eye caught the word ITINERARY at the top of the first sheet, so he read it. Cavalli had booked a flight from Syracuse, New York, tomorrow morning to Phoenix, Arizona. He looked at the second sheet. It was a car rental reservation for the lot at the Sky Harbor Airport in Phoenix. The third sheet was a hotel reservation for three days in a hotel in Scottsdale, but it began the day after Cavalli arrived in Phoenix. That meant the meeting must be in the next forty-eight hours.

He folded the papers and put them in his pocket, switched off the light, and made his way to the stairs. He went down the stairs to the first floor and moved toward the garage to see if Cavalli's car was inside, then stopped. There was an engine sound, a car approaching on the road. Then a rectangle of light appeared on the back wall. It was a headlight shining through the front window. He quickly climbed the stairs to the second floor, went to the window in Cavalli's room, and looked down.

There was a van idling in the driveway. As he watched, it pulled out and backed into the space in front of the garage. Its lights went out, and Schaeffer understood. He had called Tosca well after midnight with Cavalli's phone. Tosca had known enough to call some of his men in New York. But it took them time to find a van and drive up from New York to the bridge over the

St. Lawrence to Canada. Now was the earliest the crew could come for the body and begin the difficult job of cleaning up.

He was trapped. They were already putting a key into the lock on the front door. He could hear the door open and two men with New York accents in midsentence. ". . . smells like a fucking slaughterhouse."

"Yeah, I know. You can always smell that. I think it's the blood smell, mostly. At least he's not that old yet. And some of them shit. That's the worst."

"Jesus. Don't go on about it. I got to work in here."

Schaeffer moved back up the hall, away from the guest room. They would have to scour that room of evidence that Cavalli had been here. He moved to the large bedroom at the end of the hall and sat on the bed. He heard grunts and complaints that sounded as though the men were lifting the body, then heels scraping on a rough wood surface that could be a box, then the bang of a hammer as they nailed it shut. He heard the door open again, and from the window he saw them carry a flat, three-foot-wide wooden box out through the garage to the back of the van. They put what seemed to be a false floor over it, then went back into the house. In a moment they came back carrying the big chair that Cavalli had been sitting in, put it in the van, and closed the doors. The next sounds he heard were the careless banging of a bucket or pan in a sink, then water running. He could tell they were washing the floor and the walls.

The cleanup was taking a long time. Schaeffer moved cautiously, walking across the floor of the master bedroom only when the men made trips outside carrying things. He explored the master suite, searching in the dark for anything that might help him narrow the list of places where the meeting could be. But he found nothing in the bedroom that had anything to do with travel. It was possible that Tosca hadn't even slept here since the arrangements had been made.

He checked the two pistols he was carrying. He had assembled them in the car in the dark, but they were fine and their magazines were fully loaded. He pulled back their slides to put a round in the chamber of each one.

He was beginning to get impatient. He would have to get on a flight to Arizona as quickly as he could after those two left. That meant getting to an airport and waiting for a flight. And Tosca knew he had come here and killed Cavalli. Tosca might have people watching for him in the Toronto and Montreal airports. He resisted the idea of driving all the way back to the United States and still having to wait for a flight. It wouldn't do him any good to arrive in Arizona after Tosca and the others had left.

He heard the two men clomping up the stairs, and he felt relief. That meant they had completed the major chores. They had been working hard for nearly two hours, and he could tell by their heavy footsteps that they were tired. They went into the guest room and after a second, he heard the click of the light switch and saw the dim glow under the master bedroom door.

He stood slightly to the side of the master bedroom door listening with a gun in each hand. He heard grumbling. They had driven all the way up to Canada, and now they were risking arrest trying to clean up a crime scene and smuggle the victim across an international border. They seemed to be feeling a bit unappreciated. He heard latches being clicked, and then heard one of them drop the suitcase on the hardwood floor.

"Let's take a look in Tosca's room."

"What for?"

"Look, dumb ass. If something is missing, will he think we took it? Hell no. He'll think that psycho took it after he killed Cavalli."

"You're so right. I'm a dumb ass. It's funny, though. All the guys who came up with me who weren't dumb asses are dead. Can you possibly think that anybody who comes back from Frank's house on a job like this isn't going to be searched?"

"Tosca isn't going to be around to worry about it. He's all the way out in Arizona, probably already asleep on a feather bed at that fucking dude ranch."

"The Silver Saguaro isn't a dude ranch, genius. It's a resort. And he left Mike Pascarelli in charge. He'll have guys watching us for just this kind of thing. This week it's Cavalli. Next week, they'll find you naked in the trunk of your car with two extra holes in your head. Tosca's bedroom is right there, the door on the end. I'm not going in, but be my guest."

Schaeffer heard a set of footsteps receding down the hall. The second set of feet shifted on the hardwood floor, making it creak. Finally, a voice just outside the bedroom door called, "I'm not going in, even to look around, if you aren't. I know you'll rat me out." The second set of feet heel-stomped away down the hall and then hurried down the staircase, the man moving fast to prove to the other that he hadn't had time to go into the bedroom and steal anything.

Schaeffer stepped to the side of the window, moved the curtain slightly, and looked down. The van pulled away from the garage, and after a moment, a car pulled out after it. He decided they must have hot-wired Cavalli's rental car because he had the keys in his pocket. It was possible they would have done that anyway. They would abandon it somewhere in Canada before they crossed the border to bolster the idea that Cavalli had been killed by a stranger.

He put the two guns in his coat pockets and looked at his watch. It was after six A.M. He went downstairs and looked at the place where he had left Cavalli's body. It was about as clean as it could be and smelled like chlorine and lemons. If the cops sprayed luminol around, they would see all the blood spots appear bright purple under UV light, but there was nothing visible. They had taken the chair out so there was no place to sit and watch the television mounted on the wall. He went upstairs and left the rental-car keys and Cavalli's wallet at the back of a dresser drawer in Tosca's room where Tosca probably wouldn't find them, but a police search would.

He slipped out the door on the river side, walked down the

beach to the edge of the water, and threw the two pistols as far out into the river as he could. He jogged along the shore, then crossed the road to the place where he'd left the car. He hoped he had given the two cleanup men enough of a head start. He drove off to the east, the direction they had gone, heading for the bridge over the St. Lawrence.

13

IT WAS GETTING to be morning, and Elizabeth was still staring at the computer screens in the basement of the Robert F. Kennedy Building. It was impossible not to wonder whether she had made a mistake. Maybe she should have told the Butcher's Boy everything she knew. It would only have amounted to "They seem to be heading for the Southwest, probably near Phoenix." She hadn't said that because he knew things that she couldn't even guess. If she had said "Phoenix," he might know of some Mafioso she'd never paid much attention to, who owned a house, some piece of land, some remote ranch outside Phoenix.

She knew that what she should have done was set a trap for him. She should have said, "We know the city is Durango, Colorado," and then told the FBI he was on his way and to detain any man who fit his description. If she got them to detain all the possibles, she might have to look at a hundred photographs tomorrow, but one of them would be his.

Instead she had been stupid and slow, and made a self-righteous speech about not helping him kill people. That had accomplished nothing except to remind him that she was a law enforcement officer and he was a criminal, and that nothing could ever make her his ally. She had been unforgivably stupid. He had given her some valuable information, and in return she had shown him there was no reason for him to give her any more.

He was potentially the best witness against organized crime in forty years, and she had thrown him away in an attack of bitchiness. A witness like that had to be cajoled into believing that the officer handling him felt at least some mild favoritism toward him, some conviction that she believed he was better than the people he was telling her about. He had already told her that the agenda of the meeting included Frank Tosca asking the assembled leaders of the twenty-six families to kill the Butcher's Boy. He had very strong reasons to believe that a minor tip from her might enable him to prevent that and give him a chance to save his life. And what had she said? *I'm not helping you.*

She felt a wave of resentment toward Hunsecker. If only he'd had a mind equal to the complexity of situations in the real world, she wouldn't be completely on her own, sneaking around like a spy in the building where she had worked for twenty years. His rigid absolutism had transformed a lucky turn of events into nothing. It was worse than nothing, really. Tosca would get the Butcher's Boy killed, exactly as he wanted. The more families involved in the hunt the better. They would be cooperating on a project that he had initiated and directed. He would not only get to be head of the Balacontano family, but a national figure, a symbol of new unity. And he was a vicious thug, a man who could make the Mafia into a terrifying force of a sort it had never been in the old days.

She couldn't help feeling sorry for the Butcher's Boy. He was as alone as a human being could be, put in the position of attacking an international enemy a hundred and fifty years old, that had unlimited people and resources. He could never hope to accomplish anything but to get away and live the rest of his life in some form of hiding. And he had been retired. He hadn't worked—killed anyone for money—in about twenty years. It was hard not to make comparisons, hard not to hope that if any criminal got through this, he did.

14

SCHAEFFER WAS ON the plane to Phoenix, and it was before noon. He'd had the advantage of knowing that one of the passengers booked on the flight from Syracuse wasn't going to make it to the airport. So he had bought a standby ticket early in the morning, sat down with his computer, and waited until he had been called to the gate and assigned a seat. He spent the two hours in the waiting area across the concourse from his gate watching. If Cavalli had chosen this flight, it was possible there were others—friends of his, Castiglione soldiers, even Tosca—on the same flight. When he had determined that there weren't any passengers he had to worry about, he saw the air marshal arrive. She was about thirty-five years old, blond, wearing a business suit and carrying a leather shoulder bag. The flight attendants at the gate were not nearly ready for boarding, but they saw her enter the waiting area at a brisk pace, nodded to her as she walked into the boarding tunnel and disappeared. It all took about four seconds, and he had the feeling that if someone asked the flight attendants about the woman, they would have said, "What woman?" When he boarded the plane, he found her standing by an aisle seat about two thirds of the way back, staring at each passenger who came in the door. He had spotted marshals on his two flights into Washington, D.C., but he hadn't expected to have one on a flight to Phoenix. He just noted where she was, took his seat, and waited.

When the flight attendant had finally closed the forward hatch and brought the bar down to lock it, he was relieved. It meant that there wouldn't be four big men appearing in front of the cockpit door in a moment to drag him off the plane. Travel was always full of small obstacles and checkpoints that had to be passed through.

As soon as the plane taxied to the end of the runway and then hurtled over the pavement into the sky, he settled into the back of his seat and prepared to sleep. Sleeping whenever and wherever he could was something he had learned from Eddie when he was about twelve. "Never work when you're tired, kid. If you don't win by strength in the first couple of seconds, you have to win by stamina. You have to learn to keep resetting the clock so it's always morning for you. The other guy is so exhausted he's beginning to see things out of the corner of his eye, but you just got up."

Sleep was a trick. Just find a comfortable place, close both eyes, and mentally repeat some short, meaningless mantra a couple of times to clear the mind of distractions. Eddie had used the Lord's Prayer, but the boy had preferred writing the alphabet. He would write each letter by directing an imaginary pen in longhand until he was asleep.

After a disconnected and meaningless series of dreams, he awoke feeling rested and alert. He looked at his watch, saw that he had slept four hours, and adjusted it to Phoenix time.

While he was waiting in the airport in the morning, he had Googled the Silver Saguaro Ranch and found its website. He had taken the virtual tour and studied the maps and layouts. The place was a resort in a mountainous area with pine trees. There was a big building called the Lodge, which appeared to have two restaurants, a couple of meeting rooms, a huge open room with gigantic stone fireplaces on either end, and a wall that appeared to be all glass. There were stables and horse trails and hiking routes, and a lake with some canoes and a dock. The suites consisted of dozens of separate cabins, each with a bedroom, a living room with a bar, and a bathroom.

At the bottom of the home page of the website was small print saying the Saguaro was a Pure Gold Seam resort. He ran a Google search on the name and found that the president of the company was Sylvia Fibbiano. Of course. He was sure that she was the daughter of Jimmy Fibbiano, who had always had a construction company in New Jersey that kept changing its name every time it got to be well known. He had been fairly sure the Silver Saguaro Ranch must be owned by a Mafioso, or the others would never consent to meet there. He supposed any potential guests for the next couple of days would be told the whole place was rented out for a large wedding party or something, so there would be no out-siders around. The help would all be relatives and protégés of the Fibbianos, even if they had to be flown in from other Fibbiano enterprises. Fibbiano would have guards stationed around the pe-rimeter of the place to prevent a breach or warn of a raid.

He could only hope that the men out there would be the usual big guys with the expensive suits and Italian shoes who ran the football betting sheets, and not a few lean and silent types who spent every fall in the woods stalking deer.

When the plane landed in Phoenix, he moved quickly. He went to the curb and got on a shuttle bus to the car-rental depot. While he was inside behind the tinted windows, he studied the crowd coming out of the baggage claim for familiar faces but he saw none. When he got to the depot, he rented a Nissan Altima in an unobtrusive gray and drove.

He stopped in a sporting-goods store and made some purchases. He bought a small backpack, a .308 Remington rifle with a ten-power Weaver scope, and three boxes of ammunition. On the way out he picked up a folding hunting knife with a flat handle that was easy to conceal and came open with a flick of his thumb.

His next stop was at a military-surplus store. He bought a pair of tropical-style combat boots, a light camouflage poncho with a hood, a camouflage tarp, a backpack-style water pack with a tube for drinking on the move, a set of water purification tablets, some salt pills, and a camouflage ventilated hat with a flap to protect the back of his neck from the sun. There was a high-tech section where he found a night-vision scope and a GPS unit. He picked out a set of U.S. Geological Survey maps of southern Arizona with altitude lines and landmarks. He needed to drive out Route 87, called the Beeline Highway, past Saguaro Lake in the Tonto National Forest. That seemed to be about forty miles. From there he had to take a turnoff and go farther out into the desert toward the pine woods and hills.

As he drove farther out of the city in the afternoon, he studied the country. His plans had become specific and certain. If the Justice Department managed to figure out where the meeting was, they'd block all the roads for miles before they moved in. There was no way that most of the old men would try to take off across country in a place like this. Chi-chi Tasso or Big Al Costananza would run about a hundred yards and die.

He found the turnoff past the lake, drove another fifteen miles on the road to the Silver Saguaro Ranch, and looked for a place to hide his car. He turned off the road onto a rocky, dry streambed that curved away into an area where the rocks were as big as small houses. He parked between two of them, stretched his tarp from one to the other over the car, and anchored it on both ends with rows of stones. He tossed some loose brush over the tarp to help disguise it from the air.

He put on his camouflage hat and boots, broke down his rifle, rolled the barrel and stock in his poncho to hide them, put the rest of his gear into his backpack, and set off on foot.

It had been at least ten years since he had engaged in the level of physical activity he was about to attempt. But in England he had kept himself in reasonably good condition as a precaution, and he routinely walked nearly everywhere he went.

He began the hike tentatively, and as his muscles warmed up and loosened in the late summer heat, he worked harder. It was midafternoon when he started, and he wanted to get as far as he could while he had light. He would be virtually invisible from the air during daylight, but at night his body heat would show up on infrared sensors, and his outline would be clear in the amplified green glow of a night-vision viewer. He ran a hundred yards, then walked a hundred yards, then repeated it. The ground was gravel with a few spiky plants and rocks of every size from a pea to a car.

The desert heat made his body seem heavier, as though gravity had been augmented somehow, but he pushed on. When he was walking, he drank, checked his position with the map and GPS, and judged his progress toward the dark silhouettes of the distant hills. He could easily tell he was gradually climbing into higher country. By the end of three hours he had noticed that the vegetation was thicker, with a few woody plants with leaves, and soon there were stands of pine. He moved to the inside of the groves for shade and cover.

Before the fifth hour the sun was low in the sky and he judged he was getting close to the ranch. He found a copse in the middle of a pine woods, half covered by a rock shelf and sheltered by trees that had grown close to it. He crawled under the shelf, opened his pack, and sorted his gear. He assembled his rifle, loaded it, then put another five rounds in the spare magazine and put it into his pocket. He rechecked the adjustments of the scope and mounts to be sure they were in the midrange—essentially the factory setting. He would have liked to zero in the rifle before he tried to do anything risky with it, but that had been impossible. He would have to move in as close as he dared, fire his first round, and adjust to improve the precision of his aim. He plotted his route to the ranch and identified a mountain as the landmark he would still be able to see later in dim moonlight.

He drank more water, lay down, and slept for a time, then awoke in the dark. He looked at his watch. It was ten o'clock in the evening. He took with him his night-vision scope, his rifle and ammunition, and his camouflage poncho. He left everything else in his pack and pushed it far back under the rock shelf.

The night was quiet in the dry, rocky hills. The birds that had sung at twilight were all quiet now. His own footsteps seemed to be the loudest sounds. Now and then some small animal skittered away into the brush ahead of him. After another quarter mile he would stop occasionally in cover, take out his night scope, and study the next stretch of visible ground before he stepped into it. He searched for the shapes of men waiting for an intruder, and then for electronic devices that might have been installed around the perimeter of Silver Saguaro Ranch.

He saw nothing and heard nothing that indicated men had been here. Probably anyone on the path he was blazing would have traveled on horseback, but he could see no signs that horses had been up here. As he approached what his map indicated was the last ridge before the ranch, he became more wary. There could easily be men posted up on the high ground watching the approaches to the resort.

He knelt in some fragrant brush, put on his camouflage poncho, concealed his rifle under it, and looked through his night scope. He saw pale green rocks and trees, black sky, pale green clouds. He looked, he waited, then moved ahead to a higher plateau with a few jagged rock outcroppings on it. He sat in front of an outcropping, spread his poncho so he wasn't shaped like a human being, and stared through the night scope, looking down the slope toward the ranch.

A hundred yards ahead there was a fallen log on the ground, a big pine that had once stood at the edge of the nearby stand. After a few seconds he saw part of it move. It moved again and he made out the shape of a head, a shoulder, and then the whole shape separated itself from the background. It was a man lying down, leaning on the log, and staring up the mountainside in his general direction.

He had to find a way past this sentry. If he passed far enough to the left or the right, he might avoid this man's notice, but there would be others stationed at intervals. One sentry was like one ant—an impossibility. He studied the area with his night-vision scope, but he couldn't see a good way around. He also knew that it would be foolish to leave an armed enemy behind him. Getting past him on the way out, after things had happened, might be impossible. But if the man was dead, this spot would be clear.

Schaeffer moved to his right, away from the sentry, and slipped into the pine woods. He felt extremely lucky that the trees up here were pines. The ground had a thick, soft carpet of fallen needles, and he could walk without making a sound. As he circled back to the left, he considered the proper method. Shooting the man would bring the rest of the watchdogs. Cutting his throat would be difficult to do without some sort of a struggle and the chance of being soaked with the man's blood. The best way would be a ligature. He pulled the cord from the neck of his poncho, tested its strength, and then looked for the right sort of branch as he moved in the woods. When he found it, he used his knife to carve it into two pieces, each about an inch thick and four inches long. In the center of each he carved a groove, then put the knife away. He tied the ends of the cord to the handles, keeping the cord in the groove. Now the cord was about two feet long with a sturdy handle on each end.

He moved on through the woods, looking in his scope until he could see the sentry again. The sentry was staring up at the slope of the hill, watching for intruders. Schaeffer began to advance toward the sentry. He stayed low, but moved steadily, and soon he was directly behind him, on the other side of the log. He gripped the handles, crossed his wrists, and dropped the loop around the man's neck. He tightened it and kept it tight. The man struggled to get the cord off his neck, then to reach for the hand that held it. But Schaeffer pulled backward hard and set both feet against the fallen tree trunk.

As he tightened the strangling cord and the man lost consciousness, Schaeffer thought about strangulation. As he had thrown the loop over the man's head, the man had done the wrong thing instinctively. He had dropped the objects in his hands and used both hands to try to pull the cord away from his throat, then to wrench his attacker's hands off the cord. Before he could change his tactic and reach down for the gun in his jacket, his brain had been denied oxygen for a couple of minutes so he was already weak and dizzy. A few seconds later he was unconscious. What amateur killers didn't realize was that strangling took patience. The amateur might consider the job done right about now. But to be sure the man wouldn't start breathing again and regain consciousness after he was gone, it was necessary to deny him oxygen for much longer. Eddie Mastrewski had always insisted on seven minutes.

While he held the cord tight and waited, he watched and listened. There was no sound up here except the whisper of wind in the tall trees. He studied the view up the hill from here so he would be sure to come back past the dead sentry instead of some live one. He looked down at the sentry. He was about thirty years old, wearing new blue jeans and a black shirt cut like a cowboy's, with snaps instead of buttons. He was beginning to lose his hair prematurely, with a receding hairline and a bare spot at the back of his head about the size of a silver dollar. On his feet were a pair of clean, new hiking boots.

Schaeffer held both handles in his left hand, touched the man's wrist, and felt for a pulse: nothing. He unwrapped the rope, found the man's wallet, and looked inside. His driver's license was from New York and said he was Raymond Agnetti. There was a thick layer of hundred-dollar bills, so Schaeffer took them. Agnetti's jacket was lying on the log beside him. When he lifted it, he felt the weight of a gun. He took it out and looked at it in the moonlight. The etching on the slide said it was a Springfield Armory XD. He'd never seen this model before, and so he knew it must be new. He released the magazine and saw it held about sixteen nine-millimeter rounds in a double stack. He pushed it back in and put the pistol in his belt and its spare magazine in his pocket.

He found Agnetti's cell phone in the coat, but he had no radio for talking to all the other guards at once. Schaeffer turned the phone off, put it back in the coat, dragged the body into the low brush at the edge of the pine woods, and covered it with branches from a broken sapling. He retrieved his gear and went on.

Moving slowly and carefully, he made his way down the hill toward the ranch. There were clearly marked hiking trails now, and he stayed in the woods that bordered them. After a quarter mile he saw the complex and realized why the families had posted guards up the hill. The hill offered a good view of the whole resort. He kept moving downward looking below for ways to accomplish what he wanted to do.

When he was only a few hundred feet from the populated area, he stopped and surveyed it. From the website he recognized the Lodge, a big, barnlike building with a high roof and big windows. He could see there were many men inside it right now. Parked beside it on the side away from the main entrance were three big white Fibbiani trucks marked GOLD SEAM CATERING, with white-coated hotel staff walking back and forth unloading supplies.

There were cabins along a network of paved roads surrounding the lodge. Many cabins had cars parked in front of them, and quite a few had lights glowing in their windows. There were small knots of men who had gathered to talk at various places along the paths to the lodge or on the wooden porches of the cabins. The thing that struck him as he looked down on the scene was that every human being he saw was male. This was not the sort of conference where they brought wives and girlfriends. It looked like a military encampment.

He found a small level space on the hillside that served as a foothold for some spiky plants, sat down, and spread his poncho on the plants so his body was under it, and its shape merged into the brush. He trained the rifle scope on a group of men standing near the lodge and studied them, then moved the rifle to other groups, searching for familiar faces. It took him several more minutes before he found one he knew. It was Gino Castelletti, an old caporegima from Brooklyn. He was fat and stooped now, and Schaeffer judged he must be around seventy. His hair was so thin that it looked like lines drawn on his bald head.

The five men standing around him listening to him talk were all about twenty-five to thirty-five years old, and Schaeffer didn't know any of them. At one time he had known a great many made men across the country and a fair proportion of the bosses. But nearly all the faces he saw tonight were new. It had been twenty years ago when he had last been around people in the families. Even the oldest of these soldiers had been children then, ten or fifteen years old. None of them had ever seen him.

There were few of the older men in evidence outside the lodge. A lot of the men who had known him were probably dead by now, and others had been convicted of something and been given those comical sentences of four or five hundred years, as Carl Bala had. There were probably two hundred men gathered at the resort to-night for the conference where one of the topics was his death, but he guessed there were fewer than forty present who had ever seen him.

He carefully made his way down the hill after stowing the rifle, the scope, and the poncho underneath a ledge. He picked his way between thick bushes and rocks, trying to stay as invisible as possible. At the edge of the resort and up a short drive by itself was a cabin with a dim light glowing in a window and a rental car parked beside it. He went to the back of the building and looked in the window. There was a bedroom, and he could see a suitcase open on a folding stand and some clothes hanging in an open closet. He went to the woodpile, picked up a piece of firewood, wrapped his hat around the end to muffle the sound, broke the upper pane of glass, reached in, and unlocked the latch, then climbed in.

He went to the closet and picked out the sort of outfit that the men outside were wearing—a pair of blue jeans and a shirt, with a nylon windbreaker intended to keep off the night chill of the mountains and conceal a weapon.

He changed into the clothes, searched the suitcase, and found a brand-new Springfield Armory .45 pistol, still in the box, and a full box of .45 ACP ammunition. These people must have flown into southwestern cities, then driven straight to gun stores operated by

111

friendly owners to pick something out so they wouldn't feel powerless. Probably when they went back to catch their flights home, they would drop the guns off where they had picked them up. He already had the sentry's gun, and it was more concealable than the .45, so he left this one alone.

Through the front window he watched a group of younger men coming along the lighted drive toward the lodge. He had never seen any of them before. He waited until they were just past him, then opened the door and hurried to the road to follow them. If someone looked at him from a distance, he would seem to be a straggler from the main group.

He was very watchful, trying to avoid coming face-to-face with any older men because they were the ones who might have seen his face years ago. When he was young, not long after Eddie Mastrewski had died, he had worked for the Albanese family in Detroit for a time. By then he had a reputation, and so a few times the Albanese capo, Johnny Sotto, had used Schaeffer's face. He had gone along with an Albanese soldier to collect debts. People might stall the soldier, but as soon as he walked in the door, the money would appear very efficiently and without any discussion. After a few months he left and never did that kind of work again because he didn't like having so many people see his face.

He had also resisted the camaraderie that some of the capos who had hired him tried to foster. He had kept his distance, done his job, collected his pay, and left town before buyer's remorse set in. He made it clear that he was a free agent and that he was nobody's friend.

The group of men kept moving down the drive leading to the lodge. There were already many men gathering there. He knew that he couldn't take the chance of going inside, where the men who had seen him would be. He preferred to stay outside with the young men who had no idea who he was. The young ones would find out what was going on inside as soon as it happened anyway. They absorbed every word the old men said, analyzed it, and repeated it.

A couple of them had turned their heads and noticed him, and now they slowed to walk with him. The bigger one held out his hand. "Vic Malatesta, from Buffalo." Then he tapped his companion's shoulder. "This is my brother-in-law, Joe Bollo."

He shook their hands. "Mike Agnelli, Calgary."

"Calgary? Holy shit," said Malatesta. "Nice of you to come."

Bollo said, "You're showing your ignorance. Of course we got crews in Calgary. You think we'd leave Canada to the fucking Eskimos?"

Schaeffer smiled, and said to Malatesta, "The Castiglione family has been in Canada since Prohibition."

Malatesta seemed to wilt a little. The Castiglione family was a major power, holding the biggest piece of Chicago since Al Capone went to jail, and had colonies in lots of distant places sending tribute to the home base.

The group kept walking. Schaeffer said, "What do you think of this sit-down so far?"

"I don't know," said Bollo. "Maybe when I hear what Frank Tosca has to say, I'll have an opinion. Or more likely, when I hear what Mr. Visconti's opinion is."

"That sounds safe."

"How about you?" Malatesta said.

"I don't have an opinion yet either. I'm waiting to hear what any of us has to gain by helping Frank Tosca kill somebody and take over the Balacontano family. What's he give the rest of the families? Do they get to taste some of the profits?"

"That would be more like it," said Malatesta.

"Well," said Bollo. "Maybe even without that, making him strong might do the rest of us some good."

"Some guys are saying he's the one to run the whole country."

"Do you know him?" asked Schaeffer.

"No," said Malatesta, "but I've been hearing about him for a long time. He's supposed to be a good earner, and a little bit of a wild man too. And that doesn't hurt when something is up. People used to hear the Italians wanted a piece of their action, and they'd get maybe a little chill in their spines. It wouldn't hurt to have some of that again."

"No question," Schaeffer said. "But maybe the way to do that isn't to send the whole organization out after one small guy that nobody's seen in ten, twenty years. It doesn't feel right to me. Not in proportion, you know? Not dignified."

"It's not going up against him that's the problem. It's finding him. That's what takes a lot of people."

Schaeffer chuckled. "If he's that hard to find, maybe he's not that big a problem. Maybe he's an anaconda."

"An anaconda?"

"Yeah. You don't ever want to tangle with one of those bastards. They're twenty, twenty-five feet long. They wrap themselves around you and squeeze you to death. Only thing is, there aren't any around here, so they aren't a problem unless you go where they are and look for them."

"I see what you mean."

The group moved closer and closer to the lodge, and he slouched a little to change his walk and keep his face down to avoid the light from the lamps along the eaves of the lodge and from the tall windows of the big banquet room.

He had not yet decided what he was going to do. He was outnumbered by hundreds to one, and his only way out would be overland, down from the mountain and across the desert to his car. He couldn't predict how the old men were going to react to Frank Tosca's request for their help and support, and that would make all the difference.

He said, "I got a feeling that we need to know a lot more about this before it happens. My bosses ask me what I think, and I have to say I don't know. Either of you guys know which cabin Tosca is staying in?"

"You're just going to pop in and ask him to explain it to you?"

"Not to just me. Maybe I'll ask one of the Castigliones to come too. But I go back a ways with Tosca. I knew him a little bit in New York when we were twenty. He'll probably remember me."

"Cabin nine," Malatesta said. "Or ten, maybe. They're both together over that way. One is his, and the other is a couple of guys he brought with him."

"Thanks. I'll see who I can get to go with me." He stepped aside and headed across the road toward the lodge. He knew it was dangerous to get too close to the building where all the attention was focused, but he needed to know more. He devoted a portion of his attention to each face that turned his way. So far they were all the faces he had hoped for, the men in their twenties and thirties who had been brought along to carry the luggage and look tough. The older men, the ones who knew him or had at least seen him, were either inside the big room in the lodge or back in their home cities running the businesses that kept the supply of money coming in.

Through the huge panes of glass he could see the old men standing around with drinks in their hands. One of the Castigliones, no, all three of the Castiglione brothers, were standing around in blue jeans and hiking boots. And there was Vince Pugliese, who was their underboss now. It must be a good night for law-abiding citizens in Chicago. There was Mike Catania from Boston, and Dean Amalfi, and one of the Sottos whose first name he couldn't bring back. He was definitely a son or nephew of the Sotto who had run the Albanese empire in Detroit years ago. Mike Tragonatta was perched on a step of the big staircase with his shoulders hunched up so he looked like a vulture.

Tosca. There he was. He looked like a cheap politician threading his way through the crowd, insinuating himself and making it impossible for the others to have a conversation that wasn't with him and about him. As he passed, he punched the shoulder of Rich Martinoli and hugged the ancient, skinny frame of Paolo Canaletti. Schaeffer cringed at the stupid presumption of it. Tosca was claiming a false equality with men older than his own father.

Schaeffer couldn't spend too much time in the glow coming from the lodge windows so he moved away. He took this opportunity to go to cabins nine and ten and look in the windows. He found that nine had twin beds and two suitcases, but ten had a king and only one suitcase so he chose that one. He went to the door, pushed the blade of his knife into the space between the handle and the strike plate, and opened it. He went in and closed the door, and then searched Tosca's luggage, but found nothing useful or revealing except a nine-millimeter Beretta pistol. He decided that the rules of the conference must require the participants to come unarmed. He ejected the magazine, removed all of the bullets, and pulled back the slide to open the chamber. He took a sheet of paper from the small pad by the phone, tore off a corner, and crumpled it. He crammed it into the chamber and barrel so even if Tosca reloaded, the first round would fail to feed. He searched for other guns, but there were none in the cabin. He went out through the back window, closed it, but left it unlocked. He walked out of the small clearing on the back side so nobody would see him coming from Tosca's cabin. He passed a few men on the paved drive, but didn't recognize any of them.

He felt slightly better now because he had at least taken some steps to prepare for killing Tosca in his cabin. Any plausible plan was better than no plan. And earlier he had created a gap in the cordon of sentries so there would be at least one way out. Now he needed to learn how the old men reacted to Tosca's proposal. If they turned him down and told him to solve his own problems, Schaeffer's best move would be to get out quietly and then kill Tosca somewhere else on another day.

He got onto the lighted drive and moved toward the lodge again. As he came nearer, he could see into the big conference room and tell that the meeting had begun. The light from inside poured out onto the pavement around the building from the glass wall so he stayed back. He could see there were four large tables pushed together into a huge square. All around it sat the old men.

It occurred to him that the square was a sign of resistance to Tosca. With a rectangular table, somebody was always at the head, and somebody was at the foot. These men were all chieftains, the heads of semitribal groups composed of extended family and close friends, as well as loose collections of hangers-on, allies, and associates who were willing to follow orders because there had always been money and protection if they did. The dons from the smaller, older eastern cities were often as rich and powerful as the leaders of the families in New York or Chicago or Boston because they could control virtually all illegal activity in those places and take a percentage. They were protective of their independence and dignity, and didn't acknowledge the superiority of anyone. They also knew that while a New York family might have more made men, there was no way to project that power to do much in a tightly held city a thousand miles away.

His best hope was that these men would be too suspicious and guarded to help Tosca come to power in the Balacontano family. Why set loose a force greater than their own? Agreeing to hunt for the Butcher's Boy was a small enough thing to do, but its very smallness meant it would be worth little gratitude in the future. Once Carl Bala was satisfied and put Tosca in power, Tosca wouldn't need their help anymore.

He stood in the crowd and studied what he could see of the big room through the glass. If Tosca had wanted to preside, he had been thwarted. The participants were sitting in equal seats at the table, the old men taking turns as each of them made his own statement. Now and then a speaker would stop, raise his eyebrows inquiringly, and gesture toward one or more of the others. Most of the time, the men indicated would nod sagely or make a reply that seemed to indicate an affirmative answer. There was no telling what the topics were, but he guessed that they were using the conference as a way to settle the eternal boundary disputes and make requests for help, a share in some racket, or exclusive rights to some method of stealing in some particular place. He knew that for most of them, there was a wide range of issues that were more important than the succession of leaders in the Balacontano family or the fate of a hit man nobody had seen in years.

Agreements made openly in this company would be difficult to disavow later, and at the same time, could not be understood

117

by third parties to be conspiracies. He stood outside among the young men, the retainers and bodyguards and soldiers, who had no more idea of the outcome than he had. But then, four men came out of the door and lit cigarettes. As they talked to friends and acquaintances, he edged closer. Within a few seconds, the four were surrounded by a growing ring of the curious.

In the center was a man about forty years old. He said, "The local stuff—gambling, street dealers, fencing operations, crews that rip off trucks and trains and cargo containers, percentages of local businesses—all that stays local. You won't have a crew from a Chicago family come in and start asking a contractor in your town to pay them for protection. Trying to pull a scam on a national company or make a deal in a foreign country is open to everybody. But if you have to go to the national headquarters, and it's in St. Louis, you do the St. Louis people the courtesy of letting them know you're there and giving them a small piece of the game." He shrugged. "It's all pretty much the way it was before we were born."

Schaeffer said quietly to the man beside him, "I wonder what happened with Frank Tosca."

One of the men who had come out heard him. "They're still talking about some of it, but he'll get what he wants. They all like the idea of a mutual defense agreement. If some outsider attacks one of the families, the don asks for help, and the other families all send soldiers."

One of the listeners said, "Sounds like overkill."

"That's the point. Things used to work because everybody knew if they wanted to go head-to-head with the Mafia, they were taking on a lot more than what was in front of their eyes that day. There was no way they could win. We need that again. Say some Mexican gang starts shaking down a neighborhood in Houston. The next thing that happens is that the city fills up with goombahs. Fifteen or twenty of the Mexicans disappear one night and the problem is solved for the next ten years."

One of the listeners said, "I'd be ready for that."

118

"Right. It's the only way. We should have been doing that already."

"Damned straight."

Schaeffer said, "What's that stuff about him wanting some guy killed? Why can't he handle that himself?"

"I think it's a test, to see which of the old men are on board."

"What do the old men think?"

"They all agreed to that first thing. It's common courtesy. You'll hear everything in a few minutes. They're going to take a half-hour break after the last couple of capos finish talking."

Schaeffer drifted backward, allowing other men to slip in to listen, so he didn't appear to be moving, but was soon ten feet from the center of the conversation. Then he was in dimmer light, farther from the lodge. He turned away and began to walk. When he was near the cabins, he left the pavement and walked between two of them as though he were taking a shortcut to his own.

He went to the back of cabin ten, entered through the window, and sat down in the dark to wait for Frank Tosca. He had heard what he needed to know so there was no reason to take the risk of standing outside the lodge in the crowd, waiting for someone to recognize him. He sat in the dark and planned and rested. It was over an hour later before he heard men's voices as they passed on the paved drive outside. Maybe the formal part of the conference was over, or maybe it was just the break. But he had to be ready.

He stood and went to the doorway, stepped into the space at the hinge side of the door, took out the lock-blade knife he had brought, and opened it. He concentrated on regulating his breathing and his heartbeat, readying himself for the struggle. This was no different from the old days. There was no longer any room for negotiation or for last-minute bartering. He heard a man coming up the gravel walk. He listened for other footsteps, but there was only one set. The man climbed up the wooden steps. His leather-soled shoes clopped on the wooden porch. His key was in the lock. The door opened and he stepped inside. Tosca. He began to close it, but before it was fully closed, Schaeffer was behind him, his forearm snaking around Tosca's neck, the knife edge tilted inward. He brought the knife across Tosca's throat with as much force as he could, and then leaned into the door so it closed and locked. He released his hold on Tosca.

Tosca collapsed to the floor on his back, his blood pumping out of him rapidly. His eyes were wide with the panicky realization that he was dying, and would be dead in seconds. His shirt, the upper part of his sport coat, and the carpet beneath him were soaked already, and the blood was pooling beside him.

Schaeffer looked down and said, "I told you to leave me out of it."

A few seconds later, Tosca lost consciousness and his body relaxed. On his way to the window Schaeffer wiped the knife on the bed sheet, closed it, and put it in his pocket. He moved the pistol he had taken from the dead sentry from his belt to his jacket pocket and climbed out the window. He closed the window, took a few steps, and slipped in among the surrounding pine trees.

He walked purposefully toward the outer edge of the complex, heading upward on the hillside with his hand in his pocket on the gun. He passed within sight of two more cabins, and he could see there were lights on in their windows. He kept climbing steadily up the hill, away from the cabins. From the vantage of the higher ground, he could see that about half the soldiers were still milling around outside the lodge, and a few of the old capos seemed to have stayed in the big meeting room, standing in small groups talking, but there were many more men walking up the paved paths to cabins. He could see nobody running or making big gestures so he knew Tosca still had not been discovered. He climbed as rapidly as he could, staying in the cover of the pine groves.

He began to feel winded, to gasp for breath as he forced himself to trot up the hillside. The lack of breath was a nightmarish feeling. He was back in the world he had left twenty years ago, forced to stay alive with his wits and the weapons he could find, but he wasn't the same man anymore. He was twenty years older, far beyond the age when this prolonged physical exertion was routine.

What he was doing tonight was something that would have challenged him in his prime. He didn't allow himself to think about how much of the ordeal was ahead of him; he just kept running, putting one foot in front of the other, taking himself up the side of the mountain.

When he reached the level ledge where he'd left his gear, he retrieved the rifle, the rolled poncho, and the night-vision scope, and climbed some more. It was after a few steps higher that he became aware of a faint, almost imperceptible hum. For a second he wondered if it was some kind of vehicle straining its transmission as it drove up a parallel road to intercept him. But as it grew louder, it didn't sound like that. It was some kind of aircraft. It occurred to him that he had not heard any aircraft before. And it must be too late at night for airliners to be landing at Phoenix Sky Harbor.

He moved faster. He took off the jacket he had stolen from the sentry and ran on. He concentrated on making his way up to the crest of the mountain, where the pine forest flourished and the cover was thick. When he reached the big grove he moved off the trail to the thick carpet of pine needles to quiet his footsteps and tried to catch his breath while he walked.

The hum of engines grew into a loud, rhythmic throbbing, and the sound of rotors became a thwack-thwack-thwack in the general roar. Helicopters came in overhead, and he could see their running lights as they cleared the top of the mountain and followed the terrain down into the compound below.

He kept moving, listening to the sounds of more and more helicopters coming in and landing at the foot of the mountain. He knew there would already be federal or police vehicles blocking the private road that led away from the resort, and undoubtedly the highway beyond it. The first thing they did in a raid was take control of the roads so nobody could drive out.

There was no question in his mind that these invaders were the result of his conversation with Elizabeth Waring. He had tipped her off to the existence of a meeting and asked her to use the Justice Department's net of wiretaps and surveillance operations to find out whether a lot of capos were on their way to one place. She had refused to tell him, but of course she had found out and sent an army of federal cops to round up everybody at the meeting. Now the feds would have a wonderful couple of days photographing, fingerprinting, and identifying all the men at the meeting and trying to find out what they were up to.

But things had not worked out well for him. If he had been able to get to her more quickly, or had more specific information for her, maybe the federal cops would have arrived in time to keep Frank Tosca from making his pitch. Tosca had called powerful men here from all over the country, and if they'd all been arrested right away, they would have been angry. Maybe they wouldn't have killed Tosca, but they might have. They certainly wouldn't have agreed to make him head of the Balacontano family. For Schaeffer the timing was wrong. They had already agreed before the first helicopter had swooped in. Now Schaeffer was about as likely to get scooped up in the police sweep as the rest of them. And if the police didn't get startled in the woods and open fire on him, then he would be locked up in a big holding cell with about fifty men who would consider it a pleasure and a privilege to beat him to death.

When he reached the rock shelf where he'd left his pack, he slipped the poncho over his head. He hid the rifle under a pile of rocks, pushed pine needles over it so no part was visible, and stood. Getting out was going to depend on stealth and speed, and not on trying to win a shoot-out with the FBI.

The trail through the pines was deserted, but as he loped along, the sound of helicopters was always in his ears. Suddenly the sound grew deafening, and he threw himself down and skittered under a big rock outcropping. When the helicopter was overhead, he was blinded by the outcropping above him, but then he could see the white belly slide over and then down into the valley. It looked so near that it seemed to him he could almost reach up and touch it.

They must be still ferrying policemen into the center of the resort so they could keep swarming into the compound, detaining everybody they saw. In a few minutes that would be accomplished, and they would be free to start fanning out, searching for stray gangsters from the air.

Before he dared to slow down, he needed to get outside the perimeter the cops were establishing. He kept moving through the pine woods, fighting the stitch in his side and the difficulty he felt gasping in enough air. He reached the spot where he had left the dead sentry, and knowing he had gotten that far gave him a second wind. If all the sentries were in a long line at this altitude, that line would be the spot where the police would start. He ran harder, promising himself he would get as far as the downslope and then stop to catch his breath. *Do it now,* he thought. *Whatever you do now is worth a hundred times as much as anything you can do later.*

He found that he remembered the ground he was crossing. He knew the spots where he could risk breaking into a full run, and where he would have to trot, watching for half-buried rocks and raised roots that could injure him in the dark. Tonight a broken ankle would be fatal.

The sound of the helicopters changed again. This time the sound was coming from the north, along the spine of the mountain. He dashed to a sparse stand of pines nearby and then searched for a better place to hide. He found a deep depression on the edge of the grove. It looked as though sometime in the past a big tree had fallen, and the roots had left a hole. He sat in the depression, spread his poncho around him, pulled armloads of pine needles and twigs over on top of it, and lay down on his back.

A helicopter passed over him, bright spotlights shone down from its belly, and then it began to descend. It hovered and set down on the open meadow that lay between him and the downslope. The engine remained loud and the rotors still turned, the false wind kicking up dust and bits of bark.

The door on the side opened and two men in olive jumpsuits

ran a few feet, dropped to their bellies, and lay there sighting M-16 rifles on theoretical foes lurking in the forest. Then the rest of the team jumped out, spread, and ran for cover. A second helicopter landed farther up in the meadow, and its crew performed the same landing drill.

The two helicopters churned up even more dust and debris as they rose unsteadily to a height of about a hundred feet and then swung away along the spine of the mountain. The men on their bellies got up and ran to join their comrades, who were already setting off along the path that led to the ranch complex.

He lay still and waited. He was fairly certain that the outer edge of the sweep had been established, and this was it. The men coming along the path passed within fifty feet of him, the butts of their assault rifles resting atop their shoulders instead of against them, turning their heads one way and the other to spot a target. None of them discerned anything human about him in the hole under the poncho and the pine needles and scraps.

Moving slowly, he fed the tube from his backpack canteen up through the neck of the poncho and drank. He rested and regained his strength while he waited for the contingent of federal officers to move far enough off. After a few more minutes he didn't hear them anymore so he got up and began to walk.

Before long he reached the beginning of the downslope. It was a gradual, steady descent, but now there were no paths. Probably few, if any, of the resort's guests had ever hiked down the mountain. In the daytime, the level land at the foot was a hot, harsh, demanding place.

As he descended out of the zone of pine trees and into the levels with patches of cactus and yucca, he could feel the rocky ground radiating stored heat into the cooler night air, like a memory of scorching sunlight. He came downward at a walk. When he reached the level ground and could see ahead far enough to spot the variations that were rocks and desert plants, he worked his way up to a trot. He could just catch the faint sound of helicopters on the moving air now and then from the far side of the mountain.

By now they were probably ferrying passengers to some police facility in the area. A lot of the men at the conference would draw some charges. Nearly every cabin would have a gun or two in it. A lot of the men were violating their paroles just by being in the same place as a hundred other convicted felons. There would undoubtedly be lots of other minor charges he couldn't anticipate—possession of this or that drug, carrying false identification, and so on. If the police found Frank Tosca, his body alone was adequate justification for holding all of the men for questioning.

Now that he was off the mountain there was little cover. He was tired, but he forced himself to stretch and take longer strides. His fast walk turned into a trot, and his trot accelerated into a jog. He kept up the pace for a mile or more before he slowed to a walk. When he caught his breath again, he worked up to a jog. He felt his age more than before. It wasn't that he couldn't perform quick, strong movements. It was his stamina that was diminished. He felt tired, used up now, and keeping up the pace was difficult.

The desert was black and silent and empty, but he knew that was an illusion. He was probably running past lots of desert creatures. He hoped he wasn't coming close to any rattlesnakes. They tended to slither into holes and crevices at night, but if he stepped in the wrong place, he was likely to draw a bite.

The only sounds now were his breathing, his footsteps, and the quiet rush of air past his ears. He kept on until he wondered if it was possible that he had missed the road in the dark and was going into an endless stretch of desert. But then he saw the dim, pale line of gravel a shade lighter than the surrounding desert. He stepped onto it, turned, and followed it. After a few minutes more he spotted the tall rocks with the tarp stretched between them where he had left his rental car. His navigation had been a bit off, but he must have diverged from his trail only a degree or two. He felt relieved. He had made it all the way into the mountain resort on foot, done what he had planned to do, and made it all the way back.

He took off his poncho and his hat and rolled them into a compact bundle, then drank the last of his water. When he reached his car, he put the bundle into the trunk with his small suitcase. He opened the suitcase and took out a set of street clothes and changed into them. He stuck the small pistol he had taken off the sentry in the back of his waistband and covered it with his shirt.

He remembered a 1950s-era hotel in Scottsdale that he used to like so he drove there and found that it didn't look as though it had changed much. He asked if they had a vacant room at this hour, checked in, and went to his room for a shower. After standing under the heavy stream of hot water for a few minutes getting the dust off and soothing his aching muscles, he ran a bath and soaked for a long time. He lay there with the water to his chin, and then his head jerked in a reflex and he realized he'd dozed off. The water had already begun to cool. He stood, dried off, went to the door to be sure he'd put out the DO NOT DISTURB sign, and locked everything that would lock. He propped a chair under the knob to buy himself a few extra seconds if someone battered in the door. Then he made sure the nine-millimeter pistol was fully loaded and ready. He put it under the spare pillow on the side of the bed nearest the door, got under the covers on the other side, and let himself fall into a deep sleep.

15

SHE RECOGNIZED SPECIAL Agent Holman's voice on the phone instantly. It was before dawn, and she had been waiting for most of the night for his call. But what he said was unexpected. "Frank Tosca is dead."

"So he found the meeting," she said.

"I thought the theory was that he was the one who asked for it."

"Not Tosca," she said. "The other one. The Butcher's Boy. He certainly wasn't invited, but he found out where it was and went there to kill Tosca."

"It's a little early to be sure of that," Holman said. "I remember that was your interpretation of the break-in and killings at Tosca's house. But anytime one of these guys is on the edge of getting really powerful, his enemies get anxious. There were sure to be others who thought they should be the head of the Balacontano family, a few with the name Balacontano. There's also the fact that calling a meeting of the old men is an inherently dangerous thing to do. They're touchy, and a couple are borderline psychotic."

"You're right, of course," she said. "How was Tosca killed?"

"He was found by the raiding party in his cabin, lying on the floor with his throat cut."

It was exactly as she would have expected—the kind of silent attack a solitary killer with all the skills would choose. "I'll wait until the preliminary investigation is over before I say anything more. What's going on out there now?"

"We're moving into the mop-up stages, I think. There are more than two hundred of them in custody right now. We're trying to process them in small groups by airlifting some of them to the Phoenix Police Department. We're also bringing in buses. I expect before the night is over, we'll be farming them out to local lockups all over the area. It's the biggest thing since Apalachin—much bigger, if you just count the number of men we picked up."

"I wish I were there."

"So do I. We could use your help keeping the names straight and how they relate to each other."

"Well, I'd better let you get back to that."

"As soon as we've got more on the Tosca thing, or anything else, I'll get back to you."

"Thanks."

"The thanks go to you. I'm not forgetting that you were the one who figured this out and turned it over to us."

"We're on the same side. It may not seem that way sometimes, but we are."

"I'll talk to you later."

She sat in her dimly lighted office staring at the telephone. She shouldn't have blurted it out that way. She hated working with people who immediately accepted the first interpretation that came to mind and then stuck to it because it was theirs. And now she had probably given Holman the impression she was one of those people. She was sure the Butcher's Boy had done it, but she shouldn't have said it until she'd given the FBI a chance to work their way to the same conclusion.

He had told her that was what he wanted to do, and as far as she knew, he had never failed to accomplish his goal when all it entailed was killing someone. He had managed to get past two hundred men, all of whom had, at some point, made their bones. He had gotten past them and killed Frank Tosca. The big question in her mind now was, Had he also gotten out?

128

If he had been scooped up in the sweep, he would be photographed and fingerprinted like everyone else. But if he was then placed in a holding cell with a big group of Mafiosi, one of them would recognize him, and they would immediately gang up and kill him. That was what they did best. But if Elizabeth Waring arrived and took him out of that danger, wouldn't he be grateful? Wouldn't he be happy to be her informant? Getting as many of the men who knew him as possible into prison would be his best way of making himself safe. And he had already begun to tell her things. He didn't have any reluctance about that. As he'd said, he hadn't taken an oath of omertà. He wasn't in the Mafia.

She had to take steps to exert control of his fate before he was lost to her forever. First, she would have to be in Phoenix. She would have to get permission from Hunsecker, but her chances of receiving it were nil.

The situation was infuriating. She was the head of a section. If, in the course of any other organized crime case, she'd needed to send a Justice Department investigator to identify and divert a prisoner in the hope of turning him into an informant, she could have done it without permission from anybody. But this man, the professional hit man who had just killed the most potent and dangerous mob boss since Carl Bala himself, evidently wasn't acceptable to the department.

And even if, as probably would happen, the deputy assistant was forced by the avalanche of publicity on his superiors to take an interest, it would be a distant, tepid interest in what the FBI was up to. And the one person who must not be directly involved was Elizabeth Waring. Not only did she have a distinctly supervisory post that precluded her going out into the field, but she was tainted. She had spoken with the killer alone before the three murders at Tosca's house. If Hunsecker knew that she had spoken with the killer a second time, she would be fired.

Elizabeth was in an impossible position, and she had no method for handling it. She had been through twenty years of bureaucratic civil wars, and she had never needed more than one strategy—look at every detail and tell the truth about it. In her first big case she had relinquished forever the chance to endear herself to the upper echelon of the hierarchy by dissenting from their view of the chaos that got Carlo Balacontano convicted of murder. And by being the lone dissenter, she had denied herself the chance to be popular with her equals. When she had been asked for an opinion, she had told the truth. Each time someone who had embraced an opposing view questioned her assessment, she would supply the evidence—as much of it as was necessary to overwhelm him and make him move on to score his points on some other issue.

The strategy of telling the truth would not work this time. She had broken rules, argued with her boss, deceived him, and done things he had forbidden. The truth would destroy her. She had crossed a line and didn't see a way back. She had already begun to console herself the way lunatics and fanatics did—by telling herself that some day everyone would see she was right. She thought about her husband, Jim. He would have told her to concentrate her efforts on persuading the rest of her section. "Bring the team along," he would have said. "If you get too far out there ahead of everybody, the main thing you are is alone."

She woke up her computer and surfed the websites of the various packagers, searching for the best flight from Reagan International in Washington to Sky Harbor in Phoenix. She was about to select a flight when she remembered the rest of the ritual—her itinerary would be sent to her computer and printed. The computer would tell anyone who wanted to look exactly what she'd done and when.

She looked at her watch. It was five-thirty already. The sun was rising on the other side of the building, and the facades across the street were bathed in a red-orange glow. She picked up the telephone on her desk and started to dial, then hung up. She had no proof that her phone calls weren't being recorded. Maybe they weren't, but the numbers anyone dialed would appear on the bill. She used her cell phone and called Delta Airlines. She got a ticket for the flight at ten A.M. Then she wrote a memo to her second-tier people, saying she was taking a personal day or two. She thought about the kids. Amanda and Jim were exceptionally mature and self-reliant, and they had each other. But she would have to do some thinking before she went through with this.

When she got home, she spent a few minutes examining the physical evidence of how her two children had operated without her last night. The dishes in the dishwasher were clean and indicated they'd cooked something that required a pot. The storage container indicated they'd finished the homemade pasta sauce, and the package in the garbage identified the pasta as penne. She was shocked to see the trimmed bottoms of asparagus and a few wilted leaves of Romaine lettuce. They were growing up.

Before she woke them for breakfast, she wrote a note explaining where she was going and approximately why, with a reminder that they were never to answer any questions about her, regardless of who asked. She said she was going to try to contact a suspect, separate him from other prisoners in a jail, and persuade him to cooperate. Then she went upstairs, woke them, and told them she had to leave for a couple of days. Neither seemed especially interested, and certainly not impressed.

She took some cash out of her hiding place in her closet, which was a tall pair of hiking boots she never wore, and left them half of it. She also left them both cars, but didn't tell them that the reason was that if anyone drove past in the daytime, one would be there, and late at night she wanted them to notice that neither was missing.

When she had kissed them good-bye and watched them get into the Volvo to head off for school, she showered, dressed, packed, and called a cab. When she got to the airport, she met a couple of colleagues from the Justice Department. They were both flying to some case in Florida, and they all checked in and declared their weapons, then were taken on a detour around the metal detectors before they parted company.

In two hours Elizabeth was on a plane watching the baggage

carts go forward past her window as the tractor pushed the plane away from the gate. The plane taxied out to its spot, bumped along the runway into the wind, and lifted. It was still tilted sharply upward and leaving identifiable buildings and streets below when her night of staring at a computer screen exacted its price. She fell asleep.

She woke six hours later as the plane went into its final descent over Phoenix. The strange, hot Arizona winds always gave planes landing there sudden rises and drops, and then, as the plane touched down, batted it from the side to force the pilot to set it down fast and hard. She was shocked and embarrassed. She would no more have slept on a plane than in any other public place.

She endured a few minutes of feeling awful and half asleep, took out her hairbrush and makeup, and did her best to repair her appearance. She was almost at the rear of the airplane so she had a long wait to get into the aisle and leave. She used the time to recover from taking her night's sleep in an airplane seat. After she got out and visited the ladies' room, where she finished her makeup and hair in front of big, well-lighted mirrors, she walked toward the baggage claim while she called Special Agent Holman's cell phone number.

"Holman."

"Hi. This is Elizabeth Waring. I'm in Phoenix. I realized I didn't have anything more important than this to do. I'm on my way to the baggage claim. If you'll tell me where you are, I'll join you and see what I can do to help."

"I'm sending a man for you. His name is Agent Krause. What airline?"

"Delta."

"Give him about a half hour."

"Thank you. I'll watch for him."

Agent Krause was there in twenty minutes, and he wasn't difficult to spot. He was probably thirty, about six foot one, and looked

132

a lot like a former running back for a small college. He wore a good gray suit and carried a sheet of paper that said WARING.

She stepped up to him and held out her hand. "Waring."

"Krause," he said. "The car's at the curb." He took her bag and led her there. It was the usual Ford Crown Victoria Interceptor. Krause drove the way they all did, with a slightly aggressive certainty that came from the driver training they got. She had always been a little bit nervous and distrustful of her husband Jim's way of pushing the speed, but nothing had ever happened, so she was resolved to ignore it now.

"You know why I'm here, right?"

"Yes, ma'am," he said.

"Is there any way I can go straight to where the prisoners are and look at them all at once?"

"Not at once. They're in about a dozen different places—precinct jails, mostly. We've got seven regional offices in Arizona, and we've been bringing in agents from all of them to help out with this."

"Have the prisoners been booked and photographed?"

"Yes. We're collecting the booking files for you right now in a conference room at the FBI building on Indianola Avenue in town."

"That should be fine."

When they arrived at the FBI field office, she recognized it from other trips to Phoenix. It was a low redbrick building that dominated the street corner, with high windows on two sides that seemed designed to save on artificial lighting. He set her up in the conference room. The room was what they all were, a long room with windows on one side and a long table surrounded by chairs that looked comfortable but weren't. She realized she had been in this room once before, about ten years ago. It had been for a briefing on information the Phoenix office had obtained in wiretaps of the phone of old Vito Sangiovese while he was exiled to Arizona.

She sat down beside the pile of files and attacked them, going through them as quickly as she could, just opening each one, glancing at the snapshot, closing the file, and setting it on top of the pile to her right so she could go to the next one.

Krause said, "What are you looking for?"

"A particular face, a man who might be using any name or no name. I think he was there. If he got picked up, I want to talk to him."

She had seen thousands of arrest files in the twenty years since she had gone to work for the Justice Department. The men in today's collection of files were unusually well dressed and neatly shaven, but otherwise they looked like booking photographs always did—one profile, one facing the camera, with height lines behind the irritated subject and a black square in front with his name. In this group there were men as old as eighty, and men who at nineteen or twenty could barely be called men. They were a year or so older than her own son, Jim. She had seen many of these faces before—most in surveillance photographs, a few in person.

She read the name in front of her, below the face of a middle-aged man. "This says he's Dominic Ippolito. He's actually Salvatore Gappa, and he lives in Detroit. He even lied about his age. This says he's fifty-one, but he's at least sixty."

"Another one?" said Krause. "We've already found about twenty who had false ID. Credit cards and everything."

She gave him the Gappa file and went to the next. She kept moving through the files quickly, scanning the pictures. She had a sense of the men who had attended the meeting. The heads of the twenty-six families that ran cities had come, as well as a few heads of crews that ran particularly important businesses. Each had brought two or three young soldiers as bodyguards and one or two consiglieres or underbosses. That group of thirty or so old men and their hundred and fifty retainers made up the central group, the people essential for a national consensus on anything. The other fifty or so were probably petitioners who had grievances, or disputants with issues they wanted the old men to decide, or heads of crews who wanted permission to do various things. In a system where the penalty for overstepping was always death, a meeting must be a great opportunity to avoid problems.

As Elizabeth went through the files, she kept searching for the face of the one man who had not been invited to the conference, but whom she believed had come anyway. She stared once at each photo of a face, unable to avoid seeing each name too, but pushing herself to get through them and find him.

If he had been there, his picture should be with the others. He was a man, not a ghost. Fifty years ago at Apalachin, at least a few important capos had evaded the police by running through the fields of nearby farms. But that had been a different kind of operation. A New York State trooper had simply noticed that there seemed to be a lot of big fancy cars parked at a local farmhouse. This time there had been a few hours' advance notice, so the might and sophistication of a modern military-style federal operation had been applied. There had been helicopters with infrared imaging, advanced night-vision scopes. How could he have gotten away? Something occurred to her and she turned to Krause.

"Holman said they'd found Frank Tosca's body in one of the cabins."

"That's right. He was killed with a knife. His throat was cut."

"What's been found since then? Were there any other bodies?"

"Yes. There's a file on it over here."

She felt the breath go out of her. Why hadn't she thought of it before? Being able to get in and kill Tosca didn't mean he could get out afterward. He wasn't in these files because they'd killed him.

Krause got up and walked to the corner of the long table, brought back a file, and handed it to her.

She opened it, almost certain whose face she would see. She looked down. It was a young man of Italian descent, twenty years younger than the man she had expected, and his name was Agnetti. "Any others?"

"Not yet. It's a big crime scene. There's the ranch, all the cabins and facilities, miles of trails, and so on. And all around is just empty mountains and desert."

"Okay." She returned to the photographs, looking for his. If he had been swept up with the others, there might still be time. All of them would have been handcuffed during the first few hours. There may not have been a moment when a group of them could strangle him or stomp him to death in a cell.

As she looked at file after file, she quietly became more and more frantic. The time she had spent looking at the ones who were not him seemed wasted. She flipped through files at an increasing rate, even when part of her mind was telling her that the odds against his being in one of the last few files were enormous.

She reached the last file, and his picture was not there. She looked up and said, "That's it, right? There aren't any men detained but not photographed, or stopped and released as innocent bystanders or something?"

"No, ma'am. I believe the thinking was that La Cosa Nostra wouldn't have let anyone like that get near their little retreat. Everybody there was considered to be invited. And there isn't much chance that anybody got away unnoticed."

"That's my next question. Why do you say that?"

"Because before the order came to move in, the roads had all been blocked with patrol cars waiting for the word for nearly an hour. We didn't want anybody driving in and saying they'd seen a whole bunch of cops. The raid was a complete surprise. When the helicopters landed, the meeting in the main building was still in session. Nobody was running away."

"Who killed Frank Tosca?"

"I don't know, but I'm guessing it was somebody working for whoever ends up as boss of the Balacontano family. Probably with the approval of the council of old men, or at least some of them."

"Who killed this other man, the young one?" She opened the file. "The diagram of the scene puts him up on the mountain, at the crest above the ranch. He was strangled with a rope or a cord."

"Maybe he was a Balacontano soldier who came to the ranch with Frank Tosca."

"The most logical reason to be up on the mountain is to stand guard, to protect the meeting from intruders. And strangling a young, healthy man is a lot of work. If it was an execution, why not do it the way they've always done it, a bullet at the base of the skull?"

"I don't know."

"I think it wasn't an execution. I think it was the killer taking out a guard in the most silent way."

"Why?" asked Krause.

"So he could get into the complex where Frank Tosca was, kill him—also silently, with a knife—and then walk out the same way, past a dead guard."

He looked skeptical. "You think the FBI screwed this up, don't you?"

"Absolutely not."

"But you think we let the one who killed Frank Tosca slip away. We apprehended over two hundred men, including the heads of twenty-six families, and about a hundred of their best people, none of whom got away. Doesn't it make more sense to think one of the two hundred made members of the Mafia we caught within a hundred yards of the body did it, and not someone we can't prove was even there?"

"Do we have a time of death for Tosca yet?"

"He was dead no more than an hour before we got there."

"So it doesn't tell us much about who did it."

"No, but it makes an outsider who did it and slipped away before we moved into the area a lot less likely. We already had cars blocking the road by then."

"If he was there, he didn't come or go by road. Do we have a murder weapon for either victim?"

"No. We have a few knives, but nothing that has any trace of blood on it, and most of them are too small to be the one. Nothing on the strangling cord, which could have been any kind of rope, strip of leather, or even rolled fabric."

"So what's been found doesn't prove anything at all."

"Agreed."

"I'm beginning to think I can't prove my theory with what we have," she said. "But if this were my raid, I would have forensics people examining the clothing of each of the men who have been detained and searching the grounds for clothing that's been thrown away. It's highly unlikely that somebody could cut Tosca's throat and not get some droplets of blood on his own clothes or shoes. Since nobody heard a struggle or shouting or anything, the attacker probably took him by surprise, and that usually means from behind. It's hard to cut a man's throat without getting a hand or arm around his head to tilt it back. By the time the throat is fully cut, the carotid artery is shooting blood out a couple of feet, and it gets messier after that."

"You're right," Krause said. "They're treating the whole ranch as the crime scene, so they'll be searching it foot by foot."

Elizabeth Waring corrected the misinformation in the files and wrote in relevant details. There were a large number of obfuscations and lies in the answers the detainees had given to direct questions. Danny "the Monkey" Strachello listed his occupation as "casino operator" even though he had been barred from entering a casino in all the states that had them. Paul Mascone from New Jersey had planted some nonsense about being in the insurance business, which was only true if extortion was a form of insurance.

But there were also genuine bits of information. Anthony Barino, the head of the family in Tampa, had listed a holding company that owned four restaurants as his employer. Jerry Sorrenti from New York had a monopoly on refuse collection in part of the city, and he listed his occupation as "garbage man." If this meeting could be shown in court to be what it was—a meeting of the men who ran the Mafia—these businesses could be broken up or confiscated under the RICO statute.

She used a computer in the outer office to examine the list of men who were on parole and were not allowed to be within speaking distance of other convicted felons. There were a dozen who weren't even supposed to leave their home states without the permission of a judge. There were fifty-six who had been taken into custody with concealed firearms, and over a hundred firearms had been found that hadn't been tied to anyone in particular. Nineteen men had been carrying cocaine and thirteen had medications with false or suspicious prescriptions on the labels.

The count she liked best so far was the telephones. Thirty-seven men had been carrying cell phones that were stolen or were clones of phones registered to other people. That apparently was their current way of keeping their calls from being monitored. But it also reminded her of something she had learned in her first days at the Justice Department. Gangsters were all thieves at heart. A capo who made millions of dollars a year on rake-offs and tributes still couldn't resist a stolen television set that ran on a cable diverted from a neighbor's yard. A case of scotch was a hundred times better if it was boosted from the back of a truck.

By now all of them must have had a chance to make a telephone call so the flights coming into Phoenix for the next twenty-four hours would be delivering the largest influx of legal talent that Arizona had ever seen. But there was still time to find more vulnerabilities in these detainees and more opportunities to ask questions.

There were men in the meeting who had so many policemen, prosecutors, and judges on their payrolls that they would have had to commit massacres in public to get arrested in their home cities, and something more than that to get anything but a suspended sentence. Immunity had made some of them careless, so many of them were going to be in serious trouble for things they habitually did at home — carrying guns and drugs, and spending time with people just like them.

She spent several more hours working with the U.S. attorney's people in the office preparing charges to be filed against the heads of the twenty-six families and then oversaw the work of the staff in filling out the papers for some of the lower-ranking men.

Holman came in looking for her late in the afternoon, and when he saw her, he grinned and called, "Waring!" He rushed up to her and extended his arms to give her a hug, but then restrained himself and lowered his hand to shake hers. "Thank you so much for coming to help us out."

"It's my pleasure," she said. "We hardly ever have too much of a good thing—so many suspects that we can hardly push the paper fast enough."

"That's the truth. I heard you've been at this all day without stopping."

"We all have. But as a result, we're getting down to the simple stuff now—the ones who didn't have the sense to throw away their guns and drugs. Nothing subtle or arguable."

"Thank you very much for doing this. I've been tied up for most of the day processing the crime scene in the Tosca murder and the one up the hill. If we could just tie the bodies to one or two of these guys—"

"I'm afraid that's not going to happen," she said. "The killer is long gone. He got out before the FBI arrived."

"How did he do that?"

"How? Probably he came on foot, avoiding the roads, and killed one of the guards along the crest so he'd be able to leave the same way."

"And where would that put him now?"

"Believe me, if I find out, you'll be the first one I call."

16

SCHAEFFER AWOKE IN the filtered sunshine that had invaded his room. For a second he thought he was in Bath, and that he and Meg had been sleeping in the bedroom of his house in the center of town with the wall of glass bricks high above his bed, rather than the darker bedroom in her family manor. But the sun was only streaming through a narrow space in a set of hotel curtains. Then he remembered where he was and felt so disappointed that he could hardly bear it.

It was two o'clock. He had been deeply asleep since around five-thirty A.M. He stared at the ceiling and felt grateful to the people on the hotel staff who had spared him the irritating knocks on the door and the reminders that checkout time was noon. He moved his legs tentatively, and felt pain and stiffness in his knees and hips. His feet were sore in some complex way. The many small bones seemed to have been subjected to strain that was separate from the surface damage to the ball and heel from running so many miles over rough ground. As he moved his torso a little to sit up, he learned that the news from his back and arms was not good either.

He considered flopping back down on the bed, but he had slept so long that he was sure the inactivity had contributed to the stiffness. He also sensed that he didn't want to waste the effort it had taken to sit up the first time.

He walked to the shower and ran the water to heat it up, and then stood under the strong stream for a few minutes. He moved his arms, then swung them, and finally raised them over his head and stretched. With a bit of trepidation he bent over to touch his toes, stretching his tight muscles under the hot water. After fifteen minutes of attention to the various strained regions of his body, he began to feel better.

Every stitch or kink or abrasion brought back to him the motion that had caused it. Both of his hands had a soreness across the palm, where the nylon cord from his poncho had been attached to the homemade handle. He had gripped the handles hard, keeping the loop as tight as he could around the sentry's neck. It had been a very long time since he had strangled a man, and the muscles had gone soft. He had gone soft.

He was over fifty years old. If, by some miracle, the life he had led in the United States had not been interrupted—had not been ended by his client's betrayal and attempts to kill him—he would still have retired by now. He wouldn't have spent last night on a mountain in Arizona strangling and knifing people. It would have been impossible for anybody to stay in the killing trade for that long without being killed. The only old hit men were people like Little Norman in Las Vegas, making the rounds each day to check his sources and be sure nothing had come in off the desert to disturb the tranquil atmosphere of the casinos. Norman wasn't a killer anymore. He was a weather man. Each day he would reassure the dozen or so powerful old capos in town that the weather in Vegas was still just fine.

When Schaeffer was very young, Eddie Mastrewski had warned him to make himself strong. "Now is the time to train yourself. Today you can make yourself the winner of whatever happens thirty years from now. If you die in that fight, it's because you didn't work hard enough today." Eddie had been strong. He was a Pennsylvania Polack from the coal country. He always corrected that. "I'm a Ukrainian." When he had taken the boy on a visit to his hometown in Pennsylvania, everybody for fifty miles around seemed to be built like a pile of rocks. Whichever godforsaken place in the Balkans their parents came from, they must have had to fight their way out because there weren't any weaklings. There were only people who had been injured or worked themselves into old age.

Eddie had drilled him in all of the basic techniques of depriving an enemy of his breath and heartbeat. He had also taught him the rest of the trade — how to read the signs in a neighborhood to tell whether the job was going to be a simple walk-in or a risky, drawn-out battle for the victim's life. What had happened last night was that he had fallen back on Eddie's most important lesson — that everything that went on was only a series of steps to his inevitable victory.

Eddie never permitted the idea of failure to enter his consciousness. "We're the wolf, they're the deer. Are they going to eat us? No. It might take a while to get them, but the universe isn't going to change so they win."

He was still the wolf. He had gone to get Frank Tosca, and so Tosca was dead. But his exhaustion today was disturbing. He wasn't the same as he had been. Time had gone by and he hadn't noticed, but it had still gone by.

He wanted to rest and recover, but it was time to get out of Phoenix. He packed his small suitcase and turned on his laptop computer. He made a plane reservation from Tucson to Houston in the name Charles Ackerman and a hotel reservation for the next two nights at a hotel he knew near the Astrodome.

As he passed the front desk, he left his checkout card and key in front of a clerk who was on the telephone and went outside. He got in his rental car and drove to a bank not far down the street in Scottsdale. He rented a safe-deposit box and paid three years' rent in advance. He opened the box in a small windowless room and put in the pistol he had taken from the dead sentry and the extra magazine and the knife he had used to kill Tosca.

The route to Tucson was flat, straight, and easy to drive. He passed a prison crew in orange jumpsuits working on a weedy patch along the highway under the eyes of a guard with a lever-action .30-30 rifle like a movie cowboy would have used. It reminded him of something else Eddie had told him. "One thing we have to do is stay out of jail. A lot of the guys we deal with spend half their lives getting in or getting out. It's something between a religious retreat and a family reunion. They've got old friends, cousins, and in-laws in there. And half of the rest of the place is people who want to suck up to them, including the guards. If you go in, there will be people who knew somebody you killed. There will be people who want you to kill somebody in there for them, and others who want you to kill somebody when you get out. There will be guys so crazy they want to know what makes you so tough so you have to kill them to show them."

The speed limit was sixty-five, so he went sixty-five, going faster only in the stretches where the rest of the cars did and a slower car would have stood out. He never stood out. He had always dressed neatly and conservatively, and since he had been in England he had been forced to replace his clothes gradually, so he had the wardrobe of a man of Meg's social level. He could stand close inspection without raising suspicion, but he had perfected his pose of the taciturn American husband. He had good manners and a smile, so there was little scrutiny. People paid attention to the beautiful and lively Lady Meg Holroyd, but less to her husband. It was simply a new version of the way he carried himself in the United States. He was a master at being the one the eye passed over in a crowd.

He arrived at the Tucson airport two hours early, returned his rental car, and rode the shuttle to the terminal. He bought a newspaper and sat in the middle of a crowded waiting area. He pretended to read the paper, but devoted most of his attention to the people around him and the people walking past on the concourse.

There, as soon as he looked, was the short, stocky shape of Mickey Agnoli walking along in a Hawaiian shirt and a pair of tan slacks, his shoes a pair of topsiders with no socks, looking as calm as though he had stepped off a yacht into the Tucson terminal. There seemed to be nobody with him.

As soon as Agnoli had passed and gone on along the concourse, Schaeffer got up, folded his newspaper and stuck it under his arm, and followed at a distance. Agnoli walked on the right side of the concourse so Schaeffer stayed on the left side, moving against the flow of people but a few paces inward so he wouldn't meet anyone head-on.

He had seen Agnoli from a distance on the ranch last night and had studied him for a moment before turning away to avoid him. He had looked very happy and prosperous, standing just outside the conference room. Agnoli had been a Strongiolo soldier in Miami since he was about nineteen, but over the years he had grown up a little. He had saved the money his crew picked up on their regular business of stealing luggage from airport baggage claims and selling fake tickets to cruises, and he bought parking lots. Ten years ago he had already been the parking king of Miami.

Schaeffer had met him on one of the worst nights of Agnoli's life. Agnoli's brother Jimmy had been found in a Dumpster behind one of their parking lots. Mickey had sent word up the ranks in the Strongiolo family that he wanted revenge. The response was a torn scrap of paper with a telephone number on it. He called the number, and a week later he met Schaeffer in a small Italian restaurant near the ocean.

They sat in a booth at the back of the dining room. Agnoli was a broad, short man, and he nearly took up the whole side of the booth that faced the wall. Schaeffer could see he'd been crying. Agnoli said, "Thank you for coming to see me. I've heard you're a busy man and don't like to spend a lot of time talking."

"I heard about your loss. I'm not in a hurry. If you want to talk, I'll listen."

Agnoli was surprised. "I didn't think you'd be . . . I don't know. So human."

Schaeffer's face showed nothing.

Agnoli's eyes widened. "I'm sorry. I should have said you're a decent guy and then shut up."

"I'm not a decent guy. A decent guy wouldn't be much use to you."

"No, I didn't ask you here to insult you. Even if I feel like committing suicide, this isn't the way I wanted to do it. I want to hire you."

"You already have. Mr. Strongiolo sent me a retainer, or I wouldn't be here. Tell me who I'm going to see."

"Three weeks ago a Cuban named Montoya came to my office and said he represented a syndicate of investors who wanted to buy a fifty-one percent share of the parking business. I said, 'How much?' and he said, 'Twenty grand ought to be enough,' and I said, 'I've got six lots, and each of them is worth ten times that. Maybe you have my company mixed up with another one.'"

"What did he say?"

"He said he knew all that. He said I was just resisting because I didn't know who he represented. He works for Hektor Cruz."

"Do you know who Hektor Cruz is?" Schaeffer asked.

"He's in the drug business. There are lots of people in Miami in the drug business." He took a deep breath and let it out. "I said, 'I've heard of Mr. Cruz. Please give him my regrets. My partners and I aren't interested in selling out.' And just so there wasn't any misunderstanding I said, 'One of those partners is Victor Strongiolo, and the others are close associates of ours.' It was true. Mr. S. gets a quarter cut of my action. You know how things work."

"I do."

"I made it clear who I was, and who my silent partners were. I mean, this guy might just not know who he was talking to. It could be an honest mistake. And I was polite. There was no reason to rub his face in it. I even stood up and held out my hand to shake. He stood too, but he didn't take it. He just gave a little wave and said, 'I'll be talking to you very soon.'"

Schaeffer could see Agnoli had come to the hard part because his eyes had started to water. "The next day we found my brother Jimmy dead. He was shot nine times and dropped in the Dumpster."

"How do you want this done?"

"I want to keep it simple. You get Hektor Cruz."

"Just Cruz?"

"Cruz is not easy. These guys are never alone. But once he's gone, the rest will be disorganized, scared, indecisive. We'll erase them over a period of a few days."

"What does this pay?"

"Two hundred thousand."

"Don't start your war until I tell you Cruz is dead."

"You have my word."

He stood up. "I'll talk to you after it's done."

"Wait," Agnoli said. "Don't you want half up front?"

He smiled for the first time. "No need. Nobody forgets to pay me."

He had located Cruz by finding a newspaper photograph of him and then waiting outside Montoya's office until he appeared. He followed him home, then watched him from a distance for two nights. He was a short man with wavy black hair and big brown eyes who wore light-colored tailored tropical suits and traveled with two bodyguards who looked a lot like him. They spent each night moving from one club to another in a black Lincoln limousine, dancing and drinking and picking up women. The women might stick with them for hours, or just ride with them to the next club, or come out with them to the parking lot, kiss them good-bye, and then go back inside. But Cruz was never alone.

On the third night he saw his chance. When the driver left the car for a few minutes while he waited outside a club, Schaeffer got into the back seat. He broke Cruz's driver's neck, then took his place in the driver's seat. When Cruz came out of the club with his two men, Schaeffer waited until they were a few feet away, then shot all three. It looked to the parking attendants and the confused line of customers as though an unseen sniper must have done the killing, and he was just returning fire. Because he was in the driver's seat of Cruz's car, he must be on Cruz's side. When he got out to drag Cruz's body into the back seat and drove off, people thought he was saving Cruz.

He drove the car only six blocks to the back of a closed restaurant, where he parked the car and hoisted the body into the Dumpster. Then he walked one more block to the residential street where he had left his rental car, got in, and drove off.

The Agnoli he followed now in the Tucson airport was twenty years older and a happier man. He was a little pudgy, but he looked good. Agnoli's step had some spring to it as he walked down the concourse. Near the end he turned into a men's room.

It was remote, at the far end where there were only a few gates, and the flights were mostly international ones that left late in the day. When Schaeffer stepped into the men's room, he saw that it was empty, except for Agnoli at the urinal. Agnoli finished and stepped to the sink and washed his hands. As he reached for a paper towel to dry them he looked up into the mirror, and their eyes locked. Agnoli's eyes went wide and he began to shake.

"I guess you remember me."

Agnoli stood still, with the towel in his hands.

"Give me your cell phone."

Agnoli reached into his pocket and handed it to him. "Are you here to kill me?"

"I hope not. You were at the ranch. How did you get away?"

Agnoli looked as though he were having trouble translating a phrase in a foreign language. After a pause, he said, "I hid. Two of the catering trucks were still there. I went and hid in the back of one of them, behind a bunch of big plastic food containers and cases of empty liquor bottles. I went behind them and then set a few others in front of me. I heard the cops come by and look in the back, and then somebody rolled the door down and locked it. I sat there for hours. Then I heard the engine start, and we began to move. Then the truck stopped, and somebody opened the door and unloaded some of the stuff on a dolly. When they pushed the dolly away, I got out. I was at a loading dock behind a restaurant in Phoenix. I knew they'd never hire a caterer for a meet like that if he wasn't a friend of ours, so I went to the back door. They set me up with a ride so I could get home."

"Congratulations. I doubt that many others got out."

"What do you want from me?"

"Information. If you tell me the truth, we'll both go away and forget we saw each other." He paused. "You know my word is good."

"It is to me. You did better than you promised. I remember when you put that son of a bitch Hektor Cruz in the Dumpster and killed two of his men. I owe you something for that extra touch. My family owes you. That was worth more than money to my poor mother."

"I need to know where I stand. When Frank Tosca asked everybody to join in and find me, what did they say?"

Agnoli sighed. "I want you to know I had no part in this. I run one little crew—all middle-aged fat guys like me. The rest of the world tolerates us because we've always been good earners. We're not greedy. We like a little wine, maybe have a woman we don't eat breakfast with now and then. I don't get a vote on anything at a sit-down, and if I did, I wouldn't use it to try to take over the world—about which I don't give a shit. You know I'd never vote to kill you. That stuff about you was courtesy of Frank Tosca."

"I know. What did the old men decide?"

Agnoli took two deep breaths and held on to the sink to steady himself. "They all said they'd do it."

Schaeffer had known that much. He nodded. He had tested Agnoli, and Agnoli had told him the truth. He patted Agnoli's shoulder. "It must have been hard to say that to me. Thank you."

"Hard? If I hadn't just gone, my pants would be wet."

"Have you heard what happened to Tosca?"

"I just heard it on the phone. A friend of mine said it was on television in Miami. The news people didn't know who that was."

"It doesn't matter now," Schaeffer said.

"No, it sure doesn't."

"Tell me where I stand now. The old men might have said yes to a request from Tosca when he was alive because they didn't want to be on his bad side if he took over the Balacontano family. Now that he's dead, what are they likely to do?"

"Jesus," Agnoli said. "Jesus."

"Don't be afraid. It's my last question. Tell me the truth and I'm gone."

Agnoli took some more deep breaths, and a drop of sweat curled down from his temple to his chin. "I'm sorry."

"What does that mean?"

"I called home to check on my guys. My underboss said they'd already gotten a call. The cops let Victor Strongiolo see his lawyer. He told him to pass the word down to us that the old men want you dead."

"Even with no Frank Tosca to thank them?"

Agnoli shrugged. "You were right about why they agreed. They didn't want Tosca to take over the Balacontano family and then hold a grudge because they didn't help when he needed it. But the rest of this pissed them off. It pissed them off that you knew about the meeting, that you got in, and that you killed Tosca. And I think it scared them. If you could do that to Tosca, what's to stop you from killing them?"

Schaeffer said, "If they changed their minds and left me alone, that's what would stop me. Nothing else. Do you understand?"

"I understand perfectly. I've seen your work."

Schaeffer said, "You've treated me honorably. I'll do the same to you. When does your flight board?"

"About a half hour."

"Stay here for fifteen minutes. Don't call anybody or try to find me. I won't tell anyone we talked."

"Thank you," Agnoli said.

Schaeffer went out the door. Agnoli steadied himself on the sink. After a few minutes of trying to regain his composure, he realized he hadn't looked at his watch to be sure when the fifteen minutes had started. He looked, and started the fifteen minutes then.

17

ELIZABETH WARING CALLED Jim and Amanda at one o'clock in the afternoon so she could catch them right at four eastern time when they arrived home from school. "How was school?" brought vague reassurances but no actual information. "Do you have everything you need for dinner? If you don't, you're welcome to go out to pick up something at Koo Koo Roo or California Pizza Kitchen" brought reminders that they had too much homework to waste time on that. She gave up, issued motherly benedictions, and went back to work. She stayed in the Phoenix field office until after midnight and then accepted a ride to a hotel near the airport. As she lay down on the bed, it occurred to her that midnight in Phoenix was three A.M. in Washington. It was a feeble, passing observation, the last before sleep took over her brain.

When she awoke, it was nearly ten. She called the FBI field office, identified herself, and asked for Special Agent Holman. The woman at the other end said, "I'm sorry, Ms. Waring. This is Agent O'Brien. He had a flight out at eight. He and his team were ordered back to Washington."

"Then the operation here is over?"

"Hardly. We have two murders, two hundred persons of interest in custody all over the place, and a wide variety of charges are being filed this morning."

"I know. I did some of the paperwork last night."

"That's right. I'm sorry. But I think what's happened is that the rest of this is going to be left to us—permanent party Arizona."

"Are you feeling overwhelmed?"

"Everybody is eager. This is a big chance. But this office doesn't see many La Cosa Nostra types except a few retirees and the guys who buy the drugs that are brought in through the desert."

"I'll be there in about an hour," Elizabeth said. "I can spare another day or two."

Elizabeth took a cab to the field office, entered the conference room, and began resorting the files on the long table. After a half hour, Krause came in. "Ms. Waring. What are you doing?"

"I'm going to make some charts so the U.S. attorneys here will know who's who. Do you think you could get me a few more office supplies?"

"Sure. What do you need?"

"Twenty-six sheets of poster-size paper. A ruler, a few pens. Black is best, but anything will do."

He returned just as she finished sorting the files into twenty-six piles. She took the first one, wrote CHICAGO and a horizontal line that said CASTIGLIONE FAMILY. She put horizontal lines in a row below it and wrote JOSEPH, PAUL, AND SALVATORE CASTIGLIONE. Directly under them were eight underbosses, and to their right were three consiglieres. She wrote in the names of four underbosses who had been arrested in Arizona. She went below to the caporegima and then to the soldiers. Below them were the names of the young bodyguards each of the bosses had brought with him.

By one she had filled in the names of all of the men who had been detained. Each appeared on his line in the hierarchy of his home city. Krause came into the conference room and looked at the charts. He brought with him a woman in her early thirties with red hair. "This is Agent O'Brien," he said. "Elizabeth Waring of the Organized Crime and Racketeering Division of Justice."

"Oh, yes," Elizabeth said. "We introduced ourselves on the phone this morning."

"Yes, we did," said O'Brien. "Everyone knows who you are, of course. It's a pleasure to meet you in person."

Elizabeth was taken aback for a second, but then she realized it was probably true that young agents knew the names of the people who had been on this detail for so many years. "Thank you."

Krause looked at a few of the organizational charts. "You knew who every one of these guys was?"

"We knew the big players, of course—the 'old men' is what people call them—because even the ones who aren't exactly old have been around a long time. They're either heads of families, or in a few cases they're underbosses who run some semi-independent group or the Mafia contingent in a small city, and they all have long records. The place where we're going to gain some ground is the two-thirds who aren't famous. Some haven't even been arrested before. We not only have their names, photographs, and addresses, but now we can tell who they work for and where they must fit in. It's a huge update."

O'Brien said, "So we should assume they're important if they were invited to the conference?"

"Not important right now. A twenty-two-year-old doesn't run anything in the Mafia, any more than he would at any other major American business. But if he was there, he's trusted. The old men, as a rule, are very suspicious and wary. If they're invited to travel anywhere, they don't necessarily assume it's safe. The young men they bring with them are the ones they would want with them in a fight. Our experience is that these are the men we'll keep seeing for the next twenty or thirty years."

"Are they the ones we try to pressure to tell us more?"

"None of these people will talk. Not the bosses, and not the young bodyguards. They take omertà seriously. The only ones we've

154

ever had any luck with were middle-aged soldiers who have done their jobs and kept the secrets for thirty years and have nothing to show for it. That's the only group that isn't invited to this kind of meeting. They're all at home making money for the bosses."

"Are we wasting our time talking to these men?"

"No. They sometimes reveal useful information without knowing it. I think what we've got to try for is what they were talking about at the conference. They don't meet like this very often, and anything that might give us the agenda is worthwhile. And relationships are important, particularly blood relations. If you find out Mike Morella in Los Angeles is a cousin of Gaetano Bruni in Chicago, some day that might be important information, so make sure it gets into their intelligence files."

"Ms. Waring?"

She turned her head. Agent Collazo was in the doorway. "There's a call from the deputy assistant AG for you. Would you like to take it in my office? It's quieter."

He meant more private. "That would be great." She got up. "Excuse me." She went into his office and he closed the door after her.

"Waring," she said.

"Please hold for Mr. Hunsecker." After a few seconds, a click brought him. "Ms. Waring."

"Yes?"

"I understand we reached you in Phoenix."

"That's right. I'm at the FBI field office."

"What are you doing there?"

"There's been an important FBI operation near here in the mountains, a big meeting of the crime families at a resort. It's sort of a dude ranch, and they took over the whole place for a meeting. The FBI did a sweep to see who was there and so on."

"I asked what *you* were doing there."

"When I learned what was happening, I realized that this was a time when they could use my help to figure out who they had. It was also an occasion for us to find out things we might need to know about changes in the current power structure and the up-and-coming generation we don't know a lot about. So I took a couple of personal days and flew out to lend a hand."

"You left Washington without asking permission or approval from higher authority and flew across the country to attach yourself to an operation by another agency. Is that about right?"

She couldn't tell him that the operation was hers as much as the FBI's. She had learned about it from a source he had already ordered her to drop and gone around him to get the FBI involved because she knew he wouldn't. "Mr. Hunsecker. I took steps in order to avoid any ambiguity about my actions and to prevent the suspicion that I was using Justice Department time or money. I took two personal days to be here, and paid for my own flight and lodging."

"You left your post without leave."

"In order to get here while it still mattered, I had to make the arrangements overnight and be on an early morning flight. If my acting alone offended you, I apologize. Often things have to happen before office hours, and Justice Department employees have to act on their own initiative. If one of the people in my section learned that something this big was happening and didn't realize it was more important to be here than to clear it with me, I'd be angry."

"We're well into the second business day, and the only reason I know about this is that the deputy director of the FBI called to thank me for sending someone to Phoenix."

"That was thoughtful of him," said Elizabeth. "May I ask what you said to him?"

"This is beginning to try my patience. We can go into all of it when you return. Make an appointment with my assistant to see me at eight A.M. tomorrow morning."

"But I'm still accomplishing things here. Can we make it the day after?"

"No. Consider yourself recalled. Be here at eight A.M."

"Yes, sir." She heard him hang up, not a click, but the incidental air noise went away, a sound like a door closing.

She decided she shouldn't be surprised that he had insisted on eight A.M. That was five A.M. Phoenix time, and it meant she would have to take a red-eye flight that arrived at seven. Even then she would have to go from the airport directly to the office to be on time. To be berated for doing her job.

18

HE GOT OFF THE plane at George Bush Intercontinental Airport outside Houston and rented a dark blue Buick LaCrosse. He drove to the comfortable old hotel near the Astrodome where he'd made a reservation and checked in. Instead of sleeping on the plane, he had remained alert because his conversation with Agnoli had been disturbing. He could have killed him in the men's room where there were no cameras and probably could have gotten away with it. But his previous dealing with Agnoli had convinced him that Agnoli wouldn't invite trouble he didn't need. And he had the feeling that a man who wasn't one of the capos who had agreed to his death should be left alone right now. There was going to be enough killing soon.

Two hours later he had dinner in the fish restaurant beside his hotel. He sat in the dark wooden booth thinking about the rest of his life. If he were to stop right now and fly back to the UK, what would happen? He might be able to fit in a few months with Meg before another enterprising young soldier managed to find him. It was possible, if he was very careful about his movements, to make it last a bit longer. He had killed Tosca's first three scouts in Brighton, but dumped their bodies in London. It was difficult for him to know if anyone in the United States knew they'd even been in Brighton.

It had been bad luck that they found him. He and Meg seldom went to Brighton, partly because that was the city where one of the Talarese family had spotted him ten years ago. For him it had seemed an unnecessary risk, and for Meg Brighton had unpleasant associations. But there he had been again, down in Brighton for the races with Meg, and he had been spotted. He wished there could have been a way to get rid of the three or elude them without killing them. Then nothing more would have happened. Carl Bala could have died of old age after a few more years in prison, and Tosca could have succeeded him, with no personal interest in the Butcher's Boy.

He hadn't seen the three men coming, and so he hadn't had a chance to do something different — go to a more remote part of the United Kingdom to stay out of sight, or go to France. Even as these thoughts formed, he knew they were lies. If he had noticed the three men looking for him in England, he wouldn't have concocted some clever way to hide. He simply would have killed them sooner and more efficiently.

The whole issue would have gone away without the old men. It was typical of bosses to listen to Tosca's request and see some advantage in it for themselves that made them indifferent to the risks. Did those fat bastards forget who Tosca was talking about? Didn't they take a moment to reflect on why a man who commanded over three hundred soldiers wanted to share the credit for killing one solitary enemy? And now, even after he had found his way into their meeting to kill Tosca and walked out again, didn't even one of them remember who he was?

He looked at the window. It was dark out and getting to be evening, time to get busy. He finished his dinner and went out to his rental car to begin his search for the necessary weapons. In the old days he'd had connections in many cities who would sell him guns. Now he was alone, and he would have to scavenge.

He thought about how he was going to find a gun. At times he had bought guns at garage sales, or from street drug dealers, who he had found would sell just about anything. He'd once known a gunsmith who sometimes had people leave guns with him to be fixed or modified and then never come back for them. Once he'd bought a compact .32 Beretta from a gas station owner outside Las Vegas who had taken it from a busted gambler in exchange for a tank of gas to get home. He knew he would have to work a little harder this time. He would have to prepare.

He had passed a big thrift store on his way into town from the airport, and he drove back now and went inside. The sales floor looked like a hurricane had blown through and deposited the contents of twenty houses. There were various unmatched pieces of furniture, toys, books, vases, clothing of every sort and size, costume jewelry, old magazines, small appliances, recordings in every format since Edison. The other shoppers were as various as the merchandise. Some appeared to need a cheap way of staying warm, while others scrutinized and evaluated each item like antique collectors.

In the clothing section, he picked out four different baseball caps, a few T-shirts in dark colors, a couple of zip-up sweatshirts with hoods, an olive drab canvas messenger bag with a shoulder strap, and a navy blue work shirt with an embroidered patch over the left pocket that said BOBBY. At a counter he bought a pair of aviator sunglasses. He bought a screwdriver, a pair of pliers, an adjustable crescent wrench, a cold chisel and hammer, a lock-blade knife. When he got to the car, he put all of his purchases in the trunk.

His next stop was a huge Home Depot. He bought a short section of sheet metal heating duct, a pair of tin snips, and a roll of electrical tape. A few blocks from the store he parked and used the tin snips to cut a strip of sheet metal about eighteen inches long and two inches wide with a slight hook on the end. He wished he could show Eddie Mastrewski that he still remembered how to do this.

When Schaeffer had turned sixteen, Eddie had taken him to the Department of Motor Vehicles and signed the papers so he could get a learner's permit. Eddie had sat in silence with beads of sweat running down his forehead while the boy drove up and down the streets, narrowly missing parked cars and stopping so abruptly at each intersection that Eddie was nearly catapulted out of his seat. He endured the lessons for two months, until the boy's test date came along and he passed. The next day Eddie said, "Come on. I want you to meet somebody who knows a lot about cars."

The boy thought it would be a mechanic who was going to show him about car maintenance. Eddie was particular about his car because he sometimes used it to get away after he and the boy had done a job. It was unthinkable that it wouldn't start and run smoothly. Instead, the man was a thief. He was tall and rangy with blond hair like a clump of hay, and he had a southern accent. He taught the boy how to cut a piece of thin sheet metal into a slim-jim, a tool for opening locked car doors. He showed him how to use a screwdriver and hammer to pop out the ignition switch to hot-wire it.

On the way home Eddie said, "I can't buy you a car right now, kid. People would wonder where the money came from. Maybe in a couple of months, after we've mentioned to the right people that you're saving for one. But after today, if it's a matter of life and death, you know how to get one."

He took his messenger bag and one of the hats and one of the sweatshirts out of the trunk and set them on the car seat, then drove a little farther down the street and stopped near a Starbuck's coffee shop. He opened his laptop computer, found the Starbuck's Internet network, and typed in "Gentlemen's clubs, Houston, Texas." Several addresses appeared, and he began to drive. The place he wanted was easy to imagine. It had to be big, and it would have to have a parking lot that was vast enough so the cameras and patrols wouldn't easily see him. It had to be a loud, popular sort of place with men coming in constantly at this time of the evening and very few leaving yet.

He drove out of the city on the beltway that surrounded it and found the first club. He drove past and decided it wasn't the sort of place he wanted. There was a small, dark-looking parking lot behind a windowless box of a building. He drove to the second, and it was better. There was a warehouse-size building with a big sign on the roof with a picture of a mischievous-looking pony and the word MUSTANG, and beneath it, HUNDREDS OF BEAUTIFUL WOMEN. He assumed the beautiful women didn't all dance there on one night.

He stopped down the road, removed the bulb that illuminated his license plate, and put a few pieces of black electrical tape on the plates so I became T, P became B, 5 became 6, and 9 became 8. He put the messenger bag over his shoulder, a hooded sweatshirt over the bag, and a baseball cap on his head, then drove back to the lot.

The parking space he selected was as far from the sprawling building as possible. He got out of the car and walked two rows closer to the club. The row where he had parked was still filling up with new arrivals. The one where he stood was full, but the drivers probably hadn't been here very long. He touched the hood of the nearest car as he walked, and it was still hot.

He stopped and looked back as though he were waiting for a friend. He leaned against the nearest car, inserted the slim-jim he'd made into the door beside the passenger window, jerked it up, and unlocked the door. He took out his car keys, pretended to unlock the door, and opened it. He leaned in and performed a quick search. He felt under the driver's seat, under the dashboard to the right of the steering wheel for a hidden pistol holder, used his screwdriver to pop the glove compartment, relocked the car, and moved on.

After three cars he began to wonder if he had made a mistake. Maybe the practice of carrying guns was one more thing in America that had changed since he'd left. But the fourth car held what he needed. In the pocket at the front of the driver's seat was a compact Sig Sauer P238 with two full magazines. He put the gun and ammunition in the messenger bag, locked the car, and moved on. His next car was empty, but then he hit two in a row. One had a Glock 17, and the other an M92 Beretta. He kept moving from car to car. When fifteen minutes had passed, he sensed that the odds were getting too high that he would be noticed.

He turned and walked back toward his rental car. The lot was filling up now, and he had to walk close to several groups of men while he was trying to keep the stolen pistols invisible. He had seven pistols in his messenger bag, which was bulging and weighed at least fifteen pounds. He got into his car, set the messenger bag on the floor in front of the passenger seat, started the car, and slowly made his way up the aisle toward the exit.

He had not been wrong. The last time he had thought about the gun laws in Texas had been quite a few years ago, but at that time it was legal to carry a loaded, concealed weapon if the gun owner was in his car. That was pretty much an invitation to keep a gun in the glove compartment, and he'd just verified that many people were in the habit. He drove out onto the highway and headed eastward toward central Houston and his hotel. Tonight he was grateful that some things were eternal.

The hotel was quiet and pleasant, and he felt glad to be back in his room. He opened the newspaper the staff had left outside his door and scanned the pages. There was a small article, no larger than four column inches, about a joint police and FBI raid on an Arizona resort, in which they'd arrested dozens of guests on parole violations, illegal drug and weapons charges. Orders from Washington must have been to keep from releasing too much. He hoped it was because the government was planning to do something more to disrupt the old men's attempts to reorganize themselves. Anything the government could do to frustrate those bastards and keep them off balance right now would help him.

He spread the newspaper on the desk and set the bag on the surface, then took out the seven stolen guns, one at a time. There was the Sig P238, the Glock 17, two Beretta M92s, a Browning Hi-Power .45, a Kimber .45, a Springfield Armory .40. All of them were fully loaded, and three had an extra loaded magazine or two.

It had been a good fifteen minutes' work. Now it was time to sleep and get ready for the next part of the trip. He showered and then soaked his body in the tub, as he had done in Arizona. He was going to do some difficult things in the next few days, and he couldn't afford to be slowed down by any aches or angry scratches or blisters once it began. When the water had cooled, he dried off and went to bed. As soon as he dozed off, he dreamed he was in England again. The strange part was that the dream wasn't strange at all. He did all the things he usually did—woke with Meg in the old manor house, went to the big dining room for breakfast, then went into the library for an hour to read the newspapers while Meg completed her letters and her e-mails. The library was his refuge because it had been hers, and her father's before her. When Schaeffer and Meg had begun to live here after her parents died, he had begun reading his way through the books in the shelves. He had read his way through in about five years and then began to buy books. In the dream-day he and Meg packed a bag and went into Bath, ate at a restaurant, went to a play, and met some friends for a drink afterward. As he looked around in the hotel bar where they had stopped, he noticed that all of the other tables and the stools at the bar were occupied by members of the Mafia he had seen at the ranch. They didn't recognize him, but he kept waiting for one to turn and look at him, then stand and point at him.

At eight in the morning he awoke, got up and dressed, then drove to an electronics store, bought a prepaid cell phone, and dialed Meg's number in London.

"Hello," she said.

"Hi. It's me."

"I've been wishing it would be you every time, but I always remind myself that you would never call in these circumstances. Do you have new circumstances?"

"They're a bit worse than before. I wanted to tell you that I'm doing my best to get through this, but you should be prepared for the probability that it won't work out."

"Oh, my God, Michael. Please. Is there any way to simply leave? If you and I met in a village in Paraguay or one of the thirty thousand islands of the Maldives, couldn't we live some kind of life together? Because I'd do that without hesitation."

"So would I. The problem is that the people I'm worrying about have branches and subsidiaries in a great many countries, and very close ties with a lot of other organizations everywhere. Right now, today, the word is being spread that finding me is worth a lot of money. The figure will be high enough so quite a few people in different places will begin to search."

"What are you going to do?"

"Make getting me seem like a hard way to make money."

"The only other time you went back there, you made up such a pretty story for me. Do you remember? You were with the CIA, and the two boys who had been killed when the Bulgarians came after you would be awarded posthumous medals by the queen?"

"I remember."

"I never bought a word of it. But I loved you for making it up. I've always loved you, from the time you took me to tea after that meeting in Bath, and we talked. I didn't know anything about you—what you had done before, who you knew, and so on. I could see everything about you without any facts to obstruct the view. You do your best to come back to me. If you make it, I'll be here waiting for you. If you don't make it back, then know that I don't regret anything. If I had it to do again, I'd give myself to you in a heartbeat."

"What's going on now reminds me that I have a few things to regret, but I've never felt anything but lucky I met you. I love you."

"I feel as though we didn't get to say that enough times."

"If I get back, I'll say it every morning before I do anything else."

"I'll remind you."

"I'm sorry, but I've got to keep moving, so I'd better go. Stay safe. Be alert. If anything around you seems odd, assume it's trouble. Visit friends in faraway places for a few weeks. One way or another, this will be over by then. If they find me, they'll stop looking."

"I'll be waiting for you."

He disconnected the call, took the phone apart, and dropped the pieces in trash cans as he walked along the street. When he reached the hotel, he checked out and began to drive northward out of Houston.

19

ELIZABETH HAD A STRANGE, disconnected feeling as she looked down at Washington from the air. She wasn't feeling the way she usually did when she flew into Reagan International—a mixture of comfortable familiarity and pride at how beautiful the place was. She was somewhere else in her mind, and she realized that she was feeling what the Butcher's Boy must be feeling.

He had killed Frank Tosca in the midst of the biggest conference of bosses in fifty years. He must be wondering, as she was, what kind of reaction the old men were having. Most of them were probably busy dealing with the problem of being detained in Arizona. Even if nothing else was lost, each of the old men would be aware that he had been made to look ridiculous—not only careless, but gullible. He must be feeling very alone right now.

Looking foolish was a very serious matter if you were trying to keep a couple of hundred soldiers cowed and respectful. Looking weak had probably been the foremost cause of death in their families for the past five generations. Who would they be blaming today for what had happened in Arizona? The one who had insisted on the meeting was Frank Tosca. But it must be terribly unsatisfying to be angry at a dead man.

Most of them would have no choice but to settle on the

Butcher's Boy. He was safe to hate. He was an outsider. None of them would have to deal with retaliation from his cousins and in-laws. When he had killed Tosca, he had robbed the meeting of its purpose. He had contributed to the number and gravity of their potential legal troubles. He had also contributed to the spectacle they presented as a group of impotent, half-senile old men trying to reconstruct a past that could never return. It had been one against two hundred, and once again, the two hundred looked like idiots. That alone would make them want him dead.

She knew, and the Butcher's Boy must know too, that the death of a man like Frank Tosca wasn't entirely bad news to the other bosses. They were the veterans of a great many vendettas and coups. The older ones had lived through a couple of disputes that in some countries would have seemed like civil wars. They knew that a strong man like Tosca might revitalize an organization that had been stagnating for years. But the more success Tosca had and the more people flocked around him, the less power the other bosses would have. He would become the first among equals, and then, ultimately, the boss of bosses—*Il capo di tutti capi.* Soon they would have been paying percentages to him for the privilege of running businesses, and after that, they would have begun to take orders from him and serve at his pleasure. Many of them must have been delighted that he had not made it home from Arizona.

None of that would help his killer. Getting the killer would be a way to overcome their new image problem and keep their power from leaking away. By killing the Butcher's Boy, they would console any of their own men who had been hoping a new golden age for the Mafia would start when Tosca took over. They would complete this single small accomplishment in concert with all of the other families who had agreed to it, and maybe acting together would bring better things later. These were men who killed on a suspicion, an impulse, a whim. Death always seemed to be the solution to every problem.

If only the Butcher's Boy was astute enough to understand his predicament, he might be ready for an approach from her. He just might be feeling the right kind of desperation. If she offered the kind of sanctuary that only the U.S. government could offer, he just might take it.

As her plane banked and leveled its wings for the approach, she was already trying to think of a way to contact him. He would be watching television and looking at newspapers to find out anything he could about the aftermath of his killing Tosca. She needed to let him know that she understood his predicament and sympathized. She stopped herself. No, that wasn't right. Did she feel sympathy for him? She detected a temptation to feel sorry he was going to suffer, even though she knew the feeling was wasted on him. There were insane serial killers who murdered fewer people than he had just since he'd turned up again, and they served as the models for horror movies.

Still, there had never been an underdog who had worse odds. His opponents were all grown-up men who had needed to commit a murder in order to be "made," and they all had been trying to kill him when he'd attacked them. But she had to resist the impulse to defend him. It made her confused and, if anyone knew, would make her seem crazy, like the women who wrote love letters to convicted serial killers.

The plane landed, gave its usual bounce and shudder, rattled down the runway to a stop, then taxied toward the terminal. By the time the lights came on to illuminate the impatient passengers popping up to get their bags from the overhead compartments, she had composed what she wanted to say.

"I've known about you for twenty years, but only met you on August 30. You've got troubles, so talk to me."

She wrote it out on a page torn from her address book while she was in the cab to the Justice Department building. She got out in front of the building, paid the driver, and went inside, still thinking about what she was going to do. When she walked into the office, she almost handed the little torn page to Geoffrey. *No,* she thought. *This has to be unofficial. No unwitting accomplices to get destroyed if it blows up.* She said to him, "Hi, Geoff. Give me fifteen minutes before I see Hunsecker," and went into her office and closed her door.

She sent text messages to her children. "I'm back and will be in the office for the day. If you need me, don't hesitate to call. Love, Mom."

Then she turned on her laptop and went to the site of the *Arizona Republic* in Phoenix and placed her personal ad. Next she went to the *New York Times*, the *Washington Post*, the *Los Angeles Times*, and the *Chicago Tribune*.

20

IT TOOK HIM two days to drive the eleven hundred miles from Houston to Denver and a night to recover, but now it was morning and he was a guest in the Brown Palace Hotel in the center of Denver. The hotel was old, with lots of dark, polished wood. He had always thought of it as what some of the old hotels Eddie Mastrewski had stayed in must have looked like before they fell into ruin. Eddie had liked those old hotels, and he would have loved the Brown Palace, with its old-fashioned wallpaper and the antique architecture of the place. It had a central stairwell, so a person on the upper floors could look down into the square enclosure of railings all the way to the lobby.

A few of Eddie's hotels were built that way, but they were all creaky, with stains on the worn carpets that the boy could only make guesses about. Eddie had liked them because they were so devoid of paying guests that he could go to the upper levels and occupy a floor of his own. That way he could use the hallway as his front porch, sit in a chair, read the papers, and look down to see if any of his horde of enemies showed up. He was especially partial to the places where the management wouldn't be too shocked if he left suddenly. He always paid in cash at the start of a stay so any consternation he caused was emotional and had no legal implications.

This morning he missed Eddie more than usual. He would have loved to have Eddie out there in the hallway, tilting back in a desk chair with a cigarette burning in the big sand-filled ashtray and the two .45 automatic pistols in his coat.

Schaeffer took the elevator to the lobby, went into the hotel shop, and bought the *New York Times,* the *Los Angeles Times,* and the *Chicago Tribune.* He walked into the hotel restaurant and went to a booth near the back where he could see the doorway. He was aware of the two other ways out of the dining room — through the bar and past the men's room, and through the kitchen to the alley. He had scanned the room from the doorway and seen no reason to worry, but he looked at all the faces once more before he opened the *New York Times.*

He ran his eyes down each page, looking for some reference to what had happened in Arizona. He saw nothing. By now the federal cops must have identified the men they had cornered in their raid. It seemed odd that more wasn't being made of it. Maybe the right person at the *Times* had not yet seen the list and noticed that many of the names were recognizable names of New York gangsters. He opened the *Tribune.* There was a brief story that said FBI officials had raided a compound in Arizona and arrested "dozens of men" on weapons and drug charges. The story was out. In a day or two, when reporters saw the names, it would probably blow up a bit.

It was possible the *L.A. Times* would be ahead on this one because Arizona was a bit closer to their orbit, but he found nothing. When the waitress came, he ordered his breakfast, then looked idly at the papers he'd already seen. He wondered if any of the old men still used the personal ads. That had once been the way that people like Eddie knew they were wanted for a job. Eddie would not have liked it if a couple of Mafia soldiers had come to his butcher shop to offer him a contract.

Something caught his eye. An ad said, "BB: Sorry I missed you at the ranch. I'll see what I can do, if you want. VP"

VP had to be Vincent Pugliese. They always used the guy you

liked best, the one you'd trust if you had to trust anyone. Pugliese worked for the Castigliones, so the one who had ordered Pugliese to do this was a Castiglione, probably Joe, the oldest brother. He would have asked if anybody thought he could be the one, and Vince had done that silent nod of his—a serious man's gesture, not bobbing his head up and down like a windup toy, but a single dip of the head.

Schaeffer remembered that nod from the old days, when the Castiglione family had summoned him to Chicago. Old Salvatore Castiglione hired him to go to Milwaukee and demonstrate to the small Mafia contingent there that their way of declaring independence from the Castiglione family in Chicago had been a bad idea. Instead of paying their regular percentage, they had killed the bagman. Salvatore had decided that the one who should pay was Tony Fantano, the boss of the Milwaukee crew.

The boy was twenty years old and he didn't know Tony Fantano by sight or where to find him. He was already resigned to having to find the right bar and start asking questions. But Castiglione said, "We'll give you a guide." The old man looked around the room at the men who were sitting there. That was the first time Schaeffer had seen the nod. Vince Pugliese was the same age as he was, but he had an intelligent, quiet gravity even then. Vince simply nodded once. "Done," said the old man. "Vince will go with you."

They drove to Milwaukee that night. They had a Chevy Impala stolen from Oklahoma City with Illinois plates that were also stolen. They had a pair of .45 pistols, two among the millions of copies of the Colt 1911 model that were issued by the U.S. Army until the end of World War II and then passed from hand to hand for forty years until there was no way of guessing who the recorded owner had been.

He remembered riding into Milwaukee while Vince drove the car. They had talked about everything but the job. They had both been feeling at that time in their lives that they wished they could go to college. Pugliese had noticed that Castiglione's son had sons

173

their age—the grandsons of old Salvatore—and two of the three were away at college. Old Salvatore was paying the insane tuition for both of them. For his own family, Salvatore thought education was a good idea. For the sons of other men—young guys like Vince—it was a stupid waste of time.

Schaeffer had admitted that he had been thinking about going to college for a couple of years, but he didn't see a way to accomplish it. If word got out where he was, there would be men coming to his dormitory to hire him for one more job, and others would come to kill him. Either way, staying would be impossible. Besides, his attendance record in high school had been spotty because he and Eddie had traveled so much.

Vince said, "You were taking wet jobs in high school?"

"Yeah. And how old were you the first time you had to step around a guy you shot to get home?"

"Yeah," Vince said. "I kind of forgot. I was seventeen." He drove in silence for a few minutes, looking occasionally at the lake to his right. "I suppose Mr. Castiglione is right—college is not for guys like me. I make more money than a doctor or a lawyer, and I'm not twenty-one yet. College would cost me too much in lost pay."

They had changed the subject and agreed on a plan. They would try to take Tony Fantano while he was out alone, away from his house. Vince would drive the car, and Schaeffer would do the work.

They parked a half block away from Fantano's house at four A.M. and waited. At just after seven, he backed his car out of his driveway and drove up the street. They waited until he turned and then followed him at a distance. He got onto a major street and drove across town while they kept a few vehicles between their car and his, thinking at each major intersection that soon he would reach his destination and stop. He didn't. He drove right out of the city with them following, trying to stay as far back as they could behind trucks that would keep them invisible to his rearview mirror. He went about ten miles out on a rural route, turned off into

174

the long gravel driveway of a farm, and stopped at a white farmhouse.

Vince drove past, then turned into the next farm road. Schaeffer said, "All right. Wait for me here. If it's a trap you can take off."

"If you get in trouble, try to make it back. I won't take off," Vince said. He leaned back in his seat and watched Schaeffer walk to the fence, climb over it, and make his way into the tall rows of corn beyond it. To his left, at the back of the farm, behind the cornfield, was a large, old apple orchard full of short, gnarled trees with thick, twisted trunks, but the corn rows were closer to the house.

Schaeffer took one look back at Vince and saw him in the driver's seat, his face impassive—watchful, merely waiting. Schaeffer went deeper into the cornfield, at first making his way quickly between the rows. But as he approached the gravel driveway through the cornfield, he moved more slowly and carefully, adjusting his position from row to row, not letting himself brush against the cornstalks so the leaves wouldn't make whispering sounds. He backtracked three rows so he could see Fantano's car and the house, but anyone inside could not see him. He took out his gun and aimed it down the open space between rows. As soon as someone stepped into that empty frame, the person would die.

As he thought about that bright, warm morning after all these years, he remembered the physical sensation he had felt when he realized it was a trap. Fantano had been expecting them, and he had led them to the farm. As Schaeffer was taking his position in the cornfield, eight of Fantano's men were emerging from the back door of the farmhouse and forming a line at the upper end of the cornfield.

When they were all lined up at the first row of corn, on some silent signal they began to move into the corn. They advanced one row at a time, then stopped to sight along the furrow to be sure all of them were still aligned and nobody got ahead of the others and got mistaken for a target. They were just five or six rows from

Schaeffer before he saw the light catch the white shirt one of them wore. It shone through the tiny gaps in the green cornstalks and leaves. He sidestepped to get out of the man's path and saw another, then another coming his way.

He dashed down the long corn row toward the end where he could see the porch of the house. In thirty seconds he was crouching beside the house. He knew he had one chance. He crept along the siding until he was beside a tall window.

He pivoted and stepped in front of the window. Tony Fantano was standing in the middle of an old-fashioned parlor, staring out the opposite window at the men in the cornfield. He seemed to have a sudden premonition, a discomfort that was mental, not sensory, because there had been no noise. He turned and saw Schaeffer looking in at him.

Schaeffer fired four rapid shots through the glass and caught Fantano twice in the chest as a splash of shattered glass sprayed the room. A bullet went through Fantano's neck, and the last one hit the wall as Fantano fell backward onto the floor. Schaeffer took aim at his head and fired, then ran around to the front porch and looked in the front window, across the room, and through the window where Fantano had been watching his men. As he looked, he ejected the magazine from his gun and inserted a fresh one.

He saw three men with guns in their hands run out of the cornfield and head for the back of the house. Schaeffer knelt on the porch in front of the window and aimed his pistol through it, across the living room, down the short, straight hallway to the back door.

The back door swung open and the three men ran in and stopped at the sight of Fantano on the floor. Schaeffer opened fire and dropped all three. He flung the front door open and ran to the three bodies. He snatched the guns out of the hands of two of the dead men, put them in his jacket pockets, and kept going down the hall and out the back door.

He ran to the back corner of the cornfield to get behind the remaining men. But just as he entered the field, he heard gunshots.

They seemed to be coming from the road ahead of him where he had left Vincent Pugliese and the car.

He veered away from the cornfield and into the orchard beside it. He caught sight of two men ahead of him running along the first two rows of cornstalks toward the road. He stopped, steadied his arm on a tree limb, and hit the back one, then the other, and ran on.

The firing up ahead was now heavier and more sustained. He ran through the orchard, swerving to miss tree trunks, jumping over exposed roots. He moved far enough into the orchard so the trunks of the trees provided some concealment and protection, but he could tell from the sounds that nobody was shooting at him.

At last he reached the far end of the orchard and looked out to see Vince Pugliese crouching behind the stolen Impala. Three men crouched in the cornfield shooting at him. The car's windows were almost all gone, and glittering cubes of shattered safety glass had spattered all over the road. There were bullet holes in the door panels, and at least one tire was flat.

Schaeffer slipped out of the orchard into the cornfield, stepped into the next row, then the next. He saw a man three rows ahead lying on his belly in a furrow aiming his pistol at Vince. Schaeffer shot him, then ran ahead from row to row, shot the second, then shot the third. None of the men ever heard him or looked in his direction. Even the last one he killed seemed to think to the end that the firing he heard was his companions firing at Vince Pugliese.

When the last one was dead, he yelled, "Vince!"

"Don't bother me. I've got these guys outnumbered."

"They're dead."

"All of them?"

"Yes."

Schaeffer stepped out of the cornfield and Pugliese stepped hesitantly around the trunk of the car. When there were no shots, he put his gun in his coat and pointed at the Impala. "The car's no good anymore."

"We can take Fantano's. Let's wipe this one for prints and go."

They wiped the surfaces clean, took off the Illinois plates, and trotted through the cornfield to the house. Inside the parlor Schaeffer stepped carefully around the blood, reached into Fantano's pants pocket, and took his keys.

As Vince drove them down the gravel drive to the highway, manic elation overtook the two twenty-year-olds. They sped along the rural highway, neither of them having to admit that he'd been sure they were about to die, but both feeling shock and relief that they hadn't. Each of them felt grateful to the other for being brave enough to keep half of Fantano's soldiers occupied for so long. Each of them had become the only witness to the other's victory.

Now, thirty years later, when Schaeffer read the personal ad in the newspaper, he felt an instant of sincere pleasure at the memory of the young Vince Pugliese. But the pleasure was followed immediately and overwhelmed by the unwelcome memory of how the Mafia worked. The one you liked, respected, and trusted most was always the one they sent to invite you to your death.

21

THE INVITATION WAS a trap. He looked at the personal ad one more time, let out a breath in disapproval, then started to fold the paper, but his eyes passed over another personal ad and stopped.

"I've known about you for twenty years, but only met you on August 30. You've got troubles, so talk to me."

It was Elizabeth Waring. Another trap, this one from the opposite side of the universe. Both sides had realized how vulnerable he was, and each hurried to roll him in before the other side could. He wondered if, when each of them checked the newspapers today to be sure their ad had run, they would each notice the other ad. Probably Elizabeth Waring would.

He decided that it was time to turn in his rental car and buy a vehicle that nobody was going to care about and want him to return. He drove to two used-car lots before he found the right make and model, the right color in the right condition. It was a Toyota Camry, which he had read was the most popular model in the United States. Even if it hadn't been, there were enough models that looked nearly like it to make it unmemorable. It was gray, and when it was on the road it seemed practically invisible. It was five years old, and so it was cheap but serviceable. He used the

179

bank account he had opened in Scottsdale to write a check for it and signed Charles F. Ackerman.

While the dealer was fitting permanent plates on his car and completing the paperwork, he drove his rental car to a Target store and bought some things he would need for his trip — a case of bottled water, two boxes of trail-mix bars. Then he drove down the street to a Big 5 sporting-goods store and bought a short-barreled Winchester Defender shotgun and five boxes of double-ought shells. He drove to a street near the used-car lot and parked his rental car, then walked to the used-car lot, picked up his gray Camry, and drove it to the rental car. He transferred his belongings from the rental to the trunk of the Camry and then drove the rental car to the airport car rental to return it. He took the rental agency shuttle bus to the airport terminal, then took a cab back to an address one street away from the block where he had left his new car.

As he got onto the road, he felt optimistic. He would watch carefully for anyone following him or seeming interested in him during the next long drive. He had tools to steal license plates in each new state if he wanted. He had food and snacks to prolong his road time, and a couple of baseball hats that made him look like a million other men on the highways. There was no reason for anyone to notice him. He had made himself ordinary.

He drove east on Interstate 80, heading for Illinois. From there he could take Interstate 57 the last few miles into Chicago. He slept the first night in a motel outside Omaha and let himself sleep as long as he could before he returned to the road. The invitation to his ambush had come from his old companion Vince from the Milwaukee job. The invitation from Vince had made him choose Chicago. But if all of the old men had agreed to hunt him, then there could be local Mafia soldiers in the lobbies of hotels in any city.

He drove all day, and when he crossed the line into Illinois, he headed south on Interstate 74 and went to the long-term parking lot at the Willard Airport near Urbana and stole a set of Illinois plates. He stopped the second night in a motel just south of Chicago in Watseka, Illinois, that he judged would be too small to accommodate Mafia soldiers watching the lobby. It was a one-story building with a row of rooms along the outside and a green neon vacancy sign on the tall marquee. The people he saw when he pulled into the lot were middle-class families who had left the interstates outside the big cities to find somewhere cheap and easy to stay. There was no restaurant, so he drove to a hamburger place down the street and brought food with him to eat in the room.

He ignored the parking space right in front of his motel room door and parked his car away from the building so an enemy wouldn't instantly connect it with the room and know which one he was in. He went inside and locked the door, the deadbolt, and the chain, and then pushed the desk in front of the door.

He had spent the first half of his life traveling in the trade, and the long habit of precautions had come back to him. Staying alive was often a matter of premeditation, of anticipating dangers long in advance and doing small things to make them less likely. It was always better to be as close to invisible as possible, better to cut the odds of being noticed, reported, and remembered to a minimum. Everything that could be locked, disguised, or hidden should be. He showered, ate his dinner, watched the television news with the sound on low to see if there was any mention of the incident at the Arizona ranch. When there was none, he put the two loaded Beretta M92 pistols under the spare pillow beside him and lay down to sleep. In a minute or two he dozed off.

He awoke, looked at the glowing clock on the nightstand beside him, and saw that it was only twelve-thirty. There were voices outside. He got out of bed and went to the window. He moved aside a half inch of the curtain at the corner and looked out.

It was a man with brown wavy hair and a woman with long blond hair. They looked about thirty, and wore jeans and T-shirts. The man carried a suitcase about the size of a small carry-on bag. He bent over almost double to fit the key in the door. They'd been drinking. Whenever he said or did anything, the woman would giggle. As they went inside the room beside his, he let the curtain close. The ease he had in hearing them was not good news. Once they were inside, they sounded as though he and they were in the same room. They were no more than eight feet from him, and the wall between them seemed to be without insulation.

He crawled back into the bed and closed his eyes. The two in the next room were fairly quiet. There was a little conversation, barely above a whisper, and then he heard the shower running. The sound was a soft hiss, and after a minute or two it put him back to sleep. A few minutes later he became aware of the voices again, and then the voices stopped. He heard the bed creak as somebody got in. It occurred to him that he should make a noise so they would be aware of how little privacy the wall afforded.

He coughed, and then coughed again. There was whispering. Good. They knew he was here, and they would be aware that if they could hear him, he could hear them. The bed creaked a little more. Someone was getting up. Both of them were. They moved a few feet off. In the dim light he looked at his own room to see where they could be going. There was a small, narrow couch. After a minute he heard a soft moan. "Oh yes. Oh."

"Oh shit," he whispered. He lay down on his side and put the spare pillow over his head so both ears were covered. He was surprised at how little that accomplished. The couple seemed to forget that they had a neighbor.

He sat up, switched on the television set, and watched a late-night talk show, trying to pay attention to the conversation. Over the years he had forgotten about American television, and he saw only a few American films a year so he found he had no idea who the guests were, or the host. Still, it seemed better than allowing himself to listen to the sounds from the next room. The noise grew louder and more distracting until it trailed off. He turned off the television, lay down again, and fell asleep as though he were turning off a light switch.

Then he woke again and thought about the pistols on the bed beside his head. He wished he could go next door and put those two out of his misery. Then he realized the sounds weren't com-

182

ing from the other side of the wall. They were outside. He looked at the clock again. It was just after three A.M. He went to the window and moved the curtain aside a quarter inch.

There were four men walking along the two rows of cars, looking at license plates and in the windshields and side windows. He watched two of them look at his gray Toyota Camry, then move on. He was glad he had stolen a set of Illinois plates.

The men reached the end of the rows of cars, but didn't seem to have found what they were looking for, and that increased his suspicion that what they were looking for was him. He couldn't see anything that might be their car, but he knew they would have parked it out of sight behind the building, very possibly with the motor idling. He had seen other jobs where the shooters had done that. If the keys were in somebody's pocket and he died, then nobody would get out. If the keys were in the car, then anybody who made it that far would get out.

He knew what must have happened. They had gone to various hotels and motels on the major routes into the city and asked night-desk clerks to watch for a lone man about his age and description. To the ones that had connections, they would ask for the favor of a call. At the other hotels, they would pretend to be private detectives and offer a reward. He dressed quickly.

He hoped it would take them a little time to get ready to shoot their way into his room because his idea would take a few minutes. He had learned something from the couple next door. The walls between rooms couldn't consist of anything more substantial than a frame of two-by-fours covered by two sheets of wallboard. He also knew that the room to the right of his was unoccupied. He'd heard nothing from that side.

The lock-blade knife he'd bought was in his pocket. He opened it, then chose the spot on the wall carefully. It had to be the space behind the small dresser. He quietly moved the dresser aside, then stabbed the knife into the wallboard. It punched through. The consistency was like thick cardboard. He punched through again and again, until he had cut an eighteen-inch square, pulled it out, and confirmed his theory. There was a frame holding up two sheets of wallboard. He punched through the next one with less hesitation. When he had cut the second hole, he pushed the piece through into the next room, then the other.

As he worked, he thought about the men outside. What took the longest on jobs like this was getting the men into proper positions, two on either side of the door. Two would hit the door near the knob with all their weight so it would fly open. The first two would run in low and fast, trying to get a shot in. The other two would come in a bit higher, aiming their guns over the shoulders of the first pair.

His hole was finished. He slithered through it into the next room, and then reached back through and strained to pull the empty dresser back up to the wall after him. He tugged on one side, then the other, to walk it to the hole in the wall, then lay still and listened.

There was no bang, no sound of a foot kicking the door in. Instead, there was a jingle of keys and a scrape as the deadbolt slid out. The door to his old room opened a crack, then hit the desk he'd pushed in front of it. There was a labored scrape as they pushed the desk aside, and then quick footsteps that he could feel vibrating up from the floor to his belly.

"What the fuck?"

"Where is he?"

Footsteps shook the floor again as two of them burst into the bathroom. "He's not in here."

Schaeffer aimed one of his pistols under the dresser through the hole he had cut. A man lay on the floor in his room to look under the bed. Schaeffer waited. If the man rolled and looked in his direction, he would have to kill him. The man stood up. "What if we got the wrong room?"

"Does that bathroom window open?"

More footsteps. "I don't think so. And how would he get up there?"

"The son of a bitch is famous for doing stuff like that. Jerry said

184

he killed a guy once who locked himself in a bank vault. They opened it up the next morning and there he was."

Whoever Jerry was, he had gotten the story wrong. The bank vault was just a safe room in Angelo Turcio's house in New Jersey. Schaeffer had boiled some bleach beside the air intake, and the chlorine had made Turcio sick. He had opened the door himself and tried to shoot his way out.

"Bobby, go to the desk to be sure we got the right room number and ask if he checked out already."

Somebody said, "We don't even know if he was the right guy."

"Some traveling salesman didn't figure this out and get away before we could slip a key in the door."

He took a couple of seconds to prepare himself for what was going to happen. In a minute they would suspect he'd made a hole and look for it. He saw the two sets of shoes approaching. The dresser was lifted suddenly, one man on each side.

He fired upward into the one on his right, the bullet going toward the groin. The other dropped the dresser as though it were hot, leaving himself open for a moment while Schaeffer fired into his side.

Schaeffer rolled away from the hole and dashed in the direction of the door. As he ran, the other two men fired at the hole, then moved their aim along the wall, punching small blooming holes in the wallboard behind him. He beat them to the door and stopped with both his pistols aimed at the door beside him, the only exit from his room.

The two men spilled out the door of his room, fully expecting to head him off before he got out, but they were terribly late. For a moment their faces showed identical expressions of unwelcome surprise, but he opened fire with both pistols, and left them lying in front of the door.

He sprinted to his car, got in, and drove. He was feeling alert and ready now. He swerved out of the lot onto the highway and quickly found the sign that said 57 NORTH — CHICAGO. It was time to go and see his old friend Vince Pugliese.

22

ELIZABETH WARING WAS in her office early in the morning once again. Yesterday's meeting with the deputy assistant AG had been worse than she had anticipated. A few days ago, she had been worried that she had forfeited the chance for a good working relationship with her new boss. Today, she was worried that she was about to lose her job. She was uneasy, not only because he was now openly contemptuous of her performance, but also because, from a certain point of view, she was guilty. If he chose to call a personnel hearing right now, it would be difficult to defend herself. She tried to imagine what that would be like. At the end of it, did they say, "We'll get in touch to announce our decision," or did they ask for the Justice Department identification and the gun and the office key right away?

What would she do? She was nearly fifty. She had a law degree, but could she even find a job as a lawyer at her age? Even if she didn't admit to being fired, she couldn't hide that she'd left because of trouble. All this time she had been encouraging Jim — and in a year, Amanda — to apply to the famous private colleges that would give them advantages in life. If she lost her job, that was over.

As she sat at her desk, paralyzed, trying to get herself to start on her work, she thought about Dale Hunsecker. Without ever wanting to, she had become his enemy, and he was going to try to crush her. What frightened her was that he was the champion idiot in a succession of amateurs appointed to hold that position. There was no way for her to work her way into his good graces. He combined strong, inflexible opinions with a complete innocence of facts. He had no instinct for law enforcement and a temperamental distaste for what it actually involved. He didn't want to learn anything about organized crime, but he wanted to know everything that anyone in the organized crime division was doing before they did it so he could arbitrarily veto about half of it. Each time she saw him, she was more deeply convinced that she must keep him from knowing about anything important and try to survive until he moved on. And right now, there was one thing that was more important than anything else.

Three days had passed, and the Butcher's Boy had made no new attempt to get in touch with her. She was almost certain that he had seen her ad by now. He would have wanted to see every single bit of information about the Arizona meeting and the resulting charges. The simplest places to look were the Arizona papers and the big metropolitan papers that covered organized crime. He must also be watching for any attempt by individual bosses to talk to him. No matter what the old men had promised Frank Tosca, he was dead now, and there was no benefit to be had by keeping their word to him. The Butcher's Boy, on the other hand, was alive, and there wasn't much sense in hunting him if it might get them killed.

She had made her own bid, but had she used the wrong way to get his attention? No. The personal ad from VP that she had seen in the same papers was a confirmation that this was a likely way to reach him. It had also diminished her hope. She could only succeed if he was alone and in trouble. If he had other invitations to talk, then he might think he had other options.

She had very complicated feelings this morning. She was frustrated that VP had reached out to him the same day she had, and she was sure that VP's ad would interest him more than hers. It seemed to be a chance for rapprochement and reconciliation with at least some small faction of the Mafia. Her offer could only amount to protection in some kind of confinement. If he could trust both offers, he would pick the offer from VP.

But VP's invitation was a trap. Did he know it was a trap? He must at least be suspicious and wary at this point. Who was VP, anyway? It was probably somebody he might trust, somebody he had known in the old days, when he was every family's favorite hit man. Who did he know from those days who could pose as a friend? It had to be somebody who was at least forty-five years old. The ad had said, "I missed you at the ranch." Did that mean VP had been there?

She had typed the list of names into her laptop the first day, then added notes to each entry as she learned details and what charges were filed. She opened the file and scrolled down the list to the Ps. There seemed to be three VPs—Victor Perrone, Vito Pastore, and Vincent Pugliese. She hesitated. VP might not even be a name. It could be VP for vice president, some reference to an old fake business he would understand. Or it could be one of those childish nicknames they gave each other—Pete "the Postman" Calvatti or Sammy "Antennas" Antonino.

It didn't even have to be a man. It could be a woman. In that world, it might make the invitation seem less dangerous. In his days as an active killer for hire, he couldn't have had a girlfriend that other people knew about, and he couldn't have had a relationship with any female relative of the men he met on business. They saved their sisters and daughters to marry other members of LCN, or at the very least, other Italians. Any women he had would have been prostitutes, or women he met on a temporary, semi-anonymous basis. He couldn't have had emotional ties with a woman of the sort that made his visits to her habitual or predictable, or he would be dead.

No, it felt like VP had to be one of the two hundred men at the ranch, and she had the feeling that nicknames weren't likely to be conveyed as initials. She returned to her list. Victor Perrone. He was old enough and was prominent enough to be the one they'd use as an ambassador. But he was a capo in the Balacontano family, and a brother-in-law of Antonio Talarese, a man she believed the Butcher's Boy had killed ten years ago, the last time he was active. Even if he wasn't a supporter of Frank Tosca, he would certainly not be a friend of Tosca's killer. A challenge from him might work; an invitation wouldn't.

That left Vincent Pugliese and Vito Pastore. She didn't know much about Vito Pastore. She went to the NCIC site. There were two Vito Pastores and neither was the right man. One of them had been born in 1901. He had a criminal record that began in 1919 and stretched for sixty years. He had been picked up in a bootlegging raid. He had once been convicted of robbing a train. He had been dead since 1979.

The second Vito Pastore's record consisted of convictions for importing and selling counterfeit designer clothes, watches, and handbags, extortion in connection with a music distribution deal. He was questioned and released in the killing of Ronald Sturtevant, a bass guitar player for a band called Scuffle. He was twenty-six years old. He would have been about five or six years old when the Butcher's Boy was still meeting people. It occurred to her that he might be a surrogate for somebody who was the right age, but how would the Butcher's Boy know that?

She turned her attention to Vincent Pugliese. He was just about the right age—fifty—and he was an underboss with the Castiglione family, the highest he could go without being named Castiglione. She had no knowledge of how he had met the Butcher's Boy, but she supposed all the ways were unlikely but one.

She scrolled to the thumbnail pictures and clicked on a few to enlarge them. There was a set of mug shots from 1980, when he was convicted of violating the Illinois concealed-firearm laws. On the day of his arrest he had been very well dressed, with an expensive haircut and a calm, relaxed expression. He had been handsome in those days.

The Justice Department file on him had more recent photographs, all surveillance photographs taken with a telephoto lens. There was nothing very revealing. Here he was coming out of a Chicago restaurant called Rangione's Villa Venetia. A parking attendant had just brought up a black Mercedes sedan that was probably his.

There was another of him on a golf course waiting to tee off—again looking prosperous, relaxed, and calm. He was leaning on his driver and holding his ball and a tee in his right hand. She recognized two of the men with him as Castiglione brothers. The third, who was teeing off, was unfamiliar to her. She looked at the note below. It said the man was Wilson McGee, the professional golfer. Of course, it would be somebody like that. Mafiosi loved celebrities.

She was almost positive now that VP was Vincent Pugliese. There were no other candidates who had all the qualities and who felt right. She had heard twenty years ago that the Butcher's Boy had grown up in the Midwest. To her that meant at least some relationship with LCN, most likely including some members of the Castiglione organization. Even if they weren't the employer, they would demand that anybody who made his living murdering people in their territory check in with them. They wouldn't want somebody collecting on a relative or a vital business associate. There would have been plenty of opportunities for the Butcher's Boy to meet Vincent Pugliese when they were both young.

There was also the complicated relationship between the two Chicago Mafia families and the five families in New York. From time to time for nearly a century the New York families had claimed some kind of primacy over the Chicago families. All of those claims had been denied and all incursions repelled. There had been nothing she knew of in the past twenty years, but maybe there was one Chicago capo who was not unhappy to see Frank Tosca die and the Balacontano family in confusion.

Anything could be happening, but what she believed was that there would be a moment when Vincent Pugliese would meet with the Butcher's Boy to talk about his future. It would take place within a few days, and it would be in or near Chicago, where there was some assurance that Pugliese could offer protection.

She walked down the long hallway. It occurred to her that this was the third time in about a week when she had, in advance, seen the path of the Butcher's Boy converging with the path of someone else in a certain place at a certain time and not been able to do anything about it herself.

She stopped at Ed Morris's office and knocked. Morris's assistant, Mike Tucker, looked up, then looked surprised, and stood. "Ms. Waring. What can I do for you?"

"I'd like about five minutes of Ed's time, if it's possible."

"Let me ask if he's able to see you right now." He knocked on the inner door and then stepped inside, and then came back out with Ed Morris.

Morris said, "Elizabeth, please come in." Elizabeth wasn't surprised by the way he treated her. Morris was, in his heart, a cop, and he had that almost courtly manner that a lot of them had. As he held the door for her, he appeared to almost bow.

When she was inside, he said, "Can I have Mike get you anything to drink—a coffee? Bottled water?"

"No thanks," she said. "The walk to this end of the hall is all of a hundred and twenty feet. I came to ask for some closely held information. I want to know if there's anybody—us, the FBI, the Chicago police—doing any surveillance on a man named Vincent Pugliese right now. He's an underboss in the Castiglione family."

"We're not," he said. "I mean not on him personally. We might get him because he's half of somebody else's phone call, or he might be noticed by the airport surveillance teams. But let me get Mike on this. It takes about ten minutes and a couple of phone calls, but when he gets the answer, you can rely on it."

"Thanks, Ed," she said.

He went out for a few seconds, then returned. "He's on it. If there isn't a surveillance operation on Vincent Pugliese, do you want us to start work on authorizing one?"

"I don't know yet," she said. "I'll get back to you if we need one.

Thanks, Ed." She had no probable cause for any kind of search or eavesdropping on Pugliese. "I'll be interested to know if somebody's already doing it."

As she walked back along the hall toward her office, she considered the issue of retirement. She had put in more than twenty years at this job, but she wasn't old enough yet to take retirement payments without a tax penalty. Both kids were going to be ready for college soon. She had saved for their tuition, but certainly not enough. She was going to be trapped in the Justice Department for at least the next six years. Or maybe it was seven years.

She was going to do it. She could hardly ignore a chance like this, but there was no way Hunsecker would approve an operation to turn the Butcher's Boy. The idea that she intended to lead it—go to Chicago and direct an armed arrest—would make him crazy. But she would have to find a way to do it.

She went to the computer and looked at maps of the area around the address of Vincent Pugliese, then looked at it from the air, and finally at ground level. She printed everything and put the copies into her briefcase. She would have to show Ed Morris the VP personal ad she had seen in the newspaper so she went onto the *Los Angeles Times* website and printed the ad.

Years ago, under a very different deputy assistant AG, she had been issued a carry permit. But the compact .32 she carried in her purse wouldn't do. She would have to go to the gun safe that her husband had installed in their basement and get the nine-millimeter pistol that had been locked in there for years. After that, she would have to talk Ed Morris into putting the operation under his aegis and lending her a couple of his investigators who were up to this kind of work.

23

MAYBE THE EASE of the old men's lives had made them forget how it felt to be vulnerable like other people. A human being was a small, pink, weak creature that trained itself from its first discovery of death to keep changing the subject, and they seemed to have forgotten this.

Or maybe it was the theatrical quality of their daily existence. From the time they came into power they were placed one level away from real dirt and blood and tears, and became actors in a pageant. They strutted down city streets with big stone-faced bodyguards who looked like bulls to exemplify their power. As long as they were awake, there were people opening their doors and driving their cars and pulling out their chairs as though they were eastern princes. They sat at tables in the backs of restaurants that were kept empty just in case they came in, their faces set in an imperial scowl. They were surrounded by oily advisors and lieutenants who whispered schemes in their ears while messengers stood by waiting for the chance to deliver some bad news to somebody. Now and then one of them would go into a tantrum, a barrage of threats and curses intended to make an audience feel fear strong enough so the jolt would be conducted down the branching circuits of the organization to the people who did the work.

It seemed to Schaeffer that they must have forgotten a great many things they needed to remember. The biggest of them this week was whom they had casually agreed to kill. It had been completely unnecessary, and it apparently had been decreed without much thought. Did it even occur to any of them that there might be a price to pay? They seemed to have forgotten that down at street level killing looked different.

There was a simple clarity to killing, and it was his only way forward. He had to remind a group of multimillionaires who had gotten used to thinking of themselves as immortal that death could overtake them at any time. He also had to teach them that even a solitary enemy could do them terrible harm.

During much of the long drive from Denver to Chicago, he had been considering exactly what he wanted to accomplish, and now he had decided. He stopped to buy a pair of thin leather gloves, some hooded sweatshirts, some running shoes.

He had kept the two Beretta M92 pistols he had stolen in Houston. Before he had left Texas he had bought two spare magazines and two boxes of nine-millimeter ammo. He was aware that the brass casings of the bullets loaded into the guns carried the fingerprints of the owners in Houston, and he liked that. He loaded the spare magazines wearing gloves.

He was going to have to work quickly to make the proper impression. He began by thinking about the Castiglione organization in Chicago. All three of the Castiglione brothers had been at the ranch in Arizona, and so they were all implicated in the decision to have him killed. And since Vincent Pugliese was their underboss, he had certainly put the personal ad in all the newspapers with their knowledge and approval. It was not a surprise that the brothers had no love for him. Twenty years ago, when he had been trying to cause enough confusion to get the families to believe a war had broken out, he had killed old Salvatore Castiglione, their grandfather. He had gotten old and gone to live in Las Vegas, where he did little besides meet once a month with the men who oversaw the family's interests there. The stratagem had worked. Schaeffer had gotten out of the country and lived twenty years that they would have denied him.

He drove toward the old Castiglione mansion on Lake Shore Drive. In the days before old Salvatore, the Mafia families in Chicago were insular. They lived in Italian neighborhoods, where everybody spoke Italian. The women went to the big churches in the center of the city. The men went on Christmas and Easter and never confessed or took Communion. There was always the shadow of Al Capone, who was considered to be the prime example of what publicity did to people. But old Salvatore had simply drawn the line in a different place. He bought a mansion that had been built fifty years earlier for the heir of one of the big meatpacking fortunes. He never spoke a word in public and lived conservatively like a bank president—which, for a while, he was. After he retired to Las Vegas, his son took over for him, and when the son was ready to retire, he said he didn't want his sons to split the family three ways, so they shared power.

Schaeffer drove north on Lake Shore Drive, with the bright blue lake on his right and the houses on the left. After a half mile of big old houses, the Castiglione mansion appeared. It looked just about the way it had twenty years ago. It had a shell of brownish-gray stone and sat on a big green lawn behind a fence of the same brown-gray stone. Its slate roofs were steep, like the mansard roofs of French châteaux. Maybe because of the family name, and maybe because of the way it looked, people called it the Castle.

The second time he had been inside was when Vince Pugliese brought him here to get his pay for solving the Milwaukee problem. When the rounded front door opened, he noticed that the wood was three inches thick. Later Vince had told him that the doors were designed to sandwich a quarter-inch steel plate between two layers of oak. The windows were recessed into the outer walls such that the glass was only about five inches wide. It wasn't until he moved to Europe that he recognized the design was a copy of the arrow slits of castles.

He and Vince had followed one of the bodyguards through a big room with long tables and a raised gallery that ran around the room near the high ceiling. At the end of the big room was a smaller room like a study where the old man waited. Another bodyguard stood near the door. The old man was bald with a close-cropped fringe of white hair. He had the eyes of a vulture—penetrating, but devoid of any heat except voracity and irritability.

People addressed him as Don Salvatore, and when he spoke to his men, it was in Italian. He stared at Schaeffer as he produced a manila envelope and held it out to Vincent Pugliese, who handed it to Schaeffer. He whispered, "Don't count it here."

Schaeffer nodded at Salvatore and said, "Thank you," and put it in the pocket under his left arm. Vince said a few sentences in Italian. Schaeffer could see it was an account of the gunfight in the cornfield, which ended in his holding up both hands wide-eyed and counting off eight fingers. The old man laughed and the bodyguards laughed harder. The old man opened the drawer again, selected a banded stack of bills, and tossed it to Schaeffer, who caught it. Then the old man waved his hand in a shooing gesture, and they left.

They went outside, walked to Schaeffer's rental car, and got in. Schaeffer handed Pugliese the stack of bills.

Pugliese looked at him in surprise. "You giving this to me?"

"He paid me for what I did. That was for the story."

Pugliese put it into his coat pocket and patted it to make it lie flat. "Yeah, the old man loves stories where people get killed."

As he drove past, he could see two cars in the circular driveway in front of the house and three more in the garage. Somebody was still living there. It would be Joe, the oldest of the three grandsons. Schaeffer kept going to find the houses of the other brothers. He needed to be sure they hadn't moved.

24

IT WAS STILL the middle of the night, and he had driven to look at the houses of the two younger Castiglione brothers. What he wanted to do tonight was going to be difficult. The Castigliones probably had gotten lazy and overconfident by now, but he already had evidence that Vince Pugliese hadn't. Sending men out to motels to kill him before he could make it to town was definitely Vince.

He had shown Vince some things that day so many years ago, when he had killed the eight men who had been waiting in ambush. Vince had shown him some things too—his physical courage, his intelligence, his ability to read and manipulate his bosses. Vince was a stronger, leaner opponent than the others had been. Vince would be aware within an hour or two that four of his men had been killed in the motel. It was possible that he had known they'd be killed, and had been willing to sacrifice them to know where Schaeffer was and when he would enter the city. When he knew, Vince would start moving his other men around, pulling them back toward the center of the city to protect the Castiglione neighborhoods. It was important to be on the inside of the circle before it tightened.

He was almost positive that the oldest brother, Joe, would still be living in old Salvatore's house. The Castle was an important place, a symbol of Castiglione power and legitimacy. He drove past the building and saw that all the lights seemed to be out, but side by side in front of the closed garage were three big black cars, all backed into the driveway so they faced the street. The house was definitely occupied, and the three cars looked as though they belonged to people who thought they might want to get out fast. Joe Castiglione was in the Castle, and Schaeffer was going in after him. The Castle was the hardest target he could have chosen, but that made it the one he had to hit first. Right now, Joe Castiglione would be feeling relieved to be out of Arizona and happy to be back in the big old house where he thought he was safe.

Joe was the oldest of the three grandsons who ran the family now, and he was supposed to be the smartest. The fact that he was still living in the Castle meant that he was still the leader of the three brothers. He looked a little bit like old Salvatore — thin and tall, so his expensive suits hung on him. Everything was loose. Even when he was very young, he was a little bent over, so the resemblance to the grandfather was strong.

His reputation for cunning was earned. The two rivals most likely to kill him and take over were his two younger brothers, but as soon as his father had died, he engaged them in watching his back and overseeing the details of the Castiglione businesses.

Schaeffer drove to the parking lot of a big white hotel a few blocks up Lake Shore Drive from the Castle. He opened the trunk, leaned in, and took apart the shotgun so he could fit most of the barrel and stock into his messenger bag and keep the shotgun from being identifiable from a distance. He put in a box of shells, slung the bag over his shoulder, and set off on foot. He knew it was possible that what he was doing was foolish and that he would be dead before the sun came up. But if he could get the Castigliones, none of the other old men would feel safe.

He felt the weight of the shotgun and shells. He remembered the night thirty-five years ago when he and Eddie had gone after the Mahons in Providence. They had a poker game in the back of a bar called the Pot of Gold. On the roof was a sign, a faint, chipped, and discolored painting of a leprechaun beside a big white vessel that looked like an antique chamber pot. The sign didn't light up anymore, and people just called the place the "Pot."

Eddie took two short-barreled pump shotguns out of a closet and loaded them before he put them in the car trunk.

The boy asked, "Why are you bringing those?"

"Because I don't own a machine gun."

"Huh?"

"There's a reason why a twelve-gauge shotgun is the weapon of choice for home defense. It's a hell of a lot more lethal than anything you can hide in your pants. A double-ought shell has twelve pellets, each of them the size of a .38 bullet. When you're inside a room, your shot travels maybe ten, fifteen feet before it hits something. At that distance, the twelve pellets have hardly separated at all. It's like getting hit with one big slug. It makes a hole you can almost put your hand through. At fifty feet the pattern is still only ten inches. If you shoot one of the Mahons down, he's going to stay down."

Eddie had specific instructions about everything. "We burst in, you go left, and I go right. We shoot the first ones we see. Then shoot the first one who moves. If nobody moves, just shoot the next one. You do that for six shells—one in the chamber and five in the tube—then drop the shotgun and pull your pistol out. By then everybody who's going to die that day should be dead, but if one's not, send him along. I'd like the whole thing done in ten seconds."

That night at the poker game they had burst in and seen a dozen men—seven poker players and five just hanging around—and at least half of them were in the process of reaching for a gun. The boy had shot six men and dropped the empty shotgun, then pulled out his pistol and prepared to fire, but Eddie had already killed the others. "Nicely done, kid," he said, then snatched up some wads of money from the floor where it had fallen and a few wallets from pockets that weren't soaked with blood. The room was a storeroom for beer and spirits, so it had a concrete floor with a drain in the center. The boy could hear the blood trickling into it as he watched the door. As Eddie had planned, the theft made the police think that someone had wanted to rob a poker game, and then panicked when they'd realized they'd picked the Mahons' personal club, and then killed everybody in sight. It made a good story.

Now, thirty years later, he was walking into the Castigliones' neighborhood again, this time carrying a messenger bag with a shotgun inside. He was eager to test his theory about the Castle. He had always believed that the defenses were concentrated in the front, where there was an electric motor that opened a wrought-iron gate. Beyond the gate was a set of holes in the pavement for anchoring barriers so a car or truck couldn't crash the gate and reach the house.

He walked along the stone fence. He knew there must be an alarm system on the property. As soon as he had the thought, he saw the alarm company's sign stuck in the garden, but it didn't worry him too much. There was almost always some part in every house that was too hard or expensive to wire so it was skipped, and he had a theory about this house. He went over the fence and walked to the side of the house. Then he dropped to his belly and looked in the first basement window. There was a room that held a furnace and hot water heater, but the room beside it looked like a gentleman's study. The overhead lights were off, but there were two night-lights plugged in along the cellar stairs leading to the first floor for safety. He examined the frame of the basement window. It was steel, with a latch in the upper edge. He looked closely at the material around the steel frame. It was solid concrete. There seemed to be no way that the jacketed cable for an alarm system could be run through the concrete to the window frame. He looked across the corner of the basement at the next nearest window. He could see no wires or cables running from the wooden floor above the window, and nothing coming up from below. The basement windows didn't seem to be wired into the system.

He put strips of duct tape on the glass of the small, low window, then crossed the strips with vertical ones. He opened his messenger bag, took out the butt end of the shotgun, and rammed the glass once. The glass gave a pop, but the pieces all stayed together. He pulled the glass out and lay it on the ground. He heard no alarm.

Turning to put his feet first, he lowered himself into the room with the furnace. He looked carefully for the small red and green lights that would indicate an electric beam that would set off the alarm if he broke it, but the basement seemed to be clear. He moved into the room that looked like a study, sat on a leather couch, and fitted the two halves of his shotgun together. He reached into the messenger bag, extracted five shells, and loaded the shotgun. He pumped the slide once. The "snick-chuck" sound reminded him again of the night in Providence. The rest of Eddie's instructions came back as he walked to the stairs. "Hold the butt of it tight to your shoulder so the kick doesn't punch you in the face or some damned thing. Never fire a twelve-gauge from your hip. You're a hell of a lot scarier staring down that long barrel so you can hit what you shoot at. And keep both eyes open. In a gunfight everything that's alive is moving, and that's what you've got to see." As an afterthought, he added, "And click that safety off. Once you're in somebody else's building, anybody you kill by accident is just one you won't have to kill on purpose."

He climbed the stairs quietly, switched off the night-light so there would be no glow behind him, opened the door, and raised the shotgun to his right shoulder. He looked down the barrel at the room. It was the kitchen. Big windows let in moonlight, and he could see it was empty. It was a huge room, equipped like an old-fashioned restaurant, with appliances that were heavy, not pretty, and big iron pots and pans.

Beyond the kitchen there was a hallway that led forward toward the front of the house, and he could tell the wall to the right side was the storage space under the staircase. He moved ahead. The closer he got to the heart of the house before the occupants woke, the more damage he could do.

He reached the foyer, an octagonal shape with windows up high that let moonlight in to throw a shine on the black-and-white tile. The stairway to his right was wide and had a curve that reminded him of the stairways to the loge in the movie theater he used to go to when he was about eleven or twelve. It had thick patterned carpet like that and brass rods at the corners to keep it from sliding. He sensed it was a trap. He didn't know how it was managed—an interior alarm system, a motion detector, an electric eye like the ones at the doors of stores, a trip wire, a pressure strip under the carpet—and it didn't matter. If they had an alarm system, what they'd want to protect most was the bedrooms at the top of those stairs. He backtracked toward the kitchen.

He found the other staircase between the pantry and the cellar door where he'd come in. He tested the back stairs to see if they creaked. They were old, part of the original design of the house, probably so the maids could get up and down without disturbing the owners. But they weren't creaking, and they were plain, bare hardwood with no carpet to hide anything. In a moment he was on the second floor, which consisted of a long hallway with bedrooms on either side. He went from doorway to doorway, staring in each room. All eight were furnished, but none of them was occupied tonight.

Joe's children had apparently all grown up and moved out. But it was odd that there weren't any bodyguards asleep on the second floor. He had seen cars in the space in front of the garage. It occurred to him that it was possible Castiglione wasn't at home. He might have been held for some infraction at the ranch in Arizona or decided not to be available to reporters.

Schaeffer returned to the servants' staircase and climbed to the third floor. As soon as he opened the door into the hallway, he knew this floor was inhabited. He heard snoring. There were two bedrooms at his end of the hall, and a single door at the opposite end, which he guessed was a master suite that took up one wing.

Between the ends of the hall there was one huge room with big windows facing the lake, and a wide-open portal. The room must once have been an upstairs sitting room because it offered a spectacular view. In the morning, it would be filled with sunlight. In the afternoon, when the sun was on the other side of the house, it would be a good place to look out at the boats on the lake. Probably parties had been held up here.

But this end of it had been transformed into what looked like a barrack. There were eight sets of bunk beds set up in two rows. The bunks didn't look like a recent development, something someone would do just for a couple of days. It would be too much trouble. A number of times over the years the Castigliones had been involved in rivalries and struggles for dominance. There must have been times when they gathered a group of their soldiers into the Castle to defend it and themselves. He heard more sounds of snoring and deep, unconscious breathing and stepped closer, studying the bunk beds from different angles. There was a man asleep in the big room.

Before he did anything else, he needed to clear the rooms by the back stairs to be sure his escape wouldn't be blocked. He opened the first, and it looked like a hotel storeroom with shelves full of linens and blankets and paper goods. The second was a large bathroom remodeled for multiple people, with toilet stalls and a shower room with three stations. He moved quietly back into the big room.

He looked down at the sleeping man in the bunk. The moment that he started the killing, all of this silence and stillness was going to shatter, and he would have to be in motion. He prepared himself.

He aimed the shotgun at the head of the man in the bunk and fired. The roar was deafening, and the man's body jumped on the springs, but there wasn't much left of his head.

Schaeffer's left hand was pumping his shotgun as he ran for the single door at the end of the short hall. He knew that the less time he took, the better his chances were, so he lifted his right foot and stomp-kicked the door. The door swung inward, splinters flying, and he dashed in after it, his shotgun aimed at the bed. He flicked on the overhead light.

There were two people in it, a man and a woman. The man was Joe Castiglione, but the woman was much younger, probably her mid twenties, with long bleach-blond hair. Castiglione was in the middle of a half roll, reaching into a drawer in his nightstand.

As Castiglione fumbled to get the gun in his hand, Schaeffer shot him in the back of the head. The woman screamed, her hands clawing at the sides of her head like talons.

"Shut up," he said.

She took a deep breath to scream again so he shot her, and she sprawled backward on the bed, her arms spread like wings.

He picked up the ejected shotgun shells in the bedroom and then the one he'd fired in the big room, and then went down the back stairs. He climbed out the basement window and pushed it shut behind him, and then took his shotgun apart and put it in his messenger bag. He walked quickly away from the house along Lake Shore Drive toward the parking lot where he had left his car, put the bag in the trunk, and drove off toward the next house.

The point would not be made without the other two brothers. The second one was Paul, and the youngest Sal. He knew he had no more than an hour or two to do the rest of the job and get out of town.

When he arrived in Paul's neighborhood, it was three A.M. The night air was cool and fresh, just a stealthy breeze flowing onto the land off Lake Michigan. In the evening it had seemed hot, but as he walked along the street, the air felt alive to him. It filled his lungs and gave him new energy.

Paul Castiglione lived only a couple of minutes from his older brother. His house was an old redbrick two-story cubical building that had a white wooden porch in front with Doric columns.

It wasn't quite a mansion, but the sort of house that had probably been built just after the Great Chicago Fire and painstakingly restored by whomever Paul had bought it from.

Schaeffer drove past and scanned to be sure there were no clusters of cars and that the street behind looked about the same as the last time he'd been here. He parked just around the corner, where he could reach his car quickly, but where it couldn't be seen from the house. He opened the trunk, took the two Beretta pistols, and put them in his jacket. He closed the trunk, walked up to the house, and looked into the window of the garage. There were three cars inside, a black Cadillac, a black Corvette, and a black SUV that seemed to be about seven feet tall. Even though he'd been in the United States ten years ago, the sight of those big SUVs still startled him with their ugliness and impracticality. But he was pleased. The three cars looked as though they represented three moods of Paul Castiglione—pretentious, childish, and stupid.

He walked around the building, examining window latches through the glass, testing doorknobs. Through the window near the front door he saw that there was an alarm system. It probably wasn't the kind that rang in the office of a security service or a police station because Paul Castiglione wouldn't want to give the cops a legal excuse for bursting into his house, but he was sure it would make noise. He could see the keypad lights glowing on the wall. He thought it probably wasn't necessary, but in case he made a mistake, he went to the rear of the house, opened the phone junction box, and disconnected the telephone wires.

There had to be a way around the alarm system because there always was. As he continued around the house, he found it. Set in the wall beside the kitchen door was an old-fashioned milk delivery box. There was a small wooden cabinet door with a weathered brass latch on the outside so the milkman could put the bottles of milk in it. Inside there would be another door that opened inward so the cook could bring the milk bottles into the kitchen.

It was a long-obsolete feature. Nobody now would have a little door set into the brick facing like that. The renovators must have left it there because antique details reminded people that this house was the real thing and not a copy. He reached up and turned the little knob and the milk door opened. He pushed on the inner door, but it was locked. He looked in and he could see four small brass screw heads flush with the surface of the door. He looked at the inner side of the outer door to compare, then used his lock-blade knife to unscrew the four screws. When he pushed the door inward, it moved. He jiggled it a bit, moving it inward until he could get his hand in and pull the latch free.

He studied the dimensions of the milk door. In the years since he had left the trade, he had aged, but he was still relatively flexible, and he judged that he could fit his middle through the two-foot square. He took off his jacket, heavy with his two pistols, and hung it on the brass handle on the door. He ducked to get his head and arms into the opening, turned sideways to get his shoulders in, and then pushed against the inner wall to slide in to his hips. He could reach a counter to his right now so he used it to pull himself the rest of the way in and get his left foot on the floor and then the right.

Turning to reach outside, he grasped his jacket and brought it in with him. He put it on, closed the milk door, stood with his back against the wall with the two pistols in his hands, and listened. There were only the tiny, barely audible sounds of a house—the refrigerator compressor, the air-conditioning system.

He moved forward into the kitchen. He had always preferred to take a great deal of time so a listener would not connect one of his moves or sounds with another. Tonight he had to bend time in the opposite direction, moving from place to place more quickly than anyone would expect. He had to find and kill Paul Castiglione, and then get inside Sal's defenses before he knew his brothers were dead.

He was halfway across the kitchen when Paul Castiglione materialized in the doorway in a big, loose-fitting bathrobe and bare feet. Castiglione took a couple of steps and opened the refrigerator door. The light spilled out of it onto the floor and splashed the walls.

Castiglione leaned over and squinted into the refrigerator, and then the sight he'd seen in his peripheral vision as he'd turned registered in his brain, and he jerked his head and looked. "Holy shit."

"Hello, Paul." The two pistols came up in Schaeffer's hands, so that Castiglione saw not only the shape of a man in his kitchen, but also a vaguely familiar face staring at him above the dark, gleaming muzzles of the two Berettas.

"It's you. What would you come to me for? I can't save you."

"I never asked." He shot Castiglione. In the light of the open refrigerator, he could see that the single shot had passed through his forehead. Schaeffer heard a woman's voice call from upstairs, "Paul? What was that? Did you knock something over?"

Schaeffer had to make a decision. Going through the house, first killing the woman and then maybe Castiglione's kids, would take time and do nothing for him. It was too late to preserve the quiet. He had to get to the third brother as quickly as he could. He turned, stepped out the kitchen door, and closed it again. Beyond the door he could hear the alarm, an electronic imitation of a bell ringing. He ran hard toward the car, got in, and drove off. The first time he had to stop at a traffic signal, he retrieved the shotgun from the trunk and reloaded it, then propped it on the passenger seat beside him.

It took him fifteen minutes to reach Salvatore Castiglione's house, and he could see he had not made it in time. Paul Castiglione's wife must have come downstairs, seen her husband's body, and started dialing the phone. The house was a suburban one-story ranch-style house set on a large lawn with a pine grove behind it and along the sides to form a narrow privacy barrier at the edges of the property. As he drove past, he could see that in spite of the fact that it was nearly four A.M., there were already lights on in the house and the shapes of men moving across the front windows. A big black car with tinted windows sat in the driveway with its motor idling. It had to be Pugliese's men, here to get Sal out of danger. Schaeffer kept going, heading his car to the north toward Milwaukee.

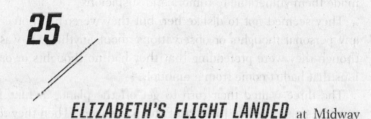

25

ELIZABETH'S FLIGHT LANDED at Midway at four P.M. She was traveling with the two Justice Department investigators Morris had temporarily assigned to her. Morris had chosen Manoletti and Irwin, both of them men about forty years old, with at least a dozen years of field experience. They inspired confidence, but they weren't very good companions for her. They were businesslike and distant. They considered themselves "sworn" peace officers, like cops and FBI agents. The fact that everyone in the Justice Department took the same oath to preserve and defend the Constitution from all enemies, foreign or domestic, meant nothing. The gun she was carrying at this moment didn't make her one of them either. It only made them more nervous about her. She wasn't entirely satisfied with them. In spite of the fact that Morris knew she wanted to do some undercover surveillance, he'd picked men who looked like cops. They both had that triangular torso that men who lifted weights often achieved, so the seams of their sport coats looked strained. They looked as though they'd gotten their hair cut on a military base.

There was never a way for them to forget she was on the other side of the department, the side with lawyers and administrators and analysts—she had become all three—and she was several levels above them on a parallel branch of the hierarchy. Worse, she was a woman. In the twenty years she'd been in Justice, women had become common, but there were still men who seemed determined to maintain a distance. Sometimes she had suspected that their aloofness was a strain of puritanical discipline left over from an earlier time. A woman, if she looked like a woman, was a temptation and a threat to their integrity. They probably knew that Elizabeth posed no threat to their chastity, but her presence still made them vulnerable to rumors and suspicions.

They seemed not to dislike her, but they weren't volunteering any personal thoughts or observations about anything. It was as though they were pretending that they had no thoughts or opinions that hadn't come from a manual.

The three waited their turn to get off the plane, inching forward in single file like the rest of the passengers. Then they rode the escalators down to get their luggage. Manoletti was the first to get his suitcase, so he went out of the baggage area, by prearrangement, to get an early place in the cab line. When Elizabeth stepped out with Irwin, Manoletti already had the cab waiting with its trunk and back door open.

At the hotel they went to their respective rooms without much consultation. Elizabeth had learned many years ago to open a suitcase immediately and hang up anything that could hang. As soon as she had her suitcase up on the folding rack, she called home and left the kids a message. "I wanted to let you guys know I'm on the ground in Chicago and I'm in my hotel, the Hyatt. When you two get home, if you feel like calling me, please do. I have my phone on. And here's the hotel number." She read it off the sticker on the telephone, then hung up. She turned on the television set and found a news program. She half listened for a weather report.

". . . savage attack at the home of Joseph Castiglione, in which two men and a woman were killed by shotgun blasts. This was followed by—"

She dialed the number of Irwin's BlackBerry with her left hand. "Turn on your TV," she said.

"We've got it on," he said. She could hear the voice of a different newscaster in the background.

"We've got to meet about this. Call me in a few minutes."

Elizabeth dialed the number of her office and Geoffrey answered, "Justice Department, Organized Crime."

"Geoff, it's me. There's something about Joseph Castiglione on the news. Did something happen while we were in the air?"

"We're trying to sort it out. Two of the Castiglione brothers are dead—Joe and Paul. There are also four men described as Castiglione associates dead at a motel south of Chicago."

"I can't believe it," she said. "What does he think he's doing?"

Geoffrey ignored the question. "Special Agent Holman from the FBI called on your personal line when you were still on the plane. I gave him your cell number. I hope that's okay."

"Of course. I thought he already had it. He hasn't called me yet. Do you have IDs for the bodies?"

"They haven't been released, but the FBI had them, and they e-mailed the list to you."

"Is there a Vincent Pugliese?"

"No. The names all sound like stops on an Italian train schedule, but he wasn't one of them."

"Good work, Geoff. I've got Holman's number on my phone, so I'll try to get back to him."

"I'll be here for a while, and I'll relay whatever comes in to you."

"Thanks. If nothing hits by seven, go home. The next shift can take over. Just tell them I'm here and I'm interested."

"I'll do that."

"Got to go." She hung up and took the call that was coming in. "Waring."

"Hi, Elizabeth. This is John Holman. I hope I didn't interrupt your dinner or anything. If so, I can—" His voice sounded different. It was openly friendly, as though she had passed some very big test.

"No, you're not interrupting. I'm in Chicago right now, and I expect dinner isn't any time soon."

"How did you get word so fast?"

"The short, honest answer is that it was a coincidence. I was flying here looking into something else, and this seems to have happened while we were in the air. I just got to the airport Hyatt and turned on the TV."

"Our people there are on it, of course, and I'll let them know you're in town. If you want anything, just call the Chicago office. Or stop by. It's on West Roosevelt. They'll know who you are. I'm flying in this evening. When you get this figured out, give me a call."

"That's flattering, but I don't expect it will be me who figures this out."

"We'll see. I'll call when I'm there."

She sat for a second, staring at her phone. This was the way Justice and the FBI were supposed to work, but sometimes didn't. She suspected that the difference wasn't a change in the institutional mentalities. It was just a matter of proving to someone on the other team that you could be trusted.

There was a loud knock on the door of her room. She got up and went to the peephole to look out. She could see Irwin and Manoletti, so she opened the door. "Come on in."

The two came inside, and she pointed to the two chairs at the small table near the window. They sat, and she turned the desk chair to face them. "Lots of news, and it's got to make for lots of changes. You know what I wanted to accomplish here. As of right now, things look a lot more difficult."

"We seem to have arrived at the beginning of a war," Manoletti said. "If he's as wily as you think he is, he won't want to be anywhere near that."

"I don't think that's what it is," she said. "It's not what I would have predicted he'd do, but I think this is still him."

"You do?" said Irwin.

"I think the reason he came to Chicago was the personal ad from Vincent Pugliese, the Castiglione underboss. It was a trap, and that made him angry, so he decided to hurt the Castigliones, to make an example of them."

"With all due respect, ma'am . . ." Irwin looked uncomfortable.

"Go ahead," she said.

"Well, it's four men in a motel, a man in Joseph Castiglione's house, Castiglione himself. That's six. Paul Castiglione makes seven. These are not pushovers either. They're all made guys who have never done anything for a living in their lives that wasn't criminal."

"You got a list of the names?"

"Morris did, from the Chicago police," he said.

Manoletti said, "And if those guys were all bunched up like that, in groups, they were expecting something. At first glance, it doesn't look like one man."

"That they were expecting? Or who did it?"

"Either," said Irwin. "Too many armed wiseguys to turn into bodies."

"What do you think might have happened?"

Irwin said, "The thing about being in a real-world gunfight is that while you're shooting one man, his four friends have time to shoot you. So unless the guys on the other side are unarmed or unconscious, the score ends at one to one. For that reason alone, I would guess this was a squad of four or five shooters moving quickly and knowing exactly where they were going, how to get in, and where their targets would be."

"And to me, that says Vincent Pugliese," said Manoletti. "I think the personal ad was for real. I don't see this as the Butcher's Boy, after twenty years, deciding to live up to his name and scare the crap out of the whole Cosa Nostra. It sounds like he and Pugliese getting together and deciding to get rid of the three little Caesars and their palace guards in one night. If they succeed, Vincent Pugliese is the sole boss of the Castiglione organization."

"What's in it for the Butcher's Boy?"

"You've been thinking that there was a contract for him because he killed Frank Tosca, and the old men didn't like it. Maybe as head of the Castiglione family, Pugliese has enough power to protect his favorite killer if he wants."

"Maybe you're right," she said. "When I asked Morris to assign you to this trip, the situation wasn't as fluid and unpredictable as it is now. I had the impression that he was alone and friendless, and that he might be ready to cooperate with the Justice Department. You were going to stand by while I raised the possibility."

"There's another wrinkle," Manoletti said. "We just got a text message from Morris. The FBI has this from here on. Irwin and I are ordered home."

"When?"

"Tonight," Manoletti said. He handed his BlackBerry to Elizabeth. She looked at the message and handed it back.

Elizabeth said, "Well, I guess you'd better get your flight arranged. I hope we actually get to work on something in the future." She held out her hand and each of them shook it.

Manoletti cocked his head. "Aren't you coming back with us?"

"No. When this mess came to light and we were on the plane, the FBI called, so now that I'm here I'm going to see what I can do to understand what's happening. I'll be back in my office bright and early Monday."

"Good luck," Irwin said. "I hope you land your informant."

"Thanks," she said. "But he's probably far away by now. We'll see what we can learn from what he left behind."

The two men went to their room to repack, and Elizabeth locked the door behind them. She called the local FBI and introduced herself. She could tell immediately that Holman must have called them. A woman named Special Agent Cable got on the line and said, "A car is on its way to you now, Ms. Waring. The two agents will take you to the scene. Their ETA is about ten minutes."

"Perfect. I'll be waiting."

"Yes, ma'am."

Elizabeth was beginning to like these people. They had a stripped, unembellished way of speaking and a direct decisiveness when they were working, just as Jim had when she'd met him. They all seemed to have an almost military sense of discipline. As she was having that thought, she realized that what she had been doing today would not have been tolerated at the FBI. By now they would have fired her about three times. Holman was undoubtedly aware of that. She was useful and helpful in this set of circumstances, but he wouldn't want her to be part of his organization. She was in terrible trouble in her own job and could easily be out of work in a week.

She went down to the lobby, sat in one of the easy chairs, and looked out the tall glass windows at the cars going by on the street, and more surreptitiously, at the cars that pulled to a stop in the circular drive.

She was in the waning part of a day when she wasn't quite sure what her job was. Her boss seemed to think it was staying at her desk in the office in Washington and collecting intelligence about the Mafia, mostly from amassing police reports and court cases and wiretap transcripts, many of them years old. Her section did perform those tasks. But every one of her people was looking for bits of information that brought them forward in time, information that could lead to arrests and convictions in the near future. They weren't simply constructing some historical archive. They were trying to keep people from being cheated and robbed and murdered.

Murder was often the avenue that was most fruitful to investigate. All kinds of suspicious things happened in the world, but not all of them involved organized crime. When witnesses disappeared and their bodies were found in fields, there was a strong likelihood that it wasn't done by a solitary perpetrator, but by one of the groups her section followed.

A car pulled up in front of the entrance and a man got out of the passenger seat and stepped into the lobby. He looked at her. "Ms. Waring?"

She stood and walked out the door with him. She shook his hand as they walked. "I'm Agent Saddler," he said. It took only thirty minutes to arrive at Joe Castiglione's big, medieval-looking stone house. The openings in the stone wall had been strung across with crime-scene tape. It looked to her as though the only ones coming in or out of the house were police technicians.

Her two companions got out of the car with her and walked toward a man in a gray suit who was standing in the driveway. Whoever went past him seemed to stop and give him some bit of information. He would nod and they would proceed. Agent Saddler said to Elizabeth, "Please wait here," ducked the tape, and approached the man in the driveway.

The man in gray came back with him. "Hello, Ms. Waring. I'm Special Agent Doug Fowles. I'll show you around."

"You're the special agent in charge?"

"Yes," he said.

"Have you had much time to look around yet?"

"We got here at seven A.M. The police called us in as soon as they had the address because they knew who lived here. But you can imagine what we've been trying to do — take fingerprints everywhere, photograph everything we can while we have access, try not to trample the scene in the process."

They went in the front door and Elizabeth stood still.

He said, "It's all right to go up the stairs. The shooter came and went on a back staircase."

"You say 'shooter.' Do you know for sure there wasn't more than one?"

"Not for sure. Never for sure at this stage. Everyone was shot with a shotgun loaded with double-ought shot. All I can say is that there was at least one."

"I think I know who he is."

He looked closely at her. "You do?"

"Not his name. He's been retired for about twenty years, but he used to be a high-end hit man. People knew of him as the Butcher's Boy. He was involved in the confusion in the Carlo Balacontano murder case. In the years since then, the old man has always wanted him dead."

"How can you tell it's him?"

"That Arizona retreat that Frank Tosca called last week was to get the families to help him find this man. He thought Carl Bala would reward him from prison by making him boss of the family. The killer found Tosca first."

"If he got Tosca, why would he come here and do this to the Castigliones?"

"I think that the other bosses didn't like it that he killed Tosca, so they're hunting him. He seems to be making his death as costly for them as possible. It's hard to know exactly what a man like him feels—what portions of his mental life haven't been permanently turned off, or what he wasn't born with. He seems to feel that once they'd agreed to come after him, they were all fair game."

Fowles took the rest of the staircase in silence. At the top of the stairs was a big room with a few metal bunk beds. Fowles said, "He came up those back stairs. He probably looked in those rooms—which are a bathroom and a closet—to be sure they were empty. Then he stepped into this area."

"Who was here?"

"One man, Jerry Grisanti, age thirty-four. He was shot once with a twelve-gauge shotgun loaded with double-ought shot. A neighbor reported hearing the shots, and it wasn't shots tumbling over one another. It was more like this: Boom. Boom. Boom. Each about a second or two apart. Which sounds like one man shooting, pumping the shotgun, and going straight to the next victim, then shooting again."

"Interesting choice, a shotgun," she said.

"He picked up the shells afterward, so there's nothing to fingerprint and no brand name to trace. The shot was the sort you'd find in a store today, nothing antique or exotic."

"I'm not surprised."

"After this man was dead, the shooter probably took a couple of quick steps to this room." He stepped to the end of the short hallway and opened the door. It was a modern, attractive master bedroom with a California king bed, a pair of matching dressers and

217

nightstands in dark-colored wood. The mattress was covered with the darkened red stain that was left when someone bled heavily. The wall beyond it had blood spatter. "Castiglione was reaching for a gun in the nightstand, but didn't have time to fire it."

"And then he shot the girl?"

"We think Castiglione was first, or he might have had time to shoot back."

Elizabeth nodded. "I appreciate your giving me the chance to see it."

"Still think it's him?" Fowles asked.

"If this and the other two scenes were the work of just one person, he'd be my leading candidate." She turned and walked toward the stairs. "Thanks again."

She descended the stairs past technicians kneeling to dust surfaces for prints and photographers taking pictures, seemingly in every room. Then she was out the front door.

The two FBI agents were waiting back at their car. Saddler said, "Would you like us to take you to the other house?"

"At the other two scenes it was a shotgun, right?"

"No, he used a pistol on Paul. One round to the forehead."

She felt a chill. He seemed to be relentless, someone who could and would do anything. "What about at the motel?"

"I understand it was a nine-millimeter pistol."

"What time of night did that happen?"

"I believe it was around two A.M., before Joe was killed. Then he went to Paul's. By then it was about four, or later."

"So the motel was the first. Can you take me there?"

"Certainly."

They drove out of town along Interstate 57 to a cheap motel. It was a relic of a generation ago, or maybe two—one long, low building with a set of doors along the side, an office near the street, and a tall sign that had NO VACANCY in neon, but the NO was probably never lit. It was easy to pick out the room because there was yellow crime-scene tape around it and the door beside it. There was a forensic team wrapping up its work when they arrived. She and her two companions got out of the car and looked in the motel-room door.

There was a woman technician just coming out holding an over-size equipment box. Saddler showed her his FBI identification. "You can take a look now," she said. "We're about done here."

Elizabeth looked inside. She saw the overturned dresser, the hole cut in the wall at the baseboard, another big blood stain. She noticed the forensic technician hadn't left. She was still there, watching Elizabeth from the doorway.

Elizabeth said, "Help me."

The woman said, "A lone man checked in at the office and came to this room in the early evening. He seems to have used the bed to sleep in. There was a couple in the next room. They say that around two A.M., some men—four of them—arrived. They walked around in the parking lot, looking in the cars, then came into his room quietly, either picking the lock or using a master key. We haven't found either yet. There was some stomping around and talking. It looks as though the man in the room had already cut a hole in the wall as an escape route and then pulled the dresser over to cover the hole. He was hiding in the unoccupied room on that side." She pointed. "They moved the dresser out of the way, and he shot two of them from the hole. The shots go up-ward into the stomach and chest of one, and the side of the other. At that point, the hiding man ran for the door of the unoccupied room to get outside. We can see bullet holes running along that wall as they tried to shoot him through it, but he must have made it and waited for them. We found the other two assailants lying outside the door of this first room. The couple in the third room waited for a while and listened until they were sure nobody was still alive, then called the police."

"And this couple—they're sure it was just one man who did this?"

"Oh, yes. As you can see, the walls aren't much. They heard him cough, but there was no talking until the assailants came."

"Thank you very much," she said. "You've helped me a lot."

She and the FBI agents walked to the car. Saddler opened the door for her and said, "I suppose he's long gone by now."

Elizabeth got into the back seat. As she spoke, she realized she was lying to an investigator who was trying to help. "I'm sure he is."

"As I recall, the last actual count we did was four hundred and forty-three soldiers in the Castiglione organization. There are probably a few we don't know about who have made their bones since. Plus assorted hangers-on, wannabes, and allies. They'll all be looking for him day and night."

"No doubt," she said. "He's probably been driving hard since about five A.M. He could be in Canada by now."

For most of her career she had never intentionally lied to another Justice Department official about anything, but now it was beginning to be a habit. In twenty years she had never pretended her opinion was different from what it really was. She had argued for her theories even when the whole Justice Department was arguing on the other side and her opinion seemed to them to be simple obstructionism. But not today. She was almost positive she knew where the Butcher's Boy was going to be tonight. If she told the FBI, they would ruin any chance she had of getting to him in time. He would be dead.

Elizabeth asked the two agents to drive her back to her hotel. It was nearly seven now. As soon as she was in her room, she locked the door, kicked off her high heels, opened her suitcase, and looked at the one outfit she had not hung up. As she usually did when she traveled, she had brought business suits—one with pants and one with a skirt that she could use interchangeably.

Now she took out the third outfit, a pair of black pants, a gray blouse, and a black cashmere jacket. The shoes were ones she had bought when she had been thinking of taking the kids to Europe. They felt as good as sneakers but didn't tell everyone instantly that she was an American tourist. They weren't stylish, but they were unobtrusive, and she could run in them.

She had almost let herself think, *Run or fight in them,* but tonight fighting would not be an option. If she was almost supernaturally perceptive and could sense when things were about to go wrong, she might be able to run.

She wondered how many other people had expected to meet him and thought about their fussy little advance preparations. Will wearing this outfit, or this one, give me an advantage? What if I bring a can of pepper spray? If I plan a route in advance that I can run efficiently from memory, will that save me? All of these decisions were nothing at all to him, the kinds of precautions he must have brushed aside a hundred times on his way to stopping somebody's heart. And the silliest of all was probably the notion that she would sense in advance that he was about to kill her, that he had weighed the options and decided that it was better for him if she died now.

Her professional self, the part of her brain that had spent twenty years studying criminals, knew that there was no way to tell if someone like him was lying. He wasn't going to telegraph anything he was thinking.

She dressed in the dark, comfortable clothes she had brought, took her pistol out of her purse and checked to be sure the magazine was full, then clicked it back in but didn't put the first round in the chamber. She had never liked guns very much, although circumstances like tonight's made them indispensable. She had an almost superstitious distrust, a feeling that they were inclined to go off unexpectedly. Their entire design was an embodiment of their purpose, and so it added a tiny physical force to an otherwise neutral object. It was hard to even pick up a gun without having your index finger slip inside the trigger guard. Keeping that finger straight along the slide took an act of will. She put the gun into her jacket, took her federal ID, her driver's license, a credit card, and a hundred dollars in cash, put them in her pockets, and locked her purse in the room's safe.

She plucked her phone out of her pocket and looked to see if she'd missed the kids' call. She hadn't. She dialed her home number, heard the ring, and then Amanda's voice. "Hello?"

"It's just your absent mother," she said. "How many people are at the party?"

"What party?"

"You mean you and your brother aren't having a huge party full of people I wouldn't approve of, doing things that would make me faint?"

"I wish. I've got a chemistry test tomorrow, and the Bad Sibling has been working on an AP polysci paper since, like, four this afternoon."

"I thought it was awfully quiet for a Festival of the Vices. How come you didn't call me?"

"You just said to call if we needed something. We were glad to know you'd landed safely and all that," she offered. "Do you want to talk to Jim?"

"No, if he's trying to concentrate on his paper, I'll let him. I'm about to go out anyway." She instantly regretted mentioning it. If something went wrong and she died tonight, she didn't want Amanda to wonder if she should have said something more or put Jim on because it would have taken up time and saved her. "If he wants to call, he's welcome. I hope to see you both late tomorrow. Love you."

"Love you."

She pocketed her phone and hooked the bow of a pair of sunglasses over her collar because the sinking sun was still bright in the west. Finally she took one last look at the enlarged street map she had printed of Vincent Pugliese's neighborhood. As a final precaution, she took the pair of police handcuffs out of her suitcase and put them in the inner pocket of her jacket. She was sure they wouldn't be of use, but carrying the proper equipment seemed to her the responsible thing to do.

As she passed the mirror, she touched her hair to get it to look fuller, but couldn't avoid looking into her own eyes. She had never planned to search for the Butcher's Boy alone. It was a stupid, risky thing to do. But things had changed radically in the past few hours. He had killed a lot of people during the night, but he hadn't

222

done what was necessary for his purposes, which was to make the sweep total. He had to get Salvatore, the last Castiglione brother. If he wanted to terrorize the old men, he had to end the dynasty and exterminate the family. And he had to get Vincent Pugliese, the man who offered him help and then sent men to kill him in his sleep. But with the city full of Castiglione soldiers and police, she could save him, offer him another way of staying alive. If he saw her with FBI agents, he would never come near her. If she was completely alone, there was a chance.

She stepped out of her room and closed the door, then walked down the hallway. She wasn't used to filling her pockets with things before she went out, particularly things as big and heavy as a pistol. Every item seemed to her to bulge or hang, but she reminded herself that there wasn't another choice this time. She was the only one who would recognize him and the only one he would recognize.

When her elevator stopped, she looked across the lobby and saw Irwin and Manoletti. They were wheeling their suitcases to the front desk. Neither of them had seen her, so she backed into the elevator and pressed the button to go to the top of the building. The doors opened and she saw the entrance to a restaurant with a small podium and a young hostess with hair that was so carefully gathered into a bun that no single loose strand showed, and it looked more like polished wood than hair. Elizabeth pressed the button for the lobby again and descended.

As she waited, she reflected that it was ridiculous to avoid the two men she had asked Morris to assign to her for this trip. She found she didn't care about being gracious. She felt a strong reluctance to talk to anyone right now. She didn't want to explain or make up a lie or answer questions or pretend. For the moment, there were only two people who mattered—her and the Butcher's Boy—and the rest of the people in Chicago were distractions or enemies.

26

HE WOKE UP in Milwaukee in the evening. He had driven out of Chicago after Salvatore Castiglione had escaped. The drive had been only a bit over an hour and took him out of Illinois and into Wisconsin. It had been a small irony to him to be taking the same drive he and Vincent Pugliese had made together the day they had broken the ambush in the cornfield.

In Milwaukee he had checked into the first large hotel he had seen, a Marriott Residence Inn, gone into his room, showered, and slept. It was now after six o'clock, and he had caught up on the portion of last night's sleep that he had lost. He felt alert and energetic and restless.

He had suffered a serious setback last night in not being able to finish the job. All three Castiglione brothers had to go. It wasn't that he had a strong feeling of dislike for Salvatore Castiglione. He had never really known young Sal in the old days. Sal had been no more than fourteen when Schaeffer had arrived to do some more work for the Castiglione family. He had seen him, but they had never spoken. He remembered young Sal in his grandfather's house when he had come in to negotiate a deal on a man named Harrow.

Harrow was a problem for the family, and old Salvatore hated to let problems go on for very long. Harrow had made some odd but unforgivable moves when he had arrived in Chicago. He had gone to a number of restaurants and demanded that they pay him a monthly fee in exchange for a guarantee that the Health Department would pass them on their inspections. He said he was an official for the public employees' union and that he was trying to work with the restaurant owners to improve conditions so the members of his union didn't have to fill out a lot of forms listing hazards and violations. He said it would help the restaurants, the city, and the customers.

Some restaurants paid him, and others didn't. The following month, the ones that hadn't paid were cited for vermin infestation, incorrect water temperature, or dirty kitchens, and closed temporarily by the Health Department. It had apparently not occurred to Harrow that he was not the first person to think of this way of making money. The ancient Romans had done it, and it was familiar to the Castiglione organization, which was already being paid to protect some of these same establishments. There were even some—the Palermo and the Bella Napoli—that were owned by people connected to the Castigliones.

Old Salvatore had not made any telephone calls or filed a complaint with City Hall, as some important men might have done. He simply told one of the young men who hung around his house all day waiting for orders to go call someone who knew how to reach the Butcher's Boy. When the Butcher's Boy arrived, they had a talk, and then Schaeffer went out to study Harrow's movements.

Two days later he reported back to old Salvatore. Harrow was not involved in any way with any union. He had simply put one of the health inspectors on his payroll. But he did have several friends, maybe relatives, who were cops. At the end of the day shift Harrow would sometimes go meet these cops at the Shamrock for a few beers.

"Cops?" said old Salvatore. "What the fuck? He hangs out with cops and they didn't tell him what he was doing to himself?"

"I don't know what they told him, or if they know about his way of getting money. But before I kill him and his inspector, I thought you should know about the cops."

"You're right. Thank you," said Castiglione. "I appreciate your manners and your good judgment. But go ahead and kill the bastards. I'd be happy if you got it done by dinnertime so those cops that drink with him will find out right away."

He went to the Health Department and waited for the inspector, followed him to his first stop, a Chinese restaurant on South LaSalle Street. He waited until the inspector left, walked up the street behind him, and shot him in the back of the head with a silenced pistol. Before the inspector collapsed onto the pavement, Schaeffer was in the middle of a crowd of people walking to the next corner. He turned at the intersection instead of waiting to cross, while some of the others turned around and went back to join the gaggle of people looking down at the fallen man.

He drove directly to Harrow's house. He knew Harrow would have some way of knowing if anyone stood on his front steps, so when he rang the doorbell, he held an envelope full of cash in his left hand, flapping it absentmindedly against his thigh. A man who was used to getting cash in envelopes would know the exact look, feel, sound, and flexibility of money. First-time blackmailers and drug thieves might be fooled by cut paper, but not Harrow.

After a few moments the door opened, and Harrow stood there looking watchful. He was a big man, about forty years old, with a fringe of strawberry blond hair above his pink face. He glowered. "What can I do for you?"

"Compliments of the Bella Napoli restaurant." He held out his left hand with the envelope.

Harrow reached for it as Schaeffer's right hand came up holding the silenced pistol. He fired one shot into Harrow's chest and pushed him backward into the house, where Harrow fell. He stood over him and fired another round through his skull, closed the front door, and walked to his car. As he reached the sidewalk, he had to stop to let three ten-year-old boys flash past on bicycles.

They were moving too fast to look at his face or to see him as anything more than a blur.

When he came back to the Castle at six, the old man was in his office. He opened his cash drawer, stood, and handed Schaeffer the money he had offered for the job. Then his black eyes, like beads, flicked to the side, and he smiled, his long, tobacco-stained teeth suddenly visible. "Come in here." He beckoned to someone in the doorway. "That's right. I saw you. Come in here now." The voice was not the hard, imperious one that he used with his men, but the softer, slightly higher, cracked voice was more horrifying because it was so forced, so false.

A boy about thirteen or fourteen appeared from around the corner and stood in the doorway. He wore jeans and high-top basketball sneakers, which was the style then, and a sweatshirt. "This is my grandson," Castiglione said. "He's the youngest, Salvatore. Named after me."

"Hello," Schaeffer said.

The boy looked at him darkly, but said nothing.

Old Salvatore said, "That's right. Take a good look. That's the scariest man you're ever going to see. Doesn't look scary, does he?"

"No."

"Well he is. Look in his eyes. You see now?"

"I don't know."

"Does he like you, or does he hate you?"

"I can't tell."

"That's because the answer is 'neither.' He looks at you the way you look at a fish. It's alive now, maybe not tomorrow, but it doesn't matter which."

"I get it."

"Good." He gave the boy a push. "You see another one like him, make sure he's on your side."

Young Salvatore had grown up. As of last night he was the reigning Castiglione. Schaeffer was irritated that he hadn't managed to kill him. It was a chore, and now it would be harder and more dangerous.

He was fairly certain that the reason Salvatore had gotten away was that he hadn't been able to get to him fast enough. As soon as he had broken into the Castle, the clock had started running. He had killed everyone he'd seen, even the girl in Joe Castiglione's bed. He'd known at the time that even she had to die. He had heard people say that killing somebody was egotism — thinking your own life was more valuable than somebody else's. Those people didn't understand either life or death. Your life wasn't better than someone else's. Your life was valuable to you because it was yours. What was egotistical was thinking you could neglect to do the smart, self-protective thing when you had the chance and still manage to survive. It was thinking your superiority gave you leeway. You could afford to leave your enemies alive because they weren't as smart or as strong or as lucky as you were. Well, you couldn't afford to think that way.

If he'd made a mistake last night, it was not going upstairs in Paul Castiglione's house to kill the woman yelling down the stairs. Presumably it was Paul's wife. He'd made the decision, not to let her live, but not to waste the time going up there to find and kill her and whatever kids there were. Apparently he had made the wrong choice. She must have called Salvatore as soon as she heard the alarm go off.

He dressed and went downstairs to eat dinner, and then came back up and used his laptop computer to find Vincent Pugliese's address. He was tentatively pleased because he knew the area in the center of the city fairly well, unless the Chicago businesspeople had torn everything down and replaced it since he'd left the country. Finally, he took the time to examine his weapons and give them a hasty cleaning. He cut up a T-shirt, stripped the pistols, and wiped them down. He used a section of a curtain rod to run a patch through the shotgun barrel. He left the shotgun in two pieces in his bag, but reassembled the pistols and reloaded them and the spare magazines.

If Eddie could have seen what he was doing, he would have thought he was crazy. He had always been against picking up somebody else's gun and using it. After Eddie and the boy had gotten to Manny Garcia by killing his two bodyguards, the boy had picked up one bodyguard's Colt Commander. Eddie had shaken his head. "That man was not a pro, or he wouldn't be dead."

The boy had replied, "His gun fired fine. There was nothing wrong with it. He just couldn't hit anything. He didn't have the balls to hold the gun steady."

"You should wipe your prints off and drop it," Eddie said. "You don't know where that thing has been."

"Are we talking about germs?"

"No. He might have killed an archbishop, four Supreme Court justices, and Miss America with that damned gun."

Now it was about nine-thirty in the evening, time to drive back to Chicago. He stepped outside and went to his car. On the drive to Chicago along Lake Michigan he could feel his alertness growing as night came on. The sky was turning dark, and a few white clouds high above the lake east of the road were illuminated by the last of the sunlight to the west.

There was really no good plan but to go to Vincent Pugliese's address in Chicago and study it for vulnerabilities. Sal Castiglione would be trying to save himself now, and the logical way was to surround himself with his own people. That meant using Vince Pugliese to reassure the soldiers and rally them. But it was possible that Castiglione would simply leave town for a time and wait until calm returned.

Seeing Vincent Pugliese's address was daunting. It was an old gray stone office building six stories high with an imposing façade built in the early part of the last century. There was a stone arch with a pair of concrete pillars, and through the glass doors he caught a glimpse of a black-and-white marble mosaic floor in the lobby. As he moved slowly past the front of the building in traffic, he saw that the bottom floor held several businesses with separate entrances—a coffee shop, a travel agency, a credit union, a restaurant called Mimi's.

After studying the place for two minutes, he could read Vince

Pugliese's intention in every aspect of it. Pugliese would want to achieve a low profile, but still have Castiglione soldiers coming and going. The first-floor businesses were sure to be a tangle of legal agreements between fourteen or fifteen different entities, all companies that didn't involve a door you could knock on or the name of an actual person. They would be as insubstantial as cobwebs. When all were brushed away, the owner would be another company owned by Vincent Pugliese.

He turned to drive around the building. It was perfect. Old Salvatore Castiglione had bought a fantasy castle for himself, but Pugliese had built a village. One reason the Mafia worked was that a powerful man could offer jobs to all of his relatives and friends, giving them all a visible means of support and lots of free time for schemes and sidelines. Pugliese had his whole first floor occupied by businesses, all of which were ones he could use for money laundering and reinvesting. And the constant presence of people loyal to him behind those ground-floor windows meant he was a very difficult man to sneak up on. The lobby was a bare marble floor with two elevators. It was guarded by a pair of security men behind a desk facing the door. If something happened, Pugliese's people could probably cut the power to the elevators and engage the locks on the door and turn the place into a slaughtering floor.

Off the alley behind the building was the entrance to an underground parking garage where Pugliese and his friends could park their cars off the street. Pugliese was as well protected as a man in Chicago could be. There were not likely to be any surprises in his life.

Schaeffer drove another two blocks farther on and parked in a parking structure beside a movie theater. It was a mild September night, with a slow stream of moving air coming in off the lake. He had already decided that the most likely way to defeat the security of Pugliese's building would be to enter through the underground garage. From there he would look for the features that he couldn't see from the outside. He knew there would be some kind of exit there. Vince was too smart to let his fortress become a prison. He wouldn't let himself be trapped by his own defenses. He would have built in a private way around the barriers. It might be a separate elevator from the sixth floor down to the garage that skipped the intervening floors. It might be a walkway that led from this building to the one beside it or even a tunnel to another building. But his guess was that somewhere in the underground garage would be a plain steel door painted the same color as the walls. On it would be a sign that said something like ELECTRICAL or STAND PIPES or SHUT-OFF VALVE, something that would help the mind move past the door because the words gave the impression that all the questions had been answered. But that door would be Pugliese's way out.

He walked toward the gray building, his eyes constantly scanning, his mind evaluating and contemplating the thousand details they passed over. He looked at traffic patterns in the neighborhood to be sure there wouldn't be a jam that kept him from getting out, searched for security cameras high on the sides of the building or in the ceiling of the garage, watched for police cars to determine the frequency of routine police patrols. He looked at the people walking along the street, and even more closely at anyone who was not walking, just standing by a building or a bus stop. He looked at upper windows for any sign of a police surveillance team or the dark silhouette of a sniper a few feet back from an open window. He studied faces, watching for eyes that stared back at him with too much interest, ones that looked away quickly, or any he had seen before. Always he had a hand close to one of the guns. As he walked he could feel the hard handgrip of the gun beneath the fabric of his coat brush the inside of his wrist.

Darkness had reclaimed the city as he approached the gray stone building. The lights were on in the travel agency and the credit union, but all the desks were empty, the surfaces cleared except for computer monitors, keyboards, and mice. The magenta neon at Mimi's Ristorante was brighter now, and the coffee shop had taken on the forlorn look they all had in the evening, empty except for a few solitary people.

Then, unexpectedly, Vincent Pugliese came out of the building, flanked by two men in dark suits. He looked almost the same as he had twenty years ago. The slicked-back hair was more gray than brown now, and his frame looked a bit broader. The expression on his face was a pinch at the eyebrows, slack skin in the cheeks. He looked as though he hadn't had much sleep. He and his two men went to the curb and looked up the street in the direction of the garage.

A gleaming black Mercedes sedan that had to be Pugliese's came out of the driveway behind the building, turned to the right, and glided toward the curb where Pugliese and his two men waited. Schaeffer kept moving along the street toward them. He stepped into the space behind an accidental grouping of five men who had just come out of a big building up the street, probably all leaving at quitting time. He kept them ahead of him like blockers as they walked toward Pugliese.

"I need to talk to you."

He turned only his eyes. It was Elizabeth Waring. She had separated herself from the stream of pedestrians beside him, appeared at his shoulder, and spoken close to his ear. He spun on his heel, put his arm around her waist, and walked her back in the direction he had come from. They walked a hundred feet or more before he said, with barely contained anger, "What do you want to talk about?"

She was aware that their body language, him embracing her that way and leaning close to her to speak, was intended to make them look like a couple. She said, "The way we start is that I tell you not to kill Vincent Pugliese."

"You've already made that impossible. Now go tell him not to kill me."

"What you did last night has made a lot of people come to this part of town who weren't here yesterday. Besides the regular contingent of FBI from the Chicago office, there are planeloads on their way from Washington and from all over the Midwest. How much more the wiseguys are doing, I can only imagine. But I'll know in another day because it's my job."

"Go do your job. You don't belong out here."

He released her and took a step that separated them by a few inches. Suddenly a shot tore the air, then four more at once, all incredibly loud, and beside him a wall of glass at the front of a closed women's clothing store had a constellation of holes. Cracks appeared to connect them, and the glass came down like a curtain at his feet.

He grasped Elizabeth's arm so hard it hurt and yanked her up into the windowless display, dragging her with him between headless manikins wearing cotton jackets and shorts. There were more shots, some blasting chips from the plaster manikins and pounding one of them backward onto the display. Elizabeth could see there were men firing from the windows of a big black car that was pulling up to the curb near where they had stood.

He pulled Elizabeth through the display of manikins, artificial grass, and colored leaves and down into the center aisle of the store. They ran toward the back of the dimly lighted building. At the end of the sales floor, there were two doors. The one he chose took them into a room full of more racks of dresses and coats, stacks of boxes, a table set up for wrapping. He saw a door to the side of the room and pulled Elizabeth through it.

They were out the side door into the alley, and they both ran hard without speaking. They knew that in a moment the black car could drive around the building and into the alley in front of them. They had to be out of sight before that happened or they would be trapped. They turned into the narrow space between two buildings and ran toward the next street. When they approached the end of the dark passageway, he held up his hand for her to stop, and she managed to do it without running into him. She turned to look behind her down the long, narrow space and put her hand in her pocket to wrap her fingers around the grips of the gun.

He grasped her arm again and tugged her out onto the sidewalk and to the right. He walked purposefully down the street with his arm around her, squeezing her affectionately. Now and then he would look around, not in a panicky, harried way, but calmly, as though he were just checking the crowds of people to see if any of their friends were among them. Elizabeth was surprised for a second at how good a physical actor he was, but then reminded herself that he'd have to be to get close to his victims and walk away after he'd killed them.

"We've got to get out of the street," he said. "Vince is probably calling everybody he knows to get them here."

There was the scream of a siren. "My side seems to be getting here quicker," she said. "They'll protect us."

"If they know who you are, they might try. But they'd fail because too many of the other side are already here. What are you doing out here alone with a gun?"

"What gun?"

"You didn't let go fast enough when I pulled your arm to get you to come along, so I saw it."

"I'm not giving it to you."

"I didn't ask. If you can hit anything smaller than a building with it, I'd rather you keep it."

"I'm competent." She pointed across the street. "Can't we just go into a restaurant like that one and wait?"

"Not that one. It's the Bella Napoli. Somebody in the Castiglione family owns it. Today they're probably using it as a command post for twenty or thirty soldiers. Keep walking, but not too fast. We're a nice, middle-aged couple going somewhere. We heard some noise a few minutes ago, probably, but we don't think it can be any big deal. We think it's a construction crew."

"At night?"

"A road crew, then. The point is, we're not the sort of people who believe we need to run from anything."

"Innocent as babes."

"This isn't funny. The family is stirred up. They aren't going to give up on us."

"Us?"

"They need more revenge than they can get with one person."

"How about that massage place?" It was a white storefront, with four Asian women in white shorts and T-shirts looking out the front window through gauzy curtains to see what the commotion was. "Who owns that?"

"Can't risk it. This close to Vince's place, they might be hookers, and that takes protection." He saw something up the street ahead of them that didn't make him happy. He took her hand and walked with her in a diagonal across the street, around a corner, and then took another diagonal onto State Street, and then up the front steps of an enormous church.

"You think a church is any safer than a restaurant?"

"It's the Holy Name Cathedral. I'm hoping there won't be anybody in there who will rat us out for a tip." He reached up to tug one of the big bronze doors and it opened automatically, powered by a hidden hydraulic system. "That gives me the creeps."

"I guess you're probably not one of their regulars." They slipped inside and the huge bronze door swung shut. The sanctuary was big and ornate, but there seemed to be nobody in it at the moment.

They moved quickly toward the altar past a screen that seemed to repeat the leaf pattern of the bronze doors, staying on the right aisle, trotting past what seemed like a hundred rows of wooden pews. They reached a row of confessional booths. When they heard the big front door opening again, Elizabeth reached for the door of one of the confessionals, but the Butcher's Boy held her arm and shook his head. He held her hand and pulled her with him to the big gallery pipe organ set on the right side of the sanctuary in its own alcove. He dragged her into the alcove where they were shielded from view by clustered marble pillars. There was a seat for the organist and four keyboards, but he went to look at the wood paneling beside the row of gold organ pipes above the keyboards. She whispered, "We could hide in the chapel. It's right up there, past the altar on the right."

He whispered, "They'll search it." He took a small pick the size of a toothpick and an equally small tension wrench out of his wallet. He was staring at a keyhole she hadn't noticed, barely visible at one side of the wooden façade of the organ. He probed the lock and picked it in a few seconds. He opened the door, pulled down a small set of folding steps, and pushed her in front of him. She climbed in, and he followed, then pulled up the steps and closed the door.

They were inside the organ. They took a few steps along a narrow walkway and stopped. Directly in front of them was the row of tall gilded organ pipes and behind them, a mesh screen. The windowless space was open far above to the ceiling of the cathedral, so there was dim light. All the way to the top there were platforms and railings and steps that connected the different levels, all of them in a light-colored hardwood. On each level she could see hundreds of organ pipes arranged in rows graded by length and diameter from the size of a ballpoint pen to the size of her waist, and mounted in wooden enclosures. Most of them were gleaming metal tubes, but others were wooden quadrangles. She and the Butcher's Boy stood side by side behind the row of façade pipes, looking out the narrow spaces between the pipes and through the fabric mesh and listening. She put her right hand on the gun in her pocket and held it there.

There were three of them. She heard them before she saw them. They wore leather-soled shoes, and they were walking along the pews toward the altar. One was on each side, brushing the walls occasionally as they moved ahead. The third came up the center aisle, where there was a long runner that muffled his footsteps. Now and then each of them would stop, bend low, and sight under a section of pews in case someone was hiding under the wooden seats. She wondered if the older one in the center could be Vincent Pugliese. Probably he wasn't. Underbosses of major families didn't do this kind of work.

The men stage-whispered as they reached the front. "I guess he didn't come in here."

"Somebody did. I saw the front door shut from the street."

"Did he have a black suit with a funny white collar?"

"It wasn't a priest. There was a woman with him."

"That's refreshing."

"You think that's funny?"

"Somebody's here, but there's nobody in the pews. Now what?"

"Take a look up there around the altar and pulpit." There was the sound of hard soles on the broad marble steps, and now Elizabeth could see them more clearly. She shuddered. Each time they eliminated a hiding place, they were more likely to find the unlocked door into the organ.

"Check the confessionals." She heard small doors opening and shutting quickly as the man moved down the line. That was where she would have been if not for him.

There were the sounds of shoes on the floor of the sanctuary again, moving off. The big front door opened and she heard traffic sounds from outside, the whisper of car tires, a distant horn, then silence.

His face was right beside hers. "They're gone."

She was so relieved that she felt like grinning, but controlled it. "I guess they don't spend as much time in churches as you do, or they'd have found us."

He said, "You wanted to talk to me. So here we are. Talk, and then we can each go about our business."

"You're in very big trouble," she said. "It looks as though everybody in the Mafia would like you to die."

"They're doing their best to make it happen."

"I can make sure it doesn't. You'll be given protection. I don't mean a guard coming by to look through a prison window at you once in a while. I mean dedicated people on duty twenty-four hours a day with nothing else to do but make sure you don't mysteriously beat yourself up and hang yourself with a bed sheet."

"Why would I be willing to go to a prison? I've never even been charged with anything."

"It wouldn't need to be a prison. It just has to be safe. Joseph Valachi was on an army base. You could be somewhere like that."

"Valachi was in prison. He was moved to an army base because he got hit with a pipe."

"That was half a century ago. We can do better now."

"So can I."

"After last night there will be nowhere you can hide. As soon as the old men know you went after the Castigliones, they'll drop everything and make sure of it. They'll be scared. Even the ones who wanted Tosca dead will be after you. You're a menace to them."

"So what you're offering is some form of protective custody in exchange for testifying against Mafia guys."

"It's my help for your help. Yes, I hope that there will be some people you can testify against—maybe a Mafioso you personally saw kill somebody. Maybe you killed somebody and he paid you. We can't bring you in to testify against somebody who did something minor. It wouldn't work well in court. But I'm hoping you'll give us tips on whatever you know was going on, and we can follow your leads and get our own evidence about what's happening now. Most likely you and I would spend some months talking every day. Then your job would be to testify in the trials of major criminals. The whole process would probably take a couple of years. You would be protected at whatever level is necessary. And I mean *any* level."

He spoke deliberately. "I'm sure you're sincere about what you're saying," he said. "But you'll have to forgive me if I don't jump at the idea of Justice Department protection."

"I know, you have good reason to believe you're better at this than either the Justice Department or the Mafia. But you have to be able to close your eyes long enough to sleep. And two or three

238

years of invisibility could make a huge difference. Some of the old men could die. Others could ask themselves why they're wasting their time on you and quit. Every day above ground is a good day. I can offer you a thousand days," she said. "Face it. If you want guaranteed survival, you're going to be my informant. Nobody else can protect you."

"You're very open and I can see you're trying to be honest," he said. "But no, thank you."

"But why? Don't you trust me?"

"I don't mean to be insulting. But you work for a huge organization. If I went in with you, within ten minutes nothing would be up to you anymore." He turned toward the doorway. "Those guys are long gone. Let's get out of here before somebody comes to play the organ."

He started to push open the door, but there was another faint hum. Someone was opening the big bronze doors at the back of the church again. "Wait." He closed the door.

Six people entered this time. She could tell because as each entered, the door would begin to shut until the next touched it and it huffed open again. There was a deep male voice that said, "Griggs, Lattimer, take the wings. Foltz, Talavera, Jackson, you take point." After about ten seconds a voice said, "Left side's clear, Agent Meade."

Elizabeth leaned close to him and whispered, "They're FBI."

He whispered back, "This is a great time to be quiet."

"We can let them know we're here, and you'd be safe."

"You wouldn't. I can hardly miss you from here."

"I've got a gun aimed at you too."

"Then we can kill each other, or we can be quiet."

They stood in silence, unmoving, as they listened to the sounds of the six FBI agents searching the sanctuary. "Right side's clear too, Agent Meade, and so are the confessionals."

"All clear in the choir loft."

"The altar is clear."

"The chapel is clear."

"Check the sacristy."

They heard leather-soled shoes trotting up the aisle toward the sacristy.

"See if there are any doors around that organ up there." One of the agents who had been by the altar came down the steps and walked back and forth in front of the organ. Now the Butcher's Boy had his gun in his hand. Through the mesh and between the organ pipes, Elizabeth watched the FBI agent moving around a few feet in front of her, but she kept the gun in the corner of her eye. If it came up to aim, she was going to drag that arm down with all her weight. But the agent didn't seem to notice the keyhole in the wooden panel.

"All right. Let's move on," said Agent Meade. The door at the rear of the church opened once, then again and again, until the church was in silence.

The Butcher's Boy pushed the organ door open, and he lowered the steps to the floor. They both came down into the sanctuary. He replaced the steps, closed the door, and inserted his pick into the keyhole to push a pin tumbler or two out of line to lock the organ door. Elizabeth looked toward the cathedral entrance, then back at him, but he was already walking toward the other side of the sanctuary. "Wait," she said.

He stopped, and when he turned toward her, the gun was already in his hand. She showed him she still had her gun, and left it pointing in his general direction, but didn't aim. "I just wanted to stay together."

"I'm going out through the rectory door. Catch up with the FBI agents on the street and you'll be fine."

"But we're not done talking."

"That's not what I want to talk about," he said. He began to back toward the other side, his gun still held steady. "You've got nothing to offer me."

"In another day or two, protective custody might sound really good."

"Then we'll talk another day." He kept moving slowly backward.

"Give me a phone number," she said.

"I don't have a phone."

"Take mine." She pulled it out and prepared to toss it.

"So you can track me by GPS satellite?"

"Then take my number. 202 555-8990. Can you remember it?"

"202 555-8990."

He turned into the space to the left of the altar and past the sacristy. After a second she heard a standard-size door open and then shut.

Elizabeth put her gun into her purse and stood still, listening. It was only after about a minute that she realized what she had been listening for was gunshots.

27

HE WAS OUT on the street alone again. There was a feeling he was getting from Elizabeth Waring that she wasn't exactly telling the truth. She wasn't telling him something that she considered important. She said she was interested in getting him into a guarded room someplace and asking him questions. That wasn't a surprise. But she was alone. When the FBI showed up, she wasn't much happier to see them than he was. She had told him the arrival of FBI agents was an opportunity to save both of them, but it had sounded like a bluff. When he had refused, she had seemed almost relieved.

She must have been making offers she hadn't cleared with any of her bosses. She was just hoping if she got him, they'd be glad enough to back her up. But for the moment, she wasn't telling anybody what she was up to because they would have stopped her. That was the way her pitch felt to him. It wasn't even a very good deal. She hadn't even offered immunity from prosecution. Was he supposed to think that was an oversight? The most peculiar part of her behavior was that she wasn't just hunting with the hounds anymore. She was hiding with the foxes too. That had to be a new experience for her, and it might make her easier to deal with later if he needed to.

He reached into his pocket and took out the little leather wallet he had picked out of her jacket pocket while he'd had his arm around her on the street. On the front was a deeply etched seal with an eagle on it. He opened the wallet and saw it was her Justice Department identification. He put it back into his pocket and kept walking to the parking structure where he'd left his car.

Parking structures were often good places to kill people. He'd used them a number of times, but it was important to check first for surveillance cameras, to be sure they were clear like this one. But he'd been in and out of this one already and it was fairly well lighted, so it was possible he'd been seen by people working for Vince Pugliese. He took a few moments to look for smudged finger marks on the car, unlocked it, and opened the hood to see if there were any signs of tampering. He didn't see any. He knew that if there was a device, there would be an attempt to place it where he wouldn't see it. He looked under the car, then closed the hood, and started the car. Searching for bombs was really only looking for an amateur's clumsy errors. A pro's work was invisible. A bomb could be set off by turning the ignition key, but it could also be done by running a wire from the brake lights or the headlights, or by making a call with a cell phone that sent a current to an initiator, or by a rocker switch that closed a circuit when the car hit a bump. Since the army had been fighting enemies for years in the Middle East who used improvised explosive devices, there were now probably thousands of young guys with fresh discharge papers who knew their way around explosives better than he did.

He backed out of his space and drove off the lot. It was ten minutes before he stopped bracing for the explosion that hadn't come. He drove a few miles away before he began searching for a twenty-four-hour mailing and copying center. When he found one in a mini-mall, he parked on the street and went inside. He used a computer to match the print font of Elizabeth Waring's ID, typed the name Elliot Lee Warren, and printed and trimmed it. He positioned it on the identification so it covered her name. He used a webcam to take his own picture, printed it in a small format, put it over her picture, and then scanned the identification and printed it. The finished identification would not have fooled experts, but he didn't intend to show it to any. He deleted everything he'd done on the computer. Then he paid his bill. He used the laminating machine to laminate it, paid for that, and left.

He drove back downtown toward Vincent Pugliese's building. He had a very strong feeling about what Pugliese was doing now that there was only one remaining Castiglione brother, and if he was right, he only had one more stop to make. He parked his car by the curb on a street three blocks from Pugliese's building. It was about nine o'clock now. The early evening traffic had drained people out of the center of the city toward the suburbs, but when he reached the area around Pugliese's building, it was still not back to normal. There were still men in the streets in twos and threes when any men walking should have been alone, heading for parking structures to claim their cars and drive home.

He was losing the time of night when he could hope to get to Pugliese. If he stayed on these streets until everyone out here was either a gangster or a cop, the only things that could happen were that he would be recognized and killed or arrested. He walked to the alley behind the building, went down the ramp into the underground parking lot, and began to search. He opened the door labeled JANITOR'S STORAGE, then tried the ELECTRICAL door, then one that was unmarked but contained an array of vertical pipes and valve wheels. Finally he found a door with RISERS stenciled on it. He opened it and saw there was a stairway leading upward into the dark. He followed it, climbing to the next floor, where he was stopped by a second steel door. He tried the knob, but this one was bolted from the other side.

He went back down, walked out of the garage to the alley and around the building. As he was walking up the street toward the main entrance, he saw three of the six FBI agents he had seen inside the cathedral. One of them was the boss, the one the others had called Agent Meade. The three men came out the front door of Vince Pugliese's building, looking as though they'd wasted

244

their time, and turned toward Schaeffer. He walked toward the building with his hands in his pockets, not showing any interest in the FBI agents. When they passed, he scanned the block as he walked and spotted the other three FBI agents getting into a car. He stopped as though he were turning into the door for Mimi's Ristorante, waited until the car was gone, then looked back up the street to see the other car gone too. Then he stepped through the glass doors to the lobby. There was one man sitting at the desk in a black sport coat tending a sign-in book and a second in an identical coat watching security monitors.

Schaeffer stepped to the desk and held up his new Justice Department identification as though he wanted both to see it at once, but so it was far enough from either to prevent real scrutiny. "Agent Elliot Warren, United States Justice Department. I'd like you both to take a step backward away from the desk, please." The two obeyed. "Now lock the front doors and escort me upstairs to see Mr. Pugliese."

The man with the sign-in book said, "There have been like, ten FBI people here in the past two hours. Let me just call upstairs—"

Schaeffer's hand rested on the man's wrist as he reached for the phone. "That would have to be the worst decision you ever make."

"Do you have a search warrant?"

"Agent Meade and the others will be back shortly with the warrant. But it's a formality. Since shots have been fired and we're in the middle of a search for the shooters, this comes under the exception of hot pursuit. Any sworn law enforcement officer can come in here without a warrant. Now lock the door and take me to Vincent Pugliese."

The two looked at each other. One stepped to the front door and locked it, and the other slid the deadbolt into the floor. The two men stepped into the elevator before Schaeffer.

As soon as the elevator door closed, Schaeffer stopped the elevator and pulled out a gun. He said, "If you cooperate, nothing will happen to you. You won't be charged with anything, and you'll remain safe. If either of you is armed, now is the time to say so and put your gun on the floor."

One of the men said, "We're not armed."

Schaeffer took the man's arm and spun him so he stood facing the wall. "Hands on the wall, feet apart." Then he turned the second man into the same position facing the wall and patted the first one down. He found a small pistol in a holster on the man's belt under his coat. He held the pistol to the man's head. "What's this?"

"It's a gun. I forgot I had it."

Schaeffer fired it into the man's head and watched him drop to the floor, then stepped over him and stood behind the second man.

"Oh, my god," the second one said. "Are you crazy?"

"Do you have a gun too?"

"Yes."

"Then you're the one who's crazy."

He found the gun and put it into his coat pocket. "Do you have any other weapons?"

"A .380 in an ankle holster."

Schaeffer bent over and took the little pistol. "Is that it?"

"That's it."

"You know the penalty for lying to me?"

"I just saw it."

"So you're clean now?"

"Yes."

Schaeffer searched him a little more, but found nothing. He pressed the button for six, the top floor, and the elevator rose.

The elevator stopped on the sixth floor and the door slid open. There was a single corridor that ran along the outer wall of the building. On the same side of the corridor as the elevator there were three doors. Schaeffer used his free hand to keep the security man ahead of him as he stepped out of the elevator. "Go up to Pugliese's door and then stop."

The man walked up to a door that had neither a number nor a name on it and stood in front of it. Schaeffer stepped to the side with his back to the wall so he could watch the other two doors, reached across the man, and knocked. A moment later, the peephole in the door went dark for a few seconds. The door opened, and Schaeffer pushed the man in and came in close behind his back.

There was a shout. "It's him!" Schaeffer's eyes were taking in everything—the four men in a huge open loft converted to an apartment—Salvatore Castiglione, two soldiers, and Vincent Pugliese. One of the soldiers already had a gun in his hand and fired. Schaeffer felt his hostage's legs buckle, and as he began to go down, Schaeffer went low with him and shot the soldier in the chest. He crouched and turned his gun in the direction of the others. Vince Pugliese popped up from his chair with his hands in the air.

"Hold it, everybody. Drop the guns so we can talk."

Schaeffer watched the remaining soldier drop his gun on the carpet, and Pugliese seemed to realize, a bit late, that Schaeffer would never believe he wasn't armed. He opened his coat wide and pinched the grips of a pistol between thumb and forefinger and set it on the floor.

Schaeffer's eyes settled on Sal Castiglione, who was still seated on a desk chair with his hands behind him. Castiglione said to him, "Don't look at me." He turned his body so Schaeffer could see he had handcuffs on his wrists attaching him to the backrest of the chair.

Schaeffer turned to Pugliese. "You didn't even wait until the other two are buried?"

"You're the one who made this possible. You changed the whole equation last night. Joe and Paul were dead, and Sal came to me for protection right away. We decided the best thing to do was to fly him to Mexico, where he would be safe and live happily on the money he's stashed away. That's our agreement."

"You wanted him to collect his money so you could kill him and steal it."

"Not me." Pugliese held his empty hands up in a gesture of innocence.

"If that wasn't the plan, he wouldn't be in handcuffs, and you would have flown him out before it was too late."

"You hear that?" said Pugliese to Castiglione. "It's too late. Sorry we didn't fly you out of here in time to save you, Sal. First it was the cops everywhere, and now my old friend. I guess he can't bear to leave until he kills you."

Castiglione looked at Pugliese. "You two deserve each other. I came to you for help after this psycho killed my brothers. You lived by my family's trust for thirty years, but when the bad hour came, you turned on me before anybody else." He turned to Schaeffer. "I remember you. I suppose you came back here because he told you he'd hide you, or smuggle you out, or something. Don't you know they always do that? The one they get to kill you is your closest friend, the one you trust."

Schaeffer moved his arm slightly and shot Pugliese, and then the last soldier. He looked at Castiglione. "I'm afraid that's the best I can do for you—let you see him die before you do."

"It's not much, but I would have hated to die with that bastard smirking at me."

Schaeffer pointed at the window, his face unsurprised. "See that?"

Sal Castiglione turned in an almost involuntary reflex to look, and Schaeffer shot him in the back of the head so he would die instantly.

Schaeffer stood still and listened. There were no sounds of sirens, no sounds of people running up the stairs. There had been plenty of time since the first gunshots. He supposed the sixth floor of the old stone building was too high up and too substantial to let the noise reach the street.

He walked across the loft to the area that was set aside as a kitchen. He couldn't help wondering if Vince had ever used any of the appliances. He began going through drawers and saw the place was fully equipped. After a moment he found what he had been looking for—a reusable fabric grocery bag. He took it and returned to the living room area. He started by taking the guns dropped by Pugliese and the two soldiers. He put them in the bag, added the three guns he had taken from the dead security men, then went through the wallets of the five men in the living room and took the cash. He dug the car keys out of Pugliese's pocket. He considered searching the loft for money, but he knew Vince would not have made finding it an easy matter. He decided he'd used up his time.

He went through the big loft apartment opening doors, searching for the secret way out, and then found it. He opened a plain door near the kitchen and saw that inside was an auxiliary heating and air-conditioning unit. A person who opened the door would normally have closed it again because all that was beyond the box-shaped HVAC unit was what looked like a plain white wall. But he stepped in and pushed it, and the wall swung away from him on hinges to reveal a space beyond. He sidestepped through it and found himself on the landing of a staircase that had apparently been closed off during remodeling. There was a small airline bag sitting on the landing beside the door. He picked it up and opened it.

He had found Pugliese's escape kit. It held a Browning .45 pistol and two spare magazines, a large stack of bills, and a few credit cards and driver's licenses and passports in different names. He put the kit into his grocery bag and went down the eleven flights of stairs to the steel door. He carefully turned the bolt so it wouldn't make a noise and opened the door a half inch to look out at the underground garage. There were the same few cars as before, but no people.

He opened the door the rest of the way and hurried to the black car that Pugliese and his men had used to go after him on the street. He used the remote control button to unlock the door. He got in, started the car, and drove it up out of the garage. He drove the three long blocks to where his car was parked, left the black car around the corner from it, and walked back carrying his bag of guns and money. He set it in the trunk of his Camry, then got behind the wheel and drove. It was late night now, and it meant there would be less traffic on the major routes out of Chicago. If he turned west at the interstate, he could be in Los Angeles in three or four days.

28

IT WAS MONDAY MORNING, and Elizabeth Waring was finally at home. Chicago had been a defeat, a horrible misstep. It had also been a searing humiliation for her. She had gone into a crucial and dangerous situation without being clear in her own mind about what was going on or what she intended to do. She had gone fact-finding with a gun in her pocket. That was about all it was. All of her years of experience and her native ability to extrapolate information from bits of available data to figure out what was going on had deserted her. No, she had deserted them. All she had done was stumble on the name of a man the Butcher's Boy was likely to visit and then rush to be there too.

She had not decided in advance what she wanted to accomplish. Did she want to prevent him from making a deal with Pugliese, or from killing him? Did she want to protect him from being killed in an ambush, or did she want to arrest him? The answer to all of those questions had been yes. She had wanted him to see spontaneously that the whole world of organized crime was always going to be arrayed against him and that his only sensible choice was to turn himself over to Elizabeth Waring of the Justice Department. She had not brought enough federal officers to make his capture even possible because she had some notion that he would go quietly and willingly. It was ridiculous. He was not capable of reacting that way. His only strategy in life was the opposite, the strategy of wild animals. If he was surrounded and vastly outnumbered, he would be more vicious than ever and kill more of the attackers. In his world, agreements were more than risky. They were usually suicidal. They were an enemy's way of disarming him so he could be killed.

She had come to him with an offer he must have seen as naive and foolish. She had hoped he would be desperate enough to consider it, but he wasn't. He could never be. Then she had toyed with the idea of pulling a gun on him and holding him in custody. That was stupid because he would always take the chance that someone wouldn't shoot in time, or would miss, or wouldn't kill him. He would always take the chance, instantly, without hesitation, moving as fast as he could to evade and counterstrike.

Now she was going to have to do the thinking she had not done before. She needed to find an unambiguous position in relation to him and then construct a plan that would induce precisely what she wanted to happen. And she wouldn't try to do it alone this time. That had been a childish reaction to the refusal of Hunsecker to see the value of an informant like this one. She would have to design an ambush for the Butcher's Boy. It would have to involve enough federal officers to overwhelm him, to swarm him and physically overpower him. It was the only way to keep him alive and hold him long enough to make a deal.

She had always liked Monday mornings. Some of the people at work had told her she liked it because she didn't drink, but that wasn't why. Monday seemed to be the fresh start that would give her a lead on all the problems she was supposed to solve. She always drove to work early and got a sense of what was happening before the others came in, then selected the most pressing problems and the most promising leads and got people working on them as soon as they arrived. During breaks and lunchtime, she would turn her attention to issues that had to do with the kids or the household that required her to talk to someone during business hours.

There had been a couple of hundred Monday evenings when she had gone home physically and mentally exhausted, but glad that she had proceeded that way because the rest of the week would be better. This morning she began by looking at the routine activity reports that her analysts had set aside because they'd seen something in them that didn't seem routine. There was often a suicide in which the deceased had more than one bullet wound, a missing boater who'd never gone sailing before, a man killed in a hunting accident wearing a business suit. Sometimes it would be a violent incident with lots of victims and witnesses who had names from a single ethnic group. Occasionally that was a sign of organized crime. It usually took only a short time each morning to clear up some misunderstanding or refer the cases to regional offices for further investigation.

This morning, as she was going through the reports, her phone rang. "Justice Department, Waring," she said.

"Elizabeth? This is John Holman, over at the FBI. I was hoping you'd be in early."

"Hi, John. Are you still in Chicago?"

"No, I got back last night. When I came in this morning, I saw some information I thought you'd be interested in —some stuff we got on a couple of wiretaps over the weekend."

"Should I go over to your office?"

"I'm sending you copies of the transcripts by e-mail, but I wanted you to be aware that they're coming. The first batch is from a tap we've had on the phone of a Castiglione soldier named Ronald Bonardo. He runs a crew that's been doing real-estate scams in Florida. They'd buy and sell the same house four or five times among themselves to jack up the price, take out a giant mortgage, and then walk away. That worked in boom times when houses were going up. Now they're taking money to prevent foreclosures. The victim signs his house over to them."

"What does he say on tape?"

"Bonardo called Vincent Pugliese in Chicago to ask what was going on. Pugliese says on Friday night that the two older Castiglione brothers were dead and he was taking over the family. He said the one who had done the killing was the Butcher's Boy. That's the nickname of the guy you've been watching for, isn't it?"

"Yes. Is there anything on the tapes that will tell us where the Butcher's Boy is going next?"

"Not on the pages I've seen. The other transcript is a phone tap on a Lazaretti soldier in California named Joe Buffone. He's talking to an associate, a Lazaretti soldier in New York named Nano Scuzzi, this morning. Scuzzi asks whether they've got things set up. He says, 'I did what I was told by Tony. I delivered the first two hundred thousand to their company. That gets them on the job. When they deliver proof that he's dead, we give them the other three hundred.' Scuzzi says, 'Tony's smart. We don't want to see our best earners following that bastard into some dark alley, like the Castigliones did. It's stupid to even try. Let the guys like him handle him. If the pros bag him, we won't have to.' What do you think?"

Elizabeth felt her morning changing rapidly. "They've hired a hit man to kill the hit man. Or a team of them. I suppose it should have been obvious that this was going to happen, but I didn't see it coming. It makes perfect sense. The Lazaretti soldiers are skilled as drug smugglers and distributors. It doesn't make them effective against a professional killer. That's why they hired people like the Butcher's Boy a generation ago."

"How do you think we should handle this?" Holman asked.

"The first thing is probably to find out what we can about this murder-for-hire team. The ones who work that way usually have some kind of cover—an office, a company that takes in money and issues paychecks. Maybe there's something earlier on the tapes that will tell you where Buffone went to make his payoff, or if he spoke with the go-between on the tapped phone, or some detail we can use."

"I'll let you know if we find anything," he said.

"Thank you, John. I really appreciate your keeping me up on this. The taps were on two unrelated cases, and they would have been missed if you hadn't noticed. I'll talk to you soon." She hung up, and she felt a headache begin around her eyes and expand and intensify. She had been in Chicago all weekend, away from her children and putting herself in danger, which she had no right to do. She had just told herself that she wasn't going to try to go off alone and ad lib a plan after she was in the street between an angry professional killer and a bunch of armed gangsters. But the Butcher's Boy might be the most promising informant in forty years. And he wasn't worth anything dead.

29

IT WAS TUESDAY, before first light on the West Coast. The mockingbirds had been singing sleepily for some time, perched unseen in the canopies of the tall sycamores, not showing themselves or flying just yet because the last of the owls were still out, gliding silently above the trees and searching for one last catch before sunrise. There were specific boundaries in time that they all had to fear. If an owl was still in flight when the sun rose, he risked having a gang of crows attack him. When they did, it was five or six of them at once, wave after wave, hurling themselves into him, trying to corner him, blinking and defenseless.

He was on foot on Marengo Avenue in Pasadena, walking along in a gray hooded sweatshirt and jeans. There were tall, old trees along the parkway and flanking the big houses that were set far up and back on their lawns. The street curved so as he walked, he saw new views, but the curves gave him a bit of invisibility too. The Lazarettis in New York had ordered the leaders of their western incursions in the 1920s to buy houses in places like this, where the quiet, the wealthy, and the respectable lived. And when the eastern bosses came for their visits, they wanted places to stay that were quiet and elegant.

He had chosen the Lazarettis. They seemed to him to be a convenient group to use to cause trouble. In the 1940s the other

256

four New York families had given them a monopoly on the drug trade in Los Angeles, with the others as silent partners. The L.A. branch supplied all five New York families with a reliable stream of cash that required no effort from them, and the others would be very concerned if that flow were interrupted. There had always been jealousies and resentments from the eastern families that didn't share in the drug business. The division had made a certain rough sense in the 1940s and 50s. The five families were each big and powerful, and together they would have been an irresistible force. Since they wanted the drug business, they got it without much discussion. But now that those families had been weakened by decades of prosecutions and the loss of most of their percentages on businesses like construction, linen supply, and garbage disposal even in New York itself, it seemed to some of the other families that the division of spoils was archaic.

The five families were no more capable of controlling the drug trade in Los Angeles than they were of controlling the weather or the tides. The drug business had become absurdly larger than they were. If they tried to control drugs now, one part of the job would be to control the hundred thousand members of the Los Angeles street gangs, who were all more or less involved in drugs, and more or less independent. Another part of the job would be to track the physical movement of drugs and money that comprised most of the economic production of six or seven countries. The Lazarettis were just one purveyor among hundreds, a brand name in a big marketplace.

As Schaeffer walked, he looked at the big houses and spacious grounds. This was what had happened to the Mafia. It wasn't defeat, it was victory. They had gotten what they wanted and they were choking on it. He had just begun to look ahead for the first Lazaretti house, the big one that belonged to Tony Lazaretti, when something whizzed past his cheek.

The first shot should have killed him. It was silenced, and the velocity was slower than the speed of sound, so there was no crack as it passed by the hood of his sweatshirt and pounded into the trunk of the tree beside him. Bark exploded off the tree, but the hood protected his ear and eye from being spattered. He dropped low, touched the ground with his palms, and spun to get behind the tree.

What the single shot had told him was not good news. The rifle had been silenced, and judging from the effectiveness of the silencer, he would guess it was factory made. Those were manufactured in small numbers for military snipers. A silencer also acted as a flash suppressor, so he hadn't seen the muzzle flash: he didn't know where the sniper was. The shot had also told him that the shooter was probably not some Lazaretti underling who spent most of his days persuading the maids on cruise ships to smuggle heroin in cases of soap or shampoo. This was somebody who had enough experience to know where to expect him and to have some idea when he would choose to arrive. The shooter had silently placed a bullet within inches of his head in the dark, had not been heard or seen, and was still out there waiting for a second opportunity now that he had the range and angle figured out.

Schaeffer considered his options. He could stay behind this tree and let the shooter try to improve his angle to get a better shot. Either the shooter would succeed or he would fail, and he might make a mistake that let Schaeffer know where he was. It was only a half hour or so before dawn. At that point the shooter would have to leave or risk being seen and caught in a police blockade that closed off all the streets. Schaeffer could try to get to better cover than this tree trunk. There were several spots not far away—a stone house was behind him and to his left, but it was set far back from the street. And there were other trees he might use as way stations for a move up the block to the next corner.

As he considered, a delivery truck appeared up the block to his left and came toward him. He looked to his right to spot any obstacles. As the truck approached, he tried to see as much as he could of the area where the shooter must be. He still couldn't see anything conclusive, but there was a thick hedge that ran along the side of the big house across the street.

He judged the speed of the delivery truck, pushed off his tree, and ran beside it. He could see the side of it now, and the logo said it was from a bakery. The truck was going about twenty miles an hour when it passed him so he couldn't quite keep up with it. But a few seconds later the brake light beside him glowed and the truck began to slow for the stop sign at the next corner. He was with it now, fully hidden by it. He had not heard the sound of a bullet hitting anything yet, but he was sure the shooter must know that he'd left his tree.

The truck reached the end of the short block and stopped for the stop sign, but he kept running, sprinting across the intersection. The truck caught up with him and he ran with it for a few yards. But the long block gave the truck driver a chance to increase his speed, and the truck accelerated away from Schaeffer, revealing an alarming sight. A man had been running with him on the other side of the truck, and he was clearly the sniper. The man held a short rifle with a silencer, and he was just slowing down, turning his head to see whether he had outrun his prey.

Schaeffer was slightly behind him, and before the man could turn and bring the rifle around, Schaeffer shot him twice in the back and once in the head. Schaeffer's shots were loud, and there was a flurry of wings as a flock of frightened birds flew off above him. He turned to the right and ran. He had left his car three blocks away in a lot beside a closed restaurant on Fair Oaks, and now he ran as though he were an early morning jogger. He kept up a steady pace with his head up and his strides long, and he was there in under two minutes. He got in and drove north toward the freeway entrance. He noticed a small piece of paper, like a business card, under his windshield wiper. At the first red light he opened the door, snatched the card, and tossed it on the seat beside him, then drove. He got on the freeway, checked his mirrors frequently for a few minutes, and then began to think about what had just happened.

The man he had just killed was a professional shooter. One of the families — probably the Lazarettis — had gotten smart and realized that they probably shouldn't sit around waiting for him. They had also apparently admitted to themselves that the middle-aged, overweight former legbreakers they had been depending on weren't going to be able to protect the bosses from a determined attacker. All the families must have learned he had killed the Castigliones by now, and they had gone into protective mode. One of the families had hired a pro.

Schaeffer hoped the man had been a solitary operator, as he had once been. He didn't want to have to begin worrying about ambushes, booby traps, and assault weapons, but for the moment, at least, he would have to. His guess was that the Lazaretti family had done this. They were the family that had the longest and deepest relationships with violent locals. Operating drug distribution rings wasn't the same as passing money to movie and music companies. The people you met were a bit more feral.

The man had been waiting in an area that was ambiguous. It was near the house of Tony Lazaretti, the one who ran the Lazaretti interests, but it was also about a block down the street from the Castiglione caretaker, Mike Bruno. The Balacontano faction's ambassador to the film industry was Jimmy Montagno, and his house was only a block to the east. The man had not been waiting at one of the houses; he had simply set himself up in the neighborhood to see if anybody came to look around. That was smart.

He couldn't let down his guard now. There were still police, and there was no guarantee that the shooter he'd killed had been alone. That was disconcerting and made him look again in all of the mirrors to be sure a second shooter wasn't in a car following him. His eye caught the little white card that had been stuck under the windshield wiper of the car. He picked it up from the seat.

He was expecting an ad of some kind, but one side was blank, and the other had small, neat handwriting in black ink. CALL ME. URGENT. The phone number was the one Elizabeth Waring had given him in the Chicago church: 202 555-8990.

She had found his car in this city thousands of miles from the place she'd last seen him. How? Was there a global positioning system the Justice Department had activated? LoJack? The car had an antitheft system. Maybe she had triggered it. Maybe in Chicago the FBI had taken pictures of the license numbers of all the cars parked around Vince Pugliese's building that night, and she had somehow narrowed down the list. He had driven to Los Angeles quickly, trying to get to the next target before everybody reacted to the deaths of the Castiglione brothers. He'd stolen some California plates this morning off a pickup truck that was up on blocks and covered by a tarp, but hadn't put them on his car yet. The Illinois plates were still on the car, and that would have made it easier to spot. But if she'd known this was his car, why hadn't there been a contingent of FBI agents waiting with body armor and automatic weapons?

He left the freeway in Silverlake, drove to a quiet hillside street where his car was shielded from the windows of the nearby houses, and removed his Illinois plates. He drove a few more blocks, stopped, and put the California plates on his car.

He coasted downhill and found a convenience store on the first major street and went to the pay phone on the outer wall. He dialed the number of Elizabeth Waring. He waited a long time while the number rang, and he knew she must have gone to sleep after she'd found his car. When her voice came on, she sounded groggy and disoriented. "Hello?"

"What did you want?"

"I found out that the Lazaretti family hired a team of hit men to go after you."

"Why didn't you try to trap me when you found my car?"

"It cost me years to intuit your existence, then to meet you and realize how much you know. I want you to live to tell me about your former friends. Meanwhile, I thought I'd better warn you about the hit men, or you might get killed."

"I had already noticed a change in strategy. Thanks for the tip, though. It tells me a lot. Take care."

"Wait. I'm in Los Angeles right now. I need to talk to you in person. Is there anywhere you're willing to meet me?"

"Where are you staying?"

"The Sheraton Universal."

"I'll be in touch." He hung up, already wondering why he had called her and regretting that he had implied that he would meet her. She was dangerous and distracting at a time when he needed to keep up the pressure on the bosses. He hoped one of them would panic and do something stupid, but no matter what, he had to keep them nervous and off balance.

He knew the flaw in his reasoning was that it committed him to a course that probably wouldn't end well. He might be able to get a couple of families to begin picking each other off, but making them that agitated would first require him to accomplish a slow-motion massacre. He would have to show up in an increasing number of places where people would be waiting for him. And if he managed to get through it, all of the families would be more interested than before in killing him. What he was doing was arranging his own last stand, not his escape.

He knew that Elizabeth Waring was not his ally and that pretending she cared about him was a police interrogation tactic she'd probably been taught in some training class. She wanted an informant, and to recruit him she needed him in trouble and desperate. She had delivered the warning about the hit team to add to the growing pile of evidence that he was not likely to make it through this without help. But that did not negate the fact that she was the only person in this hemisphere who actually preferred that he live rather than die. If he listened to her next pitch, maybe he would hear something he could use. And no matter what, she worked for the most powerful entity in this game.

He got off the freeway at Laurel Canyon Boulevard and drove along Ventura Boulevard to Lankershim, turned left and then right to go up the steep hill to the Universal Studios complex. He stopped his car on the circle at the front entrance to the Sheraton

Universal Hotel, hurried inside, picked up a courtesy phone, and asked for her room.

"Hello?" she said.

"Come and meet me in the lobby. I'll be here for five minutes. If I see anything that makes me uncomfortable, I'm gone."

"Can you give me ten minutes to brush my hair?"

"Do it in the elevator." He hung up and went to sit in a velvet chair in an arrangement near the front entrance. The hotel lobby was all white and the floor yellow with black lines in geometric shapes. He scanned, looking at the people.

In the old days he could have picked out any FBI agents in something under two seconds. On jobs like this they would have been all male, and the ones who weren't white would have looked like black members of an all-star football team. Now FBI agents didn't look one particular way. He had to watch every human being within view, and if one of them let his eyes rest on Schaeffer for more than an instant, he became a possible enemy. The surveillance systems in public places like hotels should be good enough so they didn't even have to be here to see everything he did. He saw several sets of parents with kids, a couple dressed like they were on their way to the tennis courts, a group of young women who looked like the survivors of a bachelorette party.

He looked at his watch. Three minutes had passed. He turned his attention to the doors and the corridors extending out of the lobby in various directions. He had to be sure that if one of his ways out got suddenly blocked, the others were open. Then he heard a bell and an elevator door slid open.

Waring's head was up and her eyes were scanning as she stepped out. She walked toward him, and he put his arm around her waist and guided her across the lobby to the row of glass doors in front. She knew he was pressing close to her so federal officers couldn't shoot him without the risk of hitting her so she submitted to it.

They stayed together all the way to his car, and he drove off with her. As they coasted down the long hill to Lankershim Boulevard and then over the overpass to Ventura Boulevard, they were silent, each watching for signs that the other's friends or enemies were following. Finally he said, "We can talk. I don't care if you're wearing a wire."

"Thank you. I wasn't looking forward to being groped. I'm not wearing a wire." She paused. "I thought since you came for me so quickly, you might have had some kind of change of heart."

"Not exactly. I thought that you deserved a tidbit for trying to warn me. I was with Sam Lonzio the night that Chickie Salateri died."

"Sam Lonzio the Lazaretti underboss in New York?"

"Yeah. Salateri was sent out to Los Angeles to do some work for the Lazarettis."

"I remember the case. Somebody reported him missing and the Los Angeles police looked for him for over a year."

"When it's somebody like him, the cops have a way of looking where it's easy to look, not where the body's likely to be."

"So you know what happened."

"That night I was in L.A. because I had to do a job somewhere else, and I wanted to be far away from it. So I had checked into the Beverly Hills Hotel, rented a car, taken a plane somewhere else, done the job, and come back. I wasn't tired, so I went out for the evening. I went to a restaurant right near where Laurel Canyon ends on Sunset Boulevard and ordered a late dinner. In walks Sam Lonzio. He sees me and comes to my table. He said, 'Can I sit with you?' I said, 'Sam. I'm here in case somebody ever asks me where I was tonight. Do you want me to say I was with you?'

"He said, 'You can't do that here anyway. Tony Lazaretti has a half interest in the place. If you eat here, you'll look like a criminal. But I've got a good alibi, and you can share it.'

"I said, 'What is it?'

"'Tonight I'm on a cruise ship that stops in Ensenada. It left San Pedro already, but there's a guy on it in my cabin using my name. If I need an alibi, I show up in Ensenada anytime before the boat leaves for Cabo, and he goes home. The crew says

Mr. Lonzio's been with us for the whole cruise. I've also got a cabin in the name Don Rustin. You can be him.'

"'That's a lot of trouble.' I didn't bother to tell him that good alibis are simple. He had his own theory. But I said, 'What is it you're going to do that's such a big deal?'

"'I've got to take out Chickie Salateri.'

"'Why?'

"'He's been dating one of the Lazaretti daughters. You know, Carmine's granddaughter, Catherine. She lives out here in L.A. She was married at one time to Bobby Molto, but he couldn't ever keep it in his pants, and he didn't understand why you can't cheat on a boss's child, so she got an annulment. That was, like, five, six years ago. So lately she's dating Chickie Salateri. Only she comes home from a shopping trip one afternoon, and there's Salateri with one of those little digital cameras, taking pictures. He's taking shots of the clothes in her closet, has her bank statements out on her desk and takes shots of those. She sees him, but tiptoes back outside and comes back in making a lot of noise. He doesn't know she knows, just hides the camera in his coat. When he goes to the head, she checks the camera. There are shots of her jewelry all laid out in the little velvet drawers from her jewelry case.'

"'Why was he bothering with all that?'

"'At first we all thought he must be working for the IRS. You know — helping them say that if she had five or six million in jewelry and didn't work, where did it come from? They do that, the feds. They put your children in a bind so you can stew about it until you want to kill yourself. But Carmine Lazaretti didn't get to be old by ignoring that light coming along the train tracks toward him. He sent people from New York that Chickie didn't know, and they watched him and asked around. They found out he's been casing the house for a robbery. He's got a crew, and he's got an out-of-state fence for everything in the house. He's even hired a woman who looks a little bit like Catherine to use cloned credit cards and IDs to clean Catherine out.'

"'So you think he's planning to kill Catherine too.'

"'All of this stuff takes a lot of time to pull off. If she's dead, he's got a lot.'

"'So you're killing him tonight?'

"'They said to do it, but if I do it after he gets her, I'm dead too. Now that I see you're in town, it's like a sign from God.'

"'You want a minute to think that through again?'

"'You know what I mean. You can do it for me.'

"'Not interested.'

"'Look,' he said. 'I've killed two people in my whole life. One was a son of a bitch in Brooklyn who owned a pawnshop. Somebody's niece noticed it was suddenly full of stuff that had been stolen in our neighborhood. One of the Lazaretti soldiers took people past the front window for a week or so, and they identified what was theirs. So I got sent to handle it. The guy wasn't even armed. He just sat behind his desk and I shot him in the chest. The other one I don't want to talk about. I've got no experience. I'll give you fifteen grand to go with me and act as a consultant. I'll do all the shooting. Then we'll drive down and catch the cruise. Those ships are full of pairs of women who pay good money just to meet somebody like us, dance and drink a little, and get laid. They say a weekend like that is just the thing. It sets them right up and they're good for a month.'

"I said, 'We can skip the cruise, but I'll help you out.' So we left. He drove, and we picked up a big van. Inside it was a plastic container, maybe four feet by two and a half, with a vacuum top that latched. We went by Chickie Salateri's house, then a couple of clubs. At the third we found him. The club was a problem because a lot of people stay very late. So I told Lonzio, go in and buy him a drink, act like his friend, and persuade him to go to another club with us. He went in, and about twenty minutes later they both came out. So there were now three of us in the van, and the big plastic tub. I sat on that, and Chickie seemed to pay no attention to the thing, as though it were a piece of furniture. Sam drove up into Griffith Park. The place is huge. Sam said the route we were taking was a shortcut to get from Los Feliz into the Valley, where a great new club had opened, but it didn't feel like a shortcut. The road was weird and winding, and went up into the hills by the observatory. Then Sam says he's got a tire that seems funny, so he pulls over to check it. This struck Chickie Salateri as more than suspicious. But he thought the one assigned to kill him must be me. He started to pull out a gun to shoot me so I gave him a quick jab to the nose. Sam opened the passenger door beside him and stabbed him. Sam was not good with a knife so he just kept trying to kill him while Chickie fought back. It took four or five minutes before the bleeding got to him and he died. The van was a mess, and so was Sam. His shirt was soaked. He ended up tossing it in the plastic bin with Chickie."

"Where did you bury the box?"

"We didn't. Sam knew about this old cemetery in the middle of the city. It wasn't little bronze plaques set in a lawn. It was full of big gravestones and crypts. Sam drove right to a crypt. It was the kind that looked like a little marble building. He'd had somebody come through and saw the lock off in advance. The box fit right on this shelf in there. We put it in, went out, and Sam put on a brand-new lock."

"Do you remember the name on the crypt?"

"O'Hara. The newest date carved on the wall was 1956."

"That's a pretty respectful burial for the Mafia."

"He was a made guy, and he had family still around. They don't usually mutilate the body unless the guy talked to the cops."

She changed the subject. "So if I find the O'Hara crypt in a cemetery in the middle of Los Angeles, there will be Chickie Salateri in Tupperware."

"I think it was Rubbermaid, actually. The point is, the body is in there with Sam Lonzio's shirt with his blood and Chickie's on it."

"Why are you giving this to me?"

"You're welcome. It's because, for whatever reason, you've been trying to help me stay alive. And because, when the time came to vote in Arizona, all the bosses of the Lazaretti family, including Sam Lonzio, voted to get together and kill me."

"You don't ever forget, do you?"

"It was a memorable evening."

"Maybe the vote in Arizona was a moment of weakness for Lonzio. He was surrounded by his bosses."

"Everybody gets another chance, every day. If he doesn't like what he's been doing, he can do something different—even do the opposite of what he just did."

"I hope you believe that."

"What's your pitch?"

"Things have just changed for you. Now the people after you aren't a lot of old, fat cigar puffers trying to look tough. And they're not waiting for you to turn up when you happen to get down to them on your list. They're hiring real hitters—people just like you —who will make a professional effort to hunt you down."

He shrugged. "I already knew. They have connections with people who do this kind of work, and they've got a lot of money to spend. It's not a surprise."

"The ones they hire may not be as good at it as you, but how good do they have to be?"

"I'll have to think of ways to keep them to a high standard."

"Wouldn't it be better to get out of their reach?"

"If they're good enough, and there's enough money at stake, there is no such place."

She turned in her seat and watched him as she spoke. "I'm willing to offer you not a perfect thing, but a good thing. We'll put you up in a place that's secret and that would be extremely difficult for anybody to know about, much less get to. There are classified military installations here and abroad. Nobody can overhear the name of the facility and have the faintest idea where or what it is. A lot of these places are somewhere in the middle of huge bases that are themselves remote and difficult to get into. You and I would meet once a day for a few weeks at a time, to chat. This might go on for a year or two, longer if you want. You would have to make your own deal for immunity with your own lawyer."

"You're not offering blanket immunity?"

"They approve that for people who give us suspects who are much worse than the informants are. I don't think the attorney general's office would approve blanket immunity for you. Everything you've done is a capital crime. I think I can get you some kind of immunity for the crimes you tell us about. Anything else, and you'd be fair game."

"And the court testimony?"

"You would have to testify in the cases where that's the best route to a conviction. If you're the eyewitness, it's unavoidable. But they wouldn't have you testifying against bookies and bagmen and corrupt accountants. The prosecution would look ridiculous bringing in someone like you for that. I'd say you should expect to testify against a few bosses. Just having you in a court saying you know them and have worked for them would be a big strike against them in the minds of a jury."

"There's a lot of showmanship in your business, isn't there?"

"Yes," she said. "Right now, we're talking about big, news-making prosecutions of Mafia bosses. This is how we do them. We find somebody who was on the inside, who knows enough details so there can't be a mistake, and we make a deal with him to testify."

"Is this your whole pitch?" he asked. "Your whole offer?"

"I can't give you money, except in the form of support while you're working with us."

"I don't need money."

"Good."

"And your bosses have agreed to everything else?"

"No," she said. "Right now, nobody knows I'm talking to you. This is an emergency. I have to make my best offer to you now, before you're dead. I can talk to them after you're safe."

"Then what you're offering is theoretical. Your boss isn't behind you on this, or you wouldn't be flying around the country without telling him what you're doing."

She sighed. "I'll be completely open with you. My boss, the deputy assistant attorney general in charge of my section, is a political appointee. He's still green, and has no experience making deals with informants, and feels suspicious about the practice. He'll learn as he goes. If we didn't make arrangements of this sort, we'd still be trying to prove the Mafia exists. His bosses know that, and if I can bring in the offer of your services, they'll explain it to him. But no. At this moment he doesn't know what I'm doing."

"So you haven't actually got any offer."

"What I've described is what I believe I can get approved, even over the objections of my boss. If his bosses feel reluctant to over-rule him, I have other allies I've collected over the years who would help persuade them. Some are powerful people. A call from any of them would almost certainly work wonders."

"I'm impressed by your commitment," he said. "You'll use up all your markers and call in all the one-time favors. It will leave you without the power to do much else."

"You'll give it back to me. If I can get convictions of a fair number of the old men, then I'll have more friends than I can use. It will also accomplish what you want most. Putting these people in prison forever, just like you did Carlo Balacontano, is as good as killing them, isn't it?"

He pursed his lips, and there was a pained expression in his eyes. "I appreciate the offer, and I believe it's real. But I can't accept it."

"What's wrong? What is it that's missing? I'm offering to keep you alive for as long as you want federal protection. If you don't get off the streets to a place where they can't reach you, they'll kill you."

"They'll keep trying, certainly."

She watched him as he drove back along Ventura Boulevard to Lankershim and then up the steep hill to her hotel. As he pulled into the circle in front of the entrance, she said, "Maybe this isn't the best I can do. Give me a chance. You haven't said what's missing. Just tell me, and I'll try to get it."

"Freedom," he said.

"I don't know how to give you that," she said. "The things you've done don't leave me a way."

"Exactly."

He stopped in front of the entrance and looked at her expectantly. She got out of the car and then stood for a moment, watching him as he moved the car forward and turned to leave the circular drive.

30

HE DROVE OFF the circle and onto the driveway, watching her in the rearview mirror as she turned, walked into the hotel, and disappeared. He felt a small twinge of regret as he turned from the driveway onto the sloping road down the hill. He had begun to feel a kind of interest in her. It wasn't affection, just a kind of sympathy for her position in this mess. He thought about the little he knew about her. She had, about twenty years ago, signed on at the Justice Department. Since then, she had apparently given her job an honest effort. She had lost her husband somehow—cancer, if he remembered right—before he had even become aware of who she was, and she had raised her two kids alone. He was glad she hadn't done anything foolish to try to get him captured. He would have hated killing her.

He coasted down the long hill from the Universal complex, keeping his speed from increasing too quickly. The steep road headed due west to Lankershim Boulevard, then flattened and crossed it onto the bridge over the freeway. As he reached the level pavement at the bottom of the hill at the intersection, he looked in his rearview mirror and saw something that disturbed him. The car coming down the hill behind him was a dark blue Ford Crown Victoria. There was a driver wearing a baseball cap and sunglasses, a tan short-sleeved shirt over a black T-shirt. A man in the passenger seat wore a brimmed cap that was a drab beige. He had a moustache and wore a pair of yellow shooting glasses.

It was this man that disturbed him. He was fiddling with something that rested on his lap. The fact that the car was pointed downward on the hill allowed Schaeffer to see through the windshield over the dashboard into the front seats. What the man in the passenger seat had on his lap appeared to be a small automatic weapon with a long silencer fitted on the short barrel. It looked like an Ingram MAC-10. He lifted it slightly, barrel upward, and slid a long magazine into the handle. Then he turned the weapon slightly and fiddled with the selector lever.

The light turned green, but Schaeffer didn't cross Lankershim. Instead, he quickly turned right just as the first of a large group of pedestrians was stepping off the curb into the crosswalk that led to the Universal Studios entrance from the bus and subway station across the street. He glanced in the mirror and saw that the stream of people that had spilled into the wake of his car had blocked the blue Crown Victoria. He memorized the car's exact color and shape as he sped up Lankershim.

He veered to the right at the fork onto Cahuenga, then turned right again to try to lose himself in the residential streets on that side. He had no real knowledge of the neighborhood, but he had the sense that in the flats of the east valley, there was a grid of north-south streets crossed by the big east-west boulevards — Ventura, Moorpark, Riverside, Magnolia, Burbank. He made a zigzag pattern as he sped away from Universal. He turned right on Riverside and drove east. He remembered that in this direction were Griffith Park and Burbank and Pasadena.

He had to find a telephone. As he drove along Riverside, he saw a Marie Callender's restaurant. He swung into the parking lot, trotted into the building, and put coins into the pay phone by the men's room. He dialed Elizabeth Waring's cell number. He heard her say "Hello?"

"It's me," he said.

"Have you changed—"

"No. Just listen. When I drove away from your hotel, two men in a blue Crown Vic pulled out after me. If they don't belong to you, then they're more shooters."

"How can you be sure?"

"One of them has what looks like a MAC-10 with a silencer. Are they yours?"

"No."

"They didn't follow me to your hotel today. I was watching for somebody like them. That means they knew where you were staying, and after they lost me in Pasadena this morning, they went to your hotel. They must have assumed that at some point I would show up."

"I can call the—"

"Don't call anybody. You've got to get on a plane and go home now. Right now. As soon as they realize they've lost me, they'll be back at your hotel. You're all they've got. So go."

"But I—" Even as she began to argue, she knew she was talking to dead air. She pressed the button on her phone, stepped to the closet, laid each outfit in her suitcase, and folded it over once. She went into the bathroom, got her toiletry kit, set it in the suitcase, and shut it.

She lifted the suitcase off the stand and set it on the floor, extended the handle, then picked up the hotel phone and punched the number for the front desk. "This is Ms. Waring in room 802. I'm checking out now. Could you please hold a cab for me? I'll be going to LAX."

As she rode the elevator down to the lobby, she reviewed what had just happened and what she was about to do. She was satisfied. She had no doubt that the Butcher's Boy, of all people, would recognize a pair of professional assassins if he saw them and would make a reliable guess about how they had come to be where they were. If professional killers knew who she was, then he was right that it was best for her to leave Los Angeles. If he lost them—when he lost them—they could only go back to her hotel looking for her. They seemed to see her as their easiest link to him. They probably assumed she would be a valuable hostage, or at least bait for an ambush.

They obviously didn't get it. They had no way of knowing that he was incapable of forming personal ties to people like her and that, most of the time, he cared very little which people died and which didn't. For him, death had always been a commodity to sell and be paid for. At the moment he was only interested in killing as many of the men who had voted to kill him as he could.

She strode quickly to the front desk, accepted the printed bill, and said, "Leave it on my credit card." The clerk at the desk said, "Your cab is at the door, Ms. Waring. Have a pleasant flight."

"Thank you," she said, and kept going. She had not exactly stopped, just walked along the counter on the way out. As the driver put her suitcase into the trunk, she sat in the back seat and scanned the lot, the sidewalks, the long drive. The driver got in and asked, "Which airline are you going to?" and she answered, "United. Terminal Seven." As he drove, she looked out the back window for a long time, hoping that the absence of the team of shooters didn't mean that they had caught up with the Butcher's Boy.

Schaeffer walked out of the restaurant with his head down and crossed the parking lot. He got into his car and pulled out of the lot onto Riverside Drive and headed eastward. He drove with determination, but was careful not to go too far over the speed limit. No matter what was chasing him, he couldn't afford to be pulled over with about a dozen stolen guns, all of them loaded, and some of them the property of dead men.

He drove to Victory Boulevard, turned right and then left onto the long parkway into Griffith Park. The speed limit was twenty-five, but the road was nearly empty at midday on a weekday, so he went forty. He took the long curve around the parking lot of the Los Angeles Zoo, but when he was nearly around the curve he looked across the lot and saw the blue Crown Victoria just starting toward him at the beginning of the curve.

He sped up, goading the Camry along the straight stretch that bisected the golf course. There was a stop sign ahead, and it looked like the perfect spot to hide a police car, so he stopped for it. As he did, he saw a sign that said CAROUSEL. He cranked the wheel to the right and drove up the side road in the direction the arrow pointed. There was a rise, and then the road dipped and turned into a little vale. There was a parking lot to the left, over a low grassy hill away from the carousel. He parked, got out of the car, took his messenger bag full of guns and ammunition, and ran for the wooded hillside above the carousel. He took cover and looked down at the lower ground. The carousel looked like the real thing, a relic of the early 1900s that had been restored at some point by people who at least cared how it looked. The horses had a layer of bright, shiny paint, and the brass poles were worn by hands but polished. A few feet away from it was a small ticket booth, and beyond that was a snack bar, but he couldn't see anyone inside either structure. Finally, he saw a sign on the booth that said OPEN WEEKENDS with smaller print beneath that was unreadable from this distance. He supposed that when school was in session, there was no reason to keep the carousel running.

He was still dressed in the gray hooded sweatshirt and jeans he'd worn to case the houses in Pasadena before dawn. He judged that the outfit would keep him from standing out much in these wooded hillsides, but he kept moving, climbing to improve his cover while he watched for the blue car. He didn't want to go too high, where the short live oaks were sparsely spread and there were stretches of empty brown grass. He crouched in thick brush about three hundred feet away. As he looked down on the scene, he sensed a presence, or maybe realized he'd seen something without identifying it, and moved only his eyes in that direction. It was a scrawny, intense-eyed coyote standing thirty feet off, the sunlight dappling its fur. After a few seconds, the coyote seemed to sense some change it didn't like and skulked off into the tawny brush higher up the hillside.

The dark blue Crown Victoria pulled up the drive into the lot and stopped. The two men got out and slammed the doors, then walked toward the carousel. They stood and looked at it for a minute or two, and then the one with the MAC-10 stepped to the left to the ticket booth. He craned his neck to look at the window, seemed to despair of seeing inside, and gave up. He raised his MAC-10 with its silencer on the barrel and fired a line of rounds across the front of the booth about six inches from the ground, then a second line back across the booth about two feet up. The noise was barely audible, just the gun's hot, expanded gas spitting out bullets, and the bullets punching through the wooden-board wall. The gun was so fast that after it was still, the ejected brass casings clinked as they all fell on the asphalt, bounced once, and rolled. The man removed the long, straight magazine, put it in his coat pocket, and inserted a fresh one.

Thirty rounds. If Schaeffer had been closer, he could have counted holes in the ticket booth, but he was pretty sure the man was using thirty-round magazines. The second man kicked open the door of the ticket booth, looked inside, and closed it again, but it was hanging on one hinge so he just propped it shut.

They moved to the second, larger building, the snack stand. It was hardly more substantial than the ticket booth, but they didn't spray the wall. They went to the door, and the man with the MAC-10 fired a short burst at the door lock and then shouldered his way inside. The two spent a minute or two looking behind things, but found nothing.

Schaeffer could see the MAC-10 had altered their behavior. It was such an overpowering weapon that they seemed to have forgotten that it couldn't do everything. And they seemed to think it made them bulletproof. He began to move down the hill closer to them while he waited for his moment to come. The two men came out of the snack stand and moved to the carousel. They stepped into the center where the motor was and satisfied themselves that he wasn't hiding there. While they were occupied, Schaeffer crept closer.

They walked up over the grass-covered hill to the parking lot and toward his parked Camry. They seemed not to feel any urgency about what they were doing. Schaeffer watched the one with the MAC-10 raise it and fire short bursts at the tires on the far side, then shoot out all the glass. His magazine was empty again so he put in a third. This time he aimed at the engine and fired. He walked around to the other side to get the last pair of tires. He had not noticed that the car no longer shielded him from the brush-covered hillside; he was standing in the open.

As the man began his burst, Schaeffer rested his right arm on the low horizontal branch of an oak tree, took careful aim, and fired. His first shot caught the man with the MAC-10 in the back and spun him around. As the man began to buckle, Schaeffer fired another shot and caught him in the chest. The man sprawled on the pavement.

His companion, the driver, snatched up the MAC-10, ducked, and stayed low as he scuttled to the far side of Schaeffer's car. When he got there, he learned what Schaeffer already suspected. The third magazine was empty.

Schaeffer shifted his aim to the second man. He rested his arm on the tree limb and fired whenever he saw a slice of the man appear over the hood of the Camry as he tried to spot the man who had shot his companion.

When Schaeffer had exhausted the bullets in the Beretta's magazine, he reached into his messenger bag for another pistol. He aimed it carefully at the far edge of the hood of his gray car, directly above the flat front tire. The man would be crouching there to keep from having a shot ricochet under the car and hit him. He counted to five, then began to squeeze the trigger. His trigger finger had already traveled about two-thirds of the pull when the man raised his gun hand and his head above the edge so he could return Schaeffer's fire. He was still raising his head when Schaeffer's firing pin touched off the next round. The shot barely nicked the surface of the Camry's hood, ricocheted upward slightly, and pounded into the man's forehead.

Schaeffer knew he had little time left. The MAC-10 was silenced, but his pistols were not. He ran from the woods, past the carousel, across the little parking lot, and stood over the driver, the man he had just shot. Schaeffer kicked the man's pistol away from his body, patted his pockets, and found the keys to the blue Crown Victoria. He noticed a tag on it that said ABLE SECURITY. He stepped to the car and set his messenger bag on the floor in front of the passenger seat, beside a clipboard with papers on it. He stepped back to the Camry, opened the trunk, took his suitcase, tossed it onto the back seat of the Crown Victoria, and drove.

He regretted the destruction of the gray Camry because it had been a good car for driving unnoticed and unremembered. The Crown Victoria was less common, but it had a powerful engine, and from a distance it looked like a plain-wrap police car or a fire commander's car. He took it down the park's side road away from the carousel to the main road and turned right toward the south.

Once he was on the main road through the park, he felt less urgency and tension. The park police would take a few minutes to isolate the source of the shots and then drive there and find the two bodies. There would be at least a few minutes while they tried various ways of fitting together what they saw. There were two men with guns lying nearby, one of them an automatic weapon with a silencer. Had they killed each other? Once the cops learned enough at the scene to reject that idea, they would start calling to shut down park exits, but he would be gone.

He glided past a pony ride and a little train station with a midget train circulating on a narrow track that wound through a grove of trees. The road emptied onto Los Feliz Boulevard, and he sensed that he had emerged in another part of the city. He drove south as steadily as he could, making it through the traffic signals on the green and turning right when they were red, then correcting his course when he could do it without slowing down. In five minutes he was three miles away and still moving.

He thought about what had happened today. He had been ambushed and attacked twice, and it was time to counterstrike. Judging from the car keys, the clipboard, and the car model, the two men he had just killed had been working for something called Able Security Service as a cover. He tried to guess what the rest of the shooters would do next. They wouldn't fall back to some defensive position. They weren't bodyguards hired to protect somebody. They were killers hired to find him and kill him. They would be out looking for him.

He got onto the Golden State Freeway, merged onto the 134 Freeway going east, and drove hard. He got off at the Lake Avenue exit and turned left at San Pasqual Street. He turned into a long, narrow parking lot that ran behind a row of stores, cruised up the back aisle searching for a parking space, and finally found one. He was in a busy shopping area, and shoppers were constantly leaving their cars or coming back to them, so he had to be careful not to let any of them see what he was doing. He picked up the clipboard from the floor and looked at the papers clipped to it. The sheet said ABLE SECURITY PATROL LOG. He went to the Crown Victoria's trunk, set the clipboard inside, opened his suitcase, pulled out a sport jacket, and put away his gray hooded sweatshirt. He brought the messenger bag to the front, selected two pistols, checked their magazines, and hid them in his coat. He pulled out of the lot and drove out to Lake Avenue, then turned off again.

He skirted the busy streets to stay in the quieter neighborhoods. He made it back to Marengo and studied the houses. He thought about the blue Crown Victoria he was driving. It was one of the reasons why he had suspected the shooters worked for a security company. The car looked like a police car, and they would have wanted to take advantage of that resemblance. It would be the sort of thing that would make some opponents panic, and others do what they were told.

Using the car was probably worth a try if he did it quickly and insistently enough. It was now early afternoon. He had seen Lazaretti once or twice, but he was sure Lazaretti had never noticed him. He lifted his messenger bag onto the passenger seat and found the Justice Department identification wallet he had stolen from Elizabeth Waring in Chicago and put it into his coat pocket.

He pulled in front of Tony Lazaretti's driveway and parked at an angle, blocking it the way cops did. He walked at a brisk pace to the front porch, rang the bell, and knocked loudly at the same time.

The man who came to the door was about twenty-five years old and had the watchful eyes of a store security guard, but he was wearing a black sport coat and a pair of jeans, with neoprene-soled deck shoes on his feet. "May I help you?" He said it with a scowl of contempt: this middle-aged cop, or whatever he was, had no idea who he was bothering.

Schaeffer took out the leather identification wallet with its deeply embossed Department of Justice seal and flipped it open. "Elliot Warren, Department of Justice. I'd like to speak with Mr. Anthony Lazaretti, please."

"What's this about?"

"It's about him not going to a federal prison for the meeting in Arizona last week with a couple hundred Mafia guys who were conspiring to commit murder. Think he'll be interested?"

The young man's face went blank, like a curtain falling to end a play. "Please wait here." He turned and hurried up the staircase in the middle of the foyer. The house was old, with thick wooden fixtures squared off in the California Craftsman style and a large stained-glass window that cast a glow over the first landing. As Schaeffer stood watching the young man disappear, he thought about the risk he was taking. He had never met Tony Lazaretti. But if there was somebody here who had seen him in the old days, Schaeffer would have a problem. He would be caught standing alone in this open foyer, with no escape but through the front door and down the open driveway to the car.

He kept looking up the staircase, then from the foyer where he was to the long hall that led past the staircase to the kitchen and the back of the house. There were wide doorways on either side of the foyer, and he decided he needed to know where they led.

281

He stepped deeper into the house and looked to his right. Beyond the doorway was the formal dining room with a single long table down the center of the room. It shone like the back of a violin. He looked to his left and saw a library. It had floor-to-ceiling shelves filled with books. But they weren't books for reading. They were books of the sort that decorators bought by the truckload—big old volumes in leather bindings. There was a big globe on a stand, and a small mahogany table with a copy of the entertainment section of the *Los Angeles Times* open on it.

He decided that must be where the kid who had come to the door had been stationed when he'd arrived. He lingered in the doorway, looking up the stairs at the second-floor landing. He heard a door shut and footsteps, and a moment later three men appeared at the top of the stairs. Two of them stood at the railing and looked down at him, while the other descended. When Schaeffer had seen Tony Lazaretti years ago, he had looked like what he was—a kid of college age who had been brought up thinking he was a prince, somebody who could never be harmed, never be required to do anything, but would always be in charge. He'd had the look of the Lazarettis, the thick curly hair at the top of his head and the pointed chin at the bottom so he looked like an inverted triangle.

As Lazaretti came down the steps, he said, "Mr. Warren? Or is it Agent Warren?"

"It's Mr. Warren. Can you spare me a few minutes alone, please?" He held up his Justice Department identification wallet, then put it away.

"What's this about?"

"In here?" Schaeffer pointed at the library. "Is this a good place to talk?"

"Yeah, sure," said Lazaretti. "That's fine."

They walked inside, and Lazaretti closed the big wooden door. Schaeffer stepped to the door and flipped the small lever above the handle to lock it. Lazaretti looked puzzled, but seemed not to know what to say.

"Mr. Lazaretti, I understand you were at the meeting in Arizona a week ago."

"I was in Arizona, yes. I wasn't at any meeting. If somebody else happened to be there at the same time, that's just what happens at high-end resorts. I was on the French Riviera when the Cannes film festival was going on, but that doesn't make me an actor."

"When Frank Tosca called for an agreement to help him kill a man he'd been searching for, you voted for it. Since you came back, you hired a team of hit men to go after him."

Lazaretti looked pale, and his forehead seemed to be getting damp. "You've got me mixed up with somebody else. Lazaretti sounds a lot like some other names, especially if you're listening from far away."

Schaeffer took out one of his Beretta pistols and aimed it at Lazaretti's chest. "I just wanted you to know what your mistake was. Some people like to know."

"What? What do you mean?" He instinctively backed away, but bumped against the tall, immovable bookcase behind him.

"I mean I would have left you alone until the end of time." He fired two rounds into Tony Lazaretti's chest, watched him fall, then fired a round through his head.

He stepped to the library window, reached up to unlatch it, opened it and pushed the screen out, sat on the sill, and swung his legs out. He could hear rapid footsteps on the staircase. He dropped to the garden. The first sounds of pounding on the locked library door reached his ears as he stood outside the window. He leaned into the room, fired six rapid shots through the upper panels of the door, then turned and walked quickly across the lawn to the driveway he had blocked. He got into the blue car and drove off toward the freeway.

He got on the 134 Freeway, drove to an off-site parking structure near the Burbank Airport, took his messenger bag and suitcase, and walked to the airport. He flagged a cab and had the driver take him to a big Holiday Inn on Century Boulevard, right outside Los Angeles International Airport.

As soon as he had checked in, he called for a reservation on a flight to Baltimore/Washington airport. Then he went to work preparing to travel. He laid out all of the pistols he had in his messenger bag. After examining all of them, he unhesitatingly selected the Kel-Tec PF-9 that he had taken from one of the guards at Vince Pugliese's building in Chicago. It was a nine-millimeter pistol with a single-stack magazine that held seven rounds. It was under six inches long and less than an inch wide. He dismantled it and examined the pieces, measuring them with his fingers. Then he went shopping.

He walked along Century Boulevard to a computer store on Sepulveda Boulevard, and bought a backup drive for a computer. It was only a small black metal box with a power cord and a USB connector. He saw from the one that was on display that when it was plugged in, all that could be seen was a glowing green light. He paid cash for it, and then went to a grocery store down the street and bought a few essentials — a tiny screwdriver for repairing eyeglasses and a roll of aluminum foil.

When he was back at the hotel, he used the small screwdriver to open the backup drive. He took each of the pieces of the PF-9 pistol, wrapped it loosely in aluminum foil, and then put it inside the metal housing. He took little care with the memory components, only watching to see if crushing or removing things would make the green light go out. When he had all of the pieces inside the housing, he used the screwdriver to close it. The green light still glowed. He unplugged the device, put it back in its original box, and put the box inside his suitcase. Then he took his messenger bag and went out again. He went for a walk, placing his other guns inside plastic trash bags in the Dumpsters he found at the backs of hotels and stores. When he had none left, he threw away the messenger bag too.

It was six o'clock. He had only four hours left before his redeye flight to Baltimore/Washington, so he took a two-hour nap, showered and dressed, and took a shuttle bus to the airport. He checked his suitcase in at the desk and then went through security and walked to his concourse to wait for his flight. He spent much of the half hour he had left in the back section of an airport bookstore looking at books because he couldn't be seen from the concourse there. At boarding time he bought a book, walked to his gate, and scanned the passengers who were lining up to be sure none of them was familiar.

On the plane he kept his seat straight up, leaned his head back into the padding, closed his eyes, and thought about Washington and the things he would have to do when he got there. The plane roared, then tilted backward as it climbed rapidly into the sky, and when it leveled off, Schaeffer was asleep.

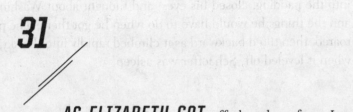

31

AS ELIZABETH GOT off the plane from Los Angeles and walked along the concourse at Reagan International, it was nearly five P.M. She had gone a hundred yards past shops and food concessions before she realized that she had made a decision without knowing that she was deciding anything. She went out through the baggage claim and stood at the taxi stand. When it came to be her turn, she said to the dispatcher, "The J. Edgar Hoover Building."

She hadn't exactly anticipated that either, but after she had said it, she realized it had been implied in her decision. She sat quietly with her suitcase beside her in the back seat of the cab, and watched the familiar buildings of the city loom and disappear. It occurred to her that she never called it the Hoover building except when she was feeling particularly intimidated by it. The fact that the FBI building was named for J. Edgar Hoover and the Justice Department was named after Robert F. Kennedy always seemed appropriate. The Kennedy building was just on the south side of the Hoover building, but they were not the same place at all. At the Hoover building she was an outsider.

The cab driver was just about to start telling her about some outrage perpetrated in Congress this week, when she said, "Excuse me, I'm sorry, but I've got to call my children." She dialed her home number and let it ring until the voice mail came on. "Hi, it's me," she said. "I'm just calling to let you know my flight has arrived and I'm on my way to the office for the last hour of the day, and then I'll be home. I thought you'd probably be home already. I hope everything is okay. If not, call me."

When the cab arrived, she got out, stood in front of the building on Pennsylvania Avenue with her suitcase, took out her cell phone, and dialed the number of Special Agent Holman.

He answered his cell phone, "Holman."

"Hi, John," she said. "This is Elizabeth Waring. I'm standing outside the Hoover building right now. I just got off a plane from Los Angeles, and I believe I need a favor."

"What are you doing out there? Come on up."

"It's embarrassing, but I lost my Justice Department ID. I've only got an out-of-date one with me. I imagine the security people will think I'm trying to test their alertness, so they'll stop and detain me."

"Probably. Using expired ID is the kind of thing the inspector general's people do as a test. I'll be right down."

She stayed in front of the ugly concrete building. The center of the city was filled with beautiful old gray stone buildings with enormous pillars and imposing steps. But the FBI headquarters looked like a computer science building in a cash-strapped Midwestern college. While she waited she faced to the side so she wasn't staring at each person who came out and wasn't blocking the sidewalk. She felt odd standing there with a suitcase, but it was a carry-on, no bigger than the wheeled carts some attorneys brought to courthouses. She hoped people who saw her invented some sensible reason for her to be here with it.

After what seemed like a long time, she saw the door open and John Holman came out smiling. "Elizabeth."

"Thanks for coming out," she said. "I can't imagine what happened to my ID. I've ordered a new one, but it takes time to airbrush out the wrinkles on the photograph."

He laughed. "I just hope there isn't some teenaged girl out arresting people with your ID."

"I'll chance it."

"Come on, and I'll vouch for your identity and get you past the skeptics."

"Thanks."

They went into the building, stopped at the security barrier to present their identification, and rode the elevator up to the third floor. She walked with him, feeling a bit out of place, like a suspect being brought in for an interrogation. But then he opened a door with his name on it and they were in an office much like hers. There was a big desk and a leather chair behind it, but he sat across from her in one of the chairs around a table.

As she sat, he got up and brought a yellow legal pad and pen from his desk and dropped them on the table, then sat again. "You said you needed a favor?"

"I did, and I do," she said. "I just got off a plane from Los Angeles. When I got there, I went to the neighborhood where some of the Mafia caretakers from the east have houses. I was pretty sure he would be there taking a look. I drove up and down the streets before dawn, checking license plates and car descriptions against the ones the FBI people had recorded around Vincent Pugliese's building in Chicago. I found his and left him a note with a number where he could reach me."

"Did he call?"

"Yes. He said he'd be in touch, and then showed up at my hotel five minutes later and demanded I go off in his car with him right away."

"And you had no time to call for a remote surveillance or anything?"

"I believed that this was the best shot I would ever get with him, to persuade him to act as a Justice Department informant. You have to realize that this man knows enough to put practically the whole older generation in jail, and I had information that might make him see the odds were against him and getting worse. I had to try."

"Didn't you worry that he might change his mind and kill you?"

"He'd had several chances to kill me and shown no inclination. So I went with him. While he drove me around, I made my best pitch to get him to come in. It was based on my experience of what the department has approved for other informants in the past. I was realistic. I said we would offer him the highest level of protection from his enemies during a two- or three-year period while he was talking to us about what he knew. I said he would testify in court against criminal defendants of a high level only if there was a case against them. He would be granted immunity only for crimes he told us about. At the end of the period he would be on his own. And I told him that we now have intelligence that at least one family has hired a team of high-end professional killers to hunt him down."

"And he turned you down?"

"Right. I realize now that unless he's sure he's about to die, it's a bad deal to him. If we had him in custody for a serious crime, a deal might seem more attractive."

"And you need FBI help to get him in custody."

"I've delayed asking for too long. As long as there seemed to be a chance of doing this simply, I kept pursuing the possibility. But today I realized that I had made a horrible mistake. I waited for him to get himself cornered so my offer would look good, but that wasn't happening. He was succeeding. He's declared a personal vendetta on the bosses who were at that meeting in Arizona, and he's killing them, one after another. He's killed Frank Tosca, all three of the Castiglione brothers, and their underboss, Vincent Pugliese. In order to do that, he's had to kill seven or eight soldiers and hired men. Today he was in Los Angeles, and I think he was after the Lazaretti family. The one to get would be Tony Lazaretti, who's not only a blood relative, the nephew of Don Carlos Lazaretti, but also the head of the western businesses."

"Is this something you know, or you're guessing?"

"You were the one who told me it was a Lazaretti soldier who said they'd hired a team of killers to find him. When I got to Los Angeles and told him there was a team of killers, he seemed to know already, and to know who had hired them."

Holman looked tired. "A couple of hours ago, we received word that Tony Lazaretti was killed in his house by an unknown assailant. There was also an associate of his killed in the gunfight and another seriously wounded. The Los Angeles field office is also looking into two men who were found dead in Griffith Park. One had an Ingram MAC-10 with a silencer. I'm sure all of this will be in your own reports, but I forwarded it to you in case."

"Oh, God." She winced and looked down.

"What do you want to do?"

"He needs to be apprehended. We can't let him go on killing people. I'd like him alive, if possible. He knows about the people who came up with him thirty years ago, the people who are running the mob right now. But he's very good at killing people, and he'll keep doing it. Even though his enemies are some of the worst people in the world, this has got to stop now."

"You shouldn't blame yourself for Tony Lazaretti or the others. They all knew what he was, and they underestimated him. In their business, that's a fatal mistake."

"Well, I've got to change the focus of what I'm doing now." She handed him a piece of paper she had torn from the notebook she carried in her purse. "Here. I wrote this down on the plane. He's in Los Angeles, or was yesterday, driving a gray three-to-five-year-old Toyota Camry with Illinois plates, number E905E 783. He was carrying two Beretta M92 pistols. And the place he's going to strike—he already has, so it's too late for that. There are a couple of other possibilities, but I don't think he'll stay in Los Angeles long enough to do any others."

"We can initiate a multistate search for the car, but if he's dumped it already, there's not much . . . wait a minute. The Camry thing sounds familiar." He stood and went behind his desk, woke up his computer, and typed in an identifier. He read for a few seconds. "Yep. Here it is. When they found the two men in Griffith Park, they were beside a shot-up Toyota Camry that had plates issued for a Ford pickup."

"Worse and worse. Now the only thing I have is my own ability to identify him. The first thing I'll do is arrange for a session with a police artist. Then I'll just have to start over. I'm ready to start planning a trap. I'll try to get a message to him using personal ads in major papers. That worked once. And I'll have to lie and say that my bosses have given me permission to improve my last offer."

"That brings up the next question. If the FBI arranges to work with you and set up this trap to get him into custody, what happens next? Does the DOJ handle the prosecution of this man and take the case from there?"

"If the Butcher's Boy left evidence at the crime scenes, or resists arrest, or an eyewitness appears once we have him safely locked away, we'll prosecute. If not, I'll still try to get him to talk. But things in the department haven't changed. Deputy Assistant Attorney General Hunsecker will not cooperate with this in any way at the moment. If he learns this is how I've been spending my time, he'll try to fire me. I'm hoping that I can persuade him not to. If I can make it clear that I intend to capture and try to convict this man, not coddle him and make generous deals with him, I think the sun will come out and Hunsecker will have a different feeling about it."

"Look, Elizabeth. People in the Bureau think highly of you, and you've earned a lot of respect. I'd hate to see your career end in departmental infighting with a political hack. Maybe this is one of those times when we have to wait for the stars to align just right before we take irrevocable action."

Elizabeth stood up. "John, you've been a terrific ally, and now you're behaving like a friend. Thanks for everything. But I don't want to wait. As soon as I'm able to think through a plan, I'll call you. I don't want to delay acting on this. I seem to be the one that opened the box, so it's my responsibility."

"All right," he said. "I'll be waiting."

She opened the office door and went out, rolling her small suitcase behind her. She headed for the Pennsylvania Avenue exit. She would be in her office in five minutes. Then she could start devising ways to betray the Butcher's Boy.

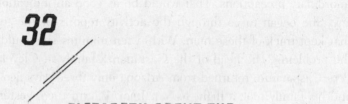

32

ELIZABETH SPENT THE last hour of the day in her office at the Robert F. Kennedy Building. She studied the reports of the carnage in Los Angeles, trying to piece together exactly what had happened. There seemed to be three shooting victims who fit the profile for high-end killers. They all had infantry experience and time overseas, but no record of promotions or decorations, then some time working as mercenary contractors—bodyguards for foreign businessmen, mostly. Two had short stints working in Los Angeles for agencies that provided temporary protection for celebrities. One had a record for assault, one had a weapons conviction. But for the past two years, none of them had any record of employment.

It was hard for her to work out the choreography. One had been in Pasadena and two in Griffith Park. The car that looked like it had been in a war was the Butcher's Boy's Camry. From the description of the car and the presence of the MAC-10, she knew that the two at Griffith Park were the ones who had waited for him at her hotel. She also knew that the one body that hadn't turned up anywhere was his. The winner was the one who walked—or drove—away. One car was found at the scene, which meant he probably took the other. He was still out there somewhere.

What was he doing? He was preparing to kill another boss of

another Mafia family somewhere. There could be little question of that. Killing the bosses was his whole strategy. It would take some thought for her to put together a list of likely candidates, and then she would probably be wrong about a few of them. If she could figure it out, so could the chosen victim.

It occurred to her that maybe the chosen victim had figured it out. Maybe one or another of the bosses was now taking extraordinary precautions. That would be as good an indication as any. She began to go through the activity reports of the teams that kept track of these men. Within ten minutes she could see the problem: "The head of the Castananza family in Cleveland, Pete Castananza, returned from Arizona only three days ago. He and his family took a flight to San Juan, Puerto Rico, yesterday. They are believed to be on a private boat somewhere in the Caribbean." "Four days ago John Mangano of the New York Mangano family was followed to a house in Telluride, Colorado, owned by New York attorney Andrew Spiegel." "Over a period of a week, beginning with the funeral of Frank Tosca, members of the Balacontano family have been gathering in Saratoga Springs on Carlo Balacontano's stud farm. At least thirty men are now in the property, and as each group arrives, they bring more supplies and groceries." It wasn't some single boss who knew he would be next. It was a general retreat to defensible places. As she looked down the long list of reports, the examples simply multiplied. Some of the old men were taking sudden vacations, and others were making preparations that seemed appropriate to some kind of siege. None seemed to be feeling less vulnerable than the others. At this point, all of them seemed to be expecting a visit from the Butcher's Boy. She checked other cities. Men in Buffalo, Rochester, Tampa, Youngstown, St. Louis, New Orleans, Denver, Biloxi, Boston, and Providence were agitated and active. If what he had been trying to do was to create a panic, he seemed to have succeeded.

She added this new information to her memory and let her subconscious mind work on it while she turned her attention to the e-mails and memos that had come in for her. She answered quickly, using few words, but being careful to say enough to re-assure her people that she had paid attention and that she cared. That was what they required—the sense that they weren't working for nothing, issuing reports that simply disappeared into a filing cabinet in the main office. Some of her replies asked for interpretations. Some directed the field people to investigate facts they'd turned up.

At the end of the day, there had been no ominous rumbling from the direction of the deputy assistant's office. She stayed an extra hour to finish the backlog of communications, and then picked up her purse and briefcase, locked the office door, put a couple of notes for Geoffrey in his in-box, called a cab, and went outside to meet it.

Elizabeth got out of the cab in front of her house and gave her credit card to the driver. While he filled out the slip, her eyes strayed to the house. She could see the light in Amanda's bedroom. It was good to know she was working on her homework. Jim's window was a bit more ambiguous. The steady white light from his computer screen bathed the ceiling and back wall of his room, but Jim was more complicated for her to understand. He seemed to think growing up meant keeping most thoughts and all activities private. Most likely he was working intensely to finish a paper, but it was also possible his computer was simply on while he texted nonsense back and forth with a new girl she had never met. She knew she was just thinking of that as a way of punishing herself for not paying much attention to her kids for two weeks.

She took her credit card back, added a tip to the slip and signed it, watched the cab move off into the night, and then extended the handle on her small suitcase and walked to her front porch. She felt a sense of guilt and loss as she pulled her keys out of her purse to unlock the door. She had spent the past three weekends away, so the time when she could have been with the two kids had been wasted. Next year Jim would be away at college, and Amanda would be a senior.

The thought brought another sick feeling. Jim had been working on his applications during those weekends, and she hadn't been around to read his essays or remind him of things he'd done that he should mention. She knew he was a good student and a straightforward sort of person. His SAT scores were high, but not remarkable. He had been elected to the student council, but was not an officer. He was on the track team, but he was by no means a star. His teachers had hinted at what their letters of recommendation would say, and the gist of their opinions wasn't too different from what she would have said. He was a good kid, the sort who became a genuine man when the time came, and thereafter did things that made his mother proud. He wasn't very different from his father. The thought made the guilt intensify. She should have been a better mother during this time. It was probably the last time he'd need, or be able to accept, heavy-duty mothering.

She unlocked the door and stepped inside. She called, "Amanda! Jim! I'm home."

Amanda came to the upstairs landing, looked down, and waved.

Elizabeth said, "I see you're rushing to help me carry my suitcase."

"No, I just wanted to be sure you weren't bringing home a pony or a stepfather for us."

Her brother appeared from the other side of the upstairs landing. "Hey, Wandering Mom. Nice to see you."

"I just stopped in to see if either of you has any broken bones or arrests." She stared at them for a few seconds. "No? Then have you both had dinner?"

"Yes," they both said.

"We didn't know you'd be home this early," Amanda said. "We would have waited for you."

"No, I'm glad you ate," Elizabeth lied.

The two came down the stairs, and Elizabeth rolled her suitcase to the laundry room and left it there for unpacking later. "Don't anybody touch that," she said. "I locked my weapon in it because I didn't want to haul it around in the office."

Jim said, "You mean your laser pointer?"

She laughed. "Yep. So what's been happening around here?"

"Your mail is on the counter," said Amanda. "I think I clinched my A in history on the test Monday. Jim stayed out with Nora Phelps until the birds started singing."

Elizabeth stuck her head in the refrigerator and said evenly, "Congratulations and shame on you, respectively. Is this asparagus still from when I left?"

"No, that's new," Amanda said. "And so is the chicken. Jim cooked that, so it's called 'Chicken della Romeo.'"

Elizabeth took the two plastic containers out and closed the refrigerator with her hip. "How are you coming on the college applications?"

"Fine," he said. "They're not due for months."

"But if you know what the essay topics are, you can write rough drafts and then have lots of time to polish them."

"I've still got to get through the first semester. Want me to start working on my law school applications too?"

"Not a bad idea," she said. "A smart guy like you could have everything done ten years in advance."

"I'll start thinking about it." He paused. "There. I'm done thinking. No."

She sat down to eat, and one at a time Jim and Amanda drifted back upstairs to their work. Elizabeth was silently grateful that they had taken her spate of absences and late nights as a small, inconsequential passing variation in the routines they had always followed since their father died. For most of those years her job had been different, an eight to five job with an hour commute on either end, and the occasional Saturday or Sunday when Organized Crime was swamped with information.

She showered, changed into a pair of soft exercise pants and an old T-shirt, and curled up on the couch with a cup of tea, her laptop computer, and her briefcase. It was good to be home. Even if she couldn't see or hear the kids from down here, just feeling them upstairs safe, working at the things they needed to do, was comforting. She had been out on the streets of unfamiliar cities with a gun in her coat pocket, but it was over now, like a fever passing. She had made an energetic but ultimately foolish attempt to turn a killer into a witness. The fact that her effort had turned out to be hopeless didn't mean it had been worthless.

The killer had given her information that would probably lead to the convictions of two Mafiosi on old homicides. That was quite a lot of success by any standard. Before she had left the office today, she had written reports on those two cases, requesting that warrants be obtained to search for the surviving evidence in the places where the Butcher's Boy had said it would be. Hunsecker would not be delighted by the way the information was obtained, but it wouldn't stop him from claiming credit if two important criminals were convicted.

Her reckless behavior had yielded some results, but she'd had enough now. Just being at home with Jim and Amanda made her wonder what she could have been thinking. She wasn't a field agent, she was a bureaucrat. If she hadn't made it home, what would have become of them? It was as though the night the Butcher's Boy had materialized in the darkness in her room, she had lost all sense of caution and judgment. He had been like a ghost returning, suddenly willing to tell her the answers to all of the things she'd been wondering about. She hadn't been able to resist.

She opened her laptop and used her password to get into her Justice Department account. She wanted to see what had been added to the continuing accumulation of details of the Butcher's Boy's visit to Los Angeles.

The federal agencies were the best in the world at the patient, almost superhumanly thorough collection and analysis of details, and her section of the Organized Crime and Racketeering Division was one of the great engines of analysis. Anything that was discovered by local or state law enforcement, or by the FBI, DEA, or any other organization, was noted, entered in the records, and cataloged. Every connection was explored, every lead followed.

There was news. The man killed on Marengo Avenue in Pasadena early in the morning was named Randall Alan Simms. He was shot in the middle of the road. At the time he was carrying a German-made Heckler & Koch rifle with the barrel machine-threaded to hold a silencer. Simms was a former soldier who had served in the first Gulf War and had been given an honorable discharge after half of a second enlistment because of unspecified medical reasons. She sensed a covered-up mental illness. That would come out too, because she would not be the only one to wonder. Simms's address was in Van Nuys, California, and he was listed as unemployed, which probably meant he was paid in cash.

The two men in Griffith Park were Stephen Fields and Brent Patterson. Fields had two DUIs, a breaking-and-entering charge that was dropped, and three domestic violence convictions. He had served six months of a one-year sentence for the third. Patterson had an assault conviction and an aggravated assault bargained down. There was a weapons charge that had put him away for two years. Fields was listed as a former employee of the Macedonian Security Group, but he'd been carrying an ID issued by the Able Security Company.

The Los Angeles FBI field office would, by now, be all over the Able Security Company, its bookkeeping, and its present and past employees. She was willing to bet that the blue Crown Victoria the Butcher's Boy had mentioned on the phone was registered to the company. There would be some connection to somebody in the Lazaretti family, even if it was only that they'd once hired the company to guard a construction site the family owned.

She wrote notes to herself to be sure that somebody in her section kept up with the investigation of the victims. It was important to know who this hit team actually consisted of. Had there been three, or thirty? Was the security company the umbrella for a lot of illegal activities, or was killing people a sideline of a few employees?

She made notes on every aspect of the events in Los Angeles. At eight o'clock she was still checking her e-mail for updates. At eleven she put away her notes and the laptop. She knew that she had to start doing some planning to set her trap for the Butcher's Boy, and it made her uncomfortable. She could only attract him to some specific place at a specific time by getting him to believe some attractive lie. He would trust her because he had treated her honorably — trusting a person he'd invested in was human nature. And she would betray him.

There must be many ways to capture him. It was possible to meet in a restaurant and have all of the workers and customers be FBI agents. She could meet him on a bus and have all the bus seats occupied by FBI agents. All they'd have to do was drive him to jail. She could meet him in an airport, where they would both have to be unarmed. She felt frustrated. People had been trying to betray and kill him for twenty years. Was there anything that he hadn't seen before and wouldn't recognize instantly? She needed something new and outlandish that would never occur to him.

She thought about the times when she had seen him. He had come into her bedroom to talk to her in the night. He had appeared suddenly when she was getting into her car at the dry cleaners. He had come to her hotel in Los Angeles. What all of those occasions had in common was that she hadn't known in advance that he was coming. He had a way in, and a better way out that nobody would be blocking. If she asked for a meeting, he might come, but not to some prearranged place at a particular time. Could she possibly guess in advance where and when he would choose to surprise her? And if the trap worked and FBI agents had him surrounded, that wouldn't mean that he would surrender.

She thought about places. There was the Washington Metro. It would be possible to fill a train car with agents looking like commuters and to flood the platform of a station with other agents, but was there any way to keep civilians out without his seeing the trap? There were restaurants, bars, stores. She just had to pick a place, find a way to isolate it from the public, block every means of escape, and persuade him to meet her there.

The trap was already beginning to feel like a chance for a stupid mistake. When a large number of people were together in one room, they had great potential for deciding on the right answer to a question. They called it the wisdom of crowds. But crowds had an even greater potential for mixed or misunderstood signals, for false alarms, for simply bumping into each other when the time came to act.

The Butcher's Boy was great in crowds. He had operated in crowds all his life, made his way to his targets in front of large numbers of people, none of whom seemed ever to have seen him kill or been able to describe him afterward. She had seen him operate in crowds, and it had been an education. He adjusted his posture, his gait, his expression to match the people around him. Even when people had suddenly begun shooting at him in Chicago, his expression was a voluntary act of muscle control.

No crowds. She would have to arrange the worst possible kind of trap and meet him alone. She would have to talk to him and get him to come to her out of trust in her word and her personal integrity. And then she would have to give some signal that brought in the hidden men with bulletproof vests and automatic weapons.

It was late. She put her notes in her briefcase with the files, locked it, and stood. It was time to get to bed. Cross-country travel was exhausting, and she'd come off her flight and put in a few hours of work afterward. Maybe tomorrow, after a night's sleep, something brilliant would occur to her. She checked the locks on the doors, set the alarm, and climbed the stairs, turning lights off as she went. When she reached the upstairs hallway, she saw the lights in the kids' rooms were off.

She went to bed so tired that the problems and worries of the day seemed to merge into a single category—things she could not solve without sleep. For a few seconds she thought about the Butcher's Boy. It occurred to her that he was probably traveling again, somewhere alone in a car on the night roads, and she wondered which city he was heading for. And then she was asleep.

At two A.M. she was startled awake. Her mind struggled to the surface, aware that there was some kind of emergency. She had been hearing noises, and there weren't supposed to be noises. Elizabeth sat up, switched on the light by her bed, kicked a little to get the blankets off, and swung her feet to the floor.

A male voice startled her. "Stay right there. Don't move." The voice was sharp, angry, coming from inside her room just on the other side of her bed.

She sat still, not daring to turn around, her eyes squinting in the light. She fought to catch up. The kids had been in the house. Had this man overlooked them? Maybe they'd heard him breaking in and gotten out. Maybe they were on the stairs trying to get out right now. She had to keep him occupied. "Who are you? What do you want in my house?"

"I'm Number One, and wherever I am, I own it. Don't try to do anything. I have a man with your son and one with your daughter. If anything happens, they'll die first."

Her chest felt like it was being crushed. She tried to breathe, but her breaths were quick and shallow, her chest refusing to expand to take in air. Her heart seemed to be pounding harder and harder. "You don't need to harm my children." She had a desperate hope. "Having them can't help you."

"They're not going anywhere," the man said. "This will be a family thing from beginning to end."

"What do you want?"

"The Butcher's Boy. You were with him in L.A. Tell us where he is and get him to come here."

"I don't know where he is," she said. "If I did, he'd already be in jail. I work for the Justice Department."

"We know where you work," he said. "You're not being helpful, so now it's time to get ready for what comes next. Get up slowly and put your hands up."

She slowly stood and turned.

He surged forward instantly, so she hadn't come completely around before he was there, delivering a bare-handed slap to the side of her head. She completed her turn and saw Jim and

Amanda at the entrance to the room, each with a man holding a pistol close to their heads.

"Oh, God," she said. "You can't."

"What do you think, guys? Think we can't?"

One of the two men, a man in his late twenties or early thirties with spiked blond hair, answered, "We can do what we want."

Number One said, "You know who's paying us. They want their money's worth. They want him dead, now."

"They're the same people who used to pay him," she said. "I'm sure they're offering a lot because they're really scared. But you're not helping yourselves by coming here."

"Why not?"

"I have no way to know where he is or where he's going. When I left Los Angeles, he was there. When I got home to Washington this afternoon, I learned that after I left he killed two professional shooters in a blue Ford Crown Victoria and then drove it to Pasadena and killed Tony Lazaretti. I'm sure after that he left town."

The three men exchanged a glance, then shifted their feet, as though they were suddenly uncomfortable. "Okay. Let's put the kids in their rooms where they can't get in the way. Keep them separate. I'll take this lady downstairs and find a way to persuade her to help us."

The young one with spiked hair dragged Amanda out the door, and the third, a man in his thirties with a cap of curly black hair and a tattoo on his hand that Elizabeth couldn't quite make out, pushed Jim hard, once, like a punch. They went along the upstairs hallway toward the other bedrooms. The older man, the leader, took Elizabeth to the staircase and down to the first floor. When she reached the bottom, she got a clearer glimpse of him. He was just under six feet, with sandy hair and a body that seemed angular and lean, with sinewy muscles in his forearms. His jaw seemed habitually clenched, and his eyes narrowed. He clutched her arm and brought her through the living room to the little den that she used as an office for paying bills and filing financial papers.

303

She said, "You must know that I don't have any power over a man like him. I can't make him do anything. He isn't my friend. You could wait forever, and he would probably never come here. I don't have a way of reaching him."

"I have confidence in you."

"He's a professional killer and he doesn't care what happens to people like me."

"I'm not actually going to tell you what to do in this situation, ma'am. Your description of him is probably right. It sounds true, anyway." He leaned closer to her. "If you can understand that much about him, you can probably understand us too. We've taken this contract. When it started, there were six of us. Now there are three. We don't care how this feels to you or what happens to your son or daughter. What we care about is this guy we agreed to kill. We want you to help us get him."

"How?"

"Like I said, I'm not going to tell you what to do. It's up to you to find a way."

"But I just told you I don't know how. I tried to persuade him to give the department information in exchange for protection. He won't talk to me because he's positive he can kill anyone who comes after him."

"Good for him. I'm going to give you time to think about what I want. But I also want you to think about us for a little while. We've killed people too. I've done a lot of them in different ways, in different places. If I have to leave you and your kids gutted like fish, I promise you I'll never lose a second of sleep over it. But I can make this an unhappy night without killing them. What are their fingers worth to you? Their eyes?"

"Please," she said. "Don't even say that." For the first time she felt helpless panic. She could form no plan, no idea of how to prevent, or even delay, this horror.

He shook his head. "I don't get any pleasure out of doing those things, or any pain either. My friend up there has already said he wants to spend a couple of hours with your daughter. In a few minutes I may tell him it's okay. While you listen to her scream, you can think about how to give me what I want before he kills her."

Maybe this was a nightmare. Was she caught in that hellish moment before the relief would flood in and she'd realize that none of it ever happened? No. If she was thinking of the possibility, then it should already be over. She was so frightened that her breathing didn't seem to be giving her any oxygen. Her arms and legs felt as though the motor neurons had been severed. She could feel them, but she couldn't get them to move.

"I can go online and find out if he's been seen anywhere since Los Angeles, or if something happened anywhere else that could be his work."

"That's a start," said the man. "I have to warn you, though. If I think you're sending a distress signal or something, I'll bring everybody down here and go to work on you in front of the kids."

She said, "My laptop is in my briefcase."

"Go ahead."

She went around him to get to the briefcase in the living room. She had gotten a better look at him in the office. He was slightly taller than average, with a bony quality—shoulders that weren't heavily muscled but square, like machined parts. His forearms, hands, and feet seemed large, his fingers long, with knotty red knuckles. His face was fair, but it had a reddish tint in some places, and he had a bony jaw and wrinkles at the eyes, as though he had spent time squinting into the sun. The eyes themselves were a flat, faded brown, and his hair a coarse, dirty blond. He spoke what she thought of as the enlisted man's dialect. Somewhere at the back of it was an accent that was vaguely southern.

She had started into the living room when his sinewy forearm hooked around her neck. She could smell his musky underarm and feel his hot breath on the back of her neck. She stopped to keep from choking.

"Go slow," he said. "If you get too far ahead, I'll start to get nervous."

She waited.

"Okay, go."

She began to move, and he was with her, his arm and part of his torso pressed against her as she walked. Her sensation was that he was attached to her like some parasitic animal about to feed. She fought the claustrophobic, powerless feeling. She bent her knees and touched the briefcase handles.

"If there's a gun in there, you'd better tell me now."

"I work in the Kennedy building in an office. I don't carry a sidearm."

She took the laptop, cradled it in her arms, and walked back toward the little office with the man keeping his hand on her left arm in a painful grasp. He tugged her to the dining room and pulled out a chair at the table. "Sit here."

She had no idea why he preferred the dining room, but it seemed that he needed to get his way about everything. She set her computer on the shiny polished table, opened it, and signed into her Justice Department account.

"Remember, I'm watching," he said. "Don't make contact with anybody."

She opened her e-mail account, then saw one from John Holman at the FBI and clicked on it. The e-mail filled the screen, and as she read it, she began to scroll down.

"Hold it," he said. "Let's read that."

She stopped and scrolled upward again. He was a slow reader. He was suspicious and irritated when she moved ahead too quickly, as though she were hiding some message she didn't want him to read.

Holman's e-mail described the men the Butcher's Boy had killed in Los Angeles. She heard the man mutter, "Damn," as he read it. Then he seemed to catch himself. "He's had quite a workout."

"It's been that way wherever he's been since Frank Tosca tried to get him killed. Is Tony Lazaretti the one who hired you?"

"What are you thinking—that we'll never get paid?"

"It had crossed my mind."

He was standing just behind her and to the side when he hit her. It was a short, quick backhand to her cheek and jaw that spun her head to the side.

"Oh!" she said, and her hand went to her cheek.

He hit her on the other side with his left hand, then pushed her back and kicked the chair forward so her back hit the floor hard. He hit her again, on the head with his gun, so hard that she saw the ceiling as a red tunnel with him coming at her down the middle of it. She went limp to keep from inciting him to hurt her more, but he hit her with his fist three times. She could tell that she wasn't just feeling the sting from slaps. He was doing damage to the bones in her face.

A red haze grew across her field of vision, and everything seemed to go quiet and dark for a second, but then she could see his face right above hers again with his teeth bared.

"You're not my equal," he rasped. "Don't tell me what's going to happen. I'll tell you what's going to happen if I feel like it."

She managed to croak, "I'm sorry. I'm so sorry." Her tongue tasted like copper, and she couldn't talk right because her mouth was pooling with blood that dribbled and bubbled out when she tried. "I'm sorry. Please. I didn't mean anything."

He glared at her, moving his head to keep his face in front of her eyes, so he looked like a snake maneuvering to strike. "You're nothing. You understand? They give women like you some fancy title like you were hot shit, but you're nothing. The best you can hope for is to be a hostage, just a piece of meat for bait. Don't imagine you're some kind of player in this. It's between us and him. You're already dead, and I'm keeping you on life support for my own convenience until I decide to pull the plug."

She lay still on the floor with the chair back under her, trying to avoid his eyes by closing hers, until he hit her again. "Look at me!"

She opened her eyes and kept them open, hoping he wouldn't see that they were unfocused because looking at him terrified her. She was weak with fear. She felt that a horrible, sudden, and unexpected change had happened to her, and it made her ashamed and disgusted with herself. She had never imagined what this kind of fear was like, never had any way of picturing herself being so totally defeated. "I understand," she said. "You're the boss. Whatever you say."

His face compressed itself into a smirk. "That's more like it." He stood. "Get up."

With difficulty, she rolled to her side and pushed herself up. She saw a shiny six-inch pool of blood where her head had been and realized her hair was wet. She resisted reaching up to touch it because he might see that as a delay in her compliance with his order, or even a complaint, and he would punish her. The pain in her scalp was no worse than the pain in her jaw or her nose. She got to her knees and then picked up her chair and sat in it.

She brushed the tears out of her eyes and went back to clicking on each of the e-mail updates about the Butcher's Boy, reading through each one slowly, giving him time to satisfy himself that she wasn't tricking him. She didn't dare try a trick. She was afraid of tricks. She only wanted to be alive and keep her children alive. This man was a brute. If she didn't find what he wanted soon, he would kill them all. She felt his impatience, his anger, the growing dread behind it that he might be failing. She slowly came to feel that she understood him and that she could almost read his thoughts. He was nearly out of patience. He needed a clue. If he didn't have a clue soon, she would begin to hear the shouts of her children.

"I've got it," she said. "He's been seen in Philadelphia. I know where he's going. He'll be there tomorrow or the next day."

33

SCHAEFFER'S FLIGHT INTO Baltimore was six hours of sleep. He dreamed that, according to some new set of government rules that made sense in his dream, if he agreed to die voluntarily, he would be permitted to be alive again at a later, pre-arranged time. The problem was that to his dream self the offer sounded like a con. He was tempted to try it because if what the government said was true, it was the only way he could ever hope to see Meg again. He was trying to construct some test of the government's sincerity when the plane descended a few hundred feet and the change in pressure woke him.

He looked out the window at the grid of lights, the yellow street lamps and blue-white headlights stretching off into the distance and then stopping at the bright edge before the black ocean. The plane swung slowly around to face the west wind and then began its approach.

It occurred to him that he had passed into a new phase of his life now. A year or two ago, Meg had forced him to go to a church for one of the occasions that the local aristocrats were expected to attend. Since the church was the Church of England, it seemed perfectly safe to him. There were no Anglican Mafiosi. The church was in a village outside Bath, where it was unlikely an American visitor would show up. The priest gave a sermon about the "end times" and what each Christian should expect. The term had stuck with him. These were his end times, the phase after the end of his world had begun but before his death. It was highly unlikely, for instance, that he would be alive in a week and almost impossible that he would last a month.

The bosses of the families had clearly figured out that he was going after all of them, and they had hired specialists to find and kill him. He had seen three specialists. It was possible that there were thirty more ranging the country and waiting for him in likely places, and when the news from Los Angeles spread, there could be sixty or seventy professional killers and hundreds of Mafia soldiers, all hunting for him.

Elizabeth Waring at the Justice Department would soon realize that while she was trying to interest him in being a stool pigeon, he had managed to keep his own schedule of kills going. When she did, her next move would probably be to have the FBI capture or kill him.

He would make the most of his final days. He would still follow the same strategy he'd devised in the beginning of this—kill the shooters and then go up the hierarchy like a ladder, killing the middlemen on the way up until he reached the boss who had sent the shooters.

The advantage he'd had on this visit to America was Elizabeth Waring. They had been using each other. He had given her a chance to solve two or three old gang murders. She had brought his knowledge of the Mafia up-to-date. It was as though without her, he was stuck in the distant past, knowing the enemies only as they'd been twenty years ago. Without him, she had to face bosses who exerted immense power, but did nothing illegal themselves. He had given her the crimes they'd committed before they got powerful.

He would use her again tonight. He couldn't avoid it. The two shooters in Los Angeles had seen him with her at her hotel. There was almost no chance that they hadn't found out which room was hers and what her name was. There were also soldiers from the

Castiglione family who had seen her with him in Chicago. Now that he had dropped out of sight again, where were the shooters supposed to go to pick up his trail? They'd go to the place where she was. He was hunting them, so that's where he was going too. If he could make a few kills in Washington to get some of the pros out of the way, it might buy him more time to bag the boss in the next city. If he could get to Boston in the morning, he might be able to hit Providence the same night.

He waited at the baggage claim for his suitcase to come down the chute to the stainless steel carousel. Out of his customary caution he watched for people who looked familiar or who seemed to look past him at something else or watched him in the reflection on the big front windows. He hadn't spotted anyone who worried him before his suitcase slid down onto the carousel. He pulled the suitcase off, swung it to the floor, and extended the handle, then walked off with a purposeful stride. He boarded the shuttle to the car-rental center and settled into a seat facing the terminals.

He looked for the sort of man who might be trouble—a man watching for something to happen, waiting for someone to appear. It was the middle of the night, and the watchers stood out more than they did in the daytime. He saw three as the shuttle moved from one airline's area to another, but he couldn't tell who any of them were. They could have been working for the drug smuggling cartels, the police, federal agencies, foreign governments. It didn't matter, because they weren't interested in him tonight.

The bus left the airport, but he never relaxed his vigilance. After being away from the country for so long, and having returned during a prolonged national security crisis, he knew he no longer had an accurate idea of what sort of surveillance might be focused on people who arrived in the airports around Washington, D.C.

His shuttle reached the lot and he entered the rental center to find it almost deserted. He picked the counter where the night man looked the least exhausted, rented a car with his Charles Ackerman identification and credit card, then drove toward McLean, Virginia. There were a lot of big hotels at Tysons Corners—Wes-

311

tin, Hilton, Marriott, Sheraton—and it was just a couple of miles along Dolley Madison Boulevard to McLean. He pulled into the driveway at the Hilton, left his car with a parking attendant, and said he'd be out in a few minutes.

He went inside and checked in, then took his small suitcase up to his room. He intended to go out tonight to take a quick look around Elizabeth Waring's neighborhood for signs that shooters might have already arrived. He knew that precautions might not be necessary, but he took them anyway. He unpacked his suitcase, took out the external computer drive that held the parts of his gun, and used the small screwdriver he'd packed with it to take off the black housing. He retrieved the parts of his Kel-Tec PF-9 pistol and reassembled them. He loaded the magazine with seven nine-millimeter rounds, inserted it, and put the small, flat gun in his right coat pocket, then shrugged his shoulders to make the coat hang right. He could feel the pistol against his right wrist, where he could reach it in a second. He put his lock-blade knife in his pocket.

He went out to the valet parking attendant to claim his car and drove out to the boulevard toward McLean. He had studied the neighborhood twice before. The first time had been ten years ago, when he had first become aware of Elizabeth Waring. He had rented a house on her block so he could watch her and decide whether or not to kill her. The second time had been a couple of weeks ago, when he had come back to the country and could think of nobody else he still knew who would be intimately familiar with the current hierarchy of the Balacontano family. Before he had gone in, he had studied every house and parked car, every spot where a shadow might be hiding an enemy.

He turned into her neighborhood four blocks from the house and approached it by driving in narrowing circles. The place looked about the same as it had weeks ago, but the hour was much later now. It was after two A.M., and all of the neighborhood windows were dark. The garages were closed and the only cars that were out on the street were the ones that didn't fit in the two-car garages.

He prepared to park and walk a bit, but he noticed something that didn't feel right to him. It was a big SUV with tinted windows. It was parked at the curb on the street behind Elizabeth Waring's house. It was exactly the spot he'd chosen when he'd come to talk to her weeks ago. It had given him a straight, sheltered path from here to there, over a stone wall that was easy to climb, then a stroll along the outer edge of her neighbor's lawn to a low fence into Elizabeth Waring's back yard, and then to the house.

He drove one more block and parked his rental car, then walked back to take a closer look. There had not been a vehicle like this when he'd been here the last time. It was almost certainly the car of a stranger to the neighborhood. He knelt to look at the license plate. It had some deep gouges in its paint, the worst of them around the brand-new set of bolts and nuts that held the plate. The plate was definitely stolen from another vehicle. He looked at the rear door. The lock was held in place by something on the inside, probably tape. It had been hammered out so the door could be opened.

He knew the safest thing to do would be to walk back to his rental car and leave. But he had come to Washington to hunt them, and here they were. He might be able to kill them before they had a chance to kill him. He walked around the SUV trying to see in the tinted windows, looking for anything left inside that might help him.

He supposed they would be set up in an ambush around the outside of Elizabeth Waring's house, like the man who had tried to kill him in Pasadena outside Lazaretti's house. He went to the low fence, looked and listened, then rolled over the fence, squatted in the deep shadow, and listened while he looked for the shape of a person.

There was nobody in this yard, so he began to move. He lingered in shadows and moved slowly, then stopped, staying still, keeping his body low. When he stopped, he kept his body in a crouch that might suggest to the eye "shrub," but never in a shape that suggested "man."

He stretched and compressed time, giving himself several minutes to sense movement, then quickly melting into a deeper darkness when he found it. When he was across the neighbor's yard, he entered Elizabeth's by going over the fence. There were lights on in the back of the house on both floors.

His heart began to beat more strongly, but he held back his eagerness. They weren't waiting for him outside. They were inside, hoping to get him when he came to the door. It was a solid, cautious way to take him. He would knock or ring a bell, they assumed, and they could open the door or shoot him through a window.

They had made a mistake and assumed that he had some kind of personal relationship with Elizabeth Waring. Maybe they had even gone into the house in the middle of the night, believing that they might surprise him in her room. He supposed that when the others had seen him at her hotel, it had given them a distorted idea of their history.

Why they had made the mistake was probably not important. The thing for him to think about was making sure it was a fatal mistake. He had a perfect chance tonight to get these people.

As he made his way to the back wall of the house, he could feel the tension of the moment. The muscles of his legs, arms, back, and stomach tightened, his breathing grew deeper to load his blood with oxygen. It was the old, welcome feeling again, the one he'd first experienced when he was a boy going out to kill with Eddie. On the first few jobs, there had been such fear and elation that it was almost impossible to separate one from the other. His mind had been activated the same way as his body—more blood pumping through his brain so he thought faster and could see things in sharper, brighter relief. It had seemed to him that he could feel the surfaces he looked at long before he touched them.

After those nights, the feeling had returned to him often. Tonight he felt it again, and it made him feel strong and quick and eager. He stood at the side of the sliding door at the back of the living room and looked in. He couldn't see anybody inside. The alarm system keypad was beside the front door, and he could just see it from here. The little lights on the keypad were off. The shooters must have shut it off somehow to get in. He could see into the dining room from here. One of the chairs at the dining room table had been moved out of line. Behind it there was a pool of blood on the light hardwood floor. Had they killed her already? No. There wasn't enough blood for a bullet wound or stabbing, and far too little for anything fatal.

They must have hit her or knocked her to the floor. It was that kind of blood. They hadn't killed her yet. They were probably trying to get her to say where he was going to be next or force her to get him to come here. He hoped she'd had the presence of mind to lie and buy herself some time. If she did, he still might be able to keep her alive if he moved efficiently and made no mistakes.

He reached into his pocket for his knife, opened it, and slid the four-inch blade between the latch and its receptacle to open the latch, then put away the knife and reached into his coat pocket for the small, flat pistol. He'd had the intention of buying a couple of spare magazines for the gun before he tried to use it, but things had happened too quickly. He slid open the door, stepped inside into the living room, and closed it again. He stood with his back against the wall, his body partially concealed by a baby grand piano.

He stood still. The gun was in his right hand, but not aimed. He simply held it pointed to his right because moving his right hand to his left was milliseconds faster than moving it to the right, and his aim would be surer. His left hand touched the wall so he could feel vibrations, and he let his eyes stare into space so anything that entered any part of his vision would be visible to him. He yawned silently so his ears were clear and listened.

Time passed, but he kept no count of the minutes, only tried to hear and feel where people were in the house. He heard and felt the sound of someone heavy walking above him near the back of the house, and a second later, someone else a few feet to the left.

315

Waring's daughter had to be under a hundred pounds and the son was tall, but thin. And kids didn't wear hard-soled shoes like that at this hour. Waring was maybe a hundred and twenty, so it wasn't her either.

It was two men, both upstairs but at least ten or fifteen feet apart, maybe in different rooms at the moment. Were they searching the place? For what? Maybe Waring and her kids weren't even home. The thought made him feel a tentative optimism, but then he heard Elizabeth Waring's voice.

It was a low "Uh, unh. No. Stop." It came from a nearby room. "Stop, please! I already told you what I know!"

Schaeffer was already moving toward her voice. It seemed to be coming from the direction of the little office off the kitchen. He kept the gun ready. There were three of them, two upstairs, probably guarding the kids. This one was downstairs with Waring.

He came to the doorway and took in the scene. The man had light, thinning hair so Schaeffer could see his pink bald spot from there as the man straddled Waring on the floor. He was in the process of tearing Waring's clothes off. He had already gotten her top off and had her bra around her waist and had her black sweatpants down to her knees, so with her pale, sun-deprived skin she looked like a classical statue that had been broken. He could tell from her eyes that she could see him.

As he stepped forward, she showed a burst of energy and tried to immobilize the man's arms by throwing hers around him in a bear hug. Two more steps and Schaeffer was there. He wrenched the man's head around to the left to break his neck, then pushed him off Waring.

Elizabeth was shaking and wide-eyed, with blood running down in streaks from her broken nose and her split lip, but he put his head close to hers and whispered. "Are there two more of them upstairs with your kids?"

She nodded. "Yes. Two." She pulled up her sweatpants, and he turned and picked up her T-shirt from the floor where the man must have tossed it. Then he handed it to her.

316

He stood, pulled out his pistol, and moved toward the door.

"Wait," she whispered. "I have a gun in the laundry room."

"Where's that?"

"Stay here." He could see she had a hard time getting to her feet. He could tell her arms and legs were tired from wrestling her vastly stronger opponent. But she went to the door, and he noticed that she was barefoot. She must have been hauled out of bed. She was a mess, just running on adrenaline now, and fear for her kids.

She padded into the room again, this time carrying a Glock 17 pistol and a magazine that he could see held sixteen gleaming bullets.

He took the gun and the magazine, inserted the magazine, and pulled the slide back to get a round into the chamber. He whispered, "Tell me the truth. Are you really good with this?"

"I'm okay. I've kept up my qualification for ten or eleven years."

"Do you have any reluctance at all to kill one of those guys up there?"

"No. None," she said.

"Okay." He handed her the gun. "I think they've got your kids in different rooms. They're probably tied or cuffed. If I go in and kill the guy in one room, his buddy will fire on your other kid. So we have to go in both rooms at once. You don't say, 'Stop or I'll shoot' or 'Freeze' or 'Drop it.' You step in and shoot him. And you have to shoot him enough times so he's beyond shooting back." He held her arm to keep her from going. "If you can't do it just like that, tell me."

"I can do it. I want to do it," she said.

He picked a piece of paper and a pencil off the desk and put it on the hardwood floor where they sat. "Draw me the two rooms. Show the door, the back window, the bed, any chairs."

He watched her draw, then nodded. "You take this one — your son's room. I'll get the girl. First we go up as quietly as we can. If anybody comes out of a room, kill him. It won't be your kid."

He put his arm around her shoulders to help her up and they

began to walk. At the doorway he whispered, "Quiet, now. Remember, we step in shooting."

"Let's go." She stepped across the big oriental rug in the living room, letting it muffle the footsteps. When she reached the foot of the staircase, she didn't hesitate. She began to climb. Her bare feet made no noise.

He followed and realized that what he was seeing was probably something she had learned when she'd gone up the stairs when her kids were babies. Nobody knew how to go through a house as quietly as the owner. He was tempted to make her stop halfway up to listen for the men, but she was doing so well he waited until they were a step from the top to put his hand on her shoulder. She stopped and looked back at him. He held his hand up to his ear, and they both listened.

There was a steady, low-level hum of talk coming from the boy's room. That seemed good. What worried him was that he wasn't hearing noises from the other room where the girl was. He hoped she wasn't dead.

He looked at Elizabeth and nodded in the direction of the boy's room. She stepped up to the second floor hallway and sidestepped toward the open door. Schaeffer moved toward the other door. He felt a sudden chill. He hadn't taken the time to tell Elizabeth some of the things she needed to know about this situation. She had to step into the middle of the doorway boldly with her eyes wide and the gun out in front of her. There was only the search for the shot and no conceivable reason to hold fire. He reminded himself that she had said she was "qualified" with her pistol, and he had to assume that federal officers were given situational training. If not, then it was too late.

He held her on the edge of his field of vision as he stepped closer to the girl's room. When he was beside the girl's room, he leaned forward just far enough to see that the door was open. He turned to meet Elizabeth's eyes.

She stood with her left shoulder touching the woodwork around the doorway, holding the gun up with both hands and her finger on the trigger. But her eyes were closed. *What the fuck was she doing?* She opened her eyes and they met his. He could tell that she'd been praying. He swallowed his irritation. He nodded to her and saw her begin her pivot into the doorway.

He launched himself into the middle of the other doorway, staying low, his right arm extended. The man was young, broad shouldered with spiked bleach-blond hair and a tan that looked as though he'd acquired it on a tanning bed. He held the girl on his lap, and his hand was under her tank top. She was crying. There was a shot from Elizabeth's gun in the next room and he jumped, saw Schaeffer in the doorway, and tried to pull his hand back and push her off his lap so he could reach his gun where it lay on the pillow.

Schaeffer fired a round into his chest, then one more into his head as he toppled back. The girl ran past him out of the room and toward her brother's room. Schaeffer picked up the man's pistol and walked after her into the other room.

Elizabeth was beside her son's bed, trying to tear at the strips of duct tape that had been used to tie him to the iron rails of the bed. Schaeffer stepped to the man lying on the floor. He had been shot twice in the chest, but there seemed to be some movement. He was breathing. Schaeffer fired a round through his head.

"You killed him! Aren't you supposed to call an ambulance?" the daughter said.

"Quiet," Elizabeth said. "We'll talk later." Elizabeth's hands were shaking so much that she couldn't get the tape off her son's wrists.

Schaeffer said, "Go talk now. I'll do this."

Elizabeth put her arm around Amanda and they went out. Schaeffer opened his pocketknife and cut the tape at the wrists and ankles. The boy sat up and then stood.

"Thanks. When he tied me up, he said it was so I wouldn't do anything stupid when I heard what they were doing to my mother and sister."

"We were all lucky they were overconfident."

The boy left the room, and Schaeffer put his small pistol away and took the one the dead man had in his belt, then found two spare magazines in the man's pocket. As an afterthought, he rolled the body over, took out the man's wallet, looked at the California driver's license, then put it back.

He walked out into the hallway and found the three standing on the hardwood floor, their arms around one another, rocking back and forth. The mother was the shortest of the three, even shorter than the daughter, who still had that sylph look that some girls had even into their late teens, that made them seem to be something thinner and lighter than flesh and bone.

"I'd better get out of here," he said.

Elizabeth let go of her children, took his arm, and walked with him down the stairs. "Nobody's coming yet."

"They don't usually call ahead. I should go."

"Not yet. I want to—"

"Stop. Jesus didn't send me. I'm here because this was the best place to hunt for those guys. And you saved your own kids." He turned to head for the back door.

"Wait, please," she said. "I know exactly what to do. You just have to trust me."

"Why would I do that?"

"Because everything changed tonight. All three of us would be dead by now, instead of the three of them. We're alive; they're not."

"I've got to go."

"On your way out, stop by the man you caught trying to rape me. Do what's necessary. Skin the fingertips, shoot him in the face a few times so they can't use it to identify him. You'd know what to do better than I do, but make sure they can't tell who he is by looking. Afterward, leave the gun here. If you need another one, take his."

He studied her for a moment.

"Go ahead. I swear you won't be sorry."

34

AT THE END of the third week, he was back in her house. She watched him looking around as he stepped in the door. "Where's the rest of your furniture?"

"Some of it is in storage, and some of it was ruined by the blood or the crime-scene people and their fingerprint dust," she said. "I'm doing some remodeling."

"What are you changing?"

"I'm having the walls knocked out in the little office and adding that space to the kitchen, which is behind it. The real estate man said having a big open space there would add to the value when I sell it."

"They know what sells."

"I decided I didn't want that room to be in my memories, or my dreams, for the rest of my life. It will help that in a few weeks it won't exist. The bedrooms upstairs are being redone, but I can't make them go away completely. So we're going away instead."

"Have you started looking for a new place?"

"Not officially, but we've seen some. Jim will be off at college in nine months, and then in another year so will Amanda. We decided that for the next phase of life a condominium with three bedrooms and a metro station nearby would be just about right."

"There must be a few of those around."

She stood silent for a few seconds, looking at him. "I've got the stuff you're going to need."

"What is it?"

"It's what I promised you." She went to the big briefcase she had left by the door. She carried it to the dining room, then stopped. "They've already moved the table out." She stepped into the kitchen and set the briefcase on the counter.

"You're not living here anymore, are you?"

"No. That first morning we checked into a hotel. The police had the run of the house for a few days, and they had it closed off. Then there was a cleanup crew, and then painters. Next it will be contractors and carpenters, more painters, and then realtors. The department is actually paying for a rental for the next couple of months until they're sure no more killers are coming back for us. We only come here to pick up things we actually need. It's surprising how few there are."

"I'm sorry my problems ruined your house for you."

"We voted, and it was unanimous that the good memories we all had would survive better without the physical house to remind us of the bad things."

"I understand."

She opened the briefcase and pulled out a big accordion file. She pulled out a blue passport, and then another. "This one is in the name Paul Foster. The second one is also you, only your name is David Parker."

He looked at the passport. "You used the picture you took of me that night."

"Are there any others?"

"None that I know of. How did you get passports made?"

"Through WITSEC. You know, the witness protection program. Nobody in the FBI or Justice had ever seen you. The man you killed when you saved me seemed about the right size and age and coloring. The others were too young. You had never left prints or DNA at any of your scenes so . . ."

"So he's me."

"He's you. Rest in peace."

"I will. How did you explain the condition of my body?"

"You ruined your fingerprints before you got here. Nobody knows if it was to keep from being tied to your recent killings or in preparation for this one. The facial damage was caused by your being shot by an inexperienced, terrified shooter who didn't know when to stop. You've been examined and documented and cremated."

"Who killed me?"

"A man named Pete Stohler, who worked for me as a gardener and handyman. Very strong, not too bright. Afterward he ran off. When he calmed down a couple of days later, he turned himself in to me at the Justice Department. Everyone agreed that the best course would be to get him out of the country right away for his own protection."

"What about the police?"

"They actually helped us cook up a cover story for him, so nothing about him had to go on the record. That story is that FBI agents killed you to rescue us. All three of you, actually. It's quite a story, only nobody will ever read the details because it was intentionally miscoded as highly classified. It's somewhere in the system, and we can prove it was entered, but you can't retrieve it. The State Department has duplicates of your picture for the passports, but they're under Foster and Parker, whom they think are real people. Only WITSEC knows they're Pete Stohler, the man who killed you."

"All these people are lying to cover up that I'm alive?"

"Oh, no. To cover up that Pete Stohler is the one who killed you so he won't have to fear retaliation from your friends in organized crime. It's hard to overestimate the amount of lying law enforcement officers will do to protect an innocent person who's saved a colleague and her kids from the Mafia. All I had to do was tell an FBI friend named John Holman something close to the truth, and he helped me navigate the bureaucracies. I had a connection with WITSEC, and he had a connection with the State Department, and we both knew people in some of the other agencies. Want to see what else is in there?"

"Sure."

"Here. A couple of driver's licenses, some credit cards, and all the other stuff people carry around — frequent-flyer cards, library cards, discount cards for supermarkets. I don't imagine you'll need them but you'll need something, so here they are."

"I hope you won't regret this."

"I'm going to be ashamed of it, but I'll never regret it." She paused. "See, I had a husband. He was something special. What's left is those two kids that we had together. I'm doing the little I can to repay you for their lives, and I'll take the guilt."

"I mean I don't want you to get caught."

"That's the least of my worries. I've involved some smart, dedicated people who now have a big reason to keep this buried. Even if there were a real Pete Stohler, doing this to protect him violates a lot of rules."

"What can I do for you?"

"You've done it. Of course, when you get in the mood to tell a few more stories, I'd like you to send me a letter or an e-mail or something. I'm sure you know how to do it without getting caught."

He picked up the file. "I'll do that." He turned and walked toward the front door.

"I told you."

"What?"

"That you'd be my informant."

He smiled at her and nodded his head, then went out the front door and closed it quietly. After a few seconds she knew that if she went out to watch him go, she'd be frustrated because he would be nowhere to be seen. And she knew that soon he'd fly to some random country as Paul Foster and then dissolve into nothingness. He would fly to wherever he was actually going under some identity she didn't know. None of the credit cards or other ID would ever be used after that first flight.

She also knew that where he was going, there was a woman waiting. He had taken off his ring before he'd come to this house to see her for the first time, and let the hand get some sun so the white band didn't show. But the indentation was still on his finger today. If he had left the ring on, she would have said it was a part of his disguise, another attempt to seem like a normal man. But since he had tried to hide it, she knew the woman must be real.

She had not told him that the guilt she felt was a problem. Probably the last emotion that he could understand was guilt. She was not going to be allowed to go on as she had been. The attorney general had already told her that he had chosen her to replace the current deputy assistant, now that Hunsecker had handed in his letter of resignation. At the end of thirty days she would be moving to a large office at the corner of the building. The two murder charges she had filed on men the Butcher's Boy had told her about had already resulted in indictments. And now that she had drawn several perfectly good FBI agents into her deception, she had become the Bureau's favorite person. What was making her uncomfortable wasn't just the shame of having done wrong. She had anticipated that. What she hadn't expected was to thrive and prosper from the lies and dishonesty. The guilt for that was much worse. After twenty years of genuine effort, she had suddenly become an impostor.

She picked up her briefcase and turned on the light that was plugged into a timer in the kitchen, reset it to go on at dusk, and walked toward the front door. She stopped and looked out through the front window before she opened the door. She had known it would be a wasted motion. He was gone, and there was nothing more to see.